DEMON CARD
ENFORCER 2

JOHN STOVALL

Published by
CS BOOKS, LLC

This is a work of fiction. Names, characters, places, and incidents either are the product of author imagination or are used fictitiously, and any resemblance to actual persons, living or dead, business establishments, events, or locales, is entirely fictional.

Cover Design: Michael Gladigau

Editors: Amy McNulty, Nia Quinn, Celestian Rince

IF YOU WANT TO BE NOTIFIED WHEN JOHN STOVALL'S NEXT BOOK RELEASES, PLEASE VISIT HIS WEBSITE OR CONTACT HIM DIRECTLY AT

John.W.Stovall@gmail.com

Dedications

*First, as always, to my wife, **Shami Stovall**, who has made this career, and many other things besides, possible. You are the most amazing person I know. With, and because, of you, my life has elevated multiple times.*

*Secondly, to the other members of my writers' group. To **Dana, Ryan, Mary, Emily, James, and Scott**, thank you for the efforts you put into this as well. Especially Ryan, whose own card game efforts led to this book directly.*

*Third, to my parents, **John and Gail Stovall**. Your support throughout my life has been over the top, and you are the perfect parents everyone else wished they had. And, in my "master's degree in English" mother's case, one of my editors as well. This dedication, unfortunately, comes too late to reach my father, who passed away. I hope you were isekai'd to some place with a really awesome map, perhaps an alternate magical Earth, to fight for the good one more time.*

*Fourth, to my editors **Celestine Rince** and **Amy McNulty**. Thanks for doing this. I know I don't make it easy.*

*Fifth, I'd like to thank **Chris Zinn,** who supported me on Patreon for multiple years as my single, sole patron, and provided bonus editing, before all this took off.*

Sixth, I'd like to thank the other people who helped me on my Discord—I got a lot of ideas from them. **Shaodwrise1, Har'Tracyn, Pancakes, True_God_of_Noobs, Seraphion, A Lazy Monster, Deltorian, jjffjhjf, Mikato1, Scion, Tristan, BonzBonzOnlyBonz, DMacks, IHaveManyAliases, KuroYuki, MagmaWave999, OliveBirdy, Section160, SuperWaffle, and Tshandrabal.** *Everyone either contributed editing, feedback, card ideas, or help with the website. To all of you: thank you, genuinely. It means a lot to see someone interested, and it helps a lot to get all your ideas for cards and concepts. This book would have been at least fifteen percent worse without you.*

CONTENTS

CHAPTER 1

STUMBLING BLOCK ON THE STRAIGHT AND NARROW

"Okay, does everyone understand what we're doing tonight?" Emmett asked as he tightly gripped the steering wheel of the blue-and-rust jalopy they were all sitting in. He was practically a caricature of a washed-up '50s pulp detective as he sat in his stained, brown suit and wrinkled shirt, running his sweaty palms over his thinning, salt-and-pepper hair before returning them to the steering wheel of a car that wasn't even turned on. He reeked of desperation and cigarettes.

Wolfe didn't mind the first scent so much, but the second one reminded him that he hadn't had a cigarette in weeks and was fiending for one.

Fiending. An appropriate term. The comforting power of Wolfe's Infernal and Beast deck was a constant presence in his chest, a feeling of hunger, power, and heat. It reminded him of his calling: to hunt those who preyed on others.

Trying to do that the right way, on the right side of the law, was what had led Wolfe to his current place in life. He was awake at two A.M., sitting in said powder-blue-and-rust jalopy, next to a fifty-year-old man who had drunk enough alcohol to be officially considered 'pickled' by the FDA, staring at a closed and rundown train station. A huge junction of tracks; old, rusted locomotives and train cars; and huge maintenance sheds, all behind a chain-like fence with razor wire on the top. The center was a cleared space where the tracks met, gravel bisected by the rusting iron lines.

"Can you go over it again?" Bart asked from the back.

Oh, right, we have a third member of our little party. Bart was some aspiring private investigator working with Emmett, trying to earn his three years of associate work—the requirement to go out on your own.

Just like I'm doing, Wolfe thought with a grimace. Becoming a P.I. had involved a few classes, but the real requirement had been practical experience. With his history, Wolfe couldn't join the police, so this was his only option.

Wolfe hated being in the same position as an obvious mook like Bart.

Emmett sighed and frowned. "We don't have much time! Okay, listen up. The plan is this: we're going to go into the trainyard, and we're going to sneak up on the people there. Then we're going to take pictures of what they're doing. That's it! Once we've done that, we're going to get out of here. Got it, Bart?"

Bart nodded.

"Got it, William?"

Silence in the car.

"William?" Emmett asked again.

It took Wolfe a moment. *Oh, right, my new name.* "I've got it."

Wolfe had been born Ethan Madison Wolfe II and gone by his surname because it had made for a solid street name. But ever since he had 'died,' he had switched his name and started over. Now he was officially William Madison, no middle name. That little change had cost him quite a bit of the money he had fled the Grimm mob family with.

Wolfe tapped the passenger-side dashboard rapidly, his desire for a cigarette making him jittery. "The real question is: Why do we need three men for a simple photography job? Or is this a bit more than that? Most normal people, even most normal criminals, don't need an abandoned train station located in the no man's land between two cities to conduct business. You only need a place like this if you're prepared to kill people to stop them from finding out what you're doing. Maybe it's truly heinous, or maybe it's just a really huge deal with a lot of money involved."

Emmett nodded with Wolfe's words and didn't appear surprised at Wolfe's knowledge. "You have some experience with these people, William?"

Wolfe clenched his fist. "My history is just that. *Mine*. Answer my damn question."

Rather than answering, Emmett reached underneath where Wolfe was tapping the dashboard and opened his glove compartment. Two Glock-17s, a 'standard' police model common throughout the country, each in a vest holster, fell partway from the compartment.

Wolfe stared at the guns for a second, then looked at Emmett, his eyebrow raised.

"I don't *want* trouble, but it could happen. The people we're dealing with are the worst of the worst, and they'll kill to keep from being dragged into the light, like the vicious, little cockroaches they are."

Wolfe chuckled darkly in the sanctity of his own mind. *Tell me how you really feel.*

Emmett took one of the holsters out, removed the eight-inch gun, checked the magazine, placed it back in its case, and handed it to Wolfe. He repeated the motions for the next one and strapped it on himself. The way that it sat on him, Wolfe was pretty sure Emmett was wearing a bulletproof vest.

Not expecting trouble, hmm?

Wolfe let it go and hefted the Glock-17 briefly. He regretted not bringing his own STI International Edge 40 caliber. He didn't have a license to carry concealed, and Illinois wasn't an open carry state. Without the protection of the Grimm family and its corrupt connections, a gun charge could land him in serious trouble—which would reveal to Damian, Wolfe's nemesis, that he was still alive.

"I don't have the permits for this," Wolfe said.

"As a trainee earning your hours under me, you can carry while on the job," Emmett replied. "Besides, I'm surprised you care about the law."

Wolfe grimaced and stared down at the police-standard gun in his hand. It was reliable, but it didn't have quite the stopping power that Wolfe's favorite gun did. Regardless, given the situation and how far they likely were from police, Wolfe decided to risk it. He strapped the gun to his chest.

"Do I get a gun?" Bart asked from the back.

Wolfe turned and stared at the other trainee. The man was about twenty, with sallow cheekbones and slightly black teeth —sure sign of someone using meth, in Wolfe's experience.

"No," Emmett said. The old P.I. rooted around in the glove compartment and took a camera from the back of it, heaved himself around in his seat, and held it out to Bart. "You get this."

Bart stared at it dubiously but took it. "I think I should carry a gun, and William here can carry the camera."

Emmett glanced over at Wolfe again. "I'm comfortable with my choices—this guy has obviously been in some fights."

"*I've* been in fights," Bart protested.

Wolfe was rapidly losing patience with the idiot. "Losing a fistfight to your sister doesn't count, jackoff. Shut up so we can get this over with—the longer we're out here, the more chance something can go sideways. I've got shit to do before I die."

"Hey, asshole—" Bart started.

Wolfe pulled the Glock and held it up, turning it in the dim light inside their vehicle.

"Whatever," Bart muttered, but he shut up beyond that.

Emmett, who hadn't said anything, let go of the steering wheel. "If you two are done arguing, let's go!"

He opened the door and exited the vehicle. Wolfe followed out his own side, Bart behind him. Bart was fiddling with the camera as he went and moved slightly forward.

Emmett fell back to walk beside Wolfe. "You *do* know how to use that, right?"

"I know my way around a firefight," Wolfe responded.

"Odd for someone whose resume listed 'lumberjack' as his only previous work experience," Emmett commented, but then he held his hands up. "I don't actually care how you know, as long as you know."

Wolfe gritted his teeth. "I've told you three times now that I can handle a gun, counting that little tiff with numbnuts over there."

Emmett nodded. "Okay. I just can't have tonight go wrong. This could make up for everything."

Wolfe just shrugged at Emmett and followed the man across the parking lot. Wolfe knew there was more to the story. The truth was, however, that he didn't want to do anything more than to collect a day of supervised training. He needed *three years* of work before he could be a licensed independent P.I., and the unfairness of sitting backseat to a bunch of wet-behind-the-ears P.I.s before he could do his own work was aggravating him.

He had been the head enforcer for the Grimm mob family for *twenty years* before Big Man Grimm's son Damian had shot his father. He could handle a little P.I. work. But *mob enforcer* wasn't something you could put on a resume, so...

The three of them ran across the parking lot until they reached the chain-link fence. The portion to which Emmett had led them was already cut, with a pair of metal cutters on the ground next to it. Bart was still fiddling with the camera.

"You prepared for this, I take it?" Wolfe asked.

Emmett just nodded, his face tense as he looked toward the trainyard.

Bart crawled through and headed into the trainyard. Before they could join him, however, Wolfe grabbed Emmett by the arm. "I don't think I want to do whatever you're doing. It isn't worth a day of training."

"I *need* you," Emmett said. "Bart can barely get his shit together."

"Well, I don't need *this*," Wolfe said. "I've got a lot of my own shit to deal with."

Emmett turned and placed his hand on Wolfe's arm. "I'll make it worth your while, William. I'll sign a *month*'s backlog of work cards to just do this. It'll probably be fine, and you'll get a month's work for an evening."

Wolfe frowned. That would save him a lot of time, despite how his instincts were telling him this was going to be dangerous. "Fine."

The two of them crawled under the cut fence, Wolfe first, and headed into the train graveyard in the center. Wolfe rounded the corner of a train car, staring down a long, open space between numerous other train cars, toward the center. It was open, and a large van was parked in the center. Wolfe could make out a couple of figures moving around in the moonlight, but he was too far away to see details.

"Bart, get back!" Wolfe hissed, but the idiot was either not paying attention or too far away to hear, about halfway from Wolfe to the van.

Emmett reached into his jacket and pulled out an old-fashioned pair of binoculars and held them up to his face. "They haven't opened the van yet. They have to open the van before we take a picture!"

Wolfe reached over and grabbed the binoculars, and Emmett let him take them. Before Wolfe could put them to his face, he heard a car approaching. He looked up to see a sportsy, black convertible with the Ferrari logo on the front pull up with a squeal in the gravel of the trainyard—Wolfe was surprised they'd even gotten close to off-roading it with a car like that, much less entered the trainyard. Infernal Realms, he was surprised they'd let it out of their garage.

He put the binoculars to his face and stared through them.

The people came into focus. Three guys Wolfe didn't recognize were waiting with obvious gun bulges beneath cheap suits, along with a fourth guy Wolfe did recognize: Piper.

"Son of a *bitch*," Wolfe said through gritted teeth.

Piper had been one of the Grimm family men and had worked with Wolfe once. Until he'd disappeared without a trace during a job that had nearly gotten Wolfe killed. Wolfe hadn't even known he'd survived, or what had happened to him.

"You know them, William?" Emmett asked.

The use of his new name floored Wolfe for a moment but stopped him from revealing anything. "No, just upset about the damage they're doing to that car."

"Fuckers deserve everything that happens to them down to the road grit," Emmett ground out. "That car is a Ferrari Mythic 2024, worth almost half a million. I looked it up. They bought it with blood."

Wolfe ignored the hyperbole and stared at the people exiting the car. One was a tall, slender man in his late twenties dressed in a perfectly tailored white suit—completely inappropriate for night-time shenanigans. The other... he was just under six feet tall, with pale-white skin and black hair. He dressed in a black hoodie and equally black skin-tight jeans, and he had a stylized skull ring on his finger.

Wolfe cussed again.

"What?" Emmett asked.

"I know the guy next to the suit," Wolfe said, pointing and passing the binoculars back to Emmett. "That's Tracy d'Ordinii. A deckbearer who will 'remove'"—Wolfe held his fingers up in air quotes, despite Emmett staring through the binoculars—"problems that the powerful crime bosses have. No offense, but we need to leave. Now."

Emmett wisely didn't ask how Wolfe knew these things. "I need to get evidence! Incontrovertible evidence of their wrongdoing. Evidence that the police can't ignore."

Wolfe pinched the bridge of his nose. "You're going to *get* dead, not evidence. Then you'll fail whatever obnoxious quest is driving you. Live to fight another day."

Emmett lowered the binoculars, his pasty face even paler in the moonlight, and Wolfe could smell the sweat and fear on him. He stared at Wolfe for a moment, then his shoulders drooped. "Let's get Bart."

Just then, there was a flash of light from the train cars near the van. Wolfe stared, dumbfounded, at Bart. He had decided to take a picture and obviously forgotten to turn the flash off.

Two of the mooks ran over to Bart, who held his hands up.

With no hesitation whatsoever, one of the mooks raised his gun and shot Bart in the head, then stomped on the camera, hard.

Chapter 2

The Dead Rise

"**N**ot another one!" Emmett yelled, moving forward. He held his own Glock out and fired rapidly, bullets heading toward the mooks as fast as the sweaty P.I. could pull the trigger.

None even came close to hitting any of their enemies that Wolfe could see.

Wolfe was nearly shocked into inaction by the ineptitude of his team. But he still had the presence of mind to grab Emmett by the back of his suit jacket and yank him behind the train car nearest them just before a hail of return fire filled the space the old detective had occupied seconds before.

"What the fuck are you doing?!" Wolfe yelled, then he ripped his own pistol free. "Never mind. Moot question. I can berate you when we're both in the Deadlands."

Wolfe stuck his hand around the edge and fired off, the lower recoil of his new pistol helping with the awkward angle.

A notification appeared in his view, and for a brief second, Wolfe thought he had hit someone, but then he cussed.

Enemy deckbearer has pulled their deck.

"Run!" Wolfe said.

"We can't leave Bart!"

Wolfe almost face-palmed with a pistol, he was so frustrated. "Bart is deader than disco! Get. The fuck. Out of here!"

"What are *you* going to do?" Emmett asked.

"What I do best," Wolfe replied before running around the other side of the train car they were hiding behind and sprinting across to another one.

He didn't see anyone, so he leapt to a ladder on the side of the car and scaled it crazy fast, feeling the skin around his chest scar stretch as he exerted himself. But he still landed on top of the train car in barely three seconds.

He waited a couple more seconds then looked over the edge.

Emmett *wasn't* running toward the gate. Wolfe silently cursed in the quiet of his own mind.

This situation was likely to go bad, and in the moment, Wolfe only wanted to hear one voice. He took his phone out and dialed.

Before the phone picked up, two of the mooks came running up the path between train cars, probably to try to flank the original position, Wolfe guessed. Wolfe hit *mute* on his phone even as Shel answered.

Wolfe couldn't hear her, but he whispered into the receiver, "If I don't make it, keep going—you're everything right in this fucked-up world."

He put his phone down and leaned over the edge of the train car. He hit the first mook with a cluster of three rapid shots to the torso, then turned and hit the other in the legs as he dived behind the other end of the same train car Wolfe had come from.

The thug screamed, "One of them is over here! And he got Pedro!"

A chill filled the air, and Wolfe glanced over. A spectral

mass of robes and rags was floating toward them, out from behind another of the train cars. Wolfe stared, and the card appeared.

Wraith
Common Tier-2 Undead/Shadow creature
1 Undead, 1 Shadow power
Health: 8
Attack: 0
Defense: 3
Magical Attack: 8
Magical Defense: 4

Special: **Incorporeal**: Immune to physical attacks
Special: **Vampiric:** This card fully heals if it kills any living card

"A common denizen of the Deadlands, the Wraith feeds on souls unlucky enough to find themselves on the plains of the Lightless Wastes."

Wolfe was torn. On the one hand, he *really* didn't want Piper or Tracy seeing him or his cards, because soon after, all of Noimoire would know he was alive. However... he *wouldn't* be alive if he fought an experienced deckbearer assassin without a deck of his own.

Wolfe would just have to try to limit the use of cards he was known for and stick with some of his lesser-known cards.

Yeah, I'll fight one-handed instead of no-handed. Screw Emmett and this job and trying to do things the right way.

Wolfe touched his hand to his chest, feeling the darkness and hunger. He held it for two seconds, then pushed his hand outward. Red and brown energy came from his chest and coalesced into five cards: first, a Tier-three Angry Hellhound;

second, Malviere, his named orphan card, which was grayed out, as she was already out back at his house; then one of his Rescue Pups; fourth, a Pack Howl; and off to the side, his companion card, Cereboo.

Wolfe barely ever used his Angry Hellhound, and it had been an extremely common card in the previous drop ten years ago—so hopefully, no one would connect it with him. It also made a small magical attack every time it made a physical attack, so it could at least fight the wraith. Wolfe reached out and touched the card, and a great dog, man-high at the shoulder, with red fur and two horns on its head, appeared. It leapt from the top of the train car and rushed the Wraith.

As soon as his new doggo had leapt, Wolfe rolled over and pointed his gun over the edge of the train again. Tracy came around the side of a train car and fired. Wolfe got a single hit, but Tracy was wearing a mantle. The magic of the mantle clearly increased his defense and prevented Tracy from being seriously hurt by the bullet—at least at the moment, when Wolfe didn't have a mantle of his own.

Tracy glanced around the corner, and in the moonlight, Wolfe could see his smile. "The deckbearer is on top of the train car at the end of the line—here. Surround him and finish him!"

Wolfe wasn't sure if the remaining people would comply, but he wasn't willing to take any chances. He rolled back to the other side and leapt down from the train car top. The ground, almost ten feet below, slapped into him and he grimaced as his ankle twisted. Wolfe collapsed from the impact. *Shit! Not one enemy has tagged me, but I just damaged myself.*

Wolfe came to his feet and limped toward the next line of cars, rolling underneath one. He touched a card and *howled*. A pulse of magic went out, giving his Angry Hellhound a boost—Pack Howl gave +2 to every single stat of any canine for thirty seconds. It was doubly effective on the Angry Hellhound, which normally made two weak attacks.

Then Wolfe dismissed his deck—the cards glowed, and he didn't need the distraction. Plus, he had an idea...

As he'd predicted, two more thugs came running around the corner—the last two, Wolfe was pretty sure. One was Piper, which made Wolfe grimace. But Piper was against him at the moment, and his loyalty had been deeply suspect from their first interactions.

Wolfe aimed carefully and shot both thugs in the chest, one bullet each, less than his usual expenditure. His notifications told him neither had died, but both hit the ground, bleeding and moaning and trying to drag themselves away. *Good enough.*

Wolfe leapt up and ran as fast as he could toward his original position: the train car he had been at when everything had gone wrong. He heard a series of gunshots as he ran.

Wolfe re-summoned his deck.

"They have a second deckbearer!" Tracy yelled. "Caine, you need to join us!"

Wolfe smiled as he came around the corner of that first boxcar. Emmett was down, and Tracy was standing over him, a spectral outline around him, his gun pointed at the detective.

Wolfe fired rapidly, hitting Tracy twice more, but again, the mantle protected him enough. Tracy turned and fled as fast as he could, however. Wolfe presumed he didn't want to face any more bullets.

The night air was penetrated by the faint sound of sirens. *Shel must have called the police.* He was glad he had joked with her about the 'stupid train mission' before leaving.

"Let's go!" the man in the suit—Caine, Wolfe guessed— yelled from near his car.

Tracy kept running, head down, dodging and weaving.

Wolfe shot a few more times but then clicked on empty. He had no more bullets or clips for his gun.

Tracy made it to the car and jumped into the passenger seat. The car spun out for a second in a massive spray of gravel before it raced out of the abandoned train junction.

Wolfe rushed to Emmett's side. The old detective was on the ground, hand over his chest. Blood leaked from a separate wound on his arm, and his already pale complexion was verging toward translucent.

"You okay?" Wolfe asked, then he grimaced. *Of course he isn't okay!*

"Never mind me," Emmett said through gritted teeth. "Are they okay?"

"I doubt it. They all have lead poisoning," Wolfe quipped. "Although Tracy got away with his suited friend—Caine, I guess. Idiot name."

"Not the *thugs*," Emmett ground out, then he slumped back to the ground. "The van..."

Wolfe wanted Emmett to relax—it appeared as if the pudgy P.I. was on the verge of losing his last health through sheer stress. "I'll check it out, Emmett. Be still. Just focus on trying not to leak everywhere."

"Ha ha," Emmett said, no mirth in his voice at all.

Wolfe got up and headed to the van, grimacing as he slowly limped through the gravel while the sirens grew louder. His old instincts were telling him to run—police were trouble. But he couldn't abandon Emmett, and besides, he thought that for once, he wasn't on the wrong side of the law, except for trespassing. Everything that had happened after had been defense of self or others, Wolfe was almost positive. Almost.

As Wolfe limped up to the back of the van, he saw that it was unlocked. He grabbed the door and threw it open even as police came blaring into the trainyard.

He was confronted by twenty long, thin coffins. One was

open, and the inside was a freezing container with a naked woman, perhaps eighteen or nineteen, lying in it. Her head was entirely shaved and her eyes closed. For a second, Wolfe thought she was dead, as she barely breathed, but he saw tubes leading from her body to a machine at the end, which included a vitals monitor that showed slow heartbeat activity.

Police poured from their cars, surrounding Wolfe and screaming at him to get on the ground, but all he could do was stare into the back of the van.

What in all the Infernal realms?

CHAPTER 3

ENTER THE HERO

Wolfe hated police stations.

Most people would assume it was because he had spent twenty years as a criminal, but they would be wrong. He had never been taken in, although he had spent a few hours in the backs of police cars from time to time.

No, it was from the huge amount of time he had spent in them as a child, the first time after his dad had beaten the shit out of him, and the second after Wolfe had killed his father. Neither had ended well, and the police had all been on the take. They had taken the money of his father's patrons—Wolfe still didn't know who—and allowed the young boy Wolfe had once been to suffer injustice. It still rankled, over two decades later.

Wolfe wasn't that great at 'letting go.'

Despite it being over twenty years—and a different city, since this was Joliet Police and not Noimoire—this police station didn't look much different than the one he remembered. It brought back unpleasant memories. Wolfe saw the same cheap-ass, hard, plastic benches bolted to the floor, the same faded, torn posters advertising various charity organizations like the David Torres Homeless Shelter, and the same bulletproof glass protecting overweight police officers with stained shirts who were so far past their prime they were calling into question whether or not said prime had even existed.

"Let go of me, pig!" a struggling junkie screamed as he was walked into the back.

Wolfe glanced at the loser being manhandled. *The same skid-row vibe of the involuntary inhabitants.*

One of the massive, metal doors in the wall opened, and an extremely cute woman, less than five feet tall with caramel skin and long, black hair, came into the room. She was dressed in the pencil-skirt version of a police uniform.

The lady glanced down at her clipboard, all frowns, then glanced up again. "Is there a William here? William?"

No one answered, and she glanced down again. "William Madison?"

Oh, right, that's me now, Wolfe thought, then he stood easily.

The woman glanced over at Wolfe and raised an eyebrow. Wolfe cut an unusual picture—he was six-foot-two-inches, two hundred thirty pounds of nothing but muscle. But his brown hair was disheveled, he was sporting a couple of days' fuzz on his cheeks, and his clothing was scuffed and torn.

Wolfe almost laughed. *She looks like she's trying to decide if I'm a bodybuilder or a vagabond.*

Wolfe walked up to the officer, limping slightly. He towered over the tiny woman by more than a foot.

She glanced up at him. "You're William Madison?"

"That's what my license says," Wolfe responded.

"Right, right... Well, if you'll come with me, please. Lieutenant Rhett Walker would like to talk to you."

Where is Shel? Wolfe pinched the bridge of his nose. "Yeah, sure, take me to him."

He would rather have shot himself in the foot, but you couldn't really say 'no' to the police when you were possibly a suspect in an investigation.

The lady frowned again but motioned Wolfe through the door.

Wolfe walked back through a ton of cubicles and a few offices until he arrived at a brown, wooden door at the back, which a sliding nameplate proudly proclaimed as the domain of Lieutenant Rhett Walker. Wolfe opened the door without knocking and strode in.

"Ah, Cara, is..." The man behind the desk trailed off as he glanced up. Then he stood.

The lady—presumably Cara—hurried past. "Sorry, Lieutenant, he just walked in! I didn't tell him to do that."

Wolfe almost laughed at the desperation in her voice—he presumed indicative of a need to have the lieutenant's approval.

The man's ice-blue eyes flickered over Wolfe, noting his walk and stance first, then meeting his eyes, then going across his clothing. The man's brow furrowed ever so slightly, as if something didn't sit right with what he saw, but Wolfe wasn't sure what.

Those eyes were what Wolfe noticed first, but the rest of the man was impressive as well. He was of a height with Wolfe —six-foot-two—and even more muscled, something Wolfe rarely encountered. His shirt was pressed, and his blond hair was in a perfect military cut. His face was smooth shaven, but for a small mustache, which Wolfe thought of as the police standard-issue mustache.

Okay, I get why she wants his approval. Wolfe disliked the lieutenant almost immediately. He was *too* perfect. Something had to be wrong with him.

Rhett's brow smoothed. "You're William? The William who was at the train station tonight?"

"That's what they tell me," Wolfe said.

Rhett raised an eyebrow at his flippant answer. "Have a seat, please."

"Do you want some coffee, Rhett?" Cara asked, her previous frown now a glorious smile, and her voice falsely cheery.

"That would be great, thanks."

"I'll get it for you, Rhett," Cara said, then she walked out of the office with a bounce in her step and a waggle in her hips.

While the two officers were talking, Wolfe's eyes flicked around the room. He saw multiple commendations and awards, including a certificate from the Elite Card Police Academy, but no pictures of family or friends—just multiple pictures of police functions and clippings from newspapers about lives saved.

There was also a huge article on the wall that read, "Deputy Chief of Police Charleston Drops Noimoire Crime Rate to Lowest Level in Fifty Years." Wolfe wondered why a Joliet detective had an article about the deputy chief of police from a neighboring town on his wall but turned his attention elsewhere.

Next to it was a second article: "Hero Cop Murdered and Ultra-Rare Grail Card Stolen," showing a picture of a smiling man who could have done duty as a recruiting poster, he appeared so masculine and wholesome both.

Rhett's desk was absolutely covered in files. The chair behind the desk was large, but not ostentatious. The one for Wolfe to sit in was a thin, cheap metal one, however.

"So, are you banging her, or do her fingers smell of her own frustration?" Wolfe asked as he pulled the chair out and flipped it around, then sat on it facing Rhett.

Rhett frowned, an expression that sat easily on his face.

"That's a very improper way to speak about a fellow human. Also, I would never sleep with a subordinate. It's deeply improper and unethical."

"Huh, your loss. She looks like she'd be fun in bed."

Rhett's frown deepened. "Also, do you have to sit in the chair that way?"

Wolfe gave the cheap chair a slap. "The ol' baby is tough. She'll hold together."

There was a brief pause before Rhett sat in his own chair and pulled out a pad of legal yellow paper from a drawer. "I wanted to ask you about your participation in tonight's events."

"You'd be better off asking Emmett—I was just hired to help him investigate a possible criminal site. He didn't tell me what we were doing beforehand, and I have no idea what that was about."

"Well, tell me your side of it, please," Rhett said. "Besides, after the barest of questioning, the EMTs ended up taking Emmett, and he's out cold at the moment."

Fuck. Even if he did get me in this mess, I hope the guy makes it. He's the kinda guy who feels as if life already took a sledgehammer to his knees.

"I already gave my statement to the officers at the scene, once they realized I wasn't a bad guy and took their pistols out of my ear," Wolfe said.

Rhett smiled at his description. "Standard police procedure when we don't know what's happening on a scene —sorry about that. But about that statement—I'd like to ask some clarifying questions. Because a few details don't add up."

Wolfe tensed slightly, although everything he'd said had been the absolute truth. "Whatever gets your rocks off."

Rhett rolled his eyes. "Right. According to Emmett, you basically saved his life. Five thugs, one of whom was a

21

deckbearer, attacked you guys when you found them engaged in human trafficking."

"That's pretty much how it happened," Wolfe said. "So, I'm the good guy, then? I can go?"

"Where did you learn to fight so well that on almost no notice, with a handgun that wasn't yours, you managed to kill two of them, deeply wound a third to the point his life is hanging in the balance as we speak, cripple a fourth, and drive the deckbearer off?"

Wolfe tensed. "I've been to the gun range."

Rhett smiled and opened a file with the name "Madison, William," on it. He glanced into it and then stared at Wolfe. "Come now, don't be modest. That was one of the most... complete, I guess, victories I have ever seen."

"Meh."

Rhett glanced up. "You told Emmett you worked at the lumber mill here in Joliet before you became a private investigator?"

"That's what it says in my file, right?" Wolfe asked. "Why do you have that, anyway? You keep files on all your citizens?"

"It was a formality, created when you applied to become a private investigator. But it does have your answers to the questionnaire here. It must have been hard."

"The questionnaire?" Wolfe asked, not sure where Rhett was going.

"Being unemployed for nearly a decade, since the last lumber mill here closed seven years ago."

Wolfe cussed in the safety of his own mind. They had needed to generate a backstory fast and loose when first getting Wolfe his fake ID, social security number, and birth certificate —things he'd needed when he'd purchased a house, even with cash.

Before he could formulate some plausible-sounding story,

the door opened, admitting the sound of yelling. "They need you in Interrogation A, Rhett," Cara said.

Rhett nodded and stood. "Don't go anywhere, Mr. Madison. We still have things to discuss. I'll be back in just a few minutes."

Wolfe nodded and Rhett left the room, following Cara.

Left alone, Wolfe reached across and opened his file. It was almost entirely incomplete. It had his questionnaire from when he'd gotten his provisional private investigator license, and some faxed copies of his fake birth certificate, his driver's license, and the death certificates for his fake parents. Nothing else.

Wolfe relaxed—nothing to connect his current life as 'William Madison' to the head enforcer of the Grimm mob family, Ethan Madison Wolfe II. Perfect.

But as he let the file go, his eye flicked across the rest of the files on the table. Most of them were files *for* the Grimm family members—including ones for Damian and Piper... and Wolfe himself.

Wolfe reached across and gently opened the file, careful not to disturb its place. At the top was his death certificate, and opposite was a blurry photo from a police cam. It didn't show him well, but...

Why is the good lieutenant looking at the file of a dead guy? Does he know, or suspect?

Wolfe closed the file and sat back. *Just more shit to deal with. Gods damn, Emmett! I really don't need the police looking into my backstory right now. Or ever.*

Wolfe glanced at the files a second time. *Why does he have the Grimm family files out? Miriam said all the money was tied up in legal proceedings, and that Damian wouldn't be able to engage in any of the family activity... Has he found an alternative source of funding? Did he have money squirreled away from before?*

Wolfe had a dark thought. *An absolute ton of good cards were left in the Grimm family mansion when I blew it all to hell. If he collected most of them—and the little card-obsessed hobgoblin could actually stand to part with a few—he could have gotten some serious seed money.*

Wolfe was so focused that he almost didn't hear the turn of the knob, but the door creaked as it opened, and Wolfe dropped the file folder flap and leaned back in his chair just before Rhett entered again.

The man walked over, sat back in his chair, and opened William Madison's file again. He read for a few moments before looking up, the folder flap held in his hand.

"Sorry about that, William. A couple of kids we removed from a car for excessive drunkenness were getting violent. Now, where were we?"

"You were about to tell me I was free to go?" Wolfe asked.

Rhett raised his eyebrow at him. "Worried I might look into your life?"

"Is this how you usually question people who just saved the lives of twenty near-kids?" Wolfe shot back.

Rhett frowned again. "I always check out all stories I don't understand, at least where my jurisdiction is concerned."

Wolfe wanted to ask about neighboring jurisdictions, like Noimoire, since the Grimm family had never had a presence in Joliet, but he held his tongue. That would have been a huge red flag for lieutenant detective over there.

Before they could continue the repartee, there was a knock at the door.

Rhett blinked at the door and muttered, "Is it too much to ask *anyone* else around here to handle something?"

Wolfe almost laughed—he could sympathize with the guy on that.

"Come in," Rhett called.

The door opened, and a vision of feminine beauty walked

in. Red hair framed a freckled, heart-shaped face with two near-emerald eyes on top of a five-foot-four, slim—but with a healthy amount of muscle underneath—frame. The vision was dressed in blue workout shorts showing off tan legs, and a T-shirt.

Before Wolfe could even greet Shel, Rhett asked, "Why are you here, Cadet Lyons?"

Chapter 4

Home Is Where the Heart Is

Wolfe blinked at Rhett's knowledge of his girlfriend but recovered quickly. "What *are* you doing here, Shel?"

Shel gave a glowing smile. "I came here to collect William—my boyfriend."

It was Rhett's turn to blink. "*This* man is the William you're dating?"

Shel nodded. Then she walked over and put her arms around Wolfe's chest from behind and kissed his cheek. "Yes. This is the man I'm with."

"I... see..." Rhett said. He dropped the folder flap. "You... vouch for him?"

Shel tilted her head slightly. "That's an odd phrase, Lieutenant. But this man has always had my back, if that's what you mean. Always."

"Even though he's way older than you?"

Shel smiled brilliantly. "I like to think of him as *more experienced*. Besides, what difference does it make, really?"

"I suppose that's as fine a way of looking at it as any," Rhett said slowly.

"Why's he here, though?" Shel asked.

"I had some questions for him, but I think I've asked enough," Rhett said. "I mean, he just saved twenty people, nearly singlehandedly, and now I've learned he's dating our cadet class's top student. I suppose that's all the answer I need, for now."

Wolfe grit his teeth at the implication that Rhett might ask more questions later.

Shel smiled again and kissed Wolfe on his other cheek. "Just like I'd expect him to do. He's free to go, right? I need to get him home and make sure he's okay."

"He has a twisted ankle that's pretty swollen, but otherwise, he's untouched."

Wolfe grit his teeth. "I can let her know how I'm doing without help, thanks."

Rhett nodded. "Sure. Let me get your number in case I have more questions, okay?"

Wolfe was tempted to refuse, but with Shel here, he didn't want to make a scene with the man who was apparently her instructor. She didn't need that shit. He grabbed a pen from the desk and wrote it on the outside of his file.

Rhett frowned—at Wolfe's disrespect for police property, probably—but didn't address it directly. "Well, take him home, Shel. I look forward to seeing you in class tomorrow, at a less infernal hour."

Shel nodded with her cheek pressed against Wolfe's.

Wolfe stood, almost shrugging out from Shel in his irritation with the situation. "Let's go."

He glanced over at Rhett and gave him sarcastic finger-guns. "Well—catch ya on the flip side."

Wolfe turned and walked from the room, Shel following. He headed out through the door and into the cheap police lobby, walking fast and fuming as he went.

Once they were outside, Wolfe turned to Shel. "That dick is your instructor?"

Shel raised an eyebrow. "I'm surprised you don't like him —you guys have a lot in common."

"Pfft," Wolfe said. "I seriously doubt that. He's a goody two-shoes cop, for fuck's sake. Or maybe one on the take, like the ones that 'helped'"—Wolfe held up air quotes—"when my father beat me all those years ago."

Shel touched his arm. "Well, no need to worry about it now. Let's get you home, where I can take care of you."

She led him out into the parking lot, to the replacement car he had purchased—cash only again, like his house. It was a slightly older Subaru Outback. Black like his old car, and it had the same set of modifications as his old car, minus the smuggling compartment. There were bulletproof windows and reinforced siding, and he had, of course, sprung for the turbocharged engine. It wasn't actually an *amazing* car, but it was one that appeared totally normal while being higher performing and more protective than it ought to have been— which he needed, since he wasn't ready to reveal to Damian that he had survived, not yet. Nor could he afford to be pulled over by curious cops. It would lead to too many encounters like the one he had just had.

"Wait, if he's your instructor, is he a member of the card police?" Wolfe asked as they got in the car, Wolfe in the driver's side, Shel in the passenger.

Shel nodded. "Yes. Although not all my instructors or fellow students are card police."

"What kind of deck?" Wolfe asked.

He pulled out of the police station and onto Jules Street, honking at someone in a Volvo who'd nearly clipped him.

Shel smiled nervously. "Don't drive angry! I think that guy had the right of way."

Wolfe didn't answer, and Shel returned to his question.

"Rhett has a Divine and Golem deck, he says, but he's never shown it. I don't know the cards or anything. That's just what he told us."

Fuck.

Wolfe looked sideways at Shel. She was still quite small, at about five-foot-four, with red hair and green eyes. But she wasn't the complete pale waif whose life he had saved in a bar fight nine months ago. She had some muscle—more tone than bulk—about her body, and a decent tan. Her gaze was steadier, and she smiled more.

When Wolfe had first met her, she had been hunting her brother's killer, and fresh out of living with family who'd beaten her. Now she was almost a year from that tragedy, in a new life as a deckbearer, with a partner in Wolfe, who, while by no means perfect, was certainly not abusive of her.

Shel probably wasn't someone the police would have recruited under normal circumstances, despite her good grades in high school—except for the fact that she had a deck. That meant that as soon as she graduated the police academy, she would be going straight to the elite—and well-paid—card police, which were exactly what they sounded like: police officers with decks. For handling a lot of situations where you needed something that could go into hostile territory, or to fight criminal deckbearers.

She's young, she's beautiful, and she has a deck. Why the hell is she still with me?

Hell, her instructor even had a Divine deck as well.

As Wolfe drove through the cool, night air, he pondered his situation. He didn't want to burden Shel with anything, but they were partners now...

He came to a decision. "We *might* have a problem. Your good buddy Rhett was looking over files on the Grimm family —including a file for me. Me Ethan Wolfe, I mean, not William Madison."

Shel grimaced. "There's nothing to connect you, right?"

"I don't think so," Wolfe mused slowly. "But I can't be sure. Some of the guys at the train station would know me on sight."

"Who? Were they Grimm family members?" Shel asked.

Wolfe shook his head, then stopped. "Actually, I'm not sure. Piper was there, and they took him into custody. He might be working for Damian. He might not. I don't know. But Tracy—Tracy d'Ordinii, an assassin for hire—would also know me. I don't think either one saw me in the dark, but I can't be one-hundred-percent positive."

Wolfe turned off Jules Street and onto Persimmon, the only entrance to a small subdivision that contained his new house—a moderately wealthy subdivision with neighbors who were mostly boring and left him alone, the way he liked it.

"What are you going to do?" Shel asked.

Before Wolfe could answer, his phone rang. Since he didn't have a good answer for Shel, anyway, he picked up the phone instead while using one hand to drive. "Yeah?"

Emmett's voice came through the phone. "William? That you?"

Wolfe frowned. "Yeah, it's me. I mean, *you* called *me*. Who did you expect it to be?"

"I can't be too careful," Emmett said, his voice going low and soft. Wolfe could imagine him glancing around with shifty eyes wherever he was. "I need to talk to you."

Wolfe rolled his eyes. "Well, I have fantastic news for you, then. You're talking to me right now! Tada! For your next trick, try to breathe. It'll also be an easy item to cross off your to-do list."

"Always with the sarcasm. I meant I need to talk to you *privately*. About what happened tonight."

"You mean the part where you dragged me into a blind

gunfight—gun and card fight—in a trainyard without warning me?" Wolfe growled out.

Shel raised her eyebrow and mouthed, "Emmett?"

Wolfe nodded to her during the brief pause.

Then Emmett cut in again. "Look, I'm sorry about that. But you saw what was going on—I needed to put a stop to it."

"So call the police," Wolfe said.

"I can't trust anyone except you. I know that you aren't with them, or I'd be dead."

"You can't trust the police? Seriously?" Wolfe asked.

"Please, just come talk to me!" Emmett said again. "I can make it worth your while."

Wolfe sighed. He doubted Emmett would make it worth his while, but he figured it wouldn't hurt to talk. "All right, tomorrow evening. It's practically morning already and I haven't been to sleep. I'll come talk to you. But I'm not promising a gods-damned thing."

"That's fair. And thank you. I'll tell you everything once you get here."

"I'm waiting with bated breath," Wolfe said with as much sarcasm as he could muster, then he hung up the phone before Emmett could say anything else.

"What did he want?" Shel asked.

Wolfe pulled into the driveway of their new home. In the darkness, even with a streetlamp a single house down, he couldn't make out many features, but it had an honest-to-goodness white picket fence, waist high, around the front. "To talk to me. Probably to ask me to do a bunch of dangerous shit for him since he got himself shot. He says he can make it worth my while."

Wolfe opened the door and stepped from the car to the sounds of paws hitting a fence over and over. Wolfe smiled as he looked at his two new dogs, then scowled as Shel got out and glanced at him.

"James and Jason are happy to see you," she said, nodding her head to the two twenty-pound apricot fluff balls masquerading as dogs that were waiting for him. Their tails were wagging so furiously, Wolfe thought they might have had motors in their butts.

"Ridiculous things," Wolfe muttered. "Their attempts to trick people into thinking they're real dogs are half-assed at best."

But he opened the gate and petted and scratched the two dogs as they jumped on him, licking at him when he bent down. The two dogs were cavapoos—a mix between Cavalier King Charles Spaniels and poodles. They were hyper-friendly, hypoallergenic, and cuddlier than the teddy bear from the detergent commercials. They were also faintly ridiculous and utterly non-threatening, with almost nothing that Wolfe would consider a normal 'dog' skill.

Wolfe glanced at Shel, who was smiling down at him as he petted and cuddled the little mop heads.

"Hey, I'm just saying *hello*. These guys are still utterly ridiculous."

"So you've said," Shel murmured, then she walked up and put her arms around Wolfe. She leaned up and licked his ear, breathing out, "Care to waste another thirty minutes before we go to sleep?"

Wolfe's heart rate quickened, and he nodded. He went to the front door, the dogs running ahead and jumping on it, and then let everyone into their house.

Wolfe pulled out his deck and touched his companion card, Cereboo.

The giant, three-headed, black-furred boxer appeared, and the two cavapoos—who had been terrified when they'd first met him—began to leap at him happily, play-bowing and then racing around.

"Keep these two idiot excuses for canines out of trouble,

huh, buddy?" Wolfe said as he reached down and scratched Jason behind his floppy ear again.

Cereboo woofed, and Wolfe stood, then picked Shel up, slinging her over his shoulder. She squealed and batted at him playfully. "Put me down!" she demanded, but there was laughter in her voice as Wolfe walked to their bedroom and kicked the door shut behind him.

CHAPTER 5

SEDUM

"Do you have any food?" the girl asked, staring up at Wolfe.

He sighed, glancing at his watch. It was almost noon. After an enjoyable evening with Shel last night, she had asked if her younger sister—the one who had left with Shel's mother when she'd fled Shel's abusive father—could come over. Wolfe had said 'yes,' and then woken up to Shel telling him that the munchkin was over, and that Shel herself needed to attend her class.

If Wolfe were being honest with himself, only Shel, his doggos, and hunting evil people brought him much happiness, and he wanted to do whatever made his girlfriend happy to return the joy she brought his life.

But he still had absolutely no idea what to do with a random rugrat.

He had been letting Papa TV handle the kid up until this point. Well, Papa TV as well as Cereboo and Malviere—the insanely creepy minion card was currently petting Cereboo in the living room. Cereboo was two hundred pounds of black-furred boxer puppy with three heads, and Malviere appeared as a skeletally thin, ten-year-old with long, brown hair who wore a tattered black dress, with equally black shadows flickering around her.

Not creepy at all.

Even more creepy was the Vengeful Orphan card that wandered around the house, earning its evolution. He appeared as a pre-pubescent boy who always carried a knife. At the moment, he was sitting on the couch near the TV.

The ten-year-old Lucy—who studiously ignored his cards—was staring up at him in his own new front room, her green eyes slightly narrowed. The house was larger than the one he had lived in before 'resigning' from the Grimm family. The front room was a full living room, with doors to both a hallway in one direction, the back yard in another, and a full kitchen in the third.

His two apricot fluff balls raced around the room, jumping and pawing at legs, trying to get someone to pet or play. The girl—Lucy—absently bent down and scratched one behind the ears, then straightened and pushed the red hair that had fallen in front of her face back behind her ears with her right hand. She kept her left arm down at her side, hiding the missing hand that ended in a stump and two very awkward pseudo-fingers.

Despite Shel's history, and Wolfe's own dark life, the hand wasn't the result of any kind of abuse, according to Shel. Lucy was just unlucky, and the gods had given her a birth defect.

"I would like some food as well," Malviere said, her voice a combination of high-pitched female child and the reverberations from... elsewhere.

"You don't even need to eat," Wolfe growled out.

"I still *like* to eat," Malviere said.

"Do you all want eggs? I make a mean scrambled egg," Wolfe said.

"You made that for breakfast," Lucy replied.

"Didn't you just eat, like, a couple of hours ago?" Wolfe asked.

"I'm a growing child and need to eat regularly," Lucy said pedantically.

Wolfe sighed and pulled out his phone. "What do you want? Because if it's not scrambled eggs, it's gonna be Chef DoorDash."

"A chicken salad," Lucy responded. "It's good for me."

"You're a weird kid," Wolfe replied, trying to find a place that would deliver what she'd asked for and settling on Applebee's.

"It's not nice to call someone 'weird,'" Lucy replied, flushing and putting her hand behind her back.

Wolfe frowned. *This is why I shouldn't be asked to watch kids.*

"I'm not talking about your damn hand, kid, and it wasn't an insult. I meant it in the sense that you're, like..." Wolfe waved his hand as he tried to think of the best way to say it. "Improbable in a good way. It's an odd ten-year-old who knows they should eat healthy. But it's a good thing. Calm your jets, or whatever the kids say nowadays."

"Oh. Sorry. I shouldn't jump to conclusions."

"I want eggs," Malviere said, and Cereboo woofed in what Wolfe knew was agreement.

"You two can have burgers," Wolfe said.

"I like my meat rare," Malviere said, licking her lips like a predator, which was extra-creepy on a ten-year-old.

A decent number of Wolfe's cards—and a few of his associates—were creepy.

Wolfe finished ordering and directed his attention back to Lucy. "All right, I'm going to go try to clean up the failure that is our back yard. You watch some more TV or play on your phone, okay?"

"Don't you have anything else to do?" Lucy asked. "I'm bored."

"You can play with Malviere."

Lucy looked over at the card that was blatantly radiating dark energy and shuddered. "Do you have anything else?"

"No. I don't have any kids' toys or know a damn thing about them. Plus, Shel will be home soon. She'll take care of you if you don't want to hang with Malviere or Cerberus."

Shel's tiny twin frowned up at him but said nothing else.

Wolfe walked to the back, opened the sliding glass door, and stepped out onto his small porch. "C'mon, you two," he called to his cards.

Malviere and Cerberus followed him out into his back yard—which could charitably be described as a 'work in progress.' Before Wolfe could shut the door, his two cavapoo pups ran out as well.

Wolfe glanced at his two companion cards, reflecting that they were the absolute backbone of his deck—both made his deck far more effective.

Cereboo

Unique Rare equivalent, Tier-7 equivalent, Beast/Infernal
[Canine] Companion
0 Power
Health: 12
Attack: 5 x3
Defense: 7
Magical Attack: 7[**Fire**]
Magical Defense: 4

Special: **Fungible [Beast, Infernal]:** While in play, Beast and
Infernal power may be spent as if they were the other.
Special: **Infernal Slayer**: +100% attack and magic attack
against other Infernal cards.

Special: **Preferred Typing [Beast, Infernal]:** Gains all the better type matchups of both Infernal and Beast.
Special: One of the 'Gate to the Underworld' cards. If all 6 are possessed in the same deck, the bearer will gain 7 Legendary Infernal or Beast card pulls. Additionally, the deckbearer may either gain the Mythic 'Gate to the Underworld' Building Card or evolve Cereboo. Each card was given to a member of the Noimoire underworld.

"A pup of Cerberus, who was born into a particularly frisky litter. Cereboo was the runt—not quite as strong, nor as tough, as his littermates. But his heart was the heart of a huntsman, and the blood of Cerberus runs in his veins. He hunted across the fiery plains of the first Infernal realm, chasing the damned who tried to escape their fates. Now, he chases many things, but his soul is still called to chase those who belong in the Infernal Realms."

Malviere, Conduit of Cerberus
Unique, no-tier Mortal/Infernal companion[Orphan, Canine]
0 Power
Health: 13
Attack: N/A
Defense: 3
Magical Attack: N/A
Magical Defense: 5

Special: Will fetch normal objects and such with a decent degree of precision and help carry up to ten pounds.
Special: **Orphan Evolution [Unique]:** If kept 'alive' for five straight years, will turn into a Tier-6 equivalent

companion card, gaining notable power. If ever 'killed,' the timer resets.

Special: **Canine Leader [1]**: All other allied [canine] creature cards gain +1 to their non-health stats while she is on the field

Special: **Canine Rush [1]**: Once per round, any one [Canine] card may take an extra attack or magical attack action.

Special: **Canine Lord:** [**Canine**] creature cards of other deckbearers will switch sides without returning their power.

"Malviere cannot remember any life except that of acting as a conduit for the great guardian of the gates of the Infernal, Cerberus. She aids his chosen hunters on the Mortal plane, to bring back those whom Hell has lost. And she gets to play with *all* the doggos. Good, and bad."

Wolfe sighed and turned his attention from his awesome cards to his less-than-amazing back yard. He looked at it in the afternoon sun of late autumn's false summer. His back yard was trashed—especially his garden. He had planted about a hundred flowers, and he couldn't remember what they all were, but only one patch of them bloomed regularly. It was a patch of flowers with a yellow center and thin, red petals sticking out around it. Not the most beautiful flower, but it was still pretty.

Wolfe walked over, grabbed the hose where it was attached to the wall, and turned on the water. He unspooled the hose and let the water hit his patchy grass as he walked over to the garden portion of his domain. Malviere ran around the yard, throwing sticks for Cereboo as well as the two apricot fluff balls. She got along better with dogs than people, most of the time, being a 'Conduit for Cerberus.'

"You're doing it wrong," a voice said from the fence.

Wolfe whirled, hand falling to where his Edge would normally have been. He saw an eye—pale blue behind smudged glasses, with wrinkles all around—staring at him through a knot in the wood.

The old bat who lives next door. Lovely.

Wolfe had never met her, but he had seen her, and some dirty-blonde-haired girl he assumed was her granddaughter, from time to time, in their front yard. It was a very nice house, and he wondered who she was that she had been able to keep it when she retired.

His two cavapoos ran to the fence and started barking at the old lady, minutes too late, like Wolfe hadn't already known she was there.

Wolfe ignored them—and her. He went back to giving his flowers some water. It pooled across the ground, not seeping in quickly.

Maybe he *was* doing something wrong.

"You should have dug the flowerbed up to about eighteen inches of depth and then broken it up before putting it back. It makes it easier for the roots and allows water to get to the flowers without problems," the lady said.

"What do you want?" Wolfe asked exasperatedly.

"Just to help you. You're floundering badly, and I feel for the plants."

Wolfe frowned. "Seriously, you old bat? You're so lonely that you want to help some random guy garden?"

The eye seemed to crinkle, as if she were smiling. "Like I said, it's a mercy for the plants."

Wolfe rolled his eyes, but he also smiled a tiny bit. He preferred people with tough skin and some bite to them.

Not enough to invite some old grandma to his house, but still.

"Look, I can handle this gardening thing. I'll figure it out. You go back to knitting, or dying in peace—whatever it is that old people do."

The lady chuckled on the other side of the fence. "So

neighborly of you. But suit yourself. I'll be here when you realize you need help."

Wolfe grunted, half-amused, half-annoyed. But he kept watering his plants. After a bit, he went and grabbed a three-pronged tool that Shel had and used it to poke holes in the ground so the water could soak in better.

After he'd checked the knot to make sure the old bat wasn't watching, of course.

Wolfe worked another hour to judge by the sun, give or take—watering, poking holes, and eventually getting their mower. It wasn't working out in the gym sense of the term, but he enjoyed the physical labor. It relaxed him, helping him to mull over Emmett, the Grimm family, Damian, and his life in general.

He also enjoyed seeing his cards and dogs playing and having fun, even if his two dogs had gotten so muddy, they had moved from apricot to brown.

The sliding glass door opened and Wolfe hunched slightly. He figured that Lucy was gonna bug him again and didn't want to deal with it.

But it was Shel's voice that called him. "Wolfe! I brought ice cream!"

Wolfe's shoulders loosened and he dropped the hose. He wasn't really an ice cream guy, but he was glad to see Shel.

"Coming!" Wolfe called.

He washed his hands off, then wiped them on a less-dirty portion of his shirt and headed inside. He turned into his kitchen, a modern-looking place done in tiles and gray, with a granite countertop. It had a section to the side with a smaller table and four chairs for eating without going to the dining room. The table and chairs were gray and theoretically fit the room, but somehow always seemed cheaper to Wolfe.

Lucy was already at said table eating ice cream and reading a book. Shel had set three more bowls out. Each was filled with piña colada-flavored ice cream, which struck Wolfe as odd, but he set it aside. He went to the fridge, grabbed a beer, and sat at the table.

There were also cold hamburgers, one on a plate on the table, and one on the floor.

"Ah, beer and ice cream, a time-honored tradition," Shel joked, smiling at him.

"Hey, I just spent an hour working in the hot sun," Wolfe said. "I'm entitled."

Malviere sat at the table and began ripping at the burger like she was feral, and Cereboo bit his in half and simply wolfed the first part down with a single gulp of the central head.

Huh, Lefty usually gets to eat. I wonder why it was different this time.

Then Cereboo bit the remainder in half and let each cavapoo puppy have one piece of it. They promptly started dragging them around the house.

Wolfe cussed and Shel laughed and went and picked up the pieces of lost burger.

"You should drink water to hydrate yourself," Lucy supplied without looking up from her book.

Wolfe rolled his eyes.

Shel sat back down and tapped her fingers together, a nervous gesture from their earlier time together that Wolfe hadn't seen in a while.

Here comes the other shoe, ready to drop.

"Just say it," Wolfe said, then he took a drink of his beer and grimaced. *I really want some good whisky, but it's too early in the day for that.*

"So... I got invited to a barbecue, by one of the other class instructors—not Rhett," Shel said.

"Good for you," Wolfe replied.

"They told me I can invite my significant other," Shel said.

Wolfe put his bottle down, staring at her for a moment, eyes wide.

"You want me to go to a *cop* barbecue?" Wolfe asked. "You forget who I am?"

"What does that even mean?" Lucy asked, staring back and forth between her sister and Wolfe.

Shel ignored her. "Well... you're William, and I think you'll get along with everyone. You have a lot in common with them. Plus, I want to tell everyone what my priorities are."

"What are they?" Wolfe asked, confused. "And why do I need to be there for you to do that?"

"My priority is you," Shel said softly.

"Gross," Lucy muttered.

Malviere chimed in with, "For the pack."

Wolfe ignored the kid—and his card—and felt his cheeks heating. "Right. Umm... sure, I guess. That's fine. But if I don't like it, I'm leaving."

Shel nodded. "That's fair. It's tomorrow afternoon."

"Great."

Shel paused as Wolfe took another sip of his beer and then some of the sweet ice cream. It wasn't the best combination.

Shel was tapping her fingers together again, like the world's most nervous evil mastermind.

Wolfe raised an eyebrow at her.

"Can I see Emmett with you as well?"

Wolfe was honestly surprised. "Of course. Why couldn't you?"

She shrugged. "You normally try to keep me out of harm's way."

Wolfe snorted. "We're gonna go see a borderline geriatric guy with a gunshot wound in a hospital. I think harm will be far away from this one." Then he tipped his beer to Lucy. "'Course, you'll need to find a sitter for this rugrat."

"Hey!" she replied indignantly.

Wolfe laughed, and Shel smiled. "I'll just have Sorenia do it. If an angel of Raphael can't take care of a child, who can?"

Shel pulled out her own deck and touched one of the softly glowing golden cards. A woman, nearly six feet tall with white hair, dove wings, and an old-timey iron lantern chain strapped to one wrist appeared.

"Thank you for bringing me out, my deckbearer," Sorenia said, bowing shallowly to Shel.

Sorenia briefly frowned at Malviere, but Cereboo woofed, ran over, and began licking Sorenia with all three heads. Lucy laughed out loud, accidentally spitting ice cream on the table as Sorenia tried to fend three heads off with one hand. Shel's sister went beet red, cleaned the ice cream up extremely fast, and then went and washed her face.

Sorenia finally managed to calm Cereboo enough to just pet him.

Wolfe glanced at the three companion cards that were all out.

Sorenia

Unique, effective Tier-7 Divine/Light companion
0 Power
Health: 10 (3 remaining)
Attack: 0
Magical Attack: 9**[Light]**
Defense: 8
Magical Defense: 8

Special: **Guiding Light [Mortal]:** While in play, all Mortal creature cards gain divine typing and +25% (minimum 1) to all stats.

Special: The benefits to Mortal cards stack with the other three named companion lantern angels. If all 4 are possessed, the card Zarachiel, Commander of the Lanterns, a 4-power mythic Tier-8 equivalent divine companion card will be gained as well as a free companion card slot.

"A particularly zealous and dedicated member of the hundred thousand lantern angels, she tries to guide mortals to right behavior—and victory over the Infernal, Undead, and Elder gods. Through her zealous efforts to make the Mortal world better, she once earned a lesson at Archangel Raphael's knee, her proudest memory."

"Yeah, odds are pretty decent she can handle anything while we're gone," Wolfe said.

CHAPTER 6

MORIBUND HOSTEL

Wolfe hated the smell of hospitals—it reminded him of his near-week-long stay after the first time his father had beaten him. There was a chemical smell that couldn't quite cover up the faintest hint of death and decay, and it reminded you that the air was likely filled with germs.

The incessant coughing of the people in the waiting room wasn't helping, either.

"Room Twenty-Three on the third floor," the stick-thin nurse acting as a receptionist said, adjusting her glasses and glancing up from the computer. She was ugly—like a stick figure drawn by someone's non-dominant hand, but her eyes were quick-moving and took details in rapidly.

Ugly, perceptive, and probably judgy. Wolfe didn't like her on sight.

The nurse continued. "He's awake at the moment, so head on up. Take the second door"—she pointed to one of numerous doors in the wall—"and I'll buzz you in. Use the elevator, and when you get off, go right. Right, got it? Right."

Wolfe blinked at her. "Yeah, I heard you the first time you said it."

The human walking stick scowled. "Well, a lot of people go the wrong way."

Shel put her hand on Wolfe's arm and stared at the badge on the lady's smock. "Thank you, Nurse Green. We really appreciate the help, and you making sure we don't get lost."

Wolfe briefly wondered how a nurse had gotten stuck working the front desk, which he was pretty sure wasn't how that was usually done.

She was still frowning but nodded to the door. "Go on, go see Mr. Dunn. No one has come to see him. We couldn't find any friends or family at all—we were worried he didn't have someone in his life, so I think he'll be happy to see you." Under her breath, she muttered, "Glad *someone* will be."

As they walked to the door, Shel smiled at Wolfe. "Why pick a fight? She's just trying to help. Be nice to the little people, remember?"

Wolfe rotated his neck and then gave her a stretching shrug. "Sorry, just feeling weird. I hate hospitals and don't want to get sick. Plus, there might be a cop here who recognizes me. Your instructor—"

"Rhett."

"—is already up my ass. Also, the Grimm family might be active in Joliet for some reason, and while they didn't see me clearly, they did get a good look at Emmett—so they might be here as well. Lady treating me like a special-needs two-year-old was just 'one more thing.'"

They reached the wall and the door buzzed. Wolfe pushed it open and hit the elevators that were immediately to the right side of the hallway they'd entered.

After the elevator doors shut, Shel said, "Well, you're *complaining* like a two-year-old. Where's the badass chosen of Cerberus who saved me at the start of this year?"

Wolfe snorted. "All right, you've got a point. I'll quit whining and just deal with the shit if it comes at us. Although I still don't like hospitals."

Shel kissed him on the cheek. Wolfe smiled.

Then Shel licked his ear.

Wolfe jerked away for a second, caught by surprise, then smirked at Shel, who was looking at him with a challenge in her eye and her hands on her hips.

Just as Wolfe was about to reach for her, the elevator dinged and opened.

Shel smirked back at him.

Wolfe rolled his eyes. "Point to you, Ms. Lyons," he said, faux serious.

"You can try again tonight," Shel said with a grin as she stepped out from the elevator.

Wolfe, already feeling ten times better than he had but two minutes ago, followed her out onto the hospital floor. The smell was just as bad, but it was almost silent in the upper wing. Wolfe took in the room number directions, then followed the signs toward twenty-three, his shoes clicking quietly on the shiny floor as he walked.

Wolfe stared at the floor, not sure what it was made of. Not linoleum, but it wasn't that different...

Shel elbowed Wolfe in the side. "Hey, speak of the Infernal, there's Rhett!"

Wolfe froze for a moment, glancing up. The good lieutenant stood in front of Room Twenty-Three—Emmett's room—and stared at a pile of paperwork attached to a clipboard, his gaze intense.

"Hey, Instructor!" Shel called out. She waved while walking forward before Wolfe could say anything.

Rhett looked up, blinked in surprise, and then smiled.

"What are you doing here, Lieutenant?" Shel continued.

"I'm here to question P.I. Emmett," Rhett said. "It's in connection to the trainyard case, of course."

"That's why we're here," Shel said, and Wolfe pinched the bridge of his nose.

"You know Emmett?" Rhett asked.

Shel motioned to Wolfe and beckoned him forward. Wolfe glared at her but walked up to the walking recruiting poster that was the lieutenant. "I work with him, remember?"

Rhett nodded, his face clearing. "Oh, of course. That makes sense."

Rhett turned to Shel, smiling at her with his perfect teeth. "It'll be officially posted tomorrow, but you scored a perfect hundred on the last test, which has solidified your position at the top of the class. You're really making something of yourself, Shel, and I can't wait to see where you go."

Wolfe found himself irritated by the lieutenant's words to Shel and threw his arm around her shoulders. "Well, it's been fun, *Sergeant*, but I have business to get to."

The lieutenant frowned, but to Wolfe's disappointment, didn't react further.

Shel leaned up to Wolfe's ear. "Actually, can I stay and talk to Rhett?"

Wolfe glanced at the stained walls of the hospital around them. "Why would you do that?"

"I don't see him outside of class very often, and Rhett is an important member of the police academy and the Joliet Police Department, a real up-and-comer. It could be a very important connection to have."

"Fine. I'll tell you whatever it is that Emmett wants when I get out," Wolfe said. He gave a nod to Rhett and then walked into Room Twenty-Three, pulling the wooden door closed behind him.

It was a pretty standard hospital room, smallish and for one person. A complex of machines with tubes and wires coming from them behind an uncomfortable-looking bed with a small, rolling desk next to it took up the center—and in the center of that nest, hooked up to just all the tubes, was Emmett.

"William!" he exclaimed, sitting up in his bed.

"You're... not looking bad," Wolfe said, blinking. It was true, and unexpected. Well, true to a degree. Emmett was still old, pale, and kinda flabby without being fat. Still, despite having a bulletproof vest, he had taken numerous shots—and one had gotten him in the arm.

Wolfe could see a bruise spreading from up under the gown across his chest, and his arm was wrapped, but he didn't seem all that more screwed up than a normal out-of-shape, pasty-white dude in his fifties would have.

"They used a weak card to heal me enough to stabilize me, but they don't have enough here to just fully heal everyone," Emmett said, his voice low. "But that doesn't matter. All that matters is that I need you to continue things for me."

Wolfe raised an eyebrow. "'Continue things'?"

"The investigation!" Emmett said. "I need you to continue the investigation!"

Wolfe hesitated. He truly wanted to get back to hunting. Cerberus had tasked him with hunting down the others who bore the 'Gate of the Damned' set cards, of which he had two —and Damian another. It seemed as if the Grimm family might have been involved in the human trafficking, and if not, Wolfe would bet one of the other families was.

But he wasn't sure if he was ready yet. He walked over to Emmett's side as he thought.

After a moment, Wolfe decided to play coy and see what he could get out of Emmett. Maybe the old private investigator would make an offer worth getting back into the field a bit early for.

"Are you crazy?" Wolfe asked. "You got *shot*. I *almost* got shot. And they had *deckbearers*. Who in their right mind would continue to investigate this? Let the police handle it."

"I can't let the police handle it," Emmett hissed, reaching out and grabbing Wolfe with his good arm. "They're *in* on it. I know some of the corrupt ones, but not most of them! I need someone to take over the investigation till I'm released from the hospital and well enough to handle it myself."

"No matter how *well* you get, you weren't *talented* enough to handle it the first time," Wolfe said.

Emmett flinched and let go of Wolfe's arm. "That's... That's true."

He sighed. "Look... What if, instead of a month of time cards, I made an entire three-year set? You handle this one thing for me, and you can be a private investigator on your own right away, instead of handling everyone else's crap for years."

Wolfe smiled inside, being sure to keep it off his face. *Perfect.*

Trying to look pensive, Wolfe nodded slowly. "All right, if you do that, I'll look into it for you. What do you need me to do?"

Emmett smiled. "I have boxes of files in my office. My clothes are hanging in the tiny closet there"—he pointed— "including my coat. Get my key, go to the office, and get the files. They have everything you need to know. You'll understand when you read them why it's so important and what to do. I need you to gather proof—incontrovertible proof—of who's really behind everything and then expose them in a way that the police won't be able to cover it up."

Wolfe nodded. "I'll take a peek at it."

Then he leaned down, his face close to Emmett's. "But if I do it, you'd better come through."

Emmett grimaced. "I said I'll do it, and I will. No need to threaten me."

Wolfe straightened. "Just so we understand each other." He was about to get the key, but he stopped and turned. "Why do you care so much, anyway?"

Emmett hesitated, then cast his eyes downward. "If you really want to know, check out the file for Jeremy. Jeremy Dunn. It's the oldest one."

He sighed. "He was my son."

Wolfe didn't know how to handle grieving people, so he just muttered "I'm sorry" and walked to the closet, rummaged through it, and found the key. He tossed it into the air where Emmett could see it, caught it, and tucked it into his pocket. *Best thing I can do for his grief is take care of the job he's left half-done.*

"Get me proof, William," Emmett said, his voice more needy than a druggie asking for his next hit. "I need proof to take all these bastards down. If I die for any reason, get the relevant files to a police officer you trust—it's better than nothing. A lot better. But not as good as I need to get them all."

"I will," Wolfe said as he walked toward the door. *Although I don't know any officers I trust. Shel can probably find one.*

He exited into the hospital hallway. Shel was leaning against the wall, scrolling through her phone, a cute look of concentration on her face.

Wolfe smiled to see her, but his mind was on something else. *Rhett left quickly. I wonder why.*

Wolfe walked over to Shel, who glanced up from the phone, caught sight of Wolfe, and smiled happily. "Hey, lover boy. How'd your meeting go?"

Wolfe grimaced at the name *lover boy* but started to answer. "Well, Emmett wants—"

A man walked around the corner of the hallway, wearing a rumpled, brown suit and carrying a bundle of flowers. He was younger, perhaps twenty-five or so, with thick, black hair. His left hand held the flowers up, in front of his chest, and his right hand was inside his jacket. He didn't appear particularly noteworthy, except that he had one blue eye and one brown— and an intense, nervous expression, with sweat beading on his forehead.

Wolfe stopped speaking, his mind on the nurse's words... something about not being able to find any family or friends of Emmett.

As the man passed, Wolfe stepped in close, conscious of not having his own gun. He placed his hand against the man's chest.

"What are you doing?" Shel asked from behind him.

But Wolfe barely heard, his hand pressed against the obvious bulge of a gun beneath the suit, just behind the flowers.

He met the other man's eyes, and there was that moment of perfect clarity, where both of them knew violence was imminent.

CHAPTER 7

BETTER CALL AN AMBULANCE, BUT NOT FOR ME

The thug's eyes widened and he started to draw the gun, but Wolfe headbutted him, forehead to nose. Something crunched, and the thug reeled away with one hand over a face splattered with blood. The assassin still drew the gun out from his jacket—but it wasn't pointing at anything, and Wolfe ripped it from the thug's hand.

But he didn't get a good grip on it himself, and the gun went skidding down the hall.

The assassin turned and ran—but not toward the gun. He hit the stairs at a near-full run, one hand on the railing, and half-leapt to the next level.

Son of an Infernal...

Wolfe followed, trying to move down the stairs fast. He made it two flights without issue, but when he reached the bottom set, he tripped at the end of the stairs. He grabbed the railing as he fell but still slammed down onto the floor of the lobby, wincing as he hit, then letting loose a string of curses.

"William?" someone asked, and Wolfe stared up to see Rhett glancing down at him with his ice-blue eyes open wide, his surprise evident to the world.

Of course it's Captain Perfect. Wolfe groaned, struggling to his feet. The same nurse from before, whose name eluded Wolfe, clicked her tongue in disapproval. "No running in the hospital! You men, I swear."

Ignoring the old nurse, Wolfe started to run from the building, but Rhett grabbed his arm.

"What are you doing?" the lieutenant hissed.

"Someone tried to assassinate Emmett, and I'm chasing him. He's getting away!"

The nurse pointed out to the parking lot. "Some white kid with blood all over his face just ran out the front door. I told him to walk, but he didn't listen, either."

Rhett didn't hesitate, withdrawing his police-issue Beretta 9mm and holding it in both hands. "Follow me!"

He rushed out the door. Wolfe hurried after him, favoring his right leg slightly. Upon exiting the hospital, however, Wolfe didn't see anyone in the parking lot.

Rhett lowered his gun slightly. "He might be hiding among the cars, but most likely, he went around one side or the other. I'll go left, you go right. What did he look like?"

"Black hair, suit, one eye was blue, the other brown, maybe twenty-five," Wolfe huffed out before turning right and rushing around the outside of the hospital.

It was dark outside, but the hospital was well lit, so Wolfe's vision was barely impaired. The hospital had a small, grass lawn and hedges around nearly the whole thing, except where there were entrances for ambulances and where they kept huge medical waste bins.

Wolfe's leg worked through whatever injury it had taken, and he was able to easily jog along the side of the hospital, keeping an eye on the hedges. As he had many times over the last day, he wished he had brought his Edge pistol, but he was still waiting for 'the man' to approve him to carry a gun.

The lack of a gun was starting to seriously irritate him, however.

Wolfe curved around the side of the hospital, coming to a break in the hedges where a couple of locked dumpsters were up against the outside of the hospital.

"Wol—William?" Shel called from somewhere behind him and around the front of the hospital, sounding slightly panicked. "Where are you, William?"

Wolfe was about to answer when he saw the assassin poke his head up from behind one of the locked dumpsters, his blood-spattered face and heterochromatic eyes instantly recognizable. Wolfe didn't hesitate, rushing at him in a full charge.

The assassin touched his chest, his five fingers splayed open.

No way... Wolfe was wide-eyed, staring at the man.

Unknown assassin deckbearer has drawn a deck near you! Three cards, all red, appeared in front of the assassin, and he reached for one.

Wolfe wasn't about to tempt fate by fighting him without a deck, and he touched his own chest. He had the satisfaction of seeing the assassin's eyes go wide in turn, but the assassin was still half a tick ahead of Wolfe. The assassin touched the card he had reached for and a pistol appeared in his hand. Not just a normal one, either—it had a pentagram on the handle, and a faint, red glow emanated from it.

Wolfe dived to the side, a moment too late. Pain ripped through his shoulder as he hit and rolled. He still had the peace of mind to throw out one of his Angry Hellhound cards instead of Cereboo, cursing the need to keep his identity hidden.

He came to his feet in a sprint for the bushes as two bullets plinked off the concrete around him. The shrubs parted as Wolfe dived headfirst into them, cussing as they ripped at him and then cussing further as he hit the ornamental rocks underneath. But it was better to be cut up from branches and bruised from the rocks than hit with another shot from the magical gun.

Wolfe glanced at his remaining two cards—his modified No Kill Pound, currently called Cerberus's Home for Wayward Hellhounds, and his Infernal Rift card.

The man touched another card and a Tormentor Imp— the Infernal card most ubiquitous to this current season —appeared.

But his Hellhound hit it and terminated it, and Wolfe waited for the perfect moment. The man shot the hellhound, and it nearly died—but for a brief moment, the assassin had no creatures.

Wolfe touched his Infernal Rift card and banished the man to a faux Infernal realm for ninety seconds.

He didn't hesitate, grabbing a rock from the ornamental garden and rushing toward where the assassin had disappeared, mentally directing the Angry Hellhound there as well.

Rhett came running around one side, and Shel the other.

"What happened to you?" Rhett called, staring at the blood pouring down Wolfe's side.

At that moment, the assassin appeared again, his eyes wide with shock and his mouth still open. But even then, he started to slowly and awkwardly raise his gun, and Wolfe slammed him with the rock as hard as he could, right in the temple, grunting as the force of his blow caused his other shoulder to throb in agony.

Unknown assassin deckbearer slain. 16 experience gained.

The man hit the ground on his back, blood leaking from his skull, and ten cards appeared on his chest.

Wolfe glanced up at Rhett, wondering what would happen now.

Rhett walked over, his gun now trained on Wolfe. "What happened? Are you in immediate danger?"

"He had a second gun—an equipment card. He used it to shoot me," Wolfe said, pointing with his right arm—which still held the bloody stone—to his left shoulder. "I had a rock. I won. I'll be fine now that Shel's here—this isn't life-threatening and she's got healing cards."

Shel touched her chest and then pushed her hand out, and her cards appeared, a slight golden color around them.

But she frowned at them and didn't use one.

Rhett walked up, then, after a moment, holstered his gun. He reached down and took the ten cards.

Damn. I could really *have used some more Infernal cards.*

Rhett briefly glanced through the cards, and when he came to the pistol equipment card—which was called Brimstone—he glanced at it.

"Try to heal him, Shel, please," Rhett said.

Shel nodded. "Of course."

She switched the cards out and this time touched one and tossed out her Rookie EMT cards.

Wolfe's minor scratches healed, but his shoulder wound remained untouched.

"I wish you could have let him live," Rhett said. "It would have been extremely helpful to question him." Then he held the cards out to Wolfe, frowning. "Here."

Chapter 8

Two Twists

Wolfe stared at the lieutenant like he had grown another head. "What trickery is this?"

Rhett's eyes narrowed. "I don't trick people, except within very specific confines the law lays out."

"Is this one of them?" Wolfe asked. "I mean, I'm not sure hearing 'I only trick people the way the man says I can' is the most reassuring thing you could be saying to me."

Rhett rolled his eyes, but a tiny smile quirked at the side of his mouth as well. "Fair. I promise, this isn't a trick—and besides, Cadet Lyons is here to make sure everything is above board. The law states that when you kill a deckbearer in single combat, in a legal manner, you get to keep the cards."

"You're shitting me," Wolfe said, thinking about the deckbearers he had killed. Although he was pretty sure those fights hadn't been legal.

"I'm not... shitting you," Rhett said. "The various religious groups combined still command almost seventy percent of the electorate, and they've kept that law on the books despite many attempts by various law and order groups, such as our own police department, to remove it.

Since multiple cards and the Great Game rules mention deckbearers killing each other for cards, we haven't been able to remove the last anachronistic rules, although we've pared them down pretty far—no voluntary duels are allowed, for example."

Wolfe only half-paid attention—he didn't really have a lot of room in his life for the politics of things. What he really heard was that he could legally keep the cards.

"Wait a minute," Wolfe said, finally reaching out and taking the cards from Rhett but staring straight into the lieutenant's eyes. "If I can keep them, how come you get to look through them first?"

"Can you guys talk and walk?" Shel asked. "You're shot, my boyfriend—how about getting some medical help while you work this out?"

Rhett nodded and started walking, and Wolfe, noticing how *much* his shoulder hurt, followed.

"I looked at the cards to confirm your story," Rhett said. "Sometimes, people shoot themselves to create a fake self-defense claim, but clearly, you were shot with Brimstone."

Wolfe glanced down at the card. The picture on the card was similar to the gun he had just seen—a modern pistol with red haze around it and a pentagram on the grip. He checked the stats.

Brimstone
Unique rare equivalent, Tier-5 equivalent Infernal persistent(equipment)
2 Infernal Power
+3 attack to the deckbearer or card equipped with this item.

Special: **Paired [Hellfire]:** This card may be equipped with

the equipment card 'Hellfire.' They empower each other, adding both totals to their wielder's attack stat.
Special: **Neutral Attack**: This equipment ignores ALL type resistances or immunities.
Special: **Injurious:** Causes damage that is immediately considered injuries for healing purposes.
Special: This card is part of the 'Banisher' card set. If both cards are gained, they will create a single rare pack of Infernal cards and give the deckbearer who possesses both 1 additional pip of Infernal power. Both cards were initially sent to members of the Noimoire underworld who are considered assassins.

"The Infernal use weapons of all sorts during both their internal wars, and their wars against other factions. This weapon started its life as a gift from Aesthma to his favorite assassin in hell and has worked its way into the mortal realm since then."

"Wow," Shel said, staring at the card along with Wolfe.

Another set card... although a lot weaker than the original one. But not weak—a permanent point of Infernal power is worth about six levels to me at the moment. Although putting in two cards that are only moderately better than normal guns is an interesting choice.

"So, I *do* have a question," Rhett said as they walked. "How did a lumberjack end up with an Infernal deck, anyway? It's extremely unusual to see in people who aren't criminals, or other... villains, shall we say."

Shel chuckled. "William is more of a bad boy than a villain."

Rhett gave a polite and perfunctory chuckle but still stared at Wolfe.

Wolfe understood—the Infernal faction was one of the

'evil' factions—perhaps the *evilest* faction. Along with the Elder faction, and to a lesser degree the Undead faction, they were widely distrusted, and usually for good reason. Few people who got god-gifted decks from those factions didn't have some remarkably evil skeletons in their closet somewhere.

But some did, and there were enough people who had done good with decks from those factions that prejudice against them was outlawed—officially. But it was still a smart move to hope your daughter didn't date an Infernal deckbearer. Even Wolfe had to admit that.

Heh, good thing that Shel's father is almost entirely out of her life.

They continued around, reaching the front of the hospital, but no one said anything. When the silence stretched awkwardly, Shel coughed again. "William got a deck from Cerberus—he's not that bad, I checked."

Wolfe gave Shel the stink eye, and she coughed and flushed visibly, even in the bad light.

Rhett ignored the byplay. "Cerberus? He's not one of the Infernal Lords I'm familiar with."

"He keeps the demons inside the Infernal realms," Shel supplied.

"Hmm…" was the only response from Rhett.

They walked into the hospital, and Rhett raised a hand and called out, "We have a shooting victim who can't be healed by non-injury healing cards. I need someone to see to him!"

Every single person in the waiting room turned to face Wolfe, and the nurse glanced up at him. "You're just going to be a problem all night, aren't you?"

She picked up a phone and talked into it briefly.

Shel giggled nervously as Wolfe clenched his teeth. "Play nice—you'll be out of here in no time."

Before Wolfe was carted away by the various nurses

coming through the door, Rhett leaned over. "Did Emmett tell you anything about the human trafficking case?"

"He told me the police were in on it," Wolfe said to Rhett's wide, ice-blue eyes.

Wolfe stared at the front of "E mett Investigations" in the bright light of the morning a mere eight hours after he had been shot, on far less sleep than he would have liked. The missing M was the least of the place's problems. The building was incredibly ramshackle, with blinds that looked as if they had been invented about the same time as bell bottoms, and not washed since then, either, blocking sight through the one window. The door was just as dirty, and the slat for mail was missing entirely, now just a random hole for bugs and weather to get in—although judging by the overhang, even the spiders wanted to stay on the outside.

Wolfe had some sympathy for not wanting to work on house stuff—his own back yard coming to mind—but he thought that Emmett needed a bit more pride. His workplace was a dump.

"Fuck it, what do I care if his place looks like a nest for three-power dust bunnies? I just need to figure out his stupid case, and then I can make my own office and not worry about someone else's dump." Wolfe pulled out the key and went to the door, unlocking it and letting himself in through a door whose hinges cried out for mercy.

The inside wasn't any different than the outside advertised. There was a waiting room with a cheap, plastic table and some equally cheap chairs that looked like refugees from the 1970s, as well as a magazine that appeared to be falling apart.

Wolfe ignored that and pushed into the back room—a small office, with a desk, two chairs, and about a hundred boxes in random piles. All of them were cardboard file boxes with the slip-on tops, and most had clear damage, from water, tearing, or probably bugs.

"Fuck me," Wolfe muttered. This was going to add hours to the case just to *find* everything, he figured. But as Wolfe's eyes ran around the room, he saw three boxes next to the desk. He could see that all were old, but they were also taped back together and carefully labeled. They'd clearly had care lavished on them that everything else in the room was lacking.

Wolfe sat down in Emmett's chair, on the other side of the desk, and looked at the boxes.

One was labeled 'Missing' and was the largest. The second, slightly smaller, was labeled 'Corruption,' and the last was labeled 'Transfer sites.'

Wolfe was pretty sure what he needed was in the last file, but he pulled the second one up first. He opened it and saw a large listing of names—last first. Each also had a designation, such as 'sergeant' or 'detective,' and Wolfe was pretty sure they were all the names of police officers.

Hoping that Shel's instructor was one of the corrupt ones, Wolfe quickly glanced through the files, but he had no luck—Rhett wasn't listed on any of them.

Emmett said that he wasn't sure of all the cops. Maybe Goody Two-Shoes is still dirty.

Wolfe wished he had spent a bit more time learning about the ins and outs of bribing cops when he'd been a member of the Grimm crime family—mostly how to spot the ones susceptible to bribing. Wolfe knew damn well that a lot of them had been in Big Man Grimm's pockets, but it had been far less than all—not even close to a majority. But it had been enough, and Wolfe assumed that was what was happening here as well. But he just had to take Emmett's word for it, and he doubted he would be able to find any more corrupt ones by himself.

After his failure to find a reason to hate Rhett—besides the fact that the man was suspicious of Wolfe, and might have eyes for Shel—Wolfe picked up the box marked 'Transfer sites.'

Before he could open it, however, the door to Emmett's business slammed open. Wolfe jumped, reaching for his Edge again before remembering he had left it home.

A man stormed into the office without even knocking. He was about five-foot-nine, scrawny, but he wore a suit that looked like it cost more than most people's monthly paychecks and radiated 'You might be able to beat me up, but my dad will sue' energy.

"You, Dunn! Where is my witness statement?" he yelled, leveling an accusing finger at Wolfe. "I've been calling and calling all morning! Why haven't you gotten it yet?"

From his own father, Wolfe could deduce that this guy was probably an attorney, which didn't endear him to Wolfe at all. He mentally settled on calling the guy 'Suit,' as it seemed his defining personality trait.

"Hey, jackass, I'm not Emmett," Wolfe said irritably. "You've got the wrong guy."

"I don't care!" Suit said, furious. "Whichever part of his office you are, I need you to get that statement, pronto. We're going to the final pre-trial this Friday, and I need it!"

Suit shouted so much, Wolfe would bet his middle name was Exclamation Mark. Wolfe was about to blow him off but stopped himself. *I'm training to be a P.I. I could get the witness statement, and besides, this guy seems like he'll become a real problem for someone if I don't.*

"Take a chill pill," Wolfe said. "I'll get the witness statement. Which case is it? Emmett didn't tell me."

"The Timo case!" Suit said, not chilling at all as he bent

over the desk and put his hands on it, his face inches from Wolfe's. "And don't forget it. I need it by the end of the day!"

"Friday is three days away," Wolfe said, frowning, restraining himself from popping the walking violation of personal space.

"I need to prepare my case and my client," Suit sneered as he pulled back. "Don't fuck this up."

"Yeah, I gotcha," Wolfe said.

"You better," Suit reiterated before turning and storming from the room.

Wolfe rolled his eyes. He checked the boxes around the desk, on the assumption the current work could be closer, and found it after just a couple of minutes looking—a box marked 'People v. Timo.'

He picked it up and glanced at the top file, which contained faxed instructions from 'Faraday, Hostler, and Chan' to interview a client about the case, and an address.

Wolfe looked at it, blinking.

No fucking way.

It was the address of the old lady who lived next to him.

CHAPTER 9

THE YOUNG AND THE OLD

Wolfe knocked on the neighbor's door with his knuckles, squinting in the afternoon sun. There was no response.

Wolfe knocked harder, knowing the old lady had to be home. There was a single beat-up car in the driveway that looked like it couldn't even handle 'once a week to church on Sundays,' and Wolfe hadn't seen any other cars in the driveway in months.

Still no answer, and Wolfe wondered if maybe she had died.

He snorted. *It would be far from the first time I've dealt with a corpse, but at the same time, it'll be funny to be able to call the cops and have them deal with it for once. That'll be new.*

The door snapped open, and the same woman from before—judging by the eyes—stared up at Wolfe. She had a general 'sunbaked' look, with light-brown skin that was wrinkled, like she wanted to win a dog show for best Shar Pei. She was a good foot shorter than Wolfe, roughly five-two, and she wore a dress that could have been a damned botanical guide, it had so many floral patterns.

The two stared at each other for a few moments before the old lady chuckled. "Finally decide to give in and get some help with your garden?"

Wolfe snorted. "No, I can handle that. I'm here on behalf of Emmett Private Investigations, and I need your statement in the case of *People v. Timo*."

The old lady glanced over her shoulder, then shuffled out of the house and closed the door behind her. "Talk quietly, please."

Wolfe blinked, confused by the odd turn of events, but he couldn't see a problem. If the old lady wanted to give her statement outside, he didn't care.

"So, you're a private dick, huh?" she said, smiling. "I wondered what you did for a living, but I guess that makes sense, based on your social skills."

Wolfe laughed—he always appreciated a good quip, even at his expense. "Look, uh"—Wolfe glanced at his paperwork again—"Patricia Timo, I need to get your statement in regards to Mr. Timo's voluntary manslaughter."

"Call me 'Grammy,' or 'Ms. Timo,' but not 'Patricia.'"

Why do people tell you how to get under their skin? Wolfe wondered, but he decided not to be a dick about it. "I just need the statement please, Ms. Timo."

Before she could answer, there was a creak of wood from inside, and a young, feminine voice called out, "Grammy? Where are you?"

Ms. Timo cracked the door open. "I'm on our front porch, honey, talking to our neighbor."

"The one with all the dead flowers you're always going on about?" the girl asked.

"The very same," Ms. Timo said.

The door pulled back to its limit, and a girl, roughly eleven or twelve based on her size and awkward proportions—the same rough age as Lucy—stared out at Wolfe. It was obvious she and Ms. Timo were related. They had the same tan-olive skin, and their eyes were an off shade of gray blue.

"This is Shannon, my granddaughter," Ms. Timo said.

Shannon's eyes roamed up and down Wolfe, obviously taking in his suit. "Are you a lawyer?" she asked out of nowhere. "Are you here about my parents' case?"

Before Wolfe could answer, Ms. Timo stepped in front of Shannon. "Honey, this is adult business. Please go inside and take care of your assignments, okay?"

Shannon's face went red. "I'm grown up enough and can handle hearing what's going on. I should know—they're my parents! I haven't heard from them in months!"

"Go inside," Ms. Timo said more forcefully, and Shannon flounced back into the house.

"Let's take a walk," Ms. Timo said, and Wolfe, irritated by the delay but unwilling to argue, followed her as she shuffled down the driveway and out onto the sidewalk that meandered through the neighborhood.

"I just need to know what happened that night," Wolfe said.

"Keep your voice down," Ms. Timo said again. "She's following us, I'm sure."

Wolfe glanced back and saw some bushes a house back rustling. He doubted Shannon could hear anything, but he humored the old lady, lowering his voice again. "Please, just tell me about the case so I can get out of here and you can get back to whatever you were doing."

Ms. Timo exhaled long and slow, took a deep, shuddering breath, and then spoke in a low voice. "My son called me, after... after he found his wife in bed with another man. Shannon was already at my house, and no one was there when it happened, except him. I drove over after he told me, telling Shannon to stay at my house."

"What did you find when you got there?" Wolfe asked, making notes as she talked.

"I found him, sitting at a table in the kitchen, a pistol in front of him. He was shaking, shaking so much. I know he didn't mean it... he had only fired a single time."

Wolfe glanced at the file. Mr. Timo had been charged with the murder of his wife. Wolfe kept taking notes.

"Did he say anything?" Wolfe asked.

"My son said he wished he could take it back. He said it'd been one moment... one moment when he'd lost control. He regretted it more than anything. I know he wasn't lying."

Wolfe was silent for a moment, then asked, as gently as he could manage, "Did you see... his wife?"

Ms. Timo looked back again, and Wolfe glanced with her, to see Shannon following, still a house behind. She spoke in a whisper. "Only very briefly. Some things... Some things you can't unsee, and I didn't want to see any more than I had to. It was as bad as the time I saw my own brother die to a monster six Drop Nights ago. Some things I don't want to look at longer than I have to."

Wolfe nodded, jotted a last few notes, and closed his file. "Thank you, Ms. Timo."

She was silent for a few moments as she continued to shuffle forward. Wolfe was about to leave when she spoke again. "Shannon is homeschooled, you know."

"What?" Wolfe asked. "I don't care how you teach your kid... Why are you telling me this?"

Ms. Timo continued. "She used to go to public school, years ago, and then she was homeschooled but at least made it to the Church of Uriel every couple of days. Now... Now she has no one. No family, no friends."

Wolfe had the sinking feeling he knew what was coming.

"Can she... visit with your daughter?" Ms. Timo asked.

Wolfe laughed. "I don't have a kid. That's my girlfriend's

younger sister, Lucy. I don't care if she visits as long as Shel—my girlfriend—approves it. But you know I'm a deckbearer, right? You've seen my cards hanging around the back yard? The Infernal ones?"

Ms. Timo nodded. "I do, and I have. More importantly, though, I see that you're always nice and respectful to your girlfriend. I want Shannon to have friends. But I also want her to have a good example of a relationship that works before... before she finds out about her parents. They were always fighting, and this situation, well... I just want her to see that some people can make it work."

Some old bag wants to use my relationship as an example for her kid? She's got to be crazy desperate.

"Look, just ask Shel, okay?"

A tiny bit of Ms. Timo's good humor returned. "I see who wears the pants in the family."

Wolfe laughed and shook his head. "Don't make me regret this."

Ms. Timo shook her head, too. "I can tell that you get it... Sometimes life is just so horrible, you have to joke about it. I hear that doctors and lawyers and cops all have a really black sense of humor—because what else can you do?"

Wolfe nodded, almost involuntarily. He couldn't deny that a lot of the time, he used humor to take the depressing edge off.

"Speaking of horrible... I really can help with your garden."

"So that's what this is all about," Wolfe said, and he shook his finger in her face. "*If* Shel says your daughter can visit, and *if* she does some afternoon when everyone is here, I won't mind if you come putter around my back yard."

"So kind, so generous."

CHAPTER 10

BEANS

Wolfe pulled his car onto the side of the road next to the relentlessly suburban house that his phone had directed him to. While it didn't technically have a white picket fence, it should have had one. The house was medium-sized, with a neatly mowed lawn and a hedge of rosebushes around the front, a minivan in the driveway, and a kid's Tonka truck toy under said hedge. The house was painted eggshell white and had a single large tree with a swing hanging down from it in the front.

"This is the place you want to go hang?" Wolfe asked, glancing over at Shel. "I mean, we hung out in the Ekron Eternal, in the VIP lounge, for crying out loud."

"No, *you* did," Shel said, smiling at him. "I hung around just outside the booth until someone decided to shoot at us, remember?"

"Ah, the good ol' days," Wolfe snarked, wiping an imaginary tear from his eye.

Shel rolled hers. "Did you ever *actually* have fun at the Ekron Eternal?"

Wolfe thought about it. "Well, not since anonymous sex

lost its appeal, back when I was in my mid-twenties, give or take."

"So give this place a chance, hmm?" Shel said, giving him another huge smile.

Wolfe snorted to himself. *Is she constantly smiling at me to put me at ease and try to make me happy? If she's been reading more of those psych mumbo-jumbo books, I'm gonna be annoyed.*

Wolfe wouldn't actually be annoyed, of course. At first, the idea that Shel was 'manipulating' him had upset him. Then he had figured out that Shel's 'manipulation' was just her doing her best to find ways to make him happy, and to conduct herself in ways he found enjoyable all the time. That, in turn, made him want to be nice to her.

Every other girl he had ever been with did it the other way around—they wanted stuff from him and were only nice if they got it.

If what Shel is doing is manipulation, sign me up to be manipulated.

"Wolfe, you there?" Shel asked, waving her hand in front of his face.

"Uh, sorry," Wolfe said.

"What were you thinking about?" Shel asked.

Wolfe smiled at her. "Believe it or not, that you're an amazing girlfriend."

Shel practically glowed, and she leaned in and gave him a kiss.

Wolfe faced the house again. "Although you pretty much need to be to justify me going to a cop barbecue. Let's get this over with."

Shel laughed. "Ah, Wolfy, I love that you can find the cloud to every silver lining."

Wolfe grimaced. "Don't. That reminds me of Miriam, which makes it... awkward."

Shel rolled her eyes. "Awkward? Why ever could that be?

Because she hits on both of us constantly and brazenly whenever we see her? Because when she isn't acting like she wants to jump in *our* bed she acts like she wants to jump into a *corpse*'s bed? Or because she's technically a criminal mastermind?"

"Yeah, that."

Shel smiled. "Well, I still like her. She's fun."

Wolfe snorted, but rather than continue the conversation, he pushed from the car, stretched once, and then walked up to the pristine house. Even the cement walkway was oddly pristine. He reached the off-white door and knocked three times.

Shel laughed and took a few double-steps to catch up, and by the time the door opened, Shel was standing next to him.

A man who appeared to be in his early thirties, powerfully muscled but with a gut and the standard issue 'cop 'stache,' stared out at them. "Shel! It's so good you could make it!"

He glanced at Wolfe, and his eyes widened the tiniest bit, but he recovered quickly. "This your boyfriend, then? William?"

Shel broke out into a huge grin, then leaned up and kissed Wolfe on the cheek. "Thank you so much for inviting me over, Charles. I really appreciate it. And yup, this is my boyfriend, best guy in the whole world!"

Charles laughed, a belly laugh that invited everyone who heard it to join in. "You only say that because you haven't tried my beans yet!"

Wolfe almost wanted to be mad—it felt like a vague challenge from his olden days—but he could pretty easily tell that Charles meant nothing by it. His eyes never even really 'saw' Shel—no looking at her body or anything, not even a flicker that Wolfe could see.

A moment later, it became clear why. A tall, thin lady with bright-blue eyes and a baby bump came to the door.

"Well, don't stand there bragging all day, Charles, invite them in!"

Charles stared at the woman with loving eyes and moved from the door. "When my wife is right, she's right! Come in, come in! Everyone is out on the back deck, and Leon is tending to the meats."

Wolfe strode inside. The house had a faint smell of roses to it—probably some fancy air freshener. Most of the furniture had faint wear and tear on it, but everything was clean and vacuumed. Wolfe went through the living room to the kitchen, past vegetable trays and a simmering pot, and then onto the back porch.

A brick porch was fronted by a small pool—also surrounded in brick—and a small but well-kept lawn and garden off to the side. About ten people—eight of whom had cop 'staches, causing Wolfe to snicker—were clustered around a barbecue and small table filled with uncooked meat. A thin man with tan skin was working the grill, and about half the people had beers in their hands that were mostly untouched.

There were two other young people there—people about Shel's age. One was a chubby, blonde girl with bottle glasses, and the other was an athletic young man with umber skin and a shaved head. They waved, and Shel walked over, calling out, "Hey, Lisa. Hey, Warren."

Wolfe walked up as well. Almost immediately, the groups reorganized around ages—the younger three in one group, and then two groups of four and five around the grill. Wolfe found himself getting a quick series of introductions—Leon was the tan guy working the grill, Carlos was a short, stocky guy with thinning hair despite being in his early thirties, Jack was so nondescript but for his mustache that his name should have been John Doe. A very elderly man, pale as snow with hair to match and a scar across his face, was named Bart, and Charles was there as well.

"What're you having?" Leon asked. "I've got some hamburgers almost ready, and we'll be putting some hot dogs on in a moment if you'd prefer—all beef. I can also do the burgers as cheeseburgers or—and hear me out here—*bacon* cheeseburgers."

At the same time, Carlos passed him a beer. "Try this. My cousin makes it—it's pretty good."

"I'll have a bacon cheeseburger," Wolfe said. "No veggies."

"Me too," Bart said. "Might as well die happy."

There were a few perfunctory chuckles around the table.

Leon nodded and slapped a couple more patties on the grill. Wolfe knocked the top off the beer on the side of the grill and took a sip. He'd had plenty of better alcohol at the Ekron Eternal, but he admitted he was an expensive whisky guy. For beer, it was pretty good, or at least flavorful for people who liked strong beer.

"Not bad," he said to Carlos's unspoken question.

Carlos nodded, evidently satisfied with the answer.

"So, how did Shel convince you to come to a party?" Bart asked.

Wolfe shrugged, not sure of the correct response. "She asked."

Bart smiled. "Wanted to see your daughter's friends, huh?"

Wolfe frowned, gripping his beer. Leon abandoned the burgers for a moment to lean over and whisper in Bart's ear.

"You're shitting me? Really? Divine be damned, maybe there's hope for me yet," the guy said, just loud enough for Wolfe to hear.

"Ha ha," Leon said. "Bart's just playing around, William. It's great that you're here supporting your girlfriend and all. How'd you guys end up together, exactly? She said it was because you saved her life and always protected her. She wouldn't tell me the details. Wanna tell me about that?"

Wolfe shrugged, doubly uncomfortable because the story

touched on personal details he *really* didn't want the cops to know and because he never looked at that story quite the way Shel did—he'd needed to kill Frankie the Frog regardless.

"Rather not, apologies."

"Well, your story, man," Charles said.

"So you guys are her instructors?" Wolfe asked.

"Just me and Rhett," Charles replied. "Everyone else here works the streets—'cept Bart, who earned his desk job with forty years and two gunshot wounds."

"Even if he sticks his foot in his mouth regularly," Leon said, nudging the older man. "Huh? Huh?"

Bart rolled his eyes.

"So, what do you do?" Leon asked.

"Nothing at the moment," Wolfe said. "But I'm working with a private investigator, Emmett Dunn, and trying to become a P.I. myself."

"How do you even take care of Shel?" Carlos asked. "That sounds like it pays squat."

Wolfe hesitated. He wasn't sure how much to reveal, but... "Well, I'm a deckbearer... and I found some cards a few days after Drop Night, and sold them. Now, I've got a house without a mortgage—"

"*So* jealous," Charles interjected.

"—that isn't even as nice as this one."

"Thanks," Charles interjected again with a smile.

"And I've got a decent car and a small amount in the bank. But I'm trying to become a P.I. to make sure there's money in a few years. *Independently wealthy*, I ain't."

Leon laughed and placed two burgers with cheese onto a thick, paper plate. At the same time, Charles' wife came out and placed a heaping helping of beans in sauce, with tiny bits of meat, along one side.

"Try the beans," Charles said.

"I'm not really a beans guy," Wolfe replied.

"Try 'em."

Wolfe sighed, picked the plate and a plastic fork up, and shoveled some beans into his mouth. He was prepared to make a noncommittal platitude to get the cop off his back about beans but stopped and really chewed.

He still wasn't sure he was a beans guy, but these were damn good. Slightly meaty sauce with a hint of honey over perfectly cooked beans. It was... wholesome, Wolfe supposed. He'd had a ton of steaks and gallons of whiskey, as well as a ridiculous amount of fast food, when he'd worked for Big Man Grimm. But nothing that had tasted... wholesome.

Charles grinned at Wolfe's expression. "See? See? I told you."

Wolfe couldn't help but smile. "Yeah. Damn good."

"Well, until you get the job, maybe you should stop by these events more often, stock up on good food."

Wolfe laughed. Every cop he'd interacted with had seemed like a dick—but maybe it was because he'd been a jackass himself. These guys seemed... not bad. Even Bart.

"Maybe I will. I could use a few free meals."

Charles chuckled warmly and clinked his bottle of beer against Wolfe's. "Yeah, it can seem like a lot of money in your bank till you think about the long term, huh?"

Wolfe nodded.

"Well, it shouldn't be long now, right?" a masculine voice asked from behind Wolfe.

He turned to see Rhett standing there in all his six-foot-two muscular glory.

"What?" Wolfe asked.

"I talked to Emmett again, and he said you've been working with him almost three years. But the other day, you told me you didn't know anything about the case and he'd picked you up to work on it recently. Care to explain?"

Well, shit.

CHAPTER 11

A CONFRONTATIONAL INTERLUDE

Wolfe stared at the lieutenant for a long moment, forking another bite of the beans into his mouth.

Emmett must be trying to lay the foundation for paying me off to keep helping him, by claiming I've been working with him for a while... but this is twice now that telling the truth is making me look like a liar.

Wolfe swallowed, about ninety percent of his attention on Lieutenant Rhett, and ten percent on how good the beans were.

"Sorry, I must have misunderstood. I thought you asked how long I've been working on this *case* for, which is not at all. I work with Emmett, but I don't have his files."

"Well, we just picked a few files up," Shel volunteered. "But we've never had his files before and haven't even opened them."

Wolfe glanced up and saw that everyone was paying attention to him now. While Wolfe wasn't bothered by attention, *per se*, he had to admit that the eyes of an entire party full of cops was a touch unnerving.

Rhett was staring at him. "You've been working with

Emmett on the case more by now, then? Anything you care to share?"

In the background, someone quietly muttered, "By the Divine, Rhett, we're at a party."

Rhett glanced around. To Wolfe's surprise, it seemed that most of the eyes had switched to Rhett, and everyone wore little frowns. Even Shel had a furrowed brow.

Rhett turned back. "Care to join me inside the house, William?"

Wolfe was tempted to refuse him but decided *fuck it*. "Fine, but I'm taking the food. I can't believe I'm saying this, but these are good beans."

Rhett blinked at the non-sequitur but didn't say anything, walking into the house.

Wolfe followed him, and Rhett led them through the kitchen and back to the living room. When they entered, he turned to Wolfe, standing stiff and tall.

His face was a stoney mask that might have been a ward against smiles. "I'm going to lay my cards on the table, William. I haven't, formally, seen anything from you that would warrant arrest, or even indicate moral turpitude. But nothing adds up with you, and I'm beginning to suspect you're not who you say you are... and that you might be a criminal, the worst of the worst."

Wolfe raised his beer in a sarcastic salute. "Hurray!"

Rhett frowned but ignored Wolfe's aside. "But even if I am wrong about all of that, you *certainly* know more about the investigation into the railyard trafficking than you're letting on. Two people are dead, three wounded, and twenty people were found naked in medically induced comas. That kind of thing doesn't happen in Joliet, and I, for one, want it to stay that way."

Rhett paused, raising an eyebrow at Wolfe, as if he expected an answer. But Wolfe had no idea what Rhett wanted, so he just set his beer down before biting into his cheeseburger. It wasn't as good as the beans, but it was pretty damn solid.

Weird that all these cops can cook.

When Wolfe didn't answer, Rhett continued. "Have you thought about how all of this is affecting Shel?"

"What? Why the hell would anything be affecting Shel?" Wolfe asked.

Rhett smiled grimly. "Finally have your attention, huh? Well, think about this. Whatever it is you're doing—and I'm pretty sure it's illegal, whatever it is—could *easily* drag her down with you."

Wolfe picked his beer back up and took a long drag before pointing the bottle at Rhett. "You leave Shel out of whatever" —Wolfe motioned the bottle back and forth between them— "this is. I don't get why you dislike me, but it's got nothing to do with her."

A sudden thought crossed Wolfe's mind. "Or does it? Is this a 'you want Shel for yourself' thing and now you're just looking for a reason to take me down? You as corrupt as the rest of the cops on this?"

Rhett spluttered. "I'm not after you to *take Shel*, whatever that means. But she's first in her class. And the class she's in isn't just the card police—there are over two hundred people there! She's going to go places and do things—unless some selfish asshole, happy he finally got one good thing in his life, drags her down!"

Rhett straightened further, something Wolfe hadn't thought possible, and cracked his neck. "And if you're going to make accusations against my fellow police officers, I'd ask that you bring proof or remain quiet. We get enough false accusations without your self-serving proclamations!"

Wolfe was feeling heated, and Rhett wasn't a problem he could punch, shoot, or Cereboo his way through. "I *know* the cops in this part are frequently crooked. But forget that. As to your ironically equally unfounded accusations against me, you're barking up the wrong tree, asshole. I haven't done *anything* illegal in this case."

Rhett's mouth quirked up at one corner. "'In this case'?"

Wolfe almost slapped his face, angry at having been baited into even that much of an admission. He was also tempted to immediately deny any illegal activity ever.

But something stopped him—he wasn't sure why, but he didn't want to run from this cocksure cop, and that was what lying would have been—it would have been running from Rhett.

Instead, Wolfe met Rhett's eyes, his voice deadly serious. "You're after the wrong guy in this case, I swear on all I hold holy. But you do you—wouldn't be the first time the supposed good guys, cops included, have absolutely wrecked my life for no reason other than their own selfish desires."

Rhett held Wolfe's gaze, and the two men stared at each other long enough that Wolfe's anger started to fade, and the whole thing started to feel awkward.

Rhett turned away first. "Well, you're either the best liar ever or you're telling me the truth about those two things, at least. I'll trust you for now. But if you're telling me the truth, why not tell me what's going on?"

Wolfe frowned. "I've told you everything I know, Lieutenant. We have some boxes of Emmett's files, and maybe I'll know more later. But he didn't tell me why we were going to that train station, I didn't know what to expect, and I still don't know what's going on. But I'm gonna lay *my* cards on the table. Even once I learn what's happening, I still may not tell you—Emmett wants things kept quiet."

Rhett frowned harder, put his hands behind his back, and tapped one foot. "When I came out, you were talking about needing money, right?"

Wolfe blinked. "Yeah, why?"

"What if I *pay* you? Once you learn things about the case, let me know."

"You want to *bribe* me? How is that not corrupt?" Wolfe asked, angry again.

Rhett let go of his pose and pinched the bridge of his nose. "I'm not *bribing* you. It's information from a paid informant. Ask Shel, it's perfectly legal."

"Still shady," Wolfe said, but he held his hand up. "Whatever. How much?"

"If you bring me his information on the case, I'll give you five thousand dollars."

Wolfe snorted, and Rhett narrowed his eyes. *I've got way more than that in the bank. Way more. And one of the weakest cards is worth ten times that.*

"I'll keep it in mind," Wolfe said.

"Please do."

There was another awkward pause, and Wolfe wasn't sure what to say. But it seemed like the conversation was done. He pointed back to the yard with his mostly empty beer. "You want to go back to the party? Charles is right—he makes some mean beans. You can fuck with me later, 'kay? Let's just eat now."

Rhett rolled his eyes, but the ghost of a smile crossed his face. "He does make some good beans."

"C'mon, admit it, you had fun at the party," Shel said, smiling at him from the passenger seat as he drove his Subaru back to his house through the moonlit streets of Joliet.

Wolfe mock-growled, "Yeah, getting interrogated by Rhett was the highlight of my month."

Shel's smile slipped and she hung her head. "Sorry, I honestly thought you and he would get along more. I'm sorry that happened."

Wolfe sighed. "I had a lot of fun at the rest of it, I'll admit. And I earned a bit, as well, listening to the cops talk stories. Tactics, methods—things like that."

Shel smiled at Wolfe again, her green eyes shining.

"I have a question," Wolfe asked. "Can Rhett bribe me to give him information on Emmett's case?"

Shel nodded. "Yeah, he can. As long as it's reasonably connected to a case, he can pay an informant—even to get information he can't go after himself legally, like Emmett's notes. Why?"

"He offered me five K to give him exactly that info."

"Why not give it to him?" Shel asked. "I mean, we don't even know what the info is yet."

"Emmett thinks the cops are dirty. Besides, we don't need them. We can solve it ourselves."

"Do you think Rhett is dirty?" Shel asked.

Wolfe sighed. "No. But I've been wrong about cops being good guys before, and I won't be shocked if he turns out to be a self-*ish* prick, as opposed to a self-*righteous* one."

Wolfe laughed at his own wordplay, mildly embarrassed when Shel didn't join in. He continued. "Also, Rhett is a lieutenant in the Joliet Police Department, and most of this is happening in Noimoire, according to the stuff I have managed to look at. The upside to helping him is very low."

Shel nodded slowly. "All right."

Wolfe had another thought. "Plus, if we really are after Grimm family members, I'm not sure I want Rhett knowing about me when we take them in. That could become a whole thing on its own."

Shel smiled at him. "I already said, 'All right.' You have to quit arguing when you win. Those are the rules."

Wolfe snorted. "We weren't arguing. Just trying to come up with a plan together."

"Of course. And whatever you decide, I've got your back."

Wolfe felt a rush of warmth. "Thank you."

They drove for a minute, Wolfe following the roads back to their house.

"Hey, so, while you were talking to Rhett, my mom called me. She needs to leave town on business for a month. Can Lucy come live with us?"

Wolfe pinched the bridge of his nose, then laughed quietly as he realized that was the same thing Rhett had done when talking to him. "Yeah, sure, the squirt can come live with us. I'm sure it'll make Malviere happy to have someone to play with."

"Besides our little apricot bundles of joy."

"Yeah, besides them."

Shel nodded. They drove in silence for a moment, until Wolfe pulled into the driveway to their house.

Shel raised an eye at him and licked her lips. "So, what's next for the evening, my hero?"

Wolfe was fairly certain that she was offering him another tumble. He had to admit, he loved the fact that Shel was into him. A woman who truly cared for him was the most precious thing in the world.

But he wasn't twenty-two anymore, and they had things to do that were more important, unfortunately. He needed to make sure everything went right, as soon as possible. "Let's go over my deck, see what I can add from that assassin's deck. If the Grimm family really is involved, I'll need to be as prepared as possible. Then we'll take a look at the files, see what we're up against. And make a real plan. Today was a good day, and I know it matters to your future that we go to these things. But tomorrow, we hunt—and we need to be prepared."

CHAPTER 12

HELLMOUTH DECK

Wolfe had his deck out as they sat at the kitchen table in his house. The new cards he had gotten from the would-be assassin—whose name had turned out to be Harvey, which made Wolfe laugh—were spread out on the table as well.

Malviere was playing with his two cavapoos, and Cereboo lounged at Wolfe's feet.

He had written down his own deck and stared at it. It was fifteen cards—he had gotten almost all his cards through the first couple of weeks after Drop Night, nine months ago, but he had been trading through the internet and a few auction sites since then.

The biggest change had been when he'd discovered how utterly cheap the Angry Hellhounds were. They had been ubiquitous last season, ten years ago, but almost no one ran Infernal and Beast combination decks, and those who did didn't want the Angry Hellhounds, which were widely regarded as 'F-tier,' 'Never Use,' or something similar, depending on which forum's lingo you were using.

Despite the normal minimum of around fifty thousand

per card, in the frenzy of buying and selling after the latest Drop Night, the price of most of them had dropped to around twenty-five thousand, and Wolfe had snatched up a ton of them. He had sold most of the spare cards he didn't need, as well as most of his share from the Frozen Tomb dungeon. He now had *four* Tier-three Angry Hellhounds.

Angry Hellhound
Common Tier-3 Beast/Infernal [Canine] Creature
Two Beast or Infernal Power
Health: 13
Attack: 8
Defense: 5
Magical Attack: 5 [**Fire or Infernal**]
Magical Defense: 5

Special: **Dual Attacker:** When this creature makes a physical attack, it also makes a Magical Attack on the same target.
Special: **Empty Mind:** Immune to all mind-affecting debuffs.
Special: **Canine Tribal [1]:** +1 to all attacks for every other canine on the field.
Special: **Hunter [Escaped Damned 1]:** Gains +1 Attack for every Escaped Damned on the field.

"It could be argued that most things in the Infernal realms are angry, but these hellhounds take it to an entirely new level—and this one has torn many a spirit to the point it needs to reform on many an occasion."

The Angry Hellhound's specialty seemed to be gaining unusually good 'tier up' bonuses and making multiple attacks —plus benefitting from other canines. Additionally, it was both Infernal and Canine, which meant every bonus Wolfe had would pretty much stack into it.

His deck also contained Cereboo and Infernal Rift, his two 'gate to hell' set cards, Malviere and Cerberus's Home for Wayward Hellhounds, which were his two cards that had been upgraded by his Infernal Rift card. He had also had two Rescue Pups that had been converted to Lost Hellhound Puppies, two Pack Howls to give large static boosts to his canine cards, his mantle, his Fireborn Hellhound, and now Brimstone—his new gun.

He pulled his stats up.

Ethan Madison Wolfe Status:
Level 19 Mortal

Deckbearer Perks:
Deckbearer Perk 1: In the Thick of it: +50% to all numerical benefits gained from mantles
Deckbearer Perk 2: Man's Best Friend's Best Friend: Gain 1 Beast Power. May have one extra card in play so long as it's a Beast (Canine or Hybrid Canine).
Deckbearer Flaw: Fallen: May not gain Divine Power, nor use Divine cards unless they are also Infernal or Corrupted.

Deckbearer Stats:
Cards in Deck: 15 (1 pip)
Cards in Hand: 4 (1 pip)
Cards in Play: 3 (1 pip)
Length of Play: 5 minutes
Specialty Cards: Companion: 1
Minion: 1 (1 pip)
Total Power: (upgraded 5 times): 8 -1 (Infernal Rift) = 7. (Total pips 15)
Type 1 and Power: 4 Infernal (5 -1(Infernal Rift))
Type 2 and Power: 2 Beast
Energy 1 and Power: 1 Fire

Personal Perks:
Inborn Perk 1: Vicious Killer: +25% to all Attack and Defense, check twice for attack modifier and take the best.
Inborn Perk 2: Tough as Nails: +10 Health
Acquired Perk 1: Crafty Street Fighter: +3 Attack and Defense

Personal Stats:
Health: 30/30
Attack: 10
Magical Attack [None]: 0
Defense: 10
Magical Defense [None]: 5

Then Wolfe spread the other ten cards he had. One was the Rescue Pup that he had replaced to put Brimstone in. The other nine were the remains of Harvey's deck.

Compared to most decks that Wolfe got, this deck was incredibly odd. It had a ton of stuff that wasn't immediately useful—Wolfe honestly wondered if Brimstone was the only thing that was useful that Harvey had pulled in his first card draw.

The first card was the Fallen Assassin mantle, which gave attack stats against Mortals—Wolfe was incredibly glad Harvey hadn't gotten that on before fighting him. Not useful to Wolfe—he already did far more than enough damage to kill most actual mortals in a single hit, and usually went after Infernal deckbearers.

Second were two copies of Infernal Creatures—the Imp and an Infernal Leech, a creature card that functioned almost like a damage over time persistent, but it had to do at least one damage in a combat round to start it. There were two copies of Pile On, a neutral card that allowed an extra creature summon when an opponent's creature was killed.

But the other four cards... Wolfe stared. They were legitimately bizarre.

One was a card called Infernal Nobility. It was an enhancer card.

Infernal Nobility
Rare Tier-1 Infernal Enhancer
0 Power cost

+1 attack, +.5 Defense, +.5 to all Infernal cards attack, +.5 Infernal Power, and +2% total lifespan per Infernal Nobility in deck. Every four Infernal transformations in the deck will give the user an Infernal feature, which may add stats.

"The Infernal Realms sometimes grant their power, and their mark, to their favorites."

"Wow," Shel commented, reading the card upside down. "That's... powerful."

"Maybe," Wolfe said, skeptically. "To get any real power from it, I would need to have at least two in my deck, and that would take out two cards I could use. Not to mention spend three leveling pips to have the two enhancer cards. Not sure it's worth it."

"What if your deck was only twenty of those cards, no power cards at all?" Shel said, staring far away. "Like Alexander the Colossus."

Wolfe nodded. If he had spent on cards only and gotten a bunch of those, he would have another thirty or so years of life and he would fight as an absolute beast himself.

"Yeah, we can't even begin to afford a bunch of rare enhancers. They go for millions of dollars, plural, each. I could start a small crime empire of my own just by selling this one."

Shel laughed, and they turned their attention back to the cards.

The next two were new minion cards called Junk Tinkerer Orphan.

Junk Tinkerer Orphan

Uncommon, no-tier Mortal/Golem minion [orphan]

0 Power

Health: 6

Attack: N/A

Defense: 6

Magical Attack: N/A

Magical Defense: 4

Special: Will fetch normal objects and such with a decent degree of precision and help carry up to fifteen pounds.

Special: **Orphan Evolution [Unique]:** If kept 'alive' for five straight years, will turn into a rare, Mortal/Golem, 2-power, Tier-4, equivalent creature card called 'Urban Outfitter.' Will also produce a common pack of mixed equipment cards.

"This young boy was born on the streets and raised by them. But he had a natural affinity for tech, and even without formal training, is a dab hand at equipping the gangs and struggling businesses around him."

"Wow, a golem orphan. I'm impressed."

Wolfe nodded. "Pretty weak for what it is, though. I mean, it basically converts to a Tier-four card, which is nice, but hardly worth writing home about."

"Maybe Rhett would want it?" Shel asked.

"We can just sell them, you know," Wolfe said irritably. "Or grow them to sell off the equipment pack cards."

He stared at the last card.

Orphanage of the Lost

Uncommon Tier-1 Mortal Building

No cost

Special: Creates a rundown orphanage of 12,000 square feet.
It may utilize power and water if hooked to an appropriate
grid and will generate food for up to 50 inhabitants, of poor
quality, every day. Any deckbearer inside gains 2 Mortal
Power.

Special: **Fast Age [3]:** All orphan cards 'age' at 3x the rate

"Well, looks like we finally found a card for you," Wolfe
said to Shel. "A sad orphanage. It'll give you a lot of power,
though, especially if people try to come for you inside the
building."

She was staring at it, not speaking. After a moment, she
glanced up. "Wolfe... I know you're gonna say I'm being a
martyr, but I want to propose something."

"Shel, I can't use the card—and I don't think we should
just sell it to buy me better stuff."

"Actually, I think you *can* use the card. Your Infernal Rift
can still convert one building card, remember? You could
make it an... Infernal orphanage of some sort. It'll be a free
specialty card for you because of the way the Infernal Rift
works."

Wolfe laughed out loud. "Are you serious, Shel?"

She nodded. "The cards get slightly more powerful each
time they're upgraded. And the Infernal Rift takes a
permanent Infernal power from you—shouldn't you get its
full benefit? Besides, it'll almost certainly make Malviere grow
far more quickly. She'll be an amazing card when she's
'grown.'"

Wolfe hesitated, but he had to admit—her mentioning
that the Infernal Rift could modify the card intrigued him.

He thought about it for a moment. "Are we sure we want
to do the orphanage? If I modify this, Infernal Rift can't
modify any other building cards. Cerberus's Wayward Pound,

the little Lost Hellhound Puppies, Malviere, and this orphanage will be the modified cards forever. I mean, I could get a dark temple or something instead, power everything up."

Shel hesitated, her lips pulled to the side. She played with her hair as she thought.

"Everyone says the orphan cards are a huge deal—although I haven't heard of anyone managing to grow one yet. I think that leaning into our Season's cards—and what will almost certainly be numerous other seasons, since the cycle of the Lost and Lonely will probably continue for a while—will be a huge benefit to us, long term. I think you should do it."

Shel smiled again. "We can try to find me an angelic orphanage or something."

Wolfe laughed at that. "All right, I'll do it. What card should I pull out, though? It's a pretty synergistic deck at the moment."

Shel considered. "I'd take either one Lost Hellhound or one Angry Hellhound out. You've got a total of seven hellhounds still in your deck, and you pull a quarter of your deck every time you swipe. You can afford to not have it."

It lined up with Wolfe's still-organizing thoughts. "Thanks, I agree... You've been getting more confident. You didn't used to suggest much about my deck before."

Shel blushed. "I'm sorry. I didn't mean—"

Wolfe held his finger to her lips. "Hey, slow your roll. I wasn't upset. Just commenting. I like you suggesting things—I wouldn't have thought to put the orphanage in my own deck."

Shel smiled. "Okay, well, don't keep a lady in suspense. Let's see what happens."

Wolfe placed his hands over his chest, his old scar itching, and felt his power. Dark and eternally hungry, somehow.

He pushed his hand out, and his cards came into existence.

Two of his Tier-three Angry Hellhounds came up, and he touched the Orphanage of the Lost and willed it into his deck.

The Hellhound popped out, and the orphanage went in. Immediately, he had the same sense as before—options appeared in his mind but were immediately picked, as he had only one qualifying card. The Orphanage of the Lost warped and turned into...

Hellmouth Institute

Unique, rare equivalent Tier-2 equivalent Infernal Building

No cost

Special: Creates an ostentatious orphanage of 24,000 square feet. It may utilize power and water if hooked to an appropriate grid and will generate food for up to 100 inhabitants, of excellent quality, every day. Minor magic within the orphanage makes the entire place far easier to live with. Any Infernal deckbearer inside gains 2 Infernal Power.

Special: Any additional Infernal Buildings gained will add bonus benefits to orphan or transformed orphan cards.

Special: **Fast Age [3], Fast Age Infernal [5]** All orphan cards 'age' at 3x the rate, unless they are Infernal or would become Infernal without the aid of this building, in which case they age at 5x the rate.

Special: **Evolve Improvement: Infernal [1]** Every orphan card that transforms that is Infernal or would become Infernal without the aid of this building gains 1 tier of equivalent power as a permanent modifier.

Special: Every Mortal orphan card that transforms becomes Infernal and is modified accordingly but gains no total increase to power.

"All right, I can see the next stage in the evolution of my deck," Wolfe said. "Or at least one possibility. And that's to get more buildings."

"Buildings cards are extremely rare and extremely expensive," Shel warned.

Wolfe nodded, but his mind was alight with ideas.

"Speaking of expensive," Shel said, holding her phone up. "I checked the prices. If we sell everything we got from Harvey except Brimstone, the Hellmouth Institute, and the Infernal Nobility card, we can afford to get a single copy of either a No Kill Pound, or a Gehennan Kennel Master for your deck."

Wolfe hesitated. They had looked at both of those as significant ways to increase the power of his deck... but he felt like he was leaving Shel out.

"Look... just humor me, okay?" he said. "Please get something for your deck, instead. Or save the money in case we need it. I know this was 'my kill,' but I feel like we've been really neglecting your deck growth. My allies—my pack—is my power too, if you're just worried about me."

Shel hesitated. "I was saving to try to get one of the other three of Raphael's companion angels. Although I can only even find mention of one of them—Aliel is owned by a coder named Sapphire Duvall in Noimoire who got a Divine deck in the last drop. I think he might be willing to sell, though. If you're serious, I'll add that to the fund... although, at this point, it'll basically *be* the fund, near enough."

Wolfe nodded. "All right. Do that."

He turned his eyes to the back room, where the boxes he had taken from Emmett's office were. "All right, let's figure out what's going on with the damn trafficking case, and see if we can start hunting Damian. I really want to be able to put my new twenty-four-thousand-square-foot ostentatious home somewhere, but I'd rather not call attention to us before we smoke him."

Chapter 13

Planning

olfe and Shel sat on the bed in their shared bedroom, the 'Sites' box from Emmett's office open off to the side and most of the files spread around them.

"So... these are the places where they make the transfers, then?" Shel asked, holding up ten files.

Wolfe nodded. "Yup. Six in Noimoire proper, one in Joliet, at the train tracks, and three more in other cities near Noimoire. If Emmett's files are anything close to accurate, half the gangs in Noimoire are involved in whatever is going on— and it's gotten far more comprehensive over the last year or so."

"So, you just have to wait for them to come back to the trainyard for an exchange?" Shel asked.

Wolfe shook his head. "It won't work like that. Now that the trainyard is compromised, they'll move on to another site. I'd also bet they pull back from the other outer sites, although I'm less sure about that. If I want to go after them, I'll have to go back to Noimoire itself, most likely."

Shel hesitated, and for a moment, Wolfe thought his

girlfriend would counsel caution, but her gaze hardened and she nodded. "I understand—and this is important. It's obvious a lot of people are having terrible things happen to them, and you should save them."

Wolfe shook his head slightly, smiling. "*You* should save them, Shel. My job is to put the ones who are doing this behind bars or six feet under."

"I will save them," Shel said. "When you go next time, I should join you. Together, we'll be far more powerful than we would be alone."

Wolfe laughed. "'*Far more powerful than we would be alone*,' huh? You sound like a Saturday morning cartoon, but I get what you're saying."

Shel smiled. "Hey, you don't have a complete monopoly on cheesy lines."

"Oof, right in the gut," Wolfe said, miming taking a bullet, and Shel chuckled.

A sobering thought crossed Wolfe's mind as he thought back to Rhett's words. "Rhett mentioned that you could lose your career, helping me. This whole situation could easily go south—it could be dangerous, but it could also end up illegal. You shouldn't kill your career before it's even started. Just let me handle it."

"You think it'll be bad?"

"A good way to figure out how much a situation will go south is to figure out how many people stand to lose what if you butt your head in," Wolfe said. "In this case, we're talking massive amounts of coordinated, RICO-level human trafficking, with what looks like half the Noimoire underground involved."

Shel twisted her finger in her hair and bit her lip.

But then her face firmed, and Shel shook her head. "I'm not leaving, and I'm not stepping back. You always try to sacrifice yourself for me, Wolfe, and I really like that about you. But we're partners. I'm going to be there for you, no matter what. My career as a police officer, especially being one of the elite card police, showing my stupid father and mother that I'm worth something... well, I really want that. But *you're* the most important thing to me. Stop trying to send me away, okay? Please?"

Wolfe smiled again. Shel's support over the day had been truly welcome. "I'll quit trying to send you away. Promise."

Shel smiled. "So, just check out the sites, then?"

Something about the whole thing was nagging at Wolfe. "Shel, has it occurred to you that we've never heard about any of this?"

Shel frowned. "What do you mean?"

"Well, the news..." Wolfe took a moment to gather his thoughts. "Let me start again. Every time the precious, cute little daughter of some rich executive or movie star or something disappears, it's national news for months, right?"

Shel nodded.

Wolfe continued. "But we've never heard about any of these people, and apparently, this has been going on for years and years, according to these files."

"Okay."

"So, the victims aren't attracting any attention. Do you know why? Do we know who the victims are?"

"I mean, not exactly. But Rhett told me they were all criminals—petty ones. Street thugs fresh out of failing high school, young whores, street-level pushers who got in because their uncles said they could make fast money—things like that. People like Kevin, or, well, me, once upon a time."

Wolfe nodded slowly. "Yeah... that's what I thought. They're the people who, if they disappear, everyone will just assume died in a way everyone expects—drug overdose, strangled by a pimp, something like that."

Shel frowned. "It still seems like *someone* should be saying something... What are you thinking?"

"I think it's time to return to Noimoire proper—and to talk to the people who know what's happening there."

Shel smiled and motioned to the darkness outside the window. "It's late—I assume you mean tomorrow?"

"Bright and early, we go see the few remaining people who like us."

Wolfe stared at the Morning After Inn from next to his car, which he had parked in one of the back-most parking spaces, to give him a tiny bit more time before someone noticed him. He had been here quite often, usually to help its owner, Melissa, with something or other, since she had done the Grimm family quite a few solids back in the day.

But he had few fond memories of the place, even if he didn't hate it. Its purpose was as cheap as its façade, which was saying something. The Morning After Inn was three stories of sleazy rooms packed into a long, thin building. The whole thing was off-white, old, cracked, and covered in dirt. A beat-up sign hanging in the front window declared, "Rooms rented by the hour, available now!"

"I get that now," Shel said, her lips pulling up on one side. "Is that a good thing, or a sign of how far I've fallen?"

"A little of Column A, a little of Column B," Wolfe said, waggling his hand.

Shel chuckled, but Wolfe didn't react after that, beyond tapping his foot.

"You okay?" Shel asked. "You seem nervous."

"This is pretty much the declaration of war, going in here. Someone is going to see me, and eventually—and I'm thinking two days, max—it's gonna make its way back to Damian. This is the end of the peaceful vacation."

Shel nodded, her finger twisting in her hair but her eyes forward and intense. "Yeah. Worth it, though. Some people need to be taken off the street."

Wolfe nodded, braced his shoulders, and walked toward the inn. He took a few steps around his car and toward the building when another car pulled into the parking lot—a fancy, red sportscar with a license plate that read, 'LeftOne.'

He stopped dead in his tracks and threw his arm out as Shel walked up beside him. She hit the arm and looked at him questioningly.

"That's Marko's car!" Wolfe said, taking his arm and pointing. "The asshole must not have changed his license plate, even though it should now read 'OnlyOne.'"

Shel let out a single gasp-snort, but she moved backward, and Wolfe followed. He rushed back behind his car and knelt. The driver- and passenger-side doors of the red sportscar both opened, and two men came out as if they had practiced synchronized car exiting. The passenger side revealed a man of middling height and weight, but the driver's side revealed a man who looked like a Viking had taken a *really* unfortunate liking to a wolf somewhere in his wood pile. He was almost six-two, with black, shaggy hair that hung loose and a physique that screamed 'work-out junkie.'

He's also wearing a wife-beater that screams 'class,' Wolfe thought to himself with a half-snort reminiscent of Shel's.

Marko added to his general dark vibe by pulling a Smith and Wesson 3566 model and racking it, like a bad B-movie villain. Then he walked into the Morning After Inn, his mook following him.

"Fuck," Wolfe growled out. "I still don't have my Edge!"

Shel raised her eyebrow. "What are you planning on doing?"

"Nothing, unless I full-on pull my deck. That freaking hand-cannon could blow a hole in a car. I could really have used a gun here. Especially since it's Marko and I deleted his brother."

Shel pointed toward the passenger side of the car. "Well... I have a gun, actually."

"What?" Wolfe asked, blinking hard.

Shel quirked her mouth. "They gave me a permit to carry a gun for purposes of training and going to the gun range—I have a Glock-17 in the glove compartment."

"Won't you get in trouble if I use that?" Wolfe asked, but he was already moving toward the side of the car.

"I... don't think so. I mean, I was transporting it correctly... I think," Shel said. "No one has to tell anyone else I allowed you to use it."

She didn't sound particularly confident, but Wolfe decided to risk it. Marko was a violent thug with almost no sense or restraint, and if he was here, there was almost certainly going to be problems of one sort or another.

He reached into the glove compartment and pulled out a small, locked gun case that had been wedged into it. Shel passed him the key, and he unlocked the case quickly, his eyes on the doors to the Morning After Inn ahead of him the whole time.

He got the gun out—the same type Emmett had given him back at the trainyard—and quickly loaded it.

He stood, feeling better with a gun in his waistband.

But before he could do anything, a gunshot sounded from inside the inn.

CHAPTER 14

OLD ACQUAINTANCES

Wolfe leapt out from behind the car door, slamming it closed, and ran toward the front door of the inn. The slap of shoes on pavement told Wolfe that Shel was keeping pace with him as he ran.

"Don't draw your deck until I've gotten my attack off," Wolfe said. "Gun still beats idiot thug."

"Okay," Shel said, her breathing easy as they hit the wall just outside the door.

Wolfe glanced in through the window in the front. Melissa was down on the ground, holding her knee, and blood seeped around her fingers. She drew breath in short, ragged gasps, and tears streamed down her face.

Marko was standing to the side of the door, half-facing it, with his pistol trained on Melissa. His partner was facing Melissa with his back to the door. The second thug had a pistol as well, but it was held loosely and pointed at the ground.

"This is a clear case of defense of others, right?" Wolfe asked Shel. "I can kill them legally?"

Shel's eyes widened, but she nodded.

Wolfe smiled a shark's smile. *About damn time.*

Wolfe touched his chest at the same time as he shouldered his way into the inn, drawing his deck with his gun pointed out in his other hand.

I need one of them.

Wolfe fired a couple of times at Marko, hitting him once in the side, but Marko was nearly as good an instinctual fighter as Wolfe. Marko managed to get one badly aimed shot off as he dived behind the counter, trailing blood. He scrambled across the floor and grabbed the screaming Melissa's arm, then dragged her with him behind the reception counter.

But Marko wasn't a tactical fighter and he had done essentially what Wolfe wanted. Wolfe slammed his gun into the head of the random thug, who hadn't managed to turn around yet. Wolfe's hit knocked the mook sideways and to the ground. Surprisingly, it didn't take him out completely, and Wolfe fired again at the counter to keep Marko's head down.

Then Wolfe kicked the mook in the same place he had hit him, putting him to sleep.

From down the hall Wolfe heard shouts and screams. *Yeah, everyone is going to know I was here.*

Wolfe's deck manifested. It showed Cereboo, his companion card, and four others—two of his Tier-three Angry Hellhounds, a Lost Hellhound Pup, and Brimstone.

Enemy deckbearer Marko has pulled his deck.

Allied deckbearer Rachel Lyons has pulled her deck.

Marko's voice came floating up from behind the counter. "I can't fight both you and your stupid cunt, Wolfe, but if you don't drop your damn gun right now, I'm gonna blow this bitch's head all over the floor—maybe she can sell the new hole to some prick. And if I so much as *smell* a summoned creature from either of you, I'm also gonna waste her."

Wolfe rolled his eyes. Marko's mouth had always been foul

even by the standards of the thugs Wolfe ran with, and it made him sound like an idiot.

But his eyes fell on his cards.

He tossed his gun to the floor so that it slid across the ground toward the counter, where Marko could see it. Shel's eyes opened wide, but Wolfe calmly reached out and touched a card.

An Angry Hellhound—one of Marko's—came around the corner, and at the same time, Marko stood up, his gun out, blood seeping from the existing wound in the thug's side.

"You dumb—" he managed to get out.

Wolfe shot him in the face with Brimstone, and Marko's head exploded across the back wall.

Melissa screamed again from behind the counter.

Wolfe rolled his eyes. *Why do so many women do that?*

The Angry Hellhound faded away, and Marko fell back to the ground.

Wolfe made a level, which surprised him. Marko had been a deckbearer for almost eleven years, but still. *When did Marko make a high enough level to give me more than a hundred percent experience?*

Wolfe pushed the thoughts aside. "Shel, make sure the guy with the concussion is alive, please, and heal him."

"My EMTs can only heal deckbearers," Shel said.

"Right," Wolfe muttered, feeling dumb. "Well, please take care of him as best you can, then. Didn't you take some basic lifesaving courses as part of becoming a cop?"

"*Very* basic," Shel replied, but she bent down and started to touch the guy's head.

Wolfe walked behind the front counter.

Melissa appeared as she always did, only wounded and terrified. Pink chemise with white bra straps showing, and she was forty and usually looked it. At the moment, with blood oozing from her wrecked knee and tears streaking her face, she currently looked closer to fifty.

Wolfe crouched down beside her. "What happened?"

"Wolfe, I thought you were dead!"

"Rumors of my demise were greatly exaggerated. But what happened, Melissa? Or why?"

Melissa was holding her leg below the knee. "Please, Wolfe, *help* me. This hurts so much!"

Wolfe picked up Marko's deck and flipped through the twenty cards. Marko had possessed a couple of Angry Hellhounds and, to Wolfe's delight and surprise, a rare Gehennan Kennel Master, as well as a couple of weaker enhancement cards. Nothing else would work for his deck and would likely just be sold, for one reason or another. Most weren't compatible, but one rare card called Aesthma's Wrath was a named card that made a single Infernal creature far more powerful—but Wolfe didn't want another named Infernal lord other than Cerberus in his deck.

"What're you doing?" Melissa asked. "Please, Wolfe!"

Wolfe ignored her for a moment. He pocketed the rare or useful cards, picking the weakest nine and the solid mantle card.

Then he held them out to Melissa. "If you want to become a mixed Infernal and Beast deckbearer, Melissa, I can give you these—but you owe me a half-million, clear? I like you, but you did choose this life, and I don't half-a-million like you. Get me? *If* you become a deckbearer, Shel can heal you."

"Those are worth a half-million?" Melissa asked, gripping her leg near the wound.

"More, actually, because I left an advanced mantle in. But I gave you a bit of a discount—close to a hundred thousand dollars."

"Wow. Thanks, hon," Melissa said, a bit of a non-sequitur to the situation. Although she was still breathing raggedly.

"Figure it out fast, though," Wolfe said. "I've got shit to do —and I need to ask you some questions."

"I didn't really want to be a deckbearer," Melissa said, sniffling. "In this life, it makes you a target... someone is gonna come gunning for me."

Wolfe waited.

She glanced at her leg. "How bad is it?"

Wolfe looked. He wasn't an expert, but he'd seen a few knee-cappings in his time. "I'm pretty sure that the knee is completely destroyed, and you'll never walk again without magic or intensive reconstructive surgery. But you could pay for a card with more powerful healing than mine, if you want to wait—and explain why you got shot."

Melissa sighed and held her hand out. "All right, give me the cards. You'll get your money. I have more than enough."

Wolfe gave her the cards, and she took all ten. "What now?"

Shel quietly walked up behind them, five golden cards floating in front of her.

"Just will them into you, I think. Aside from needing to touch your chest to pull the cards, which is true for very nearly every deckbearer out there, everything I've experienced so far, from directing my creatures at targets to pulling up my status sheet, merely requires me to will it."

Melissa scrunched her nose, and the cards disappeared. A look of wonder briefly replaced the pain written all across her face.

Shel immediately touched one of her cards, and a nervous-looking woman in her late teens appeared, dressed in a blue jumpsuit with a white plus sign on it.

Golden light washed across Melissa's knee, and her face lost its pinched, pained look and her eyes went wide. "God, that's good."

Wolfe watched the bones briefly fuse back—partially— and the flesh heal somewhat.

He waited as Shel did it twice more. By the time she was done, Melissa was able to crawl to her knees and then her feet.

"Thank you," Melissa said, hugging him. "Seriously, Wolfe, from the bottom of my heart, thank you."

Wolfe stiffened slightly but didn't pull back, nodding as he said, "Just make sure I get paid—I already discounted you."

Melissa gave him another squeeze. "Of course."

Wolfe disentangled himself from her. "I'm not really the hugging type, Melissa. If you really want to thank me, you can answer some questions for me."

She nodded.

"Let's start with—why the hell was Marko here? And shooting you?"

Melissa rubbed her knee, even though it appeared to be totally healed. "Hon... do you do body disappearing anymore?"

Wolfe shook his head. "No."

"I promise I'll answer your questions, Wolfe. But let me take care of some stuff, okay?"

Wolfe sighed, aggravated. But he had to admit that 'dead body and massive blood stains' were pressing issues.

Melissa pulled her cell phone out from a drawer and called someone. "Mr. Singh? Melissa here. I've got a dead body and a ton of blood in my downstairs lobby." She paused. "It's Marko, from the Grimm family."

Wolfe met Shel's wide eyes with his own. Both knew they had just heard confirmation that the Grimm family was still operating—and that Marko had somehow joined it. *Damian, that little bastard, must have finished unifying the families. I'm not surprised by the basics, but I'm surprised he managed to get Marko on board when his scheming—or failure to scheme well enough—got Marko's brother, Ramius, killed by me.*

Melissa was still talking. "No, I'm fine." Pause. "I don't think I can say who killed Marko." Another pause, in which she met Wolfe's eyes. "It would be bad for everyone. Yeah, I'll be here."

Melissa hung up. "Okay, hon, what was the question? Also, how are you still alive? Where have you been?"

Wolfe shook his head. "As to how I'm alive, I'll talk about it later, over a shot of whisky at some bar someday. As to my questions... Well, first, why did Marko shoot you?"

She grimaced. "I wouldn't tell him where Cherry and Delilah were."

With a name like Cherry... "Two of the working girls?"

She nodded. "Yeah. The cops, under this new Deputy Chief of Police Charleston, have been cracking down like crazy. They grab every freakin' working girl they see and send them to jail. Every minor drug pusher, too. Most are only there for a small amount of time, but no one wants to go to jail and get a rap. Anyway, I've been letting a lot of them live here—or at least work here, with assigned rooms—and the Singh family has been sending the johns here directly."

A face, thin and feminine with long, brown hair and dull, brown eyes, poked out from the hall. "Mel? Is everything okay?"

Then the girl took in the body. "By the Divine! What happened? Oh, god, are we going to be okay?"

Melissa grimaced. "Yeah. We're fine, Pearl. They came to get Cherry and Delilah, and Marko became violent, but Wolfe here handled the situation."

"Wolfe? The guy who killed all those Cobras and then died?"

Melissa smiled. "Well, *didn't* die, apparently. But Marko, at least, won't be bothering us."

Wolfe held his hands up. "Wait. Wait, wait, wait. *Why* the

heck would Marko be coming for these girls? Nothing you said explains that."

Melissa shrugged and then reached into a drawer behind the counter with shaking hands, removing a pack of cigarettes. "I don't know. But the last time he came for some girls, a month ago, only one was ever found—and she was rescued by some guy at that trafficking incident in Joliet. You know, the one in the trainyard? It made the news."

Wolfe met Shel's eyes—he could tell she knew as well. They had been suspicious, but this was absolute confirmation that Damian, that scumbag, was involved in the human trafficking.

CHAPTER 15

OLD HABITS

There was a brief moment of silence in which Wolfe, Shel, and Pearl just glanced around at the room. Melissa carefully lit her cigarette—she needed more than one try—and puffed. Wolfe felt a brief, almost overwhelming, desire to ask for one but pushed it down after a furtive glance at Shel.

There was blood and brain on the wall, blood on the cheap carpet where Melissa had been shot and leaking from the mook's mouth as well, and bullet holes all through the structure. A window behind Wolfe had a hole in it with a spiderweb crack radiating out from it.

The brief combat had really accentuated the awfulness of the place—the 'rooms rented by the hour' signs and all the pictures of half-naked women were terrible if you really thought about it, but splattering everything with blood made the horror immediate and shocking.

The Singh enforcers have their work cut out for them.

Pearl looked green and gagged once before gathering herself. "Do you think May is going to be okay?"

"I don't know," Melissa said. "I'm sorry, I haven't heard anything."

Pearl came up to Wolfe, licking her lips and looking up at him. "Wolfe?"

He tried to hold in his sigh—he just knew that someone else was going to ask something of him. "Yeah? What did you want?"

"Umm... if you're looking for missing girls, can you, maybe, um, keep an eye out for my friend Maybelle?"

"Where is she?" Shel asked. "Did she go missing?"

Pearl nodded. "Yeah. The cops took her to jail on a soliciting charge a month ago, and she hasn't come back yet."

"She got thirty days for soliciting?" Wolfe asked, surprised. "Was this a repeat offense?"

Pearl shook her head. "No, first time. She was barely eighteen, fresh in from Northridge. But she didn't get a conviction. They didn't take her to court—I've been checking every day."

"That's illegal," Shel said. "They have to take her to court within forty-eight hours or let her go, unless a weekend or holiday interferes, and then they can have ninety-six hours. No more."

"She ain't been to court," Pearl said, frowning. "I know that for sure."

"If we hear something, I'll let you know," Wolfe said.

"We'll make sure we find out, though," Shel said. "I promise, we'll find out what happened to Maybelle, and save her if we can."

Wolfe half-growled but left it. He had literally told Shel that it was her job to save people, and his to take down evil—he could hardly complain that she was following his rules.

Still, whether they saved some whore or not, they needed more information. Wolfe felt like he had ninety percent of the puzzle, and he just needed that last ten percent.

His eyes fell on the guy on the ground. *He might know something—but I can't just kill him after.*

"Shel, please bring the car up. I'm going to grab the mook—we need to question him, find out what the hell they're doing exactly. And even more importantly, how they're getting away with it all."

Shel glanced back at Pearl. "What's Maybelle's last name?"

"Fontain."

Shel nodded to Pearl and then took one last gander at the Morning After Inn. She glanced at the blood on the wall, the blood on the ground, the bullet holes in the wall. "Are they going to be able to clean this up?"

Wolfe snorted to hear his thoughts mirrored. "We can discuss the odds of their cleaning crew's success when we're on the move with the mook here."

Shel rolled her eyes but gave Wolfe a nod, heading out the front door to the parking lot.

Wolfe turned to Melissa. "You have a scarf or anything around here? Or a towel I could have?"

"Why?" Melissa asked, but she reached into a different drawer behind the counter and pulled out a thick, pink woolen scarf.

"Because I'm pretty sure that Shel won't let me kill some thug who surrendered, and I don't want him knowing who I am. It'll fix the 'knowing who I am' problem."

Wolfe took the scarf and put it around the head of the mook he had knocked out earlier—it was ridiculous-looking, but it did the job.

The action caused the mook to stir and cry out slightly as Wolfe jostled his shattered jaw, however. "Wha'—ow! —'appened?"

"Shut up," Wolfe said. "You fucked around, now you found out, with a bonus dose of *kicked so hard, you forgot the five minutes before I made your dentist rich.*"

"Wha' I evah do you? 'O ah 'u?" the thug asked.

Wolfe knew he was being a jackass, but the thug's idiot speech made him want to laugh.

Wolfe very lightly slapped the back of the mook's head. "I said, *shut up*. In case you can't tell by the blindfold, the less you know, the better your chances of living are. The more I find out from you, also the better your chances. Even a dumb fuck like you ought to be able to process this."

The thug must have been able to, because he shut up.

A second later, Shel pulled their Subaru up onto the sidewalk of the Morning After Inn and got out, opening the side door. Wolfe grabbed the mook by his upper arm—cuffed behind his back—and stood him up. The mook was wobbly, but Wolfe managed to get him to the door.

"Hey, um... thanks!" Pearl called. "Please don't forget to find Maybelle!"

Wolfe turned around, and Melissa nodded.

"Yeah," Wolfe said, glancing around one more time at the absolute mess that the front room was. "We'll do our best. Don't forget my money."

"I won't," Melissa said.

"Get in the car, you," Wolfe said, pushing the blindfolded man toward the back of the Subaru. The guy managed to carefully inch in, crying out softly once when his face hit the back cushion.

Wolfe took the moment to go back and get Shel's pistol, and then, as an afterthought, took the gun Marko had dropped when his head had exploded, and the one that his mook—Wolfe still didn't know the guy's name—had dropped as well.

Both pistols were the heavy, powerful Mark Nineteen Desert Eagle 44s, with eight-shot capacity. Wolfe was unimpressed. The gun was extremely powerful but felt more like the kind of gun Marko would use—powerful and showy, but it would run out of ammo quickly. He assumed that the mook had just copied his boss but didn't know.

Wolfe missed his Edge.

He took the guns, walked back to the car, and got in the front driver side. Shel took the passenger side. Wolfe put both guns in the glove compartment.

"You know you—" Shel began.

Wolfe waved his hands and silently mouthed, *"Be quiet."* Then he looked her in the eye and said, *"I* know."

Shel smiled, a tremulous thing that quickly faded, but she nodded. "Where are you taking him? You can hardly use the warehouse for this one."

"I had an amusing thought about that."

It wasn't even noon yet, and Wolfe stood, in full daylight, in the trainyard. Even during the day, it was semi-secluded, and so long as Wolfe didn't actually fire a gun, he was pretty sure no random passerby would see him—and he suspected that the Grimm family, and whatever organization they were selling to, had abandoned the site.

Wolfe touched the back of the mook's head with the pistol he had looted from Marko. He had already emptied the gun of bullets, and shown Shel.

Everything they were doing was illegal, but if the guy lived and walked, Wolfe strongly suspected no one would ever find out, and Shel's career would be fine.

And morally speaking, Wolfe was pretty sure the guy deserved a lot more than a broken jaw and a solid scare, which was all he would get for being part of shooting someone and a ton of kidnappings and trafficking.

"'Us' 'ell 'e wha' 'u wan' 'ow" the guy said quickly. Blood had drooled from his mouth down his shirt.

Man, listening to this guy try to talk is gonna be a huge pain. Although probably not as much a pain as talking is for him.

"Listen, and answer simply, to save us both the pain of you trying to talk. In fact, just nod yes or shake your head no. Got it?"

The mook nodded.

"Do you know how they pick which victims to kidnap?"

The mook shook his head.

"Do you know how the victims are physically being picked up?"

The mook nodded.

"Explain out loud," Wolfe said.

"On 'e'ease 'um 'ail," the man sputtered out.

"On release from jail?" Shel asked. "Like, they're being picked up right when jail releases them?"

The thug nodded again.

"Who tells you when they're being released?" Wolfe asked.

The man shrugged.

Wolfe frowned. He couldn't tell if the mook was lying, but it all seemed consistent to what he knew. The Grimm family hadn't told all the street-level enforcers how the plans were made, or who the sources of information were. They had told them to go guard a pickup at this time on this day. The same principle applied here.

"How did Cherry and the other girl not get picked up, then?" Wolfe asked.

"'A'ic," the man said.

"What?"

"'Affic," the man said, struggling to sound out the word.

"Traffic? You guys were late?" Wolfe asked.

The man nodded.

Wolfe almost laughed. It was surprising how often something simple fucked up a good crime. It was rarely a treacherous insider spilling the beans or something—it was usually some dumbass who drove twenty miles over the speed limit with a hundred thousand dollars of drugs in a car with six outstanding speeding tickets, got pulled over and got his car impounded, and all of a sudden, he's looking at ten years if he stays quiet and two if he talks.

This felt similar to Wolfe. He still wasn't sure of the truth, but it all *felt* right to him, consistent with his twenty years of experience.

But it still didn't answer the question of how they were picking whom to make victims. Wolfe still didn't have the last ten percent.

But Mr. Talkative here had given him another string to pull at.

And Pearl *had* wanted him to check on Maybelle at the jail.

CHAPTER 16

SOME TIME IN JAIL

The Noimoire jail was huge. It wasn't a part of the prison, which was even bigger—just the jail, where people awaiting trial and the people serving short sentences for baby crimes stayed. It occupied a massive block it would take minutes to *drive* around.

"I still can't believe you took that guy's pants," Shel said, trying not to start laughing again.

Wolfe didn't try, chuckling. "Best chance to get him legitimately arrested, and if he doesn't want to get arrested for having his dong out, he's gonna need to be mighty stealthy—which means longer before people find out about Marko."

"Did you check his cards?" Shel asked as Wolfe pulled into the massive parking lot in front of the jail's main entrance.

"Yeah, I glanced at them. Mostly a few extra Angry Hellhounds, which is gonna be the signature card in this deck, I swear by all the gods—"

"Appropriately signature," Shel snarked.

"—and most of his other stuff was trash. But he *did* also have a Gehennan Kennel Master," Wolfe said.

Shel clapped rapidly in front of her face, looking a bit

more like a woo-girl than Wolfe was used to. "Take it out, I want to see it!"

"That's what she said?" Wolfe asked, arching an eyebrow at her.

She chuckled. "C'mon, let's see it."

Wolfe pulled into one of the parking spaces and turned the car off, then reached into his pants and pulled Marko's deck out.

He passed it to Shel. "Yeah, sure. Here."

She flipped through the deck, pulled the card out, and held it where they could both see it.

Gehennan Kennel Master
Tier-1 Rare Infernal Creature
2 Infernal Power, 1 Fire or Beast Power
Health: 28
Attack: 8
Defense: 7
Magic Attack: 6
Magic Defense: 7

Special: **Motivation**: When this creature enters the field, any creature with a matching type may make an additional attack.

Special: **Gehennan Leadership**: +1 to attack and magical attack to any Creature [Canine] for each of the types it matches among Fire, Beast, and Infernal.

Special: **Façade [Canine]**: This card acts as a Creature [Canine] for triggering any other canine's bonuses only.

Special: **Meat for the Pack**: The first time a deckbearer with this card and at least three Hellhounds defeats a Divine deckbearer, they will gain a random Hellhound from any of the last ten sets as if drawing from a rare deck.

"The Fireborn Hellhounds that hunt Gehenna, the Lake of

Fire, are sometimes recruited to serve in the armies of the Infernal, and a magically twisted demon is put in charge of them. He motivates his pack with the flesh of angels."

"Are you going to add it to your deck?" Shel asked.

Wolfe hesitated. "It's crazy strong for my deck, but it takes *so much* power for a card that isn't a canine itself, given how my deck works."

"It takes three, and you have seven. Most of your strong cards could enter—imagine if you had this big boy and Cerberus's Home for Wayward Hellhounds. Each of the generated Lost Hellhound Puppies would be crazy strong."

Wolfe did the math—each would become a nine-attack creature. Cerberus's Home would generate five that would enter free. Still...

"If I had it out, I could either place Cerberus's Home and also spam my spare Lost Hellhound Puppy cards, or bring out two Angry Hellhounds with this guy... But I have to cut something from the deck."

"What would you cut?"

Wolfe was having trouble deciding, but... "Yeah, it's completely worth it. I'll add it. Wish I had another power or two, though, to really stack stuff."

"You need to gain another five levels to gain another power."

Wolfe nodded. "Yeah. I doubt that'll happen soon."

"It would if we fought in the Arena and gained some levels. It'd be hard, but if you got some over-level match-ups, you could make it."

Wolfe thought about it. *Maybe, but...* "Same problem as before. If I go to a major Arena, Damian will find me—and maybe the police. I've already got Rhett up my rear. I don't need the Noimoire Police Department comparing notes with him."

"Why don't you call someone, one of your old contacts? I mean, you're back on the scene, anyway, and Damian is bound to find out. Perhaps just call Victor. He likes you, even if he doesn't owe you anymore, right?"

Wolfe laughed as he imagined the look on the information broker's face. "He's gonna be shocked. But he might sell my existence to someone else, you know."

Shel shrugged and glanced back down at the card. "It's going to come out soon, Wolfe. You're hunting again."

Wolfe nodded slowly. "All right, I'll call him. But first, let's go see if we can find out what happened to one Maybelle..." He snapped his fingers.

"Fontain," Shel supplied.

"Right, one Maybelle Fontain."

The inside of the jail, at least in the front room, was less horrible than Wolfe would have guessed. The floor was clean green-and-white tile. The walls had art whose motif seemed to be almost entirely 'wholesome scenes from the 1950s.' The lady with curly, brown hair at the front desk, dressed in a prison guard's uniform and typing away at the old computer next to an even older printer was surprisingly cute, perky, and helpful.

Well, as helpful as she could be, but Wolfe was pretty sure that she wasn't going to let him go down the hallway that led past the metal detector to the visiting rooms.

She smiled up at him, her teeth so white and brilliant that Wolfe expected an announcer to pop out and say something about *ten out of ten dentists.*

Then she gave a cute, little frown. "I'm sorry, but we don't have a Maybelle Fontain in custody right now—neither the first name nor the last name are bringing up any hits right now. Your friend is lucky—she got let go."

Wolfe met Shel's eyes, and he knew they were both thinking the same thing. *The odds that was 'lucky' for her were about the same as the proverbial snowball in Gehenna.*

The smile came back. "Is there anything else I can help you with?"

"Can you at least tell me when she was released?" Wolfe asked, leaning over onto the desk.

Without a falter of her smile, the front desk guard leaned back about six inches. "I'm sorry, sir, only family with proof of relation can access that information."

Wolfe sighed, straightened, and shuffled to the side. Shel went with him, and the two moved over to the waiting room benches.

"What now?" Shel asked.

"I don't—" Wolfe started, but stopped, glancing back at that lady and then to Shel. "That lady—she just answers questions about people who are, or were, in jail, all day long, right?"

Shel pursed her lips in evident confusion but nodded. "Yeah."

"And it's hooked up to a database or whatever that tells her about all of them? Even the ones who left?"

Shel nodded.

"So all I really need is to look at the program for a few seconds..." Wolfe mused, still glancing at the lady.

"Wolfe... You can't take that nice guard's computer away from her," Shel said with a heavy sigh.

Wolfe looked up, ready to argue that he wasn't that dumb and wouldn't just hurt some random woman, but he found Shel smirking at him.

He chuckled. "Hilarious. But seriously, how do I do this?"

Shel glanced around the room they were in. It was fairly

small, with the desk and waiting benches... but it had three exits. One was the double doors back to the parking lot, one was past the metal detectors and into the facility itself, and one was to a small alcove with a bunch of vending machines and some small computers.

Before Shel could answer, Wolfe pointed back toward the computers. "What's back there?"

Shel briefly glanced at it. "It's a new electronic system they installed to check on current inmates and put money on books so they can buy food and stuff."

"Hmm..." Wolfe mused. "Perky there seems like she's *really* excited to do her job. What if I just go pay someone to pick a fight with the vending machines and check the computer when she leaves?"

"Okay—just pay them *off* camera, okay?" Shel asked.

Wolfe nodded.

Then he walked out of the double doors and back into the parking lot. He glanced around for a place he could observe easily without being observed as easily, in case someone came in who would recognize him. Two columns along the side of the entrance that were in the shadows at the moment were the best he was going to do, Wolfe figured.

He leaned on one of the columns, his profile sideways to the entrance, and scanned the people filtering in. Older long-haired lady with entirely too much makeup in entirely too little of a leather skirt, likely the girlfriend of a career criminal —too wise and jaded by half. Next, a heavy-set man in a cheap suit with a widow's peak, looking embarrassed, likely the father of some precious kid who'd taken a walk on the wild side—not even remotely criminal or desperate enough.

Then he saw him. A pale-skinned twenty-year old with a pock-marked face, dressed in baggy designer jeans that were old and worn, a black T-shirt, and scuffed sneakers that were a touch too large. He had a faux gold chain around his neck, and the skin on his face was sunken in so much, you could open a cardboard box with his cheekbones.

The kind of guy who was both idiotic and had a lot to prove. Wolfe knew the type quite well. *I'll call him Baby Thug.*

As Baby Thug walked up, Wolfe pried three hundred-dollar bills from his pocket and stepped forward.

Baby Thug turned, took a step back, eyes wide, then stepped back forward, subtly pressing his chest out.

"I've got a business proposition for you," Wolfe said without preamble as he stepped up to Baby Thug, the money visible in his hand.

"What?" Baby Thug asked, staring at the money hungrily.

"What're you here for?" Wolfe asked.

Baby Thug turned to face him. "Gonna do my ten—caught a bullshit possession case, lawyer fucked me. Why you care?"

Wolfe winced at Baby Thug's use of language—and his halitosis.

But that confirms what I needed to know about Baby Thug's judgement and station in life. "I don't actually give a shit. But I need a favor. I want you to pick a fight with a vending machine in there, make it good. Can you do that for three hundred dollars?"

Baby Thug reached for it, but Wolfe pulled it back. "I'll put it on your books, after you do what I need."

"How do I know you'll—"

"You don't," Wolfe interrupted. "You'll have to trust me. But I'll handle it. And I'm only asking you to pick a fight with a vending machine."

"I'm Reginald Hutchings," Baby Thug said. "So you can put the money on my books."

Wolfe glanced at Reginald. *He doesn't look like a Reginald —more like a train wreck.*

"I go by Reggie."

"I don't care," Wolfe said. "Just do your part, and I'll do mine."

Reggie nodded.

Wolfe followed Reggie back in, and Reggie immediately went to the side, where the vending machines were. Wolfe walked up to the desk and waited next to it. When Guard Perky gave him a questioning arch of the eyebrow, Wolfe ignored it.

"Hey, give me my soda, you fucking machine!" came from the back, followed by the sound of flesh striking glass.

Guard Perky stood, smiled briefly at Wolfe and rolled her eyes, nodding to the back like it was some kind of joke.

"Remain calm, sir!" she called.

Shel was trying not to giggle in the corner of the reception room.

A couple more slams came from the back. "I don't need your shit right now, you fucking machine!"

"Sir, calm down!" Guard Perky yelled, sounding angry now. "Don't vandalize the machines!"

Another couple of smacks and some profanities followed.

Guard Perky glanced at Wolfe while pulling out pepper spray. "Don't touch anything!"

She raced around the side of the desk and down the hall.

Wolfe immediately walked around the desk and leaned over, trying to figure the system out. It was rather intuitive, with a huge input bar next to a space titled "Inmate Lookup."

"Sir, let go of the machine, right now!" came from the back, followed by a "It took my fucking money!"

Wolfe ignored that and quickly typed out 'Fontain, Maybelle' into the search bar.

A picture came up of a cornfed Iowa cheerleader type with red-rimmed blue eyes and blonde hair, a bruise on the side of her face. Wolfe glanced through her biographical data without interest before coming to the status section. She had been picked up thirty days ago, and released the evening after, at five. The only other note was that the pretrial services package had been prepared by a company called Worldwide Decurion, carried out by its agent Caine Delacruz.

Caine... I've heard that somewhere.

Wolfe remembered his fight in the trainyard. When he had been beating Tracy d'Ordinii, the fixer had called for backup from the guy with the sportscar. He had specifically called out for Caine.

It wasn't the most common name...

"All right, all right, just give me a soda and I'll calm down. No need to pepper spray me," came from the back.

Wolfe glanced back up at the biographical information. It claimed Maybelle was homeless and had her father unlisted... and she had no emergency contact information.

Wolfe quickly exited the file and tried to remember the name of any other young working girls he knew but couldn't. He just typed in 'Smith,' and got a ton of hits. Looking for one with a female name and a release date in the last sixty days, he found a 'Marissa' and selected it.

She had been released a day after pickup, and Worldwide Decurion had done the pretrial services package. This time, Wolfe glanced at the biographical data.

Homeless, no emergency contact information, dad unlisted.

Wolfe quickly hit escape and stood, just as Guard Perky came around the corner, marching Reggie in front of her.

Wolfe met Reggie's eyes and nodded, patted his own pocket, and then walked toward the back before Reggie could say anything stupid and get them both in trouble.

CHAPTER 17

THE MUCH-ANTICIPATED
RETURN OF SUIT

"Why are we here?" Shel asked as Wolfe pulled into the parking lot outside 'E mett Investigations.'

Wolfe parked out front and turned the car off. "I don't understand how Emmett got all his information without making the connection to Worldwide Decurion—he has all these files where he has the victims listed, but I don't see anything about Worldwide in the files. I want to know what Emmett knows and how he knows it."

Wolfe opened the door and swung his feet out.

"You could call him," Shel said.

Wolfe stopped, half in the car. "That would be the easy answer. Sorry, given my history, I guess I'm not the most trusting type. I should have done that. But we're here now— I'll check his place, see what we can learn, and perhaps we'll find something. If not, we can call him after."

Wolfe stood next to the car, then walked over to the door, took his key out, put it in, and turned to unlock the door. He met no resistance and shifted down and turned the knob. The door opened.

Wolfe stepped inside. All the old magazines were missing.

"Fuck," Wolfe muttered. *Someone had been here.*

Or is here.

"Pull your deck," Wolfe whispered, touching his own chest. A second later, his deck came out, and Wolfe dropped Brimstone into his hand. He ignored the notification about Shel's deck.

Sorenia appeared behind him.

"Thank y—" Sorenia began.

Wolfe held his finger up. "Ssh!"

Although being quiet was probably pointless as a surprise tactic. Any other deckbearers certainly knew they were coming, and any ordinary thugs had probably heard them in the tiny building, anyway. But it wouldn't help to give away their position constantly.

Wolfe moved forward cautiously and kicked the door to the back office open.

It was empty of enemies, which was easy to tell because every box and scrap of paper was missing entirely, and the desk had been turned over.

Wolfe dismissed Brimstone and his deck.

He pinched the bridge of his nose. "Fuck. Someone must have come and cleaned this place out. If there was any more information, it's long gone."

"You think Damian did it?" Shel asked.

Wolfe pushed the desk back up and pushed the chair back under it. "Damian, or these Worldwide Decurion people, or maybe the corrupt cops Emmett talked about... I've got no idea. There's a whole lot of reasons for a whole lot of people to cover this up."

The door slammed open in the front room. Wolfe grabbed Shel and pulled her down behind the desk, touching his chest again as he did. She yelped as he shoved her down underneath the piece of furniture.

Then an aggravating voice he remembered all too well yelled out, "Dunn!"

Shel picked herself up off the floor as Suit busted into the room, a briefcase in one hand and a piece of paper in the other. He walked up to Wolfe like he owned the place.

Then he thrust the paper into Wolfe's face. "This is worthless, Dunn! Complete, utter garbage that I can't use! You need to get off your lazy, incompetent ass and go back and do it right!"

"What?" Wolfe asked, staring at the half-filled page. It was the statement he had gotten from Ms. Timo on her son's manslaughter case. "What's wrong with it?"

Shel glanced at it, then glanced at Wolfe.

"It's incomplete—and done improperly. It's completely inadequate, inadmissible... Pick your favorite word that means 'useless and worthless.' Now we paid you for a gods-damned statement, and I expect a good one, or I'll report you to the licensing board myself!"

Wolfe was about to pop Suit in the nose, but Shel put her hand on his arm. "We'll get this taken care of, Mr., umm...?"

"You better!" Suit said, still angry. "You damned well better."

Then he looked around. "I see you at least cleaned this dump up. Now you better clean your act up as well."

He threw the paper down on the desk.

Before Wolfe could decide how to handle the situation, Suit turned and flounced from the building.

"What. The. Fuck," Wolfe ground out.

Shel sighed. "Actually... he has a point, even if he's an ass. The statement needs to be very detail oriented, preferably with specific times. It needs to be on court paper, it needs to be signed..."

Wolfe pinched the bridge of his nose. "Why the hell does it

need all that? It says here, on the paper, plain as day, what the hell Ms. Timo did."

"Look... I can help you make a better statement," Shel said.

"I don't need your help," Wolfe ground out.

Shel reached her arms around him and hugged him. "Wolfe, when something needs beating or killing, do I ever, and I mean *ever*, try to stop you from doing it your way?"

"No."

"Because I know you're the best ass-kicker in three counties," Shel said, with the air of someone quoting a famous line, although Wolfe had no idea which one. "But I'm the one taking the police courses—including the one on statements that the prosecutor can use. Let me help, please?"

Wolfe sighed. "All right, fine. Just this once to help me learn."

Shel smiled. "Perfect. Lucy will be over tomorrow to start the month with us, and Ms. Timo asked if Shannon could come play—I said 'yes.' So I'll help you get ready tonight, and you can get it from her tomorrow, while everyone is over and I'm at class. No one will even know I helped."

Wolfe nodded. "We'll do it your way." Then he glanced around again. "I wish I *did* know who raided this place—Damian, the police, or someone else."

Wolfe pulled his phone out and dialed Emmett.

After the fourth ring, Wolfe hung up.

"No answer?" Shel said, raising an eyebrow.

Wolfe shook his head, then dialed again. This time, he waited for voicemail, but when it kicked on, he got a falsely cheery lady telling him the mailbox was full.

He hung up again, then glanced at Shel. "What was the name of the hospital?"

"The one Emmett's at?"

Wolfe nodded.

"Uriel's Sacred," Shel said, glancing around the room they were in nervously, as if the people who had raided it might come back at any time.

Wolfe knew that people committing crimes rarely hung out where they had done so once they were done, so he wasn't too worried about it. He finished looking up Uriel Sacred and dialed.

A series of menu choices led him to placing a call to Floor Two, Room Twenty-Three—but no one picked up again.

Wolfe, feeling like something might have gone south, dialed the main line again and went through the menu until he was connected with an operator.

"Hi, how may I help you?" a tired, feminine voice asked.

"I'm looking to talk to Emmett Dunn... he was brought in two days ago. I work for him and need some assistance with a job we're doing."

"Dunn, Dunn..." the voice said, along with the clackity-clack of a keyboard. "I'm sorry. Mr. Emmett Dunn is no longer with us."

"He died?!" Wolfe exploded into the phone, and Shel's eyes went wide.

The woman chuckled, then coughed. "Sorry, didn't mean to laugh. No, he was discharged early this morning, with a clean bill of health, basically. I'd look for him where you normally find him."

Wolfe glanced around the empty office. "Yeah, I'll do that. Thanks."

He hung up.

"He's not dead—he was discharged," Wolfe said. "Maybe he took the files."

"Thank Raphael," Shel said, sighing. "Do you think he came and got the files himself?"

Wolfe shook his head. "He might have, but I doubt it. And it isn't the best sign that he's not answering his phone. It's not even close to the end of working hours—why wouldn't he answer?"

Shel nodded, tapping her fingers together. "So, he might still be in trouble?"

Wolfe nodded.

"What should we do?" Shel asked.

"Well, I'm a private investigator now. I need to do some more investigation. I think it's time we investigate in a different direction. Let's go see Miriam and learn about what's been going on with Damian."

Shel snorted. "Ought to be an experience, at least."

Wolfe dialed Miriam.

Wolfe pulled to the front of the Ekron Eternal, past the garden and fountains around the main entrance, up to the steps. Once, the garden had been filled with statues of flies and demons, but now it had been redecorated with numerous barely clothed vampire statues.

Wolfe shook his head. He had been a couple of times since Miriam had assumed control of the place, but it always felt weird seeing the new décor. He thought it must also have been weird for people who had never seen the old décor, but it was extra weird for him.

What was different, however, was the front line. The last time Wolfe had been there, there had been almost no line to get into the club—the lack of criminal support and the gunfight nine months ago had made the Ekron Eternal a dying institution, and despite being appointed to run it temporarily by the probate courts, Miriam hadn't been able to turn that around.

Now, however... The front had a huge line, filled with men

Wolfe recognized from all the different crime organizations, who were waiting for their chance to ascend the ramp and enter the club.

Plus, the guys working the line were completely unfamiliar.

"What has Miriam done?" Wolfe asked.

Shel glanced at him, not understanding, but he shook his head. He would ask Big Man Grimm's daughter soon enough.

Wolfe took a deep breath. This was the final moment of truth, when his presence would be known, openly, to the underground again. Entering publicly, in front of so many of his old associates, was tantamount to declaring that he had returned.

Time to do this. I've returned to hunt, and I guess they'll know they're being hunted. Feels right, somehow.

Wolfe stepped from his car, and Shel followed on her side, staring up at the ostentatious club. Wolfe was about to head up the steps next to the ramp and enter when a man in his early twenties walked up to Wolfe. He was shirtless and covered in makeup to make him look incredibly pale. He glanced at Wolfe's Subaru and sneered.

"Do you want me to valet... this, sir?" the man asked.

Wolfe tossed him the keys and resisted the temptation to punk the kid. "Yeah, handle it."

Wolfe strode up the steps, past the huge line of people who stared at him as he walked straight up to the bouncer and his two backup men. The bouncer was even larger than Wolfe, about six-six and built like a linebacker. He held his hand up to Wolfe, palm out.

"What the hell are you doing, chump? Get in line."

Wolfe leaned in. "I'm William Madison. I believe Miriam had special instructions."

The man nodded but didn't remove his hand. "You said a name I'm going to pay attention to, but now I need some ID."

Wolfe fished into his pocket, pulled it out, and showed the man.

He lowered his hand, removed the rope, and ushered Wolfe inside. "Miriam is waiting in the back, at the VIP table, sir. Do you need an escort?"

Wolfe shook his head. "I know my way."

Wolfe and Shel strode past, with a few angry exclamations and one guy shouting, "Who the fuck is that guy?" from behind them. Wolfe didn't want to admit that it mattered to him, but he did like getting the respect he would have been given back in the day, when he'd been the Grimm head enforcer. He was getting damn tired of being a trainee P.I.

Shel chuckled. "Enjoyed that, did you?"

Wolfe gave a half-smile to his girlfriend but didn't reply directly.

Aside from the statues outside—and some matching ones inside—the club remained about the same as he remembered from his days as head enforcer. That was a huge upgrade from what it had been a couple of weeks ago. The inside was dark but lit by flashing lights that swirled through a machine-generated fog, which swirled around the statues of vampires—many of them actually nude now that they were inside the club. The twenty-somethings who danced through the club were barely more dressed, and loud, beat-heavy techno music played across the dance floor, reverberating through Wolfe's teeth.

He wove his way around the outside of the huge dance floor, avoiding any chance of collision with the various dancers, and made his way to the back, along a path he knew quite well.

He reached the end of the club, where the VIP table was. It was exactly as Wolfe remembered it, down to bullet holes in the top of the giant, oak table from when Wolfe had used it as a shield. He slid into the large, leather booth on the left side of the table, past Harry, who was still acting as guard a year later for the Grimm family. As always, he didn't bother Wolfe when Wolfe took his seat, but in a change from the past, he also said nothing when Shel slid into the booth on the right side.

Wolfe glanced around at the other three occupants.

The first was Derek, who had helped Wolfe in a couple of his final fights, including taking out Javier Garcia, the old lieutenant of the Cobras. Derek was shirtless, with his umber skin oiled, and he had an honest-to-the-gods pitchfork upright in the booth next to him.

The second was a new man, Ahmed, who had been hired by Miriam after her father had died—with cards from the Frozen Cairn dungeon Derek, Miriam, Wolfe, and Shel had completed together. Ahmed was also young, in his late twenties. But he was dressed almost like an Egyptian pharaoh —although still shirtless. He was very tan, six feet tall, and had been both a model and a military man before Miriam had cut a deal with him.

Lastly, there was Miriam herself. She was dressed in a diaphanous, silver dress that just barely hinted at her dark underthings beneath and hung very low on her frame. She had in red contact lenses, with black makeup around the eyes, and lounged back in the booth with her arms on the backrest behind her, both accentuating her sensuality and heightening the space she took up.

Miriam always managed to take up a lot of room, whether in attention, conversation, or just an old-fashioned physical space.

A black purse with white skull clasps beside her completed the image.

Wolfe glanced around. "You always manage to look like you're leading a supervillain team, Miriam. Why?"

She smiled and then licked her lips blatantly. "It's good to see you too, Wolfy. What can I do for you this beautiful evening? I was positively intrigued when *you* asked to come see *me* for once."

"Well, before I answer that, tell me what deal with the Infernal you've made to turn this around."

Miriam's smile slipped, and she grimaced but leaned in toward Wolfe conspiratorially.

CHAPTER 18

DEAL WITH THE INFERNAL

Miriam leaned in even further. "Look, you know how things were after Damian killed Dad. I really appreciate you saving me, Wolfe, truly—I'd love to be allowed to show you *how much* someday, in fact."

She licked her lips suggestively.

Wolfe snorted. "I'm not letting you distract me, Miriam. Just tell me what you did."

Miriam leaned back in the huge, leather booth, her eyes slightly narrowed, but then she shrugged her slender shoulders. "The Ekron Eternal was shut down, our house was gone, and insurance wouldn't pay for a 'probably criminal bombing.' No one could figure out where Dad had been keeping most of the loose money. We still haven't."

Wolfe raised an eyebrow—he was pretty sure Big Man Grimm had stashed the money *somewhere*—millions of dollars in cash.

Miriam picked a cocktail up with one slender hand and sipped at the edge of the glass. "I was sustaining my lifestyle—and my delicious employees"—she waved languidly at Derek and Ahmed—"by selling off the cards we got from the Frozen

Cairn dungeon. But that wasn't going to do the trick long term."

Wolfe, reminded by Miriam taking a drink, turned to Harry. "Please bring me a whisky—you know my favorite."

Harry nodded, but Wolfe reached out and touched his arm. "And a strawberry daiquiri for Shel."

Harry nodded a second time and walked off. Wolfe turned back to Miriam.

"The court made you the operator for the club since both your parents were dead and you had credible witnesses that Damian was the murderer. You couldn't make money from that?"

"Yeah, that's true," Miriam said, taking another sip. "But the club had a horrible reputation after the attacks Nico launched on it. Very few people were coming here—it wasn't the place to be anymore. The operating costs were higher than the profit, and I was in debt."

"So..." Shel asked.

"*So,* I talked to the remaining crime family leaders, starting with Benjamin Renfeldt. We made a deal. I would be their money laundering location. They send all their people through, spending a ton of money here on alcohol and entrance fees, just like with Dad. Only, I hire a bunch of fake consultants and such, transferring most of it back to the families. Very nearly everyone in the Noimoire underworld is in on it now, and a fountain of illegal money pours through this place—and I get thirty percent. Plus, the club is popular again, and a lot of legitimate money flows through it as well."

Wolfe sighed, leaning back in the booth to match Miriam.

She frowned. "Don't give me that, Wolfy. It's not like you spend a lot of time on the right side of the law—and I've got my own men, my own business, and everything."

"And law school?" Wolfe asked, gritting his teeth at the nickname.

Miriam smiled. "I'll still graduate. I doubt I'll ever do anything with it, directly, since this place makes *way* more money than most law firms, but it's a handy skill to have."

"You know I'm going to put most of the crime families out of business, right?" Wolfe asked. "Have you thought about that?"

Miriam smiled widely at Wolfe, taking her phone out and typing at it. "Oh, I definitely have. In fact, it'd be better to say I'm *counting* on it. This"—she waved around at the club—"is another of those businesses you can't leave, normally—I know too much about too many people. I suspect the other crime bosses are all hoping that I'll eventually get assassinated because of that knowledge, and then their dealings will be totally secure."

Shel laughed lightly, shaking her head.

Miriam grinned back at her and ran one finger around the edge of her drink. "Audacious, I know. But I do have what business calls asymmetric knowledge now—I know that a certified killer everyone else thinks is dead is still gunning for them. All of them. And when they do die, whatever money is currently in the pipeline will just become mine as well. It's perfect."

Wolfe glanced at her. *I really hope she doesn't go full supervillain. I would truly hate to have to kill her as well, both because she's a woman, and because I've known her since she was in diapers.*

Even as they were talking, a sixth person slid into the booth, next to Shel, who scooted over. Wolfe glanced at the newcomer briefly, then did a double take. A short five-foot-seven, almost painfully thin, pale white with faint acne scars and brilliant green eyes under greasy, black hair...

"Wolfe?!" the man asked, his eyes as wide as dinner plates. "You're alive?"

"Victor," Wolfe said. "Your information-gathering powers

are amazing—you discerned the state of my life just from looking at me."

Victor laughed, running his hand through his black hair, his eyes still wide. "It's been, like, three years since I last saw you—and nine months since we talked. I thought you were dead... where have you been?"

Miriam shook her head. "Uh-uh. No asking Wolfe about that, Victor."

Victor settled back. "Yeah, sorry. I just like to know. Well, Janine will be happy to hear that her savior managed to survive."

Miriam held her glass out to Wolfe, then motioned to Victor with it. "Victor works for me now, Wolfe. He's always had his ear to the ground for news about the Great Game within Noimoire, among other things. And I've learned some things that I want your help with. Things that can help both of us, in fact."

Wolfe held his hands up. "Wait, wait, wait. Do that second. It sounds great, but I want some information first. I didn't come here because of cards. I came here because of Damian. I think his half of the Grimm family might be involved in human trafficking."

"Yeah, Victor told me about the situation—you think that's Damian?" Miriam's mouth twisted in a tiny frown.

"Along with others. What I don't know is where the evil little dwarf is hiding, and what his connection is."

Miriam stirred her drink again, glancing down at it for a moment. "Well, as to what his connection is, I have to admit I'm not sure. I don't know what he's doing at the moment, and the few attempts I've made to infiltrate my men into his organization have failed."

Wolfe frowned.

Miriam looked up with a bright smile, her eyes glassy. "But if you're looking for revenge for Dad, I know *where* he is. His people are constantly going to an old meat-packing plant with a ton of old warehouses nearby. It's a huge complex, not at all small, bigger than anything Dad had—although I think it's his *only* base of operations."

She giggled, a sound with an edge to it. "Deliciously, I think he might live there."

Then she frowned. "But no one, from the police to the local hitmen, seems willing to do anything about the information. I assume the creep is either paid up with some important people, or working with them."

Wolfe slowly nodded. "My contact says that the police might be in on it, so that makes sense at least."

Miriam reached into her purse and pulled out a stick of red lipstick. Then she wrote an address onto a napkin.

"Do handle my dear brother as soon as you can, Wolfy."

"You don't want to help?" Shel asked.

Miriam drummed her fingers on the table. "I don't want to be anywhere near where he dies because I'm a *very* obvious suspect. How about I'll keep you in information and gear, hmm?"

Then she smiled again. "Now that that's out of the way, can we discuss my proposal?"

Wolfe nodded. "Sure, what do you want from me?"

"Well... it seems that the gods actually gave Noimoire a second Arena. An underground Arena, literally and figuratively. Neither Victor nor I have been able to find out who runs the place, for the moment, at least. I want to go participate, but I'm worried about the details."

Wolfe raised an eyebrow, his interest piqued. "'The details'?"

"Well, you get taken to the Arena blindfolded, and no one gets to bring cellphones or anything like that—so we'll be out of touch. Potentially vulnerable. No slight to Ahmed and Derek, here—"

"None taken," Derek said. "Wolfe already saved my bacon. I get it."

"Yes, exactly. I'd rather have you around in that kind of a situation."

Wolfe glanced over at Shel. She was grinning at him.

Wolfe turned back to Miriam. "Yeah, I think that could be... fun, to play the Great Game with you again. When?"

"Tomorrow afternoon?"

"Not nighttime?"

Miriam shook her head.

Wolfe nodded. "That works out—I've got business to attend to tonight. I want to check the sites, see if I can find out where they're going to do the switch, and who's involved."

Victor leaned in. "Do you know the sites? I can spy on them, as long as there are only a few."

Wolfe raised an eyebrow. "Really?"

Victor nodded. "Just because I'm part of Mistress Grimm's organization doesn't mean that I left my skills and contacts behind. If it's a limited number of sites, I can put my people on it, let you know when someone sees something. I can also get you any ordinance you might need."

Most of Wolfe was incredibly excited to hear both of those things, but a small piece of him...

"'Mistress Grimm'?"

Miriam smiled at him, took a sip of her drink, and shrugged.

CHAPTER 19

THE NEWEST SITE

A bit later, Wolfe was driving his Subaru down Main Street, headed for Industrial Avenue again. The moon still lit everything, although it was considerably higher in the night sky now, but on Main, it wasn't needed—cars were still common, and the streetlights kept everything at least dimly illuminated.

The site that had turned up a hit had been a large complex of warehouses, barely half a mile past the pound where he, Shel, and Miriam had slain Ramius and gone to their first dungeon—the werewolf one.

Now, well into the early hours of the morning, Wolfe and Shel were driving to probably stop a mass kidnapping—and hopefully gain the evidence needed to put a stop to the traffickers in general, one way or another.

About a quarter mile before they reached the site, Wolfe pulled onto a side road and then turned onto another road facing away from the warehouses. Then he pulled over to the side of the road and turned the car off.

Shel raised her eyebrow at his rapid turns.

Wolfe smiled at her, feeling in his element again. "They might have seen the car coming at this range—if they did, not seeing us turn away would raise suspicions. This way. they'll think we left if they're there and paying attention. At the same time, it's close enough we can likely get to it at a dead run, if we have to."

Shel shuddered but nodded.

Wolfe reached down and grabbed one of Miriam's gifts—a brand-new Edge STI International Pistol, loaded, with two additional clips in his belt. It felt good—just a touch heavier and more powerful than the usual pistols—the nine-mils—without being unwieldy.

Wolfe stuffed it into the belt holster he'd been given and opened the door to his car, exiting swiftly. Shel took her cadet Glock and put it in the back of her jeans before following him out.

"All right, from here on out, let's try to keep quiet—but don't *act* like you're trying to keep quiet."

"*What*?" Shel asked, laughing. "How do I do that?"

"I don't know... just walk casual."

Shel snorted, but neither said anything else as they walked down the road between the warehouses. There were very few streetlights, and almost no cars, to light things, but the moon still kept everything dimly visible in shades of gray.

An owl hooted off to the side, and a chill October wind blew down the street.

Shel shivered and then gave a forced laugh. "All we need is rain for the atmosphere to be perfect for a grizzled P.I. and his femme fatale in a crime novel."

Wolfe chuckled, but something she'd said struck him as a non-sequitur.

"Have you ever killed *anything*, Shel?" Wolfe asked.

"Well, not a person, if that's what you mean, although I've gotten credit for helping."

"Well, you might get your chance tonight," Wolfe said.

"So much for lightening the mood with some light-hearted banter," Shel muttered, shivering again.

Wolfe crooked a smile, but he was too wound up to do more.

The two of them reached the edge of the main warehouse complex. It was all asphalt, newer and quieter than the gravel at the trainyard. On the other hand, there weren't a lot of places to hide—no going under train cars, or leaping from line to line. Instead, there were ten warehouses, all around a huge parking lot, four to each side north and south with one each on the other ends.

"We go around the back of the warehouse to our right, and then we'll look around the side, between the two near ones, see what we can see," Wolfe said.

Shel nodded, and Wolfe started an easy jog along the back of the first warehouse, a couple hundred feet before he reached the turn point and glanced around.

There weren't any trucks, despite the warehouses—just a huge parking lot, empty in the dark but for a single van, almost a perfect match for the one Wolfe had seen the night this whole mess with Emmett's case and Wolfe's early return to Noimoire had started.

"They're here," Shel said, her voice a barely audible whisper in the darkness.

Wolfe nodded. "Victor said they were, and I've found his information to be reliable often enough I didn't doubt it. Shall we go?"

"Should we pull our companion cards first?" Shel asked.

Wolfe shook his head. "I think we're close enough to be detected if they have deckbearers—and I can't make out who's there in the darkness. But even if we weren't, Sorenia is a *lantern* angel. Let's get as close as we can, guns out, and then pull our decks."

Shel nodded. "We have to try to arrest them first, you know."

Wolfe hesitated but nodded. "All right. One warning. But if they go for guns or knives, I'm sending them to whatever idiot realm wants their shriveled souls. At the end of the day, there are likely another twenty people who need saving in that van, and a lot more who'll die or suffer some fucked-up fate if we don't take these guys down now. Cerberus himself showed me my purpose, and it's to end these fuckers."

Shel gave him a nervous smile. "That was almost a noble speech. Almost."

Wolfe rolled his eyes. "Let's go."

Wolfe rushed forward, crouching as he ran, trying to keep his approach a surprise. Very softly, he could hear Shel's soles hitting the pavement as she ran after him. He kept his gun in one hand—it wasn't as good a way to aim, but he wanted his other hand free to slap his chest and summon his deck.

He made it farther than he'd thought he would, closing to within a couple hundred feet before fate itself decided he wasn't going to get any closer. The same Ferrari Mythic from the first meeting sped into the parking lot, calling everyone's attention to it and shining a light directly onto Wolfe as it did.

"Deck!" Wolfe screamed, touching his chest and turning to face the Ferrari. He hoped the snazzy sportscar hadn't had the same modifications as his far more mundane car. Wishing for once that he had more of a hand cannon rather than his new Edge, Wolfe fired two shots at the radiator, based on a tip he had picked up from the police barbecue, two into the hood of the car almost for the hell of it, and then two right toward the driver's face—where they hit the bulletproof glass, spiderwebbing the windshield.

But the ones in the radiator seemed to go in—the body of the car wasn't armored, probably to keep its speed up.

The car had traveled almost half the distance to him in

the time Wolfe had fired off the six shots, and Wolfe decided to work on self-preservation, taking a step to the side Shel hadn't run, and then kicking back and leaping in the other direction as the car adjusted. He never took his hands off his chest, even as he hit and rolled—now with bullet fire around him from the direction of the van as well.

He saw his cards—an Angry Hellhound, a Lost Hellhound Puppy, Cerberus's Home for Wayward Hellhounds, the Gehennan Kennel Master, and, of course, Cereboo.

Wolfe had a sudden thought among the gunfire—what he really needed was cover. *Cereboo can physically block bullets. I wonder...*

He rolled across the ground but tossed out Cerberus's Home for Wayward Hellhounds. A series of rocks poked from the ground in a circle, and multiple dog-run-style cages formed between them, with a central area of cracked ground showing red.

A bullet ricocheted away from a rock.

Rachel Lyons, allied deckbearer, has pulled her deck.

Unknown enemy deckbearer has pulled their deck.

Unknown enemy deckbearer has pulled their deck.

Joy, Wolfe thought as he rolled to the rocks.

"Use Cerberus's Home as cover!" Wolfe screamed out. "It blocks bullets and shit!"

Shel started back toward him, golden-glowing cards in front of her. She touched one and Sorenia appeared, her lantern glowing in her hand.

Near the van, the darkness coalesced into a Wraith—but this one was larger and more powerful than Wolfe had seen before.

Malik, Soul Devourer

Unique Tier-7, Power-2 equivalent Undead/Shadow
Companion
0 Power
Health: 15
Attack: 0
Defense: 5
Magic Attack: 10
Magic Defense: 5

Special: **Incorporeal**: Immune to physical attacks
Special: **Maggot of the Soul:** If Malik gets the killing blow on
an enemy deckbearer, Malik's deckbearer gains a card as if it
were drawn randomly from a rare Undead or Shadow pack.
This only works against deckbearers who received 'god gifted'
decks on Drop Night.
Special: **Façade [Wraith]:** Considered a wraith for all things
that would affect a wraith.

"Malik, Soul Devourer, was once a mere wraith. But a
thousand years in the Deadlands, feeding on the souls of
powerful departed he was lucky enough to find, has made him
into something more."

Fuck, he has a companion, Wolfe thought.

The Ferrari screeched as it turned, and in an impossibly
badass move, a man in a tailored suit opened the door and
stepped out even as the car twisted. He flung his hand out as
his shined shoes hit the asphalt, throwing a card out.

A woman rose up, one with pink hair and old-fashioned,
ornate, slightly glowing plate armor, with a lantern strapped to
her wrist and a sword at her side, as well as wings springing
from her back.

No...

CHAPTER 20

DO WALLS COUNT?

S hel rolled over, gripping a leg leaking blood, and Wolfe felt his heart unfreeze. He touched his chest, throwing out the tier three Angry Hellhound. At the same time, a Lost Hellhound Puppy sprang into existence from Cerberus's Home for Wayward Hellhounds.

New summons appeared near his enemies as well.

Wolfe barely paid attention as he dragged Shel back, somehow avoiding the bullets from the thugs near the van.

Shel managed to touch her deck and summon an EMT to heal herself even as Wolfe dragged her behind the rocks.

He paused for half a second, taking stock of the situation.

Two thugs at the van with their deckbearer, who was almost certainly Tracy D'Ordinii. He had his companion and a Wraith out. At the same time, Caine—Wolfe presumed—had Artenia out, and he was now covered in a white glow with a fiery sword in his hand. His mantle.

Sorenia was nearly dead from gunshots and a beam of light from Artenia, who was weeping and apologizing as she fought.

Wolfe swiped sideways, bringing new cards up. He still

had Cereboo, as well as his second Lost Hellhound Puppy, another Angry Hellhound, the null card for Malviere, who was at his house, and his Soul Hunter Mantle.

Wolfe started to reach for his mantle, but even as he did, an alternative path that he thought had a better chance for victory came to him. He glanced at his hellhound...

Angry Hellhound
Common Tier-3 Beast/Infernal [Canine] Creature
Two Beast or Infernal Power
Health: 13
Attack: 9 (8 +1)
Defense: 5
Magical Attack: 6 (5+1) [**Fire or Infernal**]
Magical Defense: 5

Special: **Dual Attacker:** When this creature makes a physical attack, it also makes a Magical Attack on the same target.
Special: **Empty Mind:** Immune to all mind-affecting debuffs.
Special: **Canine Tribal [1]:** +1 to all attacks for every other canine on the field.
Special: **Hunter [Escaped Damned 1]:** Gains +1 Attack for every Escaped Damned on the field.

"It could be argued that most things in the Infernal realms are angry, but these hellhounds take it to an entirely new level— and this one has torn many a spirit to the point it needs to reform on many an occasion."

...and told it to stay behind the rocks and not fight, along with his Lost Hellhound Pup.

Wolfe stood, firing at Artenia—normally the fool's play when he could just aim for Caine, but a mortal against a mantle was a bad play. Additionally, if Wolfe put his own mantle on, he would be at disadvantage against Caine's Divine mantle.

But against a Divine creature, he had a base eight attack, with two separate chances to go to a ten or better, thanks to his perk—which would kill Artenia in thirty seconds of combat.

Wolfe also touched the Lost Hellhound Puppy in his deck, using one power that immediately returned, leaving him with two again. Another Hellhound Puppy appeared from Cerberus's Home.

Lost Hellhound Puppy
Rare Tier-1 Beast/Infernal(Canine) Creature
1 Beast or Infernal Power [Available]
Health: 8
Attack: 6 (4 x1.5)
Magical Attack: 5 (3 x1.5) [**Fire**]
Defense: 4
Magical Defense: 4

Special: **Cheap:** Does not require upkeep—is a zero-cost monster.
Special: **Innocent [Mortal, Beast]:** If slain, all Mortal and Beast cards in play gain +50% physical attack for the next 30 seconds.
Special: **Underlying Merge:** May be merged with Rescue Pup cards but advances as if Rare in quality.

"A poor, lost Hellhound, outside its normal realm."

"Shel, send your EMT forward and summon something else to take the hits!"

Shel, whose leg was partially healed, nodded from the ground. But she also raised her gun and fired at Artenia, presumably following Wolfe's lead.

Artenia went down hard—Wolfe's attack alone had been enough and Shel's just made it overkill. At the same time, the glowing Sorenia dropped as well from a hail of gunfire.

A man in a black suit with a gun appeared next to Caine—a one Mortal power Corporate Enforcer card.

Fiery wings appeared and Caine leapt into the fight, swinging viciously at Wolfe. Wolfe dodged the first three swings and shot Caine, who doubled up like he had been gut punched, twice but then clicked on empty.

As he tried to reload, the fiery sword clipped him across the arm, and Wolfe bit down to keep from screaming as the flesh burned around the cut. He dropped his clip.

But he still threw his Angry Hellhound out, bringing him to zero spare power—and Cerberus's Home spewed another out.

"What're you doing, Tracy?!" Caine screamed as he rushed Wolfe again, kneeing him in the face when he ducked the sword.

A chill fell across the battlefield, and wisps of spirits seemed to rise around them. Wolfe got a notification that a persistent card 'Ghastly Gloom' had been played, which gave all undead the ability to heal for half of all damage they dealt.

Wolfe glanced over to see that two Wraiths and Malik, Soul Devourer, had almost made it to him, with Tracy running behind.

But Tracy couldn't see what Wolfe's pack looked like now. Each Lost Hellhound Puppy had fifty percent extra attack and magical attack, overcoming the Wraiths' biggest strength. But there were now two Angry Hellhounds and *four* Lost Hellhound Puppies on the field, which meant that every single Angry Hellhound got a *five* point bonus to both attacks—and would gain another plus fifty percent if any of the Puppies died.

Angry Hellhound
Common Tier-3 Beast/Infernal (Canine) Creature
Two Beast or Infernal Power
Health: 13
Attack: 13 (8 +5)
Defense: 5
Magical Attack: 10 (5 +5) [**Fire**]
Magical Defense: 5

Special: **Dual Attacker:** When this creature makes a physical attack, it also makes a Magical Attack on the same target.
Special: **Empty Mind:** Immune to all mind-affecting debuffs.
Special: **Canine Tribal [1]:** +1 to all attacks for every other canine on the field.
Special: **Hunter [Escaped Damned 1]:** Gains +1 Attack for every Escaped Damned on the field.

"It could be argued that most things in the Infernal realms are angry, but these hellhounds take it to an entirely new level—and this one has torn many a spirit to the point it needs to reform on many an occasion."

The difference between a magical attack of five and a magical attack of ten is huge—four times the amount—and the physical attack is now a base one-hundred-and-sixty-nine damage divided by defense.

Wolfe was stumbling back, fighting defensively while he tried to reload. But he ordered his pups in. He couldn't target the deckbearers but sent his two Angry Hellhounds at Malik, Soul Devourer, and two of his Hellhound Puppies at the Wraiths, and the last two at the Corporate Enforcer.

The slaughter was universal, with the overpowered Hellhounds doing huge damage and wiping everything out but getting mostly wiped out in turn—leaving him with a single Hellhound Puppy and Angry Hellhound pair.

Caine, however, stared dumbfounded as the whole battlefield cleared.

Wolfe swiped his cards again and threw the newest Angry Hellhound onto the field while another Lost Hellhound Puppy popped out of Cerberus's Home.

Caine's eyes flicked around the field even as Wolfe pointed his gun and started firing, but it was apparently too much for him—his wings of fire flickered, carrying him from the fight even as Wolfe hit the mantled bastard with a few more shots.

Wolfe's arm mostly healed as Shel brought forth another EMT.

Caine used a card to heal the minor bullet wounds rather than summoning another creature, and Wolfe directed his pack toward his enemy.

Wolfe glanced around without stopping, feeling the battle had switched dramatically in his favor.

As if to prove him wrong, an engine roared to life. The van screeched and lurched forward over the parking lot pavement, slowly picking up speed as it barreled toward Wolfe and his pack of creatures. The thugs leaned out the window and fired, and Wolfe grit his teeth at the near misses.

Shel—who had gone through her deck, apparently—re-summoned Sorenia and started firing back, causing the thugs to duck back into the questionable protection of the Van.

Wolfe ran back toward the safety of the stones surrounding Cerberus's Home for Wayward Hellhounds, but at the last moment, stutter-stepped and rushed in the other direction as the van passed, missing the stones by a few feet and Wolfe by a few inches.

Wolfe touched Cereboo's card finally, summoning his companion *into* the van 'through' the open window, like he had summoned him outside his own car the very first time his companion had joined him in combat.

At the same time, he heard the crack of a gunshot and fell, his own leg gushing blood.

Wolfe rolled and shot toward the Ferrari, missing the mook who had been with Caine. But the Hellhounds hit the car and the mook went down, briefly screaming before going silent. Caine himself was nearly chewed to bits, but he managed to gun the Ferrari and screech out, turning an Angry Hellhound into red power that flowed back to Wolfe as he did.

There were screams, growls, and gunshots from the van as it sped forward across the parking lot, but then it veered off course and slammed into the corner of one of the warehouses, plowing sideways and tipping on its side.

The Ferrari went flying past Wolfe and out of the parking lot.

Fuck! I wanted to get that fucker.

Wolfe stood, cussing as his leg wouldn't support his weight. "Healing, Shel!"

Another EMT appeared and partially healed Wolfe's leg, to the point he could limp over to the van.

A notification told him that Cereboo had died, but he didn't see any creatures on the battlefield—and he had spare power now. He swiped his cards, knowing by process of elimination that he would see his Infernal Rift this time, waiting for the inevitable move.

Tracy D'Ordinii popped up over the van, reaching for a card and pushing his gun out at the same time. But Wolfe was just a hair faster, hitting Infernal Rift and banishing the assassin before he could do anything.

Wolfe hurried his limp, trying to decide if he wanted to kill Tracy or take him for questioning.

Wolfe was almost ashamed to admit it to himself, but the fact that Tracy was sporting an Undead deck as opposed to an

Infernal, Divine, Mortal, or Beast one was what made the decision. When Tracy appeared, Wolfe slammed the gun against the assassin's temple, almost identically to his attack on Harvey, hoping that Tracy would survive.

Tracy slumped down and then dropped back into the van.

"Please go get the ties, Shel. We'll put him in the back of the Subaru."

Shel nodded and raced away.

Wolfe went to the back of the van and opened it, staring inside.

He found ten more of the steel containers, each with a display on the side, blinking. He did a quick check—everything appeared normal, as near as he could tell.

Wolfe went back and kicked out the windshield, rooting around until he found a phone. Very conveniently, it had a thumb lock, and Cereboo hadn't eaten this thug's hand.

Wolfe dialed 9-1-1, then, before anyone could answer, hung up.

Instead, he quickly looked up and then dialed the Joliet Police Department.

"Hello?" a feminine voice answered.

Wolfe tried to make his voice higher-pitched. "Hello, um, I found a crashed van and some of those kidnapped people I read about from that trainyard story. They're in South Noimoire, near the Industrial Avenue warehouse complex."

"Who is this?"

"There are a ton of people here who need help," Wolfe said.

"Stay on the phone, please," the voice said, then the phone went quiet. But Wolfe could faintly hear the lady calling for a supervisor.

Good enough. Wolfe didn't comply with her request, instead hanging up. Then he wiped the phone with his shirt, trying to make sure any fingerprints were gone, just in case.

Shel came running back with zip ties, and Wolfe grabbed them and set to work restraining Tracy with his hands behind his back.

A few minutes later, Wolfe drove by an abandoned, and burning, Ferrari Mythic.

He chuckled darkly. "Huh, guess I got the radiator, after all."

CHAPTER 21

BROMANCE INTERRUPTUS

"You're sure you're okay to drop me off?" Shel asked. Wolfe nodded again and rolled his eyes. "Of course. I don't think I'll be in too much danger here, and I'd rather you not be there when I'm interrogating Tracy, in case someone sees."

Shel smiled nervously. "I'm supposed to be by your side."

"I'll be fine," Wolfe said. "This isn't worth the risk. We've been over this. Tracy is zip tied with his hands behind his back. I took his gun. If we're caught, I seriously doubt he'll talk, since that would get him involved in a kidnapping charge. I likely won't get in too much trouble. But if you're involved, even a small thing can get you kicked out."

Shel slowly nodded, her fingers tapping together.

"I'm right here, you know," came from the back. Wolfe glanced into the mirror to see Tracy sitting up in the car, a ripped shirt making a blindfold across his eyes, his shoulders strained with how he was sitting, his arms tied behind him. Wolfe was pretty sure that Tracy could neither see where they were, escape, pull his deck, nor attack anyone.

"Welcome back to the land of the living," Wolfe quipped.

"Is that a joke about my deck, or...?" Tracy trailed off. "Fuck, my head hurts. I assume Team Me lost?"

Wolfe chuckled. "Yeah, Team You lost. I was just commenting about how long you'd been out, which is probably why your head hurts. Or just because I hit you solidly."

Tracy glanced down at himself. "I'm cut and bruised, but no gunshots..."

Wolfe turned onto Persimmon and into their subdivision. "I have questions. If you answer them well, I'll let you live."

Tracy was silent for a moment. "You had a good name for that sort of thing... and I *am* blindfolded, I guess. But won't you kill me just so no one knows you're still alive?"

Wolfe laughed. "That's well and thoroughly out of the bag, trust me."

He turned onto his street before Tracy could respond. Wolfe was going to head to his driveway when he saw a blue Honda Civic in front of the house, interior lights on and engine idling. Wolfe narrowed his eyes. He didn't know who was at his house at night, but he would rather sneak up on them than have them know he was coming.

Wolfe stopped his car on the side of the road. When Shel glanced at him, he instinctually nodded to the car rather than talked, even though the car was two houses down and his silence was almost certainly useless.

He fished Shel's Glock-17 from the glove compartment and opened the car door, keeping it behind him as he did.

Wolfe stuck his head back in. "Stay here and stay quiet, or I promise I *will* kill you."

Tracy nodded.

Shel followed him out, and the two of them walked down to the blue Civic.

Before they reached their target, a huge man, as tall as Wolfe and even buffer, exited from the car like a cork popping free from a wine bottle, making the whole car rock a tiny bit.

Shel let out a tiny sigh of relief and waved. "Rhett!"

Wolfe was less happy about seeing the lieutenant and hissed, "Take your pistol!"

Shel bumped into him and he passed it back to her behind their backs.

Shel fumbled, gave a slight gasp, and dropped the gun.

Even though it was extremely unlikely, Wolfe tensed, figuring the universe—or Jyestha, Goddess of Misfortune—would cause it to misfire.

But nothing happened, and Wolfe breathed a sigh of relief.

"Did you just drop your gun, Cadet?" Rhett asked as he walked up. "In fact, why were you even carrying your gun?"

Shel blushed hard enough that Wolfe could see it by street lamp, and then bent to retrieve the weapon. "Sorry, sir, I wasn't sure who you were, or why you were at my house at three in the morning. My sister and her new friend are here."

Rhett scratched his chin for a moment, then looked back at his car, his face conveying dawning realization. "All right, yeah, somehow, I didn't think of it that way. You've got a point."

Wolfe almost snorted at the look on Rhett's face but held back.

Rhett returned his stare to Wolfe. "A better question is why are *you* two out here? Especially you, William?"

"Why do you care?" Wolfe asked.

"Well, I got a report from Cara—"

"Fingers?" Wolfe asked.

Rhett pinched the bridge of his nose. "*Please* never call her that again. As I was saying, I got a call from my assistant, who told me that *we* had received a call about a crime in Noimoire —involving human trafficking. I was just curious where you were."

Rhett glanced down at Shel's pants, which were torn and soaked in blood. "It seems like you might have a story to tell, Cadet."

There was a long pause as Rhett stared at Shel, then turned to Wolfe. "Care to enlighten me? Because I'm pretty sure that whatever you're up to, it ends poorly for the woman you claim to care so much about."

Wolfe squeezed his fist. *Don't attack the asshole cop. Don't attack the asshole cop.*

After another few seconds, Shel asked, "Are we being detained, Rhett?"

Rhett stared at her. "You really want to go down this path, Cadet? Tomorrow is the Gala, where you're receiving the award for the top student in your class. Captain Tennison, as well as some police captains from neighboring jurisdictions, will be there. A very bright future is ahead of you. Do you really want to throw it away?"

"People are—" Shel began, her finger twisting in her hair.

Rhett interrupted her. "I fully believe your intentions are good, Ms. Lyons. I even think there is a slightly greater than even chance that your boyfriend's intentions are good. But intentions won't matter in the face of certain methods. You'd be better served bringing your concerns to the police and letting us handle it."

"Emmett thinks—" Wolfe began.

Rhett interrupted him as well. "I know what Emmett thinks. I stand by the officers of my department fully. We're a small department, and they're all men I know personally. I trust their judgement—and their integrity."

"Do you trust everyone in Noimoire's police force?" Wolfe asked.

Lieutenant Rhett hesitated. Wolfe could tell he was an honest man, even if he was a pushy, self-righteous one.

He cleared his throat. "I don't know everyone in

Noimoire's police force. It would be impossible—there are almost fifteen thousand employed officers there. We have barely a hundred."

"Well, there you go."

"There can't be fifteen thousand corrupt cops," Rhett said with disgust. "Even if, theoretically, there are a few. If you bring the trafficking to the attention of the department, they'll deal with it."

Wolfe snorted and crossed his arms over his chest.

Rhett grit his teeth. "Fine. Drag yourselves down. But don't count on me to go easy on you when you inevitably screw up." He paused, and looked back to Shel. "I'll see you at the Gala at eight P.M. tomorrow night, Cadet."

Shel nodded, and Rhett turned and walked back to his car.

Wolfe watched as Rhett got in his car and drove away.

"Damn glad he didn't search the car," Wolfe muttered. "I probably would have said more about him showing up at my place at three A.M. except I was sweating bullets over that. Hell, all he had to do was glance in the back window."

Shel let out a near-hysterical giggle.

"I'm gonna go see to Tracy. You make sure everyone inside the house is okay. I'll be in later tonight."

Shel chewed her lower lip. After a moment, she nodded quickly and kissed him on the cheek. "Don't be too late. We have to go to the Arena with Miriam tomorrow, and we should spend some time with Lucy and Sharon in the morning."

"Who's Sharon?" Wolfe asked.

Shel smacked him on the chest lightly. "You. It's the neighbor's granddaughter. She was over so that Ms. Timo could look after both of them."

"I'll be quick, promise. I want to take one last look at the files as well."

Wolfe turned and headed back to the car, then opened the

door and sat on the driver's seat, buckling himself in and starting the car.

"Who was that?" Tracy asked.

"A cop. So be glad you kept quiet, or you'd be in on multiple kidnapping and trafficking charges and I'd be in for being me."

"So... what did you want to know?" Tracy asked, shifting around in his seat.

Wolfe drove out onto the street.

"Why do you need to drive somewhere if I'm going to live?" Tracy asked, still squirming in his seat.

Wolfe laughed. "Because it's three A.M., and I've got shit I need to do if I'm going to get any sleep at all. Let's talk while we drive, huh?"

"What do you want to know?"

"How deep is the Grimm family involved?" Wolfe asked as he turned onto Main, which even at this hour had a few cars zipping by at over fifty miles per hour. "Or at least Damian's portion of it."

Tracy somehow managed to shrug despite being zip tied. "A lot, but he's not the main guy. After you blew half the family to pieces, Damian sold a few cards, but his real source of money is someone else. He isn't calling the shots, but he's getting huge amounts of money to act as the main mover in this whole thing."

"Where does it all operate out of?" Wolfe asked.

"The huge warehouse and shipping complex he bought, of course," Tracy said nonchalantly.

Something about his voice sounded off. Wolfe glanced into the rearview mirror to see Tracy pulling the headband off his eyes with a hand carrying a small pocket knife.

How did he...?

Before Wolfe could even finish the thought, Tracy lunged over the side of the seat, knife out, wedged above Wolfe against the ceiling. Wolfe caught Tracy's arm as he brought the knife toward Wolfe's throat, but his enemy's position gave Tracy a massive leverage advantage, and the knife was cutting deep into his hand.

Wolfe slammed on the brakes as hard as he could. The car squealed and slid two lanes, turning perpendicular to traffic on the wrong-side lane. Tracy flew up and slammed into the inside, passenger side corner of the glass windshield headfirst, getting wedged in with his feet over the back of the chair. Wolfe kept his foot on the brake and let go of the wheel, touching his chest with one hand and punching Tracy with the other repetitively.

Somehow, despite enough blunt-force trauma to put a cow down for the count, Tracy managed to touch his own chest and hold for two seconds.

A deckbearer has summoned their deck.

A horn sounded, and Wolfe glanced past Tracy's flailing form to see a car heading right at them.

He tried not to tense as it slammed into his car.

CHAPTER 22

ALWAYS THE CAR

Wolfe's world went topsy-turvy for a moment as the car smashed his Subaru. The Subaru was tougher than it ought to have been, thanks to the modifications Wolfe had paid for. But it wasn't *that* tough. Tracy slammed into Wolfe, and something hit his head.

Wolfe shook himself back to full consciousness. His head hurt, and when he reached up, pushing Tracy off him as he did, his hand came back with blood. Even his arm was spotted with little pieces of glass.

Wolfe focused and saw he had a notification—Tracy was dead, and Wolfe had gained more experience, enough for another level, even after the split with 'unknown driver ally.'

Wolfe knew that ought to have been funny, but everything felt fuzzy. A card fell from Wolfe's shoulder as he moved, knocking a few more pieces of glass to the ground.

I need to get back to Shel, to get healed. But she already used her healing once on me.

Wolfe glanced up to see the person who had hit him stumbling from their car. The car had both its headlights shattered, and Wolfe counted on the extra anonymity as he put his car into reverse, praying to whatever Divine or Infernal being would help him that the car would move.

With a tortured screech of metal, Wolfe's Subaru pulled back, and he shifted it into drive. The car was pulling hard to the right, and grinding was coming from multiple places—but it was moving.

"Hey, are you all right, buddy?" the man who had stumbled from the car shouted.

Wolfe felt bad for ruining the guy's day, but if he stayed, he'd most likely end up in prison and still wouldn't do anything to help the man.

He drove back down the road at a slow pace, pushing Tracy's broken body further into the seat. Blood and other bodily fluids leaked onto the passenger seat.

I need to dump the body somewhere they won't find it, and then hide my car as best as possible.

Wolfe suddenly laughed, gritting his teeth when that hurt.

He turned on the next street, heading for Noimoire—and a certain warehouse that was still in probate court, with a back entrance onto a deep and freshwater-crab-inhabited part of the river.

"Wolfe?" Shel asked as Wolfe opened the door to their shared bedroom. "That you?"

Wolfe sat on the bed. It was near to five in the morning and he was supposed to be hanging out with Shel's family in a couple of hours.

"Aren't you supposed to be asleep?" Wolfe asked his girlfriend.

"I was worried about you. Did everything go okay?"

"No," Wolfe muttered as he sat next to her in the dark. "Tracy got free and attacked me. Cut my hand up, but that was the least of it. I got in an accident. The car is a near-total loss, and I'm pretty badly beat up. I need the remaining two EMT heals."

A few seconds later, a soft, golden glow lit the room, revealing Shel's face. Gasping, she reached out and touched Wolfe's head gently with the ends of her fingers, then pulled them back.

She touched a card and an EMT appeared, healing Wolfe a tiny bit. Shel dismissed it afterward, then, a few moments later, swiped her deck.

After the next heal, she reached over and pulled Wolfe's shirt off.

"I'm too tired, and still too hurt," Wolfe muttered, trying to lie down. "You'll have to do all the work."

Shel smiled wryly in the dim, golden light, tossing his shirt to the side. "You need to go to the bath. You are, in fact, still busted up... and you've got blood and everything else all over you. I'll take care of you."

Wolfe remembered the last time he had had a long day with a lot of wounds, and Shel taking care of him then. Nothing had happened, but it had been a very sensual scene—once he'd recovered enough to appreciate it.

He allowed himself to be led to the bathroom, where Shel closed the toilet lid and bid him sit down, which he did. He watched as she started a bath, adding shampoo as a makeshift bubble bath, and then throwing in some bath salts.

"All right, c'mon," Shel said, giving Wolfe a half-smile. As Wolfe stood and stripped his remaining clothing off, Shel's eyes widened, her smile slipped, and her brow furrowed.

He glanced at the mirror. Dried blood covered half his face, and his entire left side was a bruise. Given how the car had been hit, he wasn't even sure how or when that had happened—maybe he'd slammed back against the side, he couldn't remember. His knuckles were still bleeding, his hand was cut—although not as deep as it had been, thanks to Shel's healing.

Wolfe was shocked at *how much* damage remained across his body.

"All right, well, you lived," Shel said. "That's what's important."

Wolfe reached down to the pants he had just discarded and fished out Tracy's deck. It was harder then he would have thought. *Weird that sometimes my body just shuts down* after *a situation. Must be the adrenaline leaving my body, or something similar.*

Wolfe passed Tracy's deck over to Shel. "Here, sell these— except maybe the companion card, which we might want to offer to Miriam first. Tomorrow, after we hang with your sister and Ms. Timo and her rugrat, we're going to go to that hidden Arena our freaky little crime boss was hyping. Get the cash and let's see if anyone there is selling cards you can use."

"Sure, Wolfe, but for now, how about you just get into the bath, okay?"

Wolfe stepped into the bath, and Shel knelt down next to him. She grabbed a sponge they had kept in the house in honor of the first time, soaped it up, and began slowly and gently wiping the blood away from him. The water immediately pinked, and small chunks of blood swirled around, slowly dissolving in the warm and soapy water. Shel didn't freak out, instead continuing her ministrations. Wolfe laid his head back on the rim of the tub and closed his eyes, trying to ignore the stings in the scrapes that remained after his healing. He had noticed, through unfortunately common use, that the cards tended to heal the internal damage first, and the superficial damage second—a good thing, but it did make this process less than perfectly pleasant.

What felt like seconds later, Wolfe found himself being gently shaken awake.

Shel's voice penetrated the fog of his thoughts. "It's time to go to bed, Wolfe."

Wolfe grunted, half-tempted to explain he had been sleeping, but too tired to put the effort forth. Instead, he got up and Shel helped him from the bath. Then she toweled him off and led him to bed.

His last thought, before the darkness claimed him, was that he had gotten impossibly lucky to get a woman who would take care of him even when she, herself, had been shot not but a few hours ago.

"How come your car is all beat up? It looks like it was attacked by one of those Drop Night monsters."

Wolfe struggled to open his eyes, glancing over at the girl across from him. His eyes slid to the side. The *two* girls across from him.

Lucy and Sharon were watching him expectantly. He honestly wasn't sure who had asked the question.

Where is Shel? Wolfe honestly couldn't remember why Shel wasn't in the main room with him. *Maybe she went outside? Ms. Timo isn't here, either, and she loves to garden... I got the statement, right? And put it back in the file? I think I remember doing that.*

Wolfe tried to shake his exhaustion and sit up straighter. He stared at the two kids.

Aside from a general height and frame—gangly ten-year-olds—they shared little in common. Lucy had red hair and green eyes to match Shel, as well as a complexion as white as mayonnaise, while Shannon was darker, with black hair and gray-blue eyes. Despite that, they could practically be sisters for mannerisms as they stared up at him.

"I got in a car accident last night," Wolfe replied.

"Did you report it to the police?" Lucy asked.

"I can't bear to answer questions about it," Wolfe said dramatically, then he put his hand to his face and pretend-sobbed. "It was a traumatic loss. That car was a part of the family. I'm still processing my grief."

Lucy frowned, but Shannon laughed.

There was a brief pause as they looked at him, then Shannon asked, "Are you working on my family's case? Is that why you talked to Grammy earlier, but I wasn't allowed in?"

Wolfe frowned. Technically he was, and he had the files in his bedroom right now, but... "I don't know much, kid. I just got some statements from your grandmother for the lawyer. That's it."

"But you know what happened, right?" Shannon asked.

How do I exit the conversation without causing the kid to cry? "Look, your grandmother knows everything. Just talk to her, okay?"

Shannon slumped. "She won't tell me anything. It's my mom and my dad, and they've been gone for months. No one will tell me what's happening. Did they leave me?"

Wolfe winced. *I can't believe Ms. Timo still hasn't told her grandkid that her mom died.* "None of this is because of you, kid. You're a fine kid."

"Her name is Shannon," Lucy said.

"She's a fine Shannon," Wolfe replied, overly sweet.

In an almost déjà vu replay of the first time he'd joked, Lucy frowned and Shannon laughed.

But Shannon sobered again quickly. "Just tell me what's going on, please."

Wolfe sighed. *Someone ought to tell her. It's crazy, keeping her in the dark like this. But I'm really not the one who should be doing it.*

Wolfe settled back in his chair and crossed his arms over his chest. "Look, I think you should know, truly. But I'm not your dad. Ask your grandma."

"She calls herself 'Grammy,'" Lucy said.

Wolfe rolled his eyes. "Ask Grammy."

"She won't tell me *anything*. She just says that she's taking care of me now, and that's okay. But it's my *mother and father*." Shannon stamped her feet.

Gods damn it. "Kid, I can't tell you. I'm sorry."

"I miss them."

I miss them too, since if they were here, it'd get me out of this conversation. "Again, I'm sorry. Sometimes, things suck. Sometimes, we don't get to be with the people we want. Ask about Lucy's brother sometime."

"His name is Kevin," Lucy said.

Wolfe rolled his eyes. "What are you, the name police? Aren't there more important things to worry about than whether I'm using someone's exact name?"

"My teacher says calling people by the name they want is very important, and it matters a lot to them."

"Well, it sure as shit doesn't matter to Kevin," Wolfe growled out.

Lucy frowned again. "That was mean."

Wolfe rubbed his eyes. He really didn't want to be upsetting kids, but he was dog tired, and he had never been the best at this kind of shit regardless. "I'm sorry. I'll try to use his —Kevin's—name from now on."

There was a brief pause.

"Can Shannon spend the night?" Lucy asked.

"Yeah, sure, as long as her *Grammy* says it's okay," Wolfe said.

Shannon clapped her hands. "Can we set up a tent and sleep in the back yard?"

Do little girls like to do that? I don't remember my sister liking any outdoors stuff when I wanted to do it.

"Sure, as long as Shel says it's okay."

Shannon clapped again. "Yay! I never get to do stuff like that anymore. I miss camping and hiking and the outdoors and adventure and—"

"Take a breath, kid."

Lucy coughed.

"Take a breath, Shannon."

The glass door to the back yard opened and Shel stepped in, followed by Ms. Timo and Malviere. The vengeance orphan trailed silently afterward.

Wolfe glanced at the wall clock. "Is it time?"

Shel nodded. "Yeah. I called an Uber—they're outside."

"Where are you going?" Lucy asked.

Shel squatted a bit and hugged Lucy for some reason. "We're going to an Arena to do our three competitions each deckbearer gets every Drop Night."

"You smell like dirt," Lucy said. Then, "Can we come? I want to see you be a deckbearer and watch Sorenia in battle."

Lucy's voice was raw with jealousy when she talked about Shel being a deckbearer.

"Yeah, I want to go!" Shannon chimed in.

"There are going to be a lot of rough characters there," Wolfe said. "I don't think it's for you. I'm sorry."

"We'll take you guys to watch some of the fights at the Three Fires Arena," Shel said. "Okay?"

"Why can't you take us to this one? Or go to the Three Fires Arena yourself?" Lucy asked.

Wolfe glanced at Shel, raising an eyebrow.

She tapped her fingers together. "We just can't."

Lucy frowned. "When you do that with your fingers you're worried about something."

"Everyone ever tell you that you're too smart for your own good, sprout?" Shel said, ruffling Lucy's hair.

Lucy ducked away from her hand. "You can never be too smart."

"Well, you'll have to figure it out yourself," Wolfe said. "Because we're going."

CHAPTER 23

THE RAT ARENA

"Seriously, Miriam, *why*?" Wolfe asked, motioning around at the huge, black limousine they were all riding in. It could seat four or five people beside one another on each side of the ridiculously large vehicle. Since it was just Wolfe, Shel, Derek, Ahmed, Victor, and Miriam herself in the giant car, it felt extra ostentatious.

And that wasn't even talking about the ceiling skull motif, or the skull etched on the hood of the limo.

Miriam smiled at Wolfe as she ran one delicate hand across the plush seat. "It just fits my vibe, you know?"

"Couldn't you just get a nice, *slightly* low-key vehicle with some protection?" Wolfe asked.

Miriam just laughed and smiled at Ahmed, then turned slightly away from him in the seat. "Massage please, Ahmed."

The Egyptian man began to knead at her shoulders, and Miriam sighed contentedly, relaxing into his touch but keeping her eyes on Wolfe the whole time.

"I read about this for one of my police academy classes," Shel said, quite seriously. "It's called Deckbearer Apotheosis

Syndrome. Someone gets some cards, can order monsters and maybe minions around, they can put mantles onto themselves... it goes to their head and they kinda go crazy with the power. More than a few deckbearers end up selling their cards to cover debts they acquire."

Derek laughed, and Miriam frowned and opened her mouth.

Wolfe beat her to the punch. "It's just old-fashioned ego. You don't need a damned college degree to make up special words for it."

Miriam glared and her cheeks pinked slightly. "It's *camouflage*, assholes. I'm never going to be as scary as Dad, not in person, at least. He used fear and anger to rule and hide his intelligence and plans. It was easy for him. He was even bigger than you, Wolfe, and had a voice that sounded like the judgment of the Divine. But I don't have any of that. So I do what you do, Wolfe—I conceal."

"You conceal?" Wolfe asked skeptically.

She kept going. "Don't think I didn't notice, Wolfe. You act physically aggressive, but you're always quiet with your intelligence and plans. You pretend to be a thug to conceal your real capabilities. You have cars that look way cheaper than you can afford, but you always get them quietly upgraded. Well, this car has the same upgrades—on top of that, the seats themselves are massively armored. We can simply lie down and probably survive anything short of a tank's big gun, although the limo can't take more than pistol- and sub-machine-gun-type fire and keep functioning. But *we'll* survive. It's the same thing."

Wolfe snorted. "Again, nothing about this is hidden, Miriam. You bray your existence and importance to the world."

She was no longer glaring, but she had a serious intensity

about her that Wolfe had only seen a couple of times before, usually when she talked about her abuse at the hands of her evil older brother. Her intelligence and force of personality shone through in a way they didn't normally, and for a moment, she somehow resembled Big Man Grimm more than anyone Wolfe had ever seen.

Miriam motioned down to herself. "I'm twenty-two, a club owner, beautiful—"

"Humble," Derek muttered.

"—the daughter of a very wealthy dead man, and absolute top of my class in *law school*. No one is going to believe I'm dumb, or a ditz, or afraid... but they might believe I'm a spoiled, eccentric rich kid with idiot notions about cards and power and the games I'm playing."

She relaxed again, and old Miriam, sardonic but playful, was back. "Not that it isn't real, to a degree. I do *love* the pageantry and drama of it all, and..."

She reached her hands out, putting one finger of each hand on Shel's and Wolfe's knees and slowly dragging them back. "I would actually, for real, love to take the two of you for some playtime. Offer will be open when you guys get bored."

Shel blushed, and Miriam smiled at her and licked her lips.

Ahmed frowned but kept kneading.

Miriam leaned back into Ahmed as she finished. "But that doesn't mean a lot of my act isn't a disguise—it's my armor, Wolfe. None of the other Noimoire bosses spend too much time worrying about Thad's poor, spoiled little daughter, in over her head. And even Victor never figured out what my escape plan for all this was till you showed up."

Wolfe gave brief thought to what she had said and nodded. "All right, that's fair. I'll stop talking about it.

With that in mind, we have a present for you," Wolfe continued.

Miriam sighed and sensually stretched in Ahmed's grasp, obviously hamming it up. "I *love* presents, Wolfy. What did you get me?"

"A card—a companion card. It's called Malik the Soul Devourer. But I guess it's only half a gift, as I expect your support in turn."

Wolfe held it out, and Miriam leaned forward, all of the playfulness gone from her.

Malik, Soul Devourer

Unique Tier-7, Power-2 equivalent Undead/Shadow
Companion
0 Power
Health: 15
Attack: 0
Defense: 5
Magic Attack: 10
Magic Defense: 5

Special: **Incorporeal**: Immune to physical attacks
Special: **Maggot of the Soul:** If Malik gets the killing blow on an enemy deckbearer, Malik's deckbearer gains a card as if it were drawn randomly from a rare Undead or Shadow pack. This only works against deckbearers who received 'god gifted' decks on Drop Night.
Special: **Façade [Wraith]:** Considered a wraith for all things that would affect a wraith.

"Malik, Soul Devourer, was once a mere wraith. But a thousand years in the Deadlands, feeding on the souls of powerful departed he was lucky enough to find, has made him into something more."

"Wow, a gift? Really?" Miriam asked. "This might sell for

a million on the open market. Probably more, actually. Companion cards are crazy rare and free of power cost. I bet it'd go for at least two million. Sure you want to make a gift of this to me?"

Wolfe nodded, but he stared at Miriam. "A partial gift. Next dungeon Victor finds for you, assuming he does, Shel and I go and get equal shares. Fair?"

"Of course," Miriam said. "I owe you one whole dungeon, and one partial one already. One more won't hurt."

"Well, then, if you get your dainty little hands on any cards for my deck, return the favor. I know you're trustworthy." Wolfe paused, then smirked at her. "Even if you are a bit touched."

Miriam laughed. "Fair. I'll be sure to take care of you. What did you do with the rest of whatever deck you got this from?"

"We sold it," Shel said, holding her phone forward. "We sold it at a discount to Gavin's, the card auction company. But they gave us immediate cash for use—including when we get to the Hidden Arena. We're hoping that some people there will have decent Mortal or Divine cards for sale."

"Finally going to work on your deck, huh?" Miriam said, then she wiped an imaginary tear from her eye. "It's so good to see my little girl all grown up."

Shel blushed.

Something outside drew Miriam's gaze, and she nodded to the window. "We're almost there."

Wolfe felt himself tensing. He understood the plan, and the necessity of it—but he didn't like it. It went against all his animal instincts.

The limo turned into a parking lot surrounded by a chain-link fence. A man at the front, with a suspicious bulge under his black suit, looked at their vehicle and then unlocked a gate, ushering the limo into the parking lot.

A separate van waited there—a van that gave off 'want some candy, kid?' kidnapping vibes harder than any vehicle Wolfe had seen before. Tinted windows, duct tape on parts of it, and a large amount of wear and tear proclaimed how unsavory it was to the world.

"More camouflage?" Shel asked hopefully as they drove in.

"What?" Wolfe asked.

"Like Miriam, it's just cover... That isn't actually a van where everything terrible happens, right?"

Wolfe snorted. "Probably not."

The limo stopped, and Wolfe, Shel, Miriam, and her three men all got out of the vehicle. Two men were waiting beside the van, and the third came up behind them.

He reached up to grab Wolfe, and Wolfe batted his hands aside. "Hey, I'm not judging your personal tastes, but I don't swing that way."

"Har har," the guard said mirthlessly, a slight hint of a British accent detectable in his voice. "Pat down. No weapons allowed."

"And if I don't agree?" Wolfe asked.

"You don't agree, you don't get in. That's it. Now don't make me do a bloody cavity search."

"You know I'm a deckbearer, right? That I can summon doom at any time?"

The guard looked at him like he was an idiot.

"Yeah, fair. I suppose I am headed to an Arena," Wolfe muttered, embarrassed.

He sighed and held his hands up. The guard patted him down, finding no weapons, and then went through the others. He might not have had a sense of humor, but Wolfe noted he did have a sense of professionalism—he didn't take even the slightest liberty with Shel or Miriam.

"All right, you're either clean or you've got guns in your prison purses. Good enough. Now the blindfolds."

Wolfe tensed but allowed the other guard to come up and place a thick cloth over his eyes. He briefly wondered about the fact that even if the Arena was hidden, this transaction was semi-visible in the daylight—but he put it from his mind. If the guys running the arena got caught, it was their problem. No law against using any Arena, after all.

When the guards had tied the blindfolds in place, they carefully helped everyone into the van. Wolfe sat on what felt like a cheap, wooden bench, as if the owners were now going out of their way to make the van as unpalatable as possible. He could smell sweat and fear and tried to calm himself, adding to neither as best he could.

"Under the right circumstances, this could be hot," Miriam said, but Wolfe caught a slight undertone to her voice. He would have bet his companion card that she was playing around to hide her own nervousness.

Shel coughed, and Derek muttered, "Sorry."

A moment later, Shel leaned against Wolfe's side.

The drive lasted all of five minutes, which at least told Wolfe what district the Arena was in, roughly. He was pretty sure he heard a metal garage being pulled down before the van door opened, letting in stale, dusty air.

Then one of the guards took his arm. "Follow me."

Wolfe followed him across what he was almost positive was a parking garage cement floor, then stopped. A slight chunk of metal settling into place came a bit after, and then a slight whirr of machinery.

The guard pushed slightly on Wolfe's elbow, and Wolfe walked forward. He stepped onto what he thought was carpet, and the floor settled very slightly. Then the whole room began to move downward.

"All right, you buggers can take the eyewear off," the guard said in a bored voice.

Wolfe reached up and removed the blindfold.

"Thank the Divine, it *is* just an elevator," Victor muttered, and the guard gave a more genuine laugh.

They were, in fact, just in an elevator—one slightly old and worn-looking, but not uncared for. It had a mirror on one side, and cheap, brown paneling on the other three.

After a moment, the elevator clunked to a stop, and Wolfe saw they had reached "B2," which he assumed was the second-floor basement.

The doors opened, looking onto a huge balcony, about fifty feet wide, that curved in a circle around the top of a massive Arena. The Arena itself was in an even larger cave—smooth stone made up the ceiling and the walls on the outside of the balcony, except for a few places where concrete and faux brick had been put up, around the elevators. Wiring ran across the natural stone ceiling, held in place by metal prongs hammered into the stalactites and ceiling itself. A few parts of the walls had power lines as well, and they snaked across the smooth, wooden floor of the balcony to the tables across the balcony and the sitting bar that ringed the Arena for easy viewing. It was cool, but not cold, in the giant, natural cavern, and numerous people watched an ongoing fight in the Arena that Wolfe couldn't see.

A huge number of anthropomorphic rats, mostly women in slinky cocktail dresses that seemed like they should have come from an '80s casino floor, worked the tables that lined the place, and the bar that ran around the entire edge of the Arena, passing out drinks and snacks. Near the wall on one side, a large makeshift bar and sitting area was where the drinks were coming from, and huge, plush couches dominated that edge of the cavern.

"Wow," Shel said. "My dad took us to the Three Fires Arena once, a couple of years ago, but somehow, I never imagined that this place would have the same level of grandeur. Especially since it's nearly empty."

A man stepped up to them. He was thin and dressed in an expensive gray suit, and a cloud of cigar smoke trailed after him like a thought bubble. His hair was thinning as well, and even the hand he held out was long and bony.

"Welcome to the Rat Arena," the man said.

CHAPTER 24

THE RAT DECKBEARER

"The Rat Arena?" Wolfe asked, glancing around. He supposed the anthropomorphic rat women—a version of minion cards, he guessed—gave it that sense, but that was it. Everything else felt more like 'an underground Arena.'

"It'll make sense when you compete," the man said with a smarmy laugh. He reached out further and took Wolfe's hand. "We're Clive Faraday."

Wolfe gave the twig-like appendage a firm shake, trying not to snap the man's fingers like so many Twix bars. *'We're'?*

Clive's cigar cloud washed over Wolfe, who inhaled. Longing passed through him again. *He even has the good shit,* Wolfe thought, recognizing the scent from his days as Big Man Grimm's well-compensated right-hand man.

He saw Shel giving him the side eye and pretend-coughed. She laughed.

Clive gave them a quizzical look but didn't comment further. He turned and waved his hand at the enclosure. "Welcome to our humble home. Since the most recent Drop

Night, the auspiciously named Cycle of the Lost and Lonely, we have been providing Arena services to the discerning members of the Greater Illinois alternatively employed. We're glad you could make it, William... or should we say Wolfe?"

Wolfe frowned, more irritated by the man's ostentatious use of phrases like "Greater Illinois alternatively employed" and the *royal we* than because he knew Wolfe's name. That ship had sailed over the last day and a half.

But calling criminals and pushers 'alternatively employed' reeked of wine-swirling condescension or pretension or both.

"'Wolfe' will do fine. How do we register for a bout?"

"You find a partner here who is willing to match you, and we set it up. But be warned—we require that a card be taken at random from the deck of the loser and given to the winner."

"That's bullshit," Wolfe said loudly. A few of the patrons turned and glanced at him... and a few sets of eyes went wide in surprised recognition.

"It's the old way, and we'll all honor it here," Clive said, holding his hands out and swirling the smoke cloud around him.

He gave Wolfe a smarmy smile. "If you don't want to join us, you don't have to play with us."

This guy uses language like dragging his nails across a chalkboard.

"Whatever," Wolfe said. "If I compete, I'll register the card."

The man nodded, his smile going wider despite the cigar in his mouth. He rubbed his hands together. "Great, great. Well, have a look around."

"We have to risk cards?" Derek asked, passing his hand through his close-cut hair. "Seriously? I don't have a spare—can I even register?"

Shel nodded slowly. "The same."

Victor nodded his head. "It'll be fine. We can add a single card to the Arena, to be placed in our decks if we lose one. All the Arenas can do this, but since the usual effect is to reduce decks and make them weaker overall, most don't."

Derek slowly nodded. "Well, all my cards are cheap as hell, so it seems like a good deal for me."

Wolfe glanced at Shel. Both of them had some fantastic, nigh-irreplaceable cards. Like their companions, and the Infernal Rift. If Wolfe lost a match, there was a twenty-percent chance that he would lose a card he really couldn't get back in any legal way.

"Let's look around, see who is here, and what they have. Maybe we can find some very likely wins," Wolfe said.

"Check with Victor," Miriam said. "He knows a lot about the people of Noimoire... and all their interesting decks."

"I'll be sure to check with our very own little CIA agent," Wolfe said.

"NSA, really, if you're going for those comparisons," Victor replied.

"Uh-huh."

Even as the group was talking, a shout of excitement went up from the crowd around the bar that ringed the Arena. An announcer called over a PA system. "By all that is unholy! Elizabeth shows us what a champion is by defeating Kiera Black *without even pulling a creature!*"

Wolfe, curious, walked up to the bar and glanced over the edge.

The bottom of the Arena was on fire—nearly the whole thing. A blasted, burned corpse of a woman was on the ground, as well as charred and splintered chunks of wood. Another woman, who remained untouched, in a red-and-black dress, was watching the corpse—for a moment. Then everything dissolved, including the two people.

"Wow, Elizabeth is amazing," a thin girl who looked barely legal next to Wolfe said. She was dressed in a slinky, black miniskirt that was a mere inch or so away from dispelling *all* the mystery.

A huge tub of lard with swarthy skin one seat past her smiled, putting a ring-encrusted hand on the girl's mostly bare thigh. He spoke with an English accent. "Yes, a good show. Having an actual champion visit certainly puts all the local riffraff to shame. I'll be glad to see all the poseur deckbearers reminded of their place. You know, the ones who think they're special because they got a deck and made level six."

The swarthy tub of lard picked up a huge tumbler of whiskey with his free hand and took a draft.

"'Local riffraff deckbearers'?" Wolfe asked before he could think it through.

The corpulent man turned to Wolfe, his chair squeaking under his weight. His hand never left the thigh of the girl. Wolfe saw her briefly glance down, and her bland expression briefly went to disgust, but then her face cleared.

"Yes," the man said. "Most of the deckbearers here lack the refinement and education to put together a truly worthy deck, and most of them are, frankly, too stupid to try. Why do you bloody care? Are you one of them?"

"Never mind," Wolfe said, shaking his head disgustedly and turning away.

"A wise choice—run away from your betters, and keep your pathetic cards."

Wolfe turned back, hand falling to the space where his absent weapon had been. "Are you that stupid?"

"Me?" the man said, sneering at Wolfe, a tiny bit of alcohol spilling from his mouth onto his shirt. But his eyes glistened, and Wolfe could tell he was happy. "You're the one who came here to compete with your betters. Or do you actually think you can beat me?"

By now, Wolfe had attracted a small crowd, including Miriam and her gang. "I don't even know you, fat-ass. Who are you, and what do you do, besides paw women you could probably eat in a sitting?"

Victor stepped up and whispered in Wolfe's ear. "This is Gopal Singh, cousin to Gurjit Singh. He has recently arrived from Pakistan to help his cousin."

Ah. Gurjit Singh, the head of the Singh crime family. Why he's such a dick makes sense, as does why he has a beautiful girl with him.

Victor leaned in closer, and Wolfe almost batted him away as the information broker breathed right into his ear. "He runs an Infernal Hive rat deck—Infernal/Beast, specifically."

Wolfe briefly paused. He didn't know this guy at all. But a deck with Beasts and Infernal cards would be a perfect opponent for Wolfe. This guy might be worth risking a fight with. Plus, Wolfe wanted very much to make a few levels. Level twenty-five, specifically, to see what new perk options he would get.

Gopal was watching him closely, and Wolfe could tell he wanted Wolfe to accept his goad and fight him. *Who's tricking whom, here?*

"Are we doing this, then?" came Clive's voice from beside Wolfe, accompanied by the faint cigar smell.

Fuck it. "All right, fat man, you're on. On one condition. You add the girl for the night, and no reprisals afterward. I know Gurjit personally."

Wolfe heard Shel shuffle, but she didn't say anything.

The man sneered. "I can always get another whore. Meet me downstairs so I can quickly put you back in your place and get back to drinking."

Clive clapped his bony hands together. "Another match, then! Wolfe the Lost Enforcer vs. the New Singh Family

Purchaser! We can't wait! This way, Wolfe, please. Gopal knows the way to the other entrance to the Arena."

Wolfe nodded and followed in Clive's cigar-infused wake as the thin man led him to a set of narrow stairs with a clear-glass handrail down the side of the Arena. Shel, Miriam, and Miriam's gang all followed after him.

"Sorry, Shel. We'll look for cards after I take this asshat down a peg or two," Wolfe said.

"No, it's fine," Shel replied nervously.

Wolfe kept going down the stairs, eventually following Clive into a large room in the side of the Arena that reminded him of a fancy dugout, with a padded bench and chairs and a small bar—but the same basic design as a dugout. At the front was a glass screen with numbers scrolling across it on a stone pedestal, a weird mixing of old and new.

"Place your hand on the glass, please," Clive said.

Wolfe complied. It was warm to the touch and pulsed with power, similar to what Wolfe felt when he touched his chest to summon cards.

Nothing happened.

Clive coughed. "We've noticed before that Gopal sometimes takes a while to reach his side. Just give it a few moments."

A good three minutes later, Wolfe felt power shoot up his arm, like an electric jolt.

Two cards appeared on the glass. One was Malviere.

Malviere, Conduit of Cerberus
Unique, no-tier Mortal/Infernal companion [Orphan, Canine]
0 Power
Health: 13
Attack: N/A
Defense: 3

Magical Attack: N/A
Magical Defense: 5

Special: Will fetch normal objects and such with a decent degree of precision and help carry up to ten pounds.
Special: **Orphan Evolution [Unique]:** If kept 'alive' for five straight years, will turn into a Tier-6 equivalent companion card, gaining notable power. If ever 'killed,' the timer resets.
Special: **Canine Leader [1]:** All other allied [canine] creature cards gain +1 to their non-health stats while she is on the field
Special: **Canine Rush [1]:** Once per round, any one [Canine] card may take an extra attack or magical attack action.
Special: **Canine Lord: [Canine]** creature cards of other deckbearers will switch sides without returning their power.

"Malviere cannot remember any life except that of acting as a conduit for the great guardian of the gates of the Infernal, Cerberus. She aids his chosen hunters on the Mortal plane, to bring back those whom Hell has lost. And she gets to play with *all* the doggos. Good, and bad."

The second was a Beast persistent card

Hunter's Hunger

Uncommon Tier-1 Beast persistent
1 Beast power [available]
All deckbearers sacrifice a Beast creature every thirty seconds. This may be sacrificed as part of another effect. If they do not have a beast creature to sacrifice, they take 4 health damage every thirty seconds.

Fuck me, now I'm risking Malviere against some uncommon, one-power, Tier-one POS card? Fucking gods hate me.

Wolfe stepped out into the bare Arena. Across from him, Gopal waddled out from his side.

An announcer called out, "Gopal Singh, new purveyor for the Singh family, has taken the field with his Hive Rat Deck! Opposing him is a new challenger, a man long thought dead, Wolfe! Once an enforcer for the Grimm family, he disappeared after near-singlehandedly taking out the Cobras. But will his skills translate to having any chance against the man who has mastered this Arena?"

Mastered the Arena?

Even as Wolfe thought the question, numerous crates and piles of trash filled the area, and a squeaking filled his ears.

"The Arena has chosen the field! It's a bad one for the challenger!"

Words flashed across Wolfe's vision.

By random selection, the Rat Arena has picked the Infested Warehouse as the site of your battle. At the start of the fight, and every minute after, a single rat will appear, with a 5 health, a 3 in Attack, Defense, and Magical Defense, and a 0 in Magical Attack. They are considered part of both sides' 'fields,' 'teams,' and 'allies,' and will attack the nearest deckbearer or creature.

Wolfe touched his chest to pull his deck, and it popped into existence in front of him.

His enemy did the same and then dropped a creature onto the field. It was nearly a basic rat but had demonic features.

Demonic Hive Rat
Uncommon Tier-1 Infernal/Beast [Rodent] Creature
1 Beast or 1 Infernal Power
Health: 5
Attack: 3
Defense: 3
Magical Attack: 0
Magical Defense: 2

Special: **Swarm [Rodent]**: This creature gains +1 to all stats for every other rodent on the field, regardless of owner.

"The Hive Rats of Dis are one of the very few vermin that could bother a demon."

Wolfe looked at the two other rats crawling from behind piles of garbage, one near him, and one near Gopal. *Ah, shit.*

CHAPTER 25

A PEG OR TWO

Wolfe had his Fireborn Hellhound, an Angry Hellhound, Malviere's Null card, and Cerberus's Home for Wayward Hellhounds in his hand—and Cereboo off to the side.

For one of the few times in his life, Wolfe blanked, not knowing the exact tactic for the moment. It was clear that Gopal had suckered him into the battle before Wolfe had known what the Arena did—but Wolfe was almost positive that Gopal didn't know what Wolfe's deck did, either, or he wouldn't have been so cocky.

Not having a better play, Wolfe threw Cereboo onto the field. A rat immediately attacked Cereboo, and the other Arena rat chewed on the demonic hive rat that Gopal had summoned.

The announcer was commentating. "Gopal starts his overwhelming rat swarm as expected. No surprises there."

Wolfe ignored that, instead running as fast as possible toward Gopal. *If I can just get to him, I can beat his fat ass to death, especially if I get my damn mantle, which never shows up first.*

"And now our challenger is running toward Gopal! What does Wolfe have in mind, I wonder? I bet it'll be exciting!"

He covered most of the distance when a thought struck him. *Wait, he has that sacrifice card for a reason...*

As Gopal reached for his card, Wolfe screamed, "Dodge this, fat ass!" and held his hand out.

Gopal stopped reaching for his card and glanced up, then half-dived, half-fell behind one of the wooden crates, letting out a grunt as he hit the Arena floor.

"Ha! That was a good one—Gopal takes a self-inflicted hit to his own belly!" the announcer cried out.

Wolfe tapped his own card, his intimidation trick having gained him back the precious seconds he'd lost when he had been stunned by the Arena producing rats.

Wolfe tossed Cerberus's Home for Wayward Hellhounds out. But unlike during his last fight, he didn't use it as cover, instead placing it to his side—he kept up his dead run at Gopal.

"Wow, what a play!" the announcer called. "This will give—"

Wolfe did his best to tune the announcer out as he neared his foe.

Gopal stood and tossed another card—a rat that appeared half brain, or perhaps a brain that had a rat head and legs coming off it.

Demonic Hive Rat Coordinator
Rare Tier-1 Infernal/Beast [Rodent] Creature
1 Beast Power, 1 Infernal Power
Health: 12
Attack: 2
Defense: 5
Magical Attack: 0
Magical Defense: 5

Special: **Swarm Coordinator [Rodent]:** Every rodent on the field gets **Swarm [Rodent]**: This creature gains +1 to all stats for every other rodent on the field, regardless of owner.

Special: **Warded [Rodent]:** No Beast [rodents] will attack the deckbearer or any Hive Rats.

"The vermin of the Infernal city of Dis, the famed Demonic Hive Rats, are nearly as dangerous as the demons that rule the city. And the coordinators rule their nests, second only to the great Brood Mothers."

Well, that explains why he wanted to play in the rat Arena. Now, since the card stops any rats from attacking him or his deck, it'll be like the Arena is summoning two extra rats per round on his side.

But Wolfe smiled—he had been right.

When the Demonic Hive Rat Coordinator came out, Gopal sacrificed his basic demonic Hive Rat. But Cerberus's Home for Wayward Hellhounds meant that the sacrificed creature joined Wolfe instead. And the Home spit out a Lost Hellhound Puppy.

Suddenly, there were four Arena rats that were neutral but effectively on Gopal's side and Gopal's Hive Coordinator against Cereboo, a Lost Hellhound Puppy, and Gopal's own Demonic Hive Rat.

Gopal appeared a bit shaken but glanced around. He must have figured that his tactic still worked as long as he kept the Hive Rat Coordinator—Wolfe couldn't beat his effective three summons a round.

But Wolfe smiled viciously. Chump deckbearers who relied on money and tricks always forgot the first card that started on the field every time—themselves. And judging by how Gopal looked, 'himself' was a common, 1-power card.

Wolfe swiped his deck as he closed the last few feet,

trusting his three creatures to survive long enough to keep him alive. That was all he really wanted. Before the thirty seconds were up, Wolfe reached Gopal, whose eyes were wide with fear as Wolfe leapt. He tackled the fat man to the ground. Gopal crunched as he hit, and the two of them went down, Wolfe on top and scrambling until he was half-straddling the fat man's chest.

Brimstone didn't show, but his Soul Hunter mantle did. It would be enough. Wolfe touched it, and the red energy flowed into him, giving him slight horns and very slightly scaled skin.

While Wolfe did that, Gopal managed to maintain enough of a sense of control to hit another card, summoning it, surprising Wolfe, who had expected him to fold instantly.

Another rat appeared, this one huge and bloated with children.

Grelka Ratbearer, Demonic Hive Rat Broodmother

Unique rare-equivalent, Tier-4 equivalent Infernal/Beast creature

2 Infernal, 2 Beast power

Health: 50

Attack: 3

Defense: 10

Magical Attack: 0

Magical Defense: 10

Special: **Swarm Coordinator [Rodent]:** Every Hive Rat gains Swarm [Rodent], gaining +1 stat for every other rodent on the deckbearer's side.

Special: Every round, a single creature from an opposing deckbearer's deck is chosen randomly. That creature is 'sacrificed' as if sacrificed by the deckbearer who owns Grelka, and Grelka spawns a number of Demonic Hive Rats equal to the power of the sacrificed creature.

He didn't think that through at all—he's flustered from being attacked and just pulling randomly.

Wolfe's cards couldn't be sacrificed—and if they were considered sacrificed by Gopal, they would return to him, anyway.

Wolfe struck down, as hard as he could, slamming his fist into Gopal's face. His target's cheekbone gave way beneath his demonically empowered blow, and teeth flew across the floor of the Arena. The copper tang of blood filled Wolfe's nostrils.

"Stoph, stoph!" Gopal cried out. "Pveave!"

Wolfe received a notification that three rats had died to his team, but that everything on his side except Cereboo had also died—and two more rats had joined.

But Wolfe ignored that.

He managed to grab the flailing Gopal's hands and pin them above his head, to prevent the man from summoning more cards, and summoned an Angry Hellhound to give himself more time.

Gopal thrashed violently but couldn't dislodge Wolfe, who started to slam short elbows into Gopal's face, over and over.

Slam. His forehead split open, and something cracked.

"Stoph!" His thrashing became more panicked and animalistic.

Slam. Gopal's jaw slewed sideways.

Gopal lay stunned for second, then wept with a half-sobbing noise. "Uh huh huh."

He was barely resisting now, his thrashing minuscule. A shit stink had joined the copper tang in a miasma of gross odors.

Can he just surrender? Or is death the only way?

Wolfe took careful aim with his next demonically empowered elbow. "Time to die, prick."

Slam. Wolfe felt his opponent's skull cave in.

He noticed the experience, which was quite high—it took him to about level twenty-four, but only about seventy-five percent to level twenty-five. *Damn. That guy was around level forty-and-change.*

Wolfe glanced up, realizing that the Arena was utterly quiet, no screams of the crowd, no announcer. He wiped the blood from his face with a hand. The attached arm was itself dripping with blood.

He turned and glanced back at his dugout. Shel was staring at him, her eyes wide, her hand at her mouth. *She hasn't actually seen me kill many people. Hope this doesn't upset her.*

Then everything dissolved, and Wolfe was standing with his hand touching the glass screen he had started the fight with. But he was clutching the Hunter's Hunger card. The blood was gone, his wounds were gone—everything felt normal. But for the card in his hand, nothing might have happened.

Clive was staring at Wolfe with considering eyes. "Wow. That was... impressive. As well as impressively dark."

Wolfe only cared about Shel's opinion, and he glanced over at her. She smiled, tremulously.

"You okay?" Wolfe asked.

"Yeah. I knew what you did when we got together, and it's good to be reminded. Not that some other recent activities didn't remind me, but that was a visceral reminder of what is simultaneously the hottest and scariest thing about you."

"Nice," Clive drawled out, and Wolfe knew the man thought Shel was referring to sex as 'recent activities.'

But Wolfe knew it was last night's fight, in which they had defeated two deckbearers together, Caine and Tracy. She was just being subtle.

Didn't hurt his stock with the Arena owner, though.

"Well, shall we head up and see about your deck?" Wolfe asked.

Shel nodded and took his hand, then kissed his ear. "I like that my man can beat up all the other men."

Wolfe snorted, and the two walked up the stairs together.

When he reached the top, he found that Gopal had apparently started back early, as he was already back at the table.

Wolfe glanced at his opponent. He appeared unharmed—until Wolfe glanced at his eyes. Gopal's eyes flickered side to side, as if already seeking escape from Wolfe. His face was pale as he briefly stared at Wolfe before looking away again.

Miriam and her crew were standing around, most of them staring at Wolfe with a mixture of respect and disgust—although Miriam had the same glazed look to her eyes that she had gotten after murdering werewolves, and Wolfe bet she was going to make some kind of comment about sex soon. Speaking of, the girl in the short, black miniskirt was still there, and she licked her lips as she stared at Wolfe as well.

He had forgotten about her for a moment, until her blatant staring brought him back.

Gopal was so shocked, he didn't even try to play dominance games. "I'm, um, going to go home early today. You, um, enjoy Tiffany."

Wolfe almost laughed, remembering the girl from Drop Night. He was nearly positive this wasn't the same person, but the outfit and demeanor might as well have been.

"Um... Wolfe?" Shel asked as Gopal waddled away, his gait unsteady.

"Yeah?"

She nodded to Tiffany. "What's going on?"

Wolfe rolled his eyes. "Right. Girl, you're free for the night."

Tiffany frowned. "You didn't want me?"

Wolfe chuckled and put his arm around Shel. "No, I just wanted that asshole to get blue balls as well."

The girl frowned but didn't make more of it beside putting some sway into her hips as she walked off.

"A shame," Miriam said, staring at her. "She would have been fun to play with." Then she turned her gaze to Wolfe. "You know—"

Wolfe held his free hand up. "No. Cards and levels. You flirting later."

"You're no fun, Wolfy, but okay. While you were absolutely *brutalizing* that waste of man-flesh that just left, Victor here did his thing. There is someone here with a connection to a lot of cards—and surprisingly, most of them are Divine cards."

"Let's go see them, then," Wolfe said. "We can get Shel some new cards and see what she can do in the Arena herself."

Shel extricated herself from Wolfe's hug and nervously twirled her finger in her red hair. "Sure."

CHAPTER 26

A HAPPY HINT OF COMING DARKNESS

Victor took them to a table on the outside edge of the great balcony overlooking the rat Arena. The wall was stone in some places and brick in others, incongruous to the build. The table was lower to the ground and had multiple couches around it. A tall man, overweight but not grossly so, with brown hair and brown eyes, was sitting at the table. His only distinguishing feature, besides being big, was a huge wart on the inside of his arm that a hair was visibly growing from. Next to him sat a pretty, blonde-haired girl who was obviously trying to hide her looks. She was dressed like a pile of laundry—she had on baggy, black sweatpants and an oversized black hoodie. She wore glasses and had a black laptop with her.

Victor gestured to the pair. "This is Hans and Lisa Berwick. They move cards that have... *issues* attached to them. Issues that would make it harder to sell them through a reputable card trading company like Gavin's."

Wolfe stared at the pair. They looked like gamers, or accountants, or maybe the kind of people who had been working on a novel in a coffee shop on and off for five years.

What they didn't appear to be were fences for what was probably cards gained by murder or theft, or through the trade that still existed to third-world countries with wars, civil or otherwise, where the cards could be bought far cheaper.

I guess not every jackass I meet can look like they stamped villain *on their forehead, like poor Gopal.*

Wolfe glanced at Shel.

She nodded.

"All right, we're looking for Mortal and Divine faction cards," Wolfe said.

"Particularly civic-type Mortal cards," Shel said. "Cards that have jobs like police officer, or EMT, or have the word 'civic' in their name."

The pair nodded in near-perfect unison, briefly meeting each other's eyes.

"Lisa will see what we can do for you," Hans said.

Lisa stared at her computer, poking away at the keyboard for a minute or so. Wolfe waited, wondering what cards would be offered.

After a bit more, Lisa turned the computer around. "Okay, we have a few options in that area, but also a few other, rarer options for Mortal and Divine."

A list of cards was on the screen, with prices attached. Shel knelt next to the low table and checked the screen. Wolfe stood, reading over her shoulder as Shel scrolled. First he saw a Veteran EMT, then a couple of the Rookie EMTs, then the same for the Riot Police cards.

Then things started to get interesting.

Shel stopped the screen as she was scrolling. "Is that an enhancer?"

Wolfe glanced at the card.

Caretaker of the Lost
Rare Tier-1 Mortal Enhancer

+2 Health

Special: **Fast Age [2]:** All minion [orphan] cards grow at twice the rate. This stacks multiplicatively with any other source of minion [orphan] growth.

Special: **Find the Lost:** When any pack is opened, there is a 10% chance one card becomes a minion [orphan]. This ability does not stack, but multiple copies may each check against the pack.

Special: **Evolve Improvement [1]:** When a minion [orphan] card evolves, it gains 1 tier automatically. This does not stack with other Caretaker of the Lost cards but may stack with other sources.

Special: **Shield the Lost:** All [orphan] and [evolved orphan] cards gain +1 Defense and Magical Defense and +2 Health.

"The next generation is the future, but they stand on the shoulders of the ones that came before."

"That's... interesting," Wolfe said, eyeing it. "It feels like a *very* long-run build. Is there any stuff that's faster?"

"Let me just check the price," Shel said.

She looked. They wanted five hundred thousand for the enhancer card.

Shel scrolled a bit more. Soon, a persistent came into view.

Police Academy
Uncommon Tier-1 Mortal Persistent
3 Mortal Power

Special: **Summoner [Rookie Police L/5]:** This card produces a Rookie Riot Police every 30 seconds until 1/5 levels of the deckbearer is present on the field. If this card is dismissed or removed, they all dismiss as well.

Special: **Façade [Veteran]:** This card counts as a 'Veteran' so
long as it's on the field.

"There is no substitute for training and experience, no matter
your field. No amount of natural talent can make up for
10,000 hours of keeping your nose to the damned grindstone."

"That's more like it," Wolfe said. "That's like the 'No Kill
Pound,' which has been one of my best cards."

Shel nodded and muttered, "Mm-hmm."

But she kept scrolling. A moment later, a Barter the Soul
came up.

Shel touched the price. They wanted fifty thousand,
which was a discount—most common cards went for that
much in the open.

"Hmm..." she murmured again.

After a bit more scrolling, she came to another card.

Grail of Free Will
Mythic Tier-1 Divine Persistent
1 Divine or 1 Mortal Power

Special: **Divine Preferred Typing [Mortal, Divine]:** All
Divine cards gain the best option of being treated as Mortal or
Divine under all circumstances
Special: **Free Will [Mortal, Divine]:** While this card is out,
no Mortal or Divine card may be controlled or sacrificed
without the specific consent of the deckbearer.

"This grail contains the essence that is most Mortal—the
essence of choice."

Shel stood, leaning up to Wolfe's ear. "This was one of the

mythic Grail cards from the last three seasons. It's almost certainly the card that belonged to Officer Klinefelter!"

Wolfe remembered the poster hanging on Rhett's office wall of the missing officer. *Whoever killed him sold his cards rather than keeping them for themselves.*

Still, I wonder...

"Where'd you get this card?" Wolfe asked.

Everyone tensed. Victor didn't say anything, but Wolfe could see the disapproving look on his face.

Wolfe could tell he wasn't going to get an answer—and might get himself in trouble.

Hans's brow was furrowed, and he started to open his mouth.

Wolfe held his hand up. "Sorry, my bad. Didn't mean to pry."

Everyone relaxed, and Wolfe nodded to the laptop screen. "It's an amazing card. How much?"

Shel scrolled slightly. The number that came up made Wolfe wince.

Twenty million.

Wolfe sighed. Unless something in his life changed dramatically for the better, the grail was off the table.

"What about the other ones? The police one and maybe the Veteran EMT?" Wolfe asked.

Shel hesitated, then touched the price on the cards. A hundred thousand for the Police Academy, and fifty thousand for each of the Veterans. Far more reasonable than the other stuff.

"I'd have to use a few levels to really benefit," Shel said. "That'll put my other plan further back."

"It'll be a while before you gain three more companions, anyway," Wolfe said. "Just go with it."

Shel stared for a bit longer, then checked the prices on the

Rookie EMT and Rookie Riot Police cards. Thirty-five thousand each, a huge discount.

"I'll take three each of the Rookie Riot Police and the Rookie EMT cards," Shel said. "And also a Veteran EMT, a Veteran Riot Police, the Police Academy, the spare Barter the Soul, and the Caretaker of the Lost."

"Really?" Wolfe asked, doing the math in his head. They actually had nearly that much between the two decks they had sold one way or another over the course of the day... but it would nearly empty them again.

Shel nodded. "Yeah. I think the orphans are going to be hugely important to becoming a truly powerful deckbearer as time goes on. Adding ten percent to three categories is about a free tier upgrade, essentially. But I need power now as well—and improving my Mortal cards will give that to me."

"All right. You've supported me wholesale in my deck-building ambitions, so if this is what you want, let's do it."

The thirty minutes after they'd decided what they wanted were taken up with bank transfers and fetching the cards from hidden back rooms, but finally, Shel and Wolfe sat at a table with all her new cards—and her status sheet. Shel had gotten a pen and paper and written down everything so Wolfe could see, although they planned to burn it afterward.

"I've taken an additional five cards in deck, bringing me up to fifteen," Shel said. "I also took an enhancer slot and increased cards on field. With my five total power, I've got some decent options."

Wolfe stared at her sheet.

Rachel Lyons Status:

Level 16 Deckbearer (8 Levels pending)

Deckbearer Perks:
Deckbearer Perk 1: Divine Favor: When pulling from a Mortal or Divine pack, one random card will be a rarity higher. If pulling from a mixed deck, at least one card will be either Mortal or Divine.
Deckbearer Perk 2: Guiding Light of the Divine: Gain 1 Light Power. May have one extra card in play so long as it's a Mortal (Any EMT, Police, or card with 'Civic' in the title).
Deckbearer Flaw: Pacifist: May not gain attack from mantles

Deckbearer Stats:
Cards in Deck: 15 (1 pip)
Cards in Hand: 4 (1 pip)
Cards in Play: 3 (1 pip)
Length of Play: 5 minutes
Specialty Cards:
Companion: 1
Minion: 1 (1 pip)
Enhancer: 1 (1 pip)
Type 1 and Power: 1 Divine
Type 2 and Power: 3 Mortal (2 pips)
Energy 1 and Power: 1 Light

Personal Perks:
Inborn Perk 1: Small: -1 Attack
Acquired Perk 1: Police Training: +1 Attack and Defense

Personal Stats:
Health: 20
Attack: 5
Magical Attack [None]: 0
Defense: 6

Magical Defense [None]: 5

"What's your deck going to look like?" Wolfe asked.

Shel spoke with conviction. "I merged the three new and three old of each of my rookie cards, so I have two each of the Rookie EMT and Rookie Riot Police. Then I added the veteran of each as well as the Police Academy, which makes up half my deck right there on the 'Civic' type cards. The Vengeful Orphan and the Caretaker of the Lost bring me to ten and cover the 'future growth' of my deck for the moment. Sorenia, the linchpin of the build, makes eleven. My mantle, Resilient Martyr, makes twelve. I've got two Barter the Souls, as I think that'll be a black horse trump card, and I think for my last card, I'm going to put the Guiding Light persistent back in, as another way to improve my Mortal cards."

Wolfe nodded, considering. A mantle, two Mortal-empowering cards, and a ton of efficiently organized Mortals —and two cards to use her cheap Mortals to upgrade if the enemy brought a giant monster to the field. Not bad.

"All right, shall we find you a fight, then?"

Shel bit her lip and checked her watch. "Okay, but we need to be at the Police Gala tonight at eight P.M. If we get dropped off at a rental place and then head there, we probably have time for one more match. Sure you don't want it yourself?"

Wolfe shook his head. "No, you go. I'd like to see you make some levels."

Shel nodded to his words. "All right, let's see what we can find."

Shel looked out into the rest of the balcony, which was filled with numerous members of the Noimoire criminal underworld, and Wolfe followed her gaze. Half the punks here probably had Infernal decks. It should be easy...

But Shel was still biting her lip, and she was twisting her fingers in her long, red hair.

It took a moment for Wolfe to get it.

She's only ever had one real deck fight where I wasn't supporting her. And she very nearly died—would have if I'd been about fifteen seconds late.

She's terrified.

He reached out and put his hand on her shoulder. "It's going to be okay. You've got training now, and no one can hurt you for real. Or, at least, the hurting will stop and you'll be fine again."

Shel chuckled. "Your inspiration leaves a bit to be desired."

Wolfe chuckled along with her. "Fine. Point is, no real consequence worse than the loss of a single card will come. You can do this."

Shel stood. "I can. Let's go."

Chapter 27

Angel Trumps...

olfe occupied the place that Shel had occupied an hour before—the small dugout on the side of the Rat Arena floor. He gave Shel a quick pat on the back as she strode forward to touch the same glowing panel on the plinth that Wolfe had touched.

She hesitated briefly as her hand hovered over the panel, the only sound the impatient tapping of Clive's shoe on the ground.

"You've got this," Wolfe said.

Shel squared her shoulders and touched the panel. There was a brief pause, and then the screen flashed.

Shel's Vengeful Orphan card came up.

Wolfe felt himself tensing. *It wasn't Sorenia, but the Vengeful Orphan is a solid card.*

Shel froze in place—but at the same time, another Shel walked a few feet into the Arena.

"Is that what happened with me?" Wolfe asked, turning to Clive.

Clive nodded. "Yeah, pretty much the same for everyone."

"When I looked back, I didn't see myself," Wolfe said.

Clive gave Wolfe a crooked smile. "Well, it wouldn't feel real if you just saw yourself back there hanging out, now would it? Just be a good boy and watch the Arena selection."

"Asshole," Wolfe said with little heat, turning back to the action. *Creepy bastard. But I can't punch every idiot who makes a dog joke.*

The Arena shifted, and the announcer cried out, "Well, ladies and gentlemen, you'll need to hold on to your popcorn! Shel and Hector are in for a treat, and so is this entire audience!"

"What happened?" Wolfe asked as four massive, ancient, pitted pillars of stone rose, two on each end of the Arena away from Shel and her opponent, Hector.

"Shh!" Clive put his finger to his mouth and glared at Wolfe.

"The Arena has selected the Remnants battlefield, which I think we've seen fewer than five times before tonight! The shades of two ancient Beast deckbearers, lost in this land ages before Columbus sailed the ocean blue, will be joining the fight!"

Wolfe frowned. Beast deckbearers would be weak against the Mortal cards in Shel's deck, but still.

"How powerful?" Wolfe asked.

"For the love of all the gods, please let us watch!" Clive said.

Don't punch our host, don't punch out host, Wolfe repeated to himself as a mantra.

Shel touched her chest and tossed out a card—the Police Academy card. A brief image of her face, and the card, appeared in Wolfe's vision along the outside of the Arena.

A solid first pull. One of her best possible starts.

At the same time, he saw the face of Hector as he pulled a card—a four-winged, bird-headed demon with claws on hands and feet that stood almost ten feet tall.

Pazuzu's Get
Rare Tier-1 Infernal/Elemental [Wind] Creature
2 Infernal, 1 Wind, 2 Any power
Health: 35
Attack: 9
Magical Attack: 9
Defense: 9
Magical Defense: 9

Special: **Perfect Movement**: At any turn after the creature enters, may move instantly to any point within a 1000 feet radius that could be reached in a direct line and attack any enemy who would then be available to strike, regardless of any other rules governing targets.

Special: **Untouchable**: 50% of all physical attacks targeting this card miss.

Special: **Shared Resistance [Infernal, Elemental, Fire]**: 50% damage to deckbearer and all allied cards from Infernal and Elemental types and all Fire energy.

"While not as strong as their father, Pazuzu's Get can be found tormenting their enemies and protecting their allies in most of the desert wastelands of the old world."

"Oh my!" the announcer called. "Hector is going for the immediate kill. Pazuzu's Get was a favorite of deckbearers that was introduced at the turn of the millennium—it allows a *very* fast killing of your opponent if you get it out and hold it!"

Wolfe couldn't help but agree and groaned nervously. *Fuck, that is crazy strong—although it's a demon and won't really help with its protections. But it could go right after Shel—and possibly kill her in a single round next turn.*

Two other people with vaguely Amerind features showed up in the screen, and one pulled a Rainbow Coyote, a three-power Beast/Meta card that could deal damage as *any* energy type, and the second pulled a card called Treeline that created a Plant persistent that reduced all incoming damage from all enemy sources by twenty percent but could be removed by any Golem or Fire direct damage spell.

Near Shel, a small building rose with generic police symbols on it. She stepped so that the building blocked the line of sight of the enemy and the Pazuzu's Get card.

At the same time, a line of trees grew near the one faux deckbearer, and a medium-sized coyote with iridescent fur sprang up near the other.

A single Rookie Riot Police popped out of the Police Academy.

Unlike in Wolfe's fight, no deckbearer changed positions. Shel's phantom still stood a mere few feet in front of Wolfe, now out of line of sight of everything else.

She still had three cards in front of her, and a fourth off to the side—Sorenia, her companion. Wolfe saw her reach for it, but as she did, she hesitated.

Her enemy pulled another card while she hesitated.

Pentagram of Demonic Strength
Uncommon Tier-1 Infernal Persistent
3 Infernal Power

Special: **Demonic Empower [2]:** All Infernal cards get +50% to all stats.
Special: **Hold On! [All Infernal]:** All the deckbearer's Infernal creatures survive the first otherwise fatal attack with a single Health.
Special: **Guarded [Infernal]:** No card may remove an Infernal card except by dealing damage

"Sometimes, the power of the Infernal pours into the world, overwhelming all else."

A circle of black flames sprang up in front of Hector, and Wolfe saw the Pazuzu card alter, going to a flat twenty on its basic stats.

At the same time, it blasted sideways, appearing next to the other deckbearer in his treeline. It attacked.

Wolfe saw the hit displayed on the outside of the Arena—fourteen damage, squared, against the deckbearer's current defense of five. Wolfe was interested to see that Arena-created deckbearers didn't get a modifier to their defense like actual human deckbearers did. Instead, the thing had its hundred and ninety-six damage divided by a mere five, dropping it to thirty-eight damage, which was still nearly two times the deckbearer's life. The twenty percent Treeline card reduction did almost nothing, reducing the overkill from two-to-one to merely one-and-a-half-to-one.

"Ooo! Pazuzu's Get swings for the fences!" the announcer called amid cheering from the balcony around the side. A brief flash of blood and the deckbearer, and the trees, disappeared.

Pazuzu's Get turned to face Shel now that it had line-of-sight.

Shel withdrew her hand from where it hovered in front of Sorenia and touched another card.

The Rookie Police Officer faced skyward and screamed, then disintegrated.

Barter the Soul flashed on the Arena wall.

"This is why we watch!" screamed the announcer. "The one play that changes *everything*. Pazuzu's Get, now empowered, just changed sides!"

A second Rainbow Coyote joined the fight, as well as another Rookie Riot Police, put out by the Police Academy.

The first Rainbow Coyote was heading across toward Shel, and the second joined as well.

"Bullshit!" Wolfe called when the Arena sent both against Shel.

"Shut up!" Clive said. "It's random. Your squeeze just got unlucky!"

Wolfe wasn't *too* worried—he assumed Shel was now going to be the winner since she controlled the overpowered Pazuzu's Get.

Hector frantically swiped cards, but a look of triumph replaced his grimace of fear, and he dissolved the Pentagram of Demonic Strength and hit another card.

Bar the Gates
3 Any Power [Available]
All Divine, Elder, Infernal, and Elemental creature cards are banished. The power used remains gone for an entire extra card switch.

"'This is a world of Mortals, and our influences should be indirect. And I would trade all my influence to be rid of theirs.'—Raphael, Archangel of Kindness, protector of Mortals."

Wolfe sighed in frustration, but Shel didn't hesitate, throwing out the Guiding Light card.

Guiding Light
Uncommon Divine/Light Persistent
1 Light, 1 Divine Power
+2 to all Stats of any Mortal card

"'You must be a Guiding Light to guide Mortals to be free of the influence of the damned.'—Raphael, to the 30th Lantern Angel cohort."

At the same time, a Rookie Riot Police popped out of the Police Academy.

"Hector really saves his bacon with that pull, but now he's got no cards on the field while the beautiful Shel has four!" the announcer called. "How can he recover?"

One of the Rainbow Coyotes reached Shel but turned to attack the older of the Rookie Riot Police with its new increased stats. Even though the Wolf attacked using Death energy, the matchup was still mixed since it was a Beast attacking a Mortal, and both took damage—the Coyote more.

A "Coyote Pack" appeared by the other deckbearer. It was a beefier creature at three power, but still not amazing with the bad match-up.

Wolfe was still hopeful despite Pazuzu's Get having been vanished—Shel had the best position of the three remaining deckbearers, he thought, and not by a small margin. Each of her once-weak Rookie Riot Police was now eight attack, nine defense, and eight magical defense, with solid match-ups against Beast cards.

The next thirty seconds solidified Wolfe's certainty that Shel still had the fight. Sorenia came out, pushing the now *three* Rookie Riot Police to ten, eleven, and ten on stats and making them take half damage from Infernal Sources as well.

Hector, meanwhile, apparently didn't have enough power left for another pull, thanks to the Bar the Gates card, Wolfe assumed.

The rest of the fight was slow but certain, with Shel methodically cleaning up, maintaining field advantage with too many cards coming too fast and with too much power for Hector to ever recover. Toward the end, there was a brief moment when a Pazuzu's Get rejoined the field, but Shel had *two* Barter the Souls, and she simply took the Get again.

The end was rather anti-climactic, and the crowd's cheers were anemic. But Shel handled it well all the same. And her choice of cards in the beginning had been perfect.

The field faded and the true Shel, frozen in front of the screen, gasped, her hand holding the card that had been wagered—the Bar the Gates card. She turned to Wolfe, her eyes glowing. Then she ran and leapt on Wolfe, wrapping her legs around him and hugging him.

"I did it, I did it!" she exulted.

"I knew you could," Wolfe said, smiling and kissing her.

Clive made gagging noises. "We are not amused."

"Shh!" Wolfe said to Clive in imitation of his earlier comment and laughed.

Clive joined in, surprising Wolfe. *Okay, so a weirdo and a jackass, but at least he has a sense of humor about it.*

"You did well, young deckbearer," a woman's voice, cultured and precise, said. "Would you care to wager that card you just got against me?"

Wolfe turned, and Shel hopped down from him.

Standing across from him was a lady, dressed in a long, black lacy dress that was simultaneously sexy and demure. She had pale-white skin and long hair so blonde, it was almost white.

Clive coughed. "Surely, she wouldn't—"

"Quiet," the woman said, her voice suddenly cold and commanding. Wolfe marveled at her vocal control as Clive just shut up, and even Wolfe felt a hint of danger from her.

"Well?" the lady asked.

Shel glared at her. "You're the one we saw fighting when we came in—Elizabeth, Infernal Champion."

Elizabeth smiled. Her voice was reasonable and not threatening as she said. "Not *Infernal* Champion—

Champion of Enlil. I won't bet against anything in your deck —and if you beat me with your Divine deck, which has advantage, you'll probably go up five to six levels. I'll give you three million dollars if you win. So whatever the Arena takes, we agree to trade back in return for the specific prizes. What do you say?"

Shel glanced at her phone.

Wolfe started to speak. "I don't think—"

Shel held her hands up. "No. I'll do it."

Wolfe glanced at her. Her face was set, her expression fierce.

Elizabeth smiled, a smile not that different from Wolfe's when some baby enforcer tried to 'step' to him back in the day. "Brilliant."

CHAPTER 28

...To A Point

"Shel, that's a *champion*," Wolfe said a few minutes later, after Elizabeth had started the trek to her side. "That means she's over level one hundred. No idea what she's doing slumming here, but why would you agree to fight her?"

"I have advantage," Shel said. "Divine beats Infernal."

"Uh-huh," Clive said from where he was still standing in their dugout.

Wolfe didn't want to agree with the jackass and just raised his eyebrow at Shel. Her cheeks pinked.

"I know it won't probably be enough—but if it is, it would solve a lot of things and make us way stronger. It's worth the bet."

"I thought you had to get to the Police Gala?" Wolfe asked.

"You guys are cops?" Clive asked, his voice nervous.

Wolfe turned to face him. "Do I look like a cop, numbnuts? You know who I am."

Clive nodded, but he looked thoughtful.

Shel ignored the byplay and glanced at her phone again. "I

think we can do this, go back, get our car and clothes, and make it in time."

Wolfe shrugged. "Whatever. If you miss the Gala, it's no skin off my nose. I'm not really pro-cop, anyway."

Shel briefly frowned, then smiled. "I like that you've got my back, even when you're grumpy about it. And you're at least a little bit pro-police—you like the beans."

Wolfe rolled his eyes but played along. "They were good beans. Now let's talk strategy."

"There's no strategy for Elizabeth," Clive said. "You know she was born in 1891, right?"

"I didn't know that, but there has to be something on her," Wolfe said. "I mean, we just saw her fight."

"All I saw when we came in was an Arena entirely on fire and a lady who obviously regretted all her life choices," Shel said.

Clive laughed.

Wolfe joined in. "Wow, one personal victory and you get all sorts of cocky and funny. I like it. But I admit that's not a lot to strategize with."

Shel chuckled but nodded.

"Do you know things about her?" Wolfe asked, turning to Clive.

"We are not betraying information about an *Infernal Champion*," Clive said with a roll of his eyes.

"Champion of Enlil," Shel interjected.

"We are not amused by your sass." Clive rolled his eyes and the corner of his lip quirked upward.

Wolfe turned away from the kooky Arena owner. "She's seen your deck—do you think we can figure out what she knows, and counter her with that?"

Shel smiled. "I doubt it."

"Well... try not to, um, 'die,'" Wolfe said, holding his fingers up in air quotes.

"I'll do my best," Shel said, kissing Wolfe once and then giving him a quick hug before turning to place her hand back on the glass.

Clive made gagging noises again.

Shel's gesture felt weird to Wolfe. *Like she's going away.* He supposed he could understand it—she was 'going to battle' at some level.

"Are you fucking kidding me?" Wolfe asked in disgust as Sorenia appeared on the trade list.

"I hope, for your sake, that Elizabeth'll honor her word, because that card would go for a couple million at least," Clive said. "Even on the black market. We're sure of it."

Wolfe almost asked "Who's 'we'?" but then just rolled his eyes. *Looney bastard. I certainly don't miss the personalities of the people I used to work with.*

Then the announcer's voice boomed through the Arena and into the dugout Wolfe, Clive, and Shel occupied. "Someone has been foolish enough to challenge Elizabeth, our resident Infernal"—he coughed—"excuse me, our resident Champion of Enlil. It's the victorious deckbearer from the last round. I don't know if she's counting on her Divine typing to help her, but I think she's in for a rude surprise if she is!"

Elizabeth stepped out onto the field—although Wolfe knew she was merely projecting onto it.

Her black dress and eyes gave her a sinister demeanor, even at the distance. She flicked her long, blonde hair once.

Shel touched her chest and pulled her deck, tan and golden cards appearing in front of her.

Elizabeth did the same, a fraction of a second behind, and red and swirled cards appeared in front of her.

Shel didn't go for the building this time, instead rapidly touching Sorenia and throwing her out.

Elizabeth, in turn, touched a red card and threw a

233

scorpion-taur with a sword onto the field. Then she started to run toward Shel, dress held up in one hand.

The announcer exclaimed, "Oh my, Elizabeth brings out her patron's signature card! It was last released in the final Drop Night of the Age of Exploration and Exploitation set over a hundred years ago but has featured in at least three other set releases prior, with alternative art! This creature has *a lot* of nasty combo powers!"

Wolfe glanced at the card.

Girtablullu
Rare Tier-1 Infernal Creature
2 Infernal Power, 1 Elemental Power
Health: 30
Attack: 7
Magical Attack: 7 [**Death**]
Defense: 6
Magical Defense: 4

Special: **Elemental Boost [2]:** Gains +2 to all stats during any 30-second period after their deckbearer played an elemental card

Special: **Limited Follow Through:** This creature may normally only make physical attacks. However, when it kills an opposing creature, it immediately gains a free magical attack against another creature or deckbearer.

"The Girtablullu are the chosen instruments of punishment from Enlil, the Infernal Lord of Storms, Floods, and Disasters."

Wolfe raised his eyebrow at the card. That could be rough. Once it reached Shel, if it could do enough damage to her cards, it would gain free attacks on her—and she would go down fairly quickly.

Shel touched her cards again, and her mantle settled over her. At the same time, Sorenia used her Light beam and burned the Girtablullu, which roared more like a bull than the man its upper half was.

Elizabeth touched another card, mouthing, *"Goodbye"* as she did.

Storm of Demons
Mythic Tier-1 Immediate Infernal/Elemental
1 Infernal Power, 1 Elemental Power

When this card is played, any number of cards matching an Infernal creature on the field may be played from the deckbearer's deck, but the cost to play each must be paid at the same time. Until all creature cards have left the field, the power used to play this card remains spent.
All matching copies of the card make an immediate action, moving up to 1000 feet to do so.

"It's not *that* the wind is blowing, it's *what* the wind is blowing."

"It's the Demon Storm!" the announcer cried. "Great Game over!"

Three more of the Girtablullu appeared on field, and winds kicked up, moving all of them instantly to Sorenia.

Sorenia died as four creatures attacked her with a boost, cutting her down, and then all of them leapt over to Shel, who cringed down as they each stabbed her with their tails—tails that were now two Magical Attack stronger.

Shel screamed as the tails entered her and her flesh rotted, and Wolfe tried to surge forward, but then Shel disappeared from the field.

"And that's it, a clinic put on by a master!" the announcer called.

The Shel that had her hand on the glass gasped and pulled back, then turned and flung herself into Wolfe's arms.

But she didn't cry, just breathing raggedly as she held him.

"You okay?" Wolfe asked. "I mean, are you okay now... Obviously, you weren't a minute ago."

"I've never died before," Shel said, shaking, her voice haunted. "Not even against Frankie did I experience... this. I felt the scorpion tails enter me, a blinding pain. Pain that then spread... It was agony, Wolfe."

Wolfe pet her head, pulling his rough hands down her hair. "You're fine now... and you'll be stronger for it, as you know what it is to suffer extreme pain."

There was a brief pause in which Wolfe thought about the encounter before he spoke again. "She had *at least* fourteen power... which means, even if she started with three power, she had to spend sixty-six levels on power. That's *insane*. That card, using up two power to spend twelve, is only really useful at the insane levels."

"She might have had some really good enhancer cards as well, maybe," Shel said. "Or perks. It might not be fourteen power."

Wolfe nodded, his chin moving across the top of her head.

Shel's shaking stopped. With a tremulous smile, she glanced up at Wolfe. "Shall we head to the Gala, then? Where I'll presumably be lauded and plied with good food? We're getting close to that point, anyway."

Wolfe chuckled. "Sure... but you just lost Sorenia from your deck. We need to go trade the Bar the Gates card and then we can head out."

Shel nodded. Wolfe tried to walk out with his arm around

Shel, but the stairs were narrow and difficult to navigate—Wolfe ended up going first, with Shel and Clive, who had been uncharacteristically silent while Wolfe and Shel were talking, trailing behind.

At the top, he met Elizabeth. Against expectations, she wasn't smiling—in fact, her face was neutral, almost somber.

She immediately held out Sorenia's card.

Wolfe reached for it, but she pulled it up a few inches. "The card I'm owed, please."

Shel came out of the stairwell, slipping past Wolfe, and held the Bar the Gates card out. Elizabeth nodded and they exchanged the cards.

"What's your story?" Wolfe asked. "For an Infernal deckbearer, you don't seem that bad."

"Pot kettle, much?" Elizabeth said.

It took Wolfe a fraction of a second to parse her broken English, but then he laughed. "Fair. Feel like sharing the specifics?"

Shel put her hand on Wolfe's arm. "I'd love to hear as well, but we don't have time. We *really* need to get to the Gala."

Elizabeth glanced at the two of them. "I don't normally share my history on first meeting regardless—but I'd love a chance to talk sometime. Despite that one-sided fisticuffs, I have a feeling about you two." She handed an embossed card over, with her name and number. "Give me a call sometime."

She walked away, and Wolfe and Shel headed over to collect Miriam.

As they did, Shel glanced over at Wolfe. "You ever wonder if you just attract weird women?"

He laughed so hard, he snorted. "I would hardly say you're weird. Improbable in a very good direction, maybe, but not weird."

Shel hugged him tightly.

"We're late," Shel said, glancing at her phone. "It's already a minute past."

"You'll be fine," Wolfe said, driving the new rental—also a black Subaru, but without all his special modifications—toward the huge, waterfront hotel, the one with the giant lion statues flanking its entrance, each with a copy of the stats of the unique Nemean Lion on its base.

It wasn't called the Hercules Hotel or anything, it was just a Hilton, so Wolfe wasn't sure why—but he couldn't deny the statues added a certain oomph to the place.

Wolfe pulled up in front of the hotel. "Okay, you're here. Nobody will be upset about three minutes."

"We still have to park—this isn't valet," Shel said.

"No, *I* still have to park—I'll find their garage and then meet you inside. You go in and start meeting and greeting and kissing all those cops' asses. I'll be along shortly."

Shel rolled her eyes, leaned over, and kissed him. "All right, but be quick."

Wolfe nodded as Shel got out of the car and headed up the front steps. He admired the figure she cut in her dress uniform —she was sleek and professional, from the jacket to the slacks to the shiny shoes.

Wolfe pulled back into traffic and circled the block, not finding the garage, then did so again, starting to get frustrated. He pulled his phone out and checked—the garage was a block over, running under two hotels.

"Of course," he muttered, hoping that Shel wouldn't think he was avoiding her ceremony or sneaking a smoke or something. Not that she would say anything, but he didn't want her to even think it.

He drove around a third time, found the parking entrance,

and pulled in. It was like every other underground parking garage ever, but with a bit less random trash, and the paint wasn't scuffed.

"Fancy," Wolfe said to himself as he drove through, finally finding a parking space and then pulling into it.

He was still a ways from the elevators, past a large number of police cars. He took a brief jog to get to the elevators, to try to make up some lost time from his drive.

They were set in a small alcove in the parking garage. As Wolfe turned around the corner, he saw Rhett waiting for him, leaning back against the wall, faux-casual. But he was dressed in a tactical vest, and Wolfe could see his muscles were tensed, and there were slight pit stains on his uniform.

"What're you doing here, Rhett?" Wolfe asked in surprise. "Shouldn't you be inside, kissing ass and getting it kissed in turn?"

"I'm doing you—and Shel—a favor," Rhett said, his voice deadly serious.

"What?" Wolfe asked, confused and slightly alarmed by Rhett's demeanor.

Rhett's eyes were hard as steel, and his hand hovered in front of his chest. "You're under arrest, William, for conspiracy to murder Emmett Dunn. Or should I say *Wolfe*?"

CHAPTER 29

RHETT MEET REALITY

"What?" Wolfe asked in the still air of the parking garage, stunned on multiple levels. "Emmett's dead?"

For half a second, Wolfe thought about Emmett and imagined him dead, lying in a pool of his own blood somewhere. He wondered if Rhett had done it.

But he glanced over at the detective. The two of them were alone, and Rhett's face shone with righteous indignation. Not a hint of the smugness he would have shown if he were pinning something on Wolfe.

And he wasn't one of the corrupt cops Emmett had fingered as working with Worldwide Decurion.

Rhett continued. "Yeah, Emmett was murdered by a Peter Brown—better known by his street name of 'Piper' for some inane reason. Piper was found with fifty thousand in cash, and he claims you paid him to do in Emmett, and provided the thug with the location of the old detective. What do you have to say for yourself?"

Wolfe gave a single dark laugh. *Piper? That stupid street-level enforcer has somehow caused me no end of problems, despite a half-ass attitude about work, no deck, and not a lot of skills. I should have finished him off in the trainyard.*

"Laughing?" Rhett asked. "That's all you have to say? Why'd you do it, Wolfe? Did Emmett know about you and your bloody past?"

Rhett stalked closer, his hands remaining by his gun and chest respectively.

Wolfe, still standing perfectly still, shook his head. "Emmett had plenty of information on bad people—including corrupt cops. Information I have in a box at home now. But Emmett didn't know a damn thing about me, and whatever past you think I have. He was helping a new detective get his hours, and I was helping him catch some bad guys—including bad guys protected by the system. That's it."

"You expect me to believe you had nothing to do with this? I know you're not who you say you are, and if you're who I think, you have a truly bloody history."

Wolfe laughed, long and rich, as the full absurdity of the situation hit him. "So you believe that *Piper*, whom Emmett and I found at the scene of a mass human trafficking case, is telling the truth when he says that the guy who got him arrested after *shooting* him was definitely also the one who paid him to kill the other guy who also, let me think, *arrested him*. Yeah, Piper definitely had no motive to take care of this himself, and no motive at all to finger me. Pure chance he names me. Any other evidence?"

Rhett frowned, his brow furrowed. "I won't deny it's a bit convenient, but given everything he told me, and who you likely are, I have more than enough to take you in. In a court at trial, the evidence standard is beyond a reasonable doubt, and this probably won't hold up. But for me to detain you and investigate and see if there's anything else that will hold up, the evidence needed is only that of reasonable suspicion. Given that Piper is probably your old gang buddy, I think his accusation qualifies."

"Great," Wolfe said.

There was another pause in which neither moved. Wolfe was a bit surprised—normally, when cops wanted to take someone in, they just did it.

"Where was he?" Wolfe asked. "When he was found, I mean."

"Piper?"

"No, Emmett."

Rhett frowned again, and his hands dropped a tiny bit from his gun and chest.

"He was found in a dirty hotel room he had rented less than an hour before, tied to a chair and shot."

Wolfe sighed. "So what now?"

"Now I put you in handcuffs and we go for a ride. I'm trying to do it here so it doesn't mess up Shel. I think she can still have a great career, if we distance her from any association to you."

Wolfe was deeply, deeply frustrated. He wanted to beat the shit out of Rhett and put a stop to this.

On the one hand, if who Wolfe actually was came out formally to the cops, he might have a lot to answer for, and more importantly... Damian and his crew, or Worldwide Decurion, might find a way to shank him in jail. Wouldn't even be that hard. But Wolfe would have a chance to fight back.

But on the other hand, Wolfe knew that beating up Rhett, or killing him, would make Wolfe a permanent criminal—one who would be arrested by any cop who saw him. Plus, Wolfe would almost certainly be cleared for Emmett's murder—Piper was the worst person to finger him, and there would be absolutely no evidence to link him. Wolfe remembered enough of his father to know he would have laughed about a case like this.

And, last and final, he had told Shel he would try to be a good guy.

"Let's get this over with," Wolfe said.

Rhett tensed and stepped back, half-drawing his gun.

Wolfe smiled to see how much the huge man, obviously a bruiser, still considered Wolfe a threat. But he turned around and placed his hands behind his back.

Rhett stepped up and pulled on Wolfe's arm. Wolfe snarled.

"Sorry," Rhett said. "Don't make a scene, though—for Shel's sake, if nothing else."

"Am I cooperating, or am I cooperating?" Wolfe asked.

"Surprisingly, you're cooperating, which reflects well on you," Rhett said as he snapped handcuffs onto Wolfe's wrists. Quite loosely, which surprised Wolfe in turn. Maybe Rhett wasn't as sure Wolfe was a bad guy as he was letting on.

Rhett straightened, putting a key to the handcuffs in his back pocket. "I have a transport team nearby to take you in. You'll get a fair hearing."

"Hurray," Wolfe sardonically said, wishing he weren't cuffed so he could do the most sarcastic jazz hands ever.

Rhett gripped Wolfe's upper arm and slowly pushed him out toward the main, open portion of the parking garage.

"A word of advice. Don't make up any bullshit about dirty cops. The judges prefer honesty, and anything you say will come out."

"Me and judges have a lot in common, then."

"Don't start," Rhett said, his voice irritated. "You've already said too much."

"Emmett wanted to catch his kid's killers. He gave me all the evidence—dates, times, locations, contacts, payments, even pictures—of the cops working with the traffickers.

Problem was, he could never find out who was really behind it all. I still haven't, not a hundred percent, although I have a damn good idea. But Emmett said I should turn it all over if he died. I'm guessing there is going to be a shitstorm in Noimoire when it all goes out."

Rhett stopped. "You have evidence of dirty cops? Hard evidence?"

"Yeah, it's all in a box that Emmett kept in his office—which was ransacked by someone, I might add. But I got there first, and now the box is in my house." Wolfe glanced back over his shoulder. "Want to make a detour on the way to the slammer, Lieutenant?"

He loaded the last word with as much sarcasm as possible.

"It doesn't really matter. Either we get it now, or Shel will turn it over tomorrow when she hears what happens. I'm sure you're very excited about that."

"Shel shouldn't openly involve herself in this," Rhett repeated.

"So you've said," Wolfe muttered. "We'll stop by, then?"

"Of course not. I know that Wolfe, who I think you are, was once a deadly killer with outcomes far above his supposed capabilities. So I'm not going to give you a chance to escape and try something. I'll go get it later tonight with Shel, and I'll turn it in."

Wolfe felt a twinge of rage at the statement, as if Rhett being with Shel in Wolfe and Shel's house were natural, but he pushed it down. *She's never betrayed you.*

"Is that what this is about? Being with Shel?" Wolfe asked, trying to control his rising rage.

"I would never, ever, arrest someone for personal gain. Not ever," Rhett said, his voice angry.

A large police van drove into the parking garage and pulled up to Wolfe and Rhett. Both stiffened at the same time, and Wolfe knew Rhett was seeing the same thing that Wolfe was—the van had *Noimoire* Police Department on its side, not Joliet.

The passenger door opened and a huge man stepped out. Wolfe was six-two and muscled, and Rhett was about the same. But neither held a candle to the man who squeezed his way out of the front door.

If someone had told Wolfe this man had been born of a woman who had figured out how to mate with an ogre card, he wouldn't have been surprised. The man looked like he ate steroids for lunch rather than taking them, per se. He was a good two inches taller than Wolfe and must have weighed nearly three hundred pounds, the vast majority of it bulging muscle—his biceps were beyond cut, and thicker around than most people's thighs. Sweat glistened on his bald head, offsetting his thick veins, probably from the heat of wearing a huge tactical vest over his police uniform.

"Deputy Chief Charleston," Rhett said with wide eyes. "How did you even...?"

Deputy Chief Charleston was one of the people on the dirty cops list...

"Thompson called me," Charleston said, pulling an assault rifle out from the car and then turning back again and walking over to Wolfe. "No need for you to do anything else, Lieutenant. We'll take it from here."

As if in time to his words, the back of the van opened and another eight men leapt out and came over, all holding guns on Wolfe.

Rhett blinked. "Isn't this a bit much?"

Charleston glanced around. "This man is a dangerous criminal, wanted for conspiracy for murder. He was once an enforcer for the Grimm mob family. Aren't you doing this with a bit too little?"

"I had a team waiting, but William—or Wolfe—was reasonable."

"Well, either way, I'm head of the task force investigating the situation in Noimoire. I'll take it from here."

"Of course," Rhett said, stepping back.

Charleston came over and grabbed Wolfe by the lower arm, wrenching him toward the giant deputy chief. Wolfe growled.

They have no intention of taking me in. I could cause far too many problems for them. I'm not going to make it to jail.

Wolfe wasn't afraid, he told himself. But he *was* becoming very concerned. Jail he could handle. Handcuffed with ten armed men around him would be... a stretch.

Wolfe stared at the police chief, trying to figure a way out of the situation. But without the ability to summon a deck, or even get a gun, Wolfe wasn't sure what to do.

The police chief must not have liked the way Wolfe was staring at him.

He growled out, "Lowlife like you doesn't deserve the comfort of our prison system. If it were up to me, you'd have a fast track right to the electric chair."

The hypocrisy of the comment almost floored Wolfe, but he didn't call it out. It wouldn't do him any good at the moment, and besides—Charleston might actually think he was doing good by getting criminals off the streets, even if the method itself was criminal.

Plus, Wolfe was handcuffed and the other guys were packing all the heat. Now wasn't the moment.

"There's one other thing," Rhett said, obviously not with Wolfe when it came to keeping quiet. "William—Wolfe—mentioned that Emmett Dunn, the victim, had some information regarding dirty cops."

By all that is Divine, why can't anyone keep their damn mouths shut?

The air in the parking garage seemed to get three degrees chillier, and all eight of the other officers exchanged glances with at least one of their fellows. Instantly, Wolfe knew that they were all in on it, although of course they were if they were all taking him in when he wouldn't make it.

But it solidified for Wolfe that Rhett wasn't in on it, even though Wolfe had already been pretty sure. None of the other officers so much as glanced at him afterward.

Wolfe was sure Rhett should never have admitted he knew about the dirty cops. If they were willing to kill Emmett to keep their secret, they would most likely be willing to kill Rhett, too.

"Is this true?" Chief Charleston asked. "You tried to disparage my fine fellow brothers and sisters in blue?"

Wolfe had no idea what to say, so he just grit his teeth and remained silent.

Without warning, without any hint in eyes or body, Deputy Chief Charleston slammed his fist into Wolfe's undefended stomach. The blow shocked him, and he felt as if things inside him were crushed. His breath exploded from him and he dropped to his knees, then fell forward and hit the cool parking garage floor, the blow to his face a welcome distraction from the agony in his gut.

The single punch had done *seven* damage, a fourth of his life—no way Charleston didn't have enhancers of some kind in his deck. Magical steroids, so to speak. Because that kind of damage wasn't normally humanly possible.

"Charleston!" Rhett barked. "What're you—"

"He was resisting." The deputy chief chortled. Some of the men with him laughed as well, but most just kept their guns vaguely pointed in Wolfe's, and now Rhett's, direction.

"No, he wasn't!" Rhett said. "He's been nothing but cooperative till this point! It's an abuse of your authority, not to mention generally morally reprehensible, to strike a man in custody!"

Rhett knelt down and placed a hand on Wolfe's back, then

tried to help him to stand. He only got Wolfe to his knees before Wolfe vomited what little food he had eaten, surrounded by a fair amount of blood. *Man, he did a number on me.*

"Leave the filth alone," Deputy Chief Charleston said. "He's a criminal with the sheer audacity to say we're like him. He's as slimy as they come. Don't be a chump manipulated by his pathetic attempts for pity."

That annoyed Wolfe. He hadn't tried for *pity* from anyone since he'd been a kid.

"He says he has proof," Rhett said, still evidently oblivious. "Physical proof. And Emmett did work with numerous police departments. I think we should take this seriously."

Wolfe almost laughed again. Rhett was such a damn Boy Scout—but he was also the only one in the entire freaking parking garage playing this straight. Wolfe almost liked the guy, but he also couldn't help but be a little amused at the idiocy wrought by Rhett's combination of naiveté and sheer bravado.

Charleston looked down at Rhett where he knelt beside Wolfe. "Rhett, you've been helpful in this investigation, but I'll take it from here. I'm handling the case, which occurred in Noimoire, I'll remind you—my jurisdiction. Just forget you ever met this lowlife scum."

Rhett stood, tall and proud. "Well, Joliet—where we are now—is *my* jurisdiction. It's also where Emmett had his office. You can take Wolfe and question him, but I'm going to investigate his claim. We need to know if someone in our ranks is using their post for personal gain. Especially if it involves human trafficking."

Charleston didn't say anything, merely staring balefully at Rhett.

Rhett continued. "To be frank, it also disturbs me how

quick you were to manhandle someone in custody. You're the deputy chief of police for all of Noimoire, for the Divine's sake. Everyone here looks to you as an example, and you're setting a terrible one. I have half a mind to report you."

Wolfe smiled where he knelt on the ground. *He's naïve as fuck, but Rhett has some testicles on him.*

Deputy Chief Charleston surprised Wolfe by laughing, his voice suddenly jolly. "You know what, Rhett? You're right. Maybe I'm overworked and taking it out on the little guys. You take this guy over to the Noimoire station, and I'll speak to Chief Huang on the subject. Maybe we can use some of the Internal Affairs guys."

Rhett took a deep breath, calming himself. "All right. I'll take him in and get you the report as soon as possible."

"Good man."

Rhett bent down and took Wolfe's upper arm.

Before Rhett could straighten, and again without warning, Deputy Charleston threw a punch impossibly fast at Rhett's face, which was at Charleston's gut level. Rhett turned away but still took most of the force to his head. He went sprawling, rolling and reaching for his gun and deck, but he was rattled and slow.

As Rhett fell, Wolfe saw his opportunity, and he went with the fall, acting as if he had been pulled down with Rhett by the hand on his shoulder. He rolled onto his side, back against Rhett, and took the key from the cop's pocket.

A cop shot Rhett with a Taser, and Rhett spasmed. Then three more descended on him, turning the lieutenant over and handcuffing him. They grabbed Wolfe as well, but no one checked his hand.

"Take them to the boathouse," Charleston said. "Have Caine's man figure out what they know. Then dispose of them."

"Even Rhett?" the officer yanking Wolfe to his feet asked.

Poor, stupid officer didn't learn the lesson.

"You want to join him?" Deputy Chief Charleston asked, his voice pure menace.

The officer finally got the clue and shook his head.

"Then shut the fuck up. No one was here, and no one saw Rhett. Write the report that he went rogue on this—that he went to apprehend this piece of shit and never came back."

Weirdly, the thing that worried Wolfe the most as he was taken away was the possibility that Shel might actually *believe* he had been responsible for Rhett's death.

CHAPTER 30

TAKING A TRIP

"You don't have to do this," Rhett said, his back to the corner of the van, his arms handcuffed and restrained to the reinforced steel siding while four officers watched. "Anderson, Thompson... you both have wives, kids. What would they say if they saw you—"

"Shut up!" one officer shouted. Then he got up, pulled his sidearm, and put it to Rhett's head. "Don't you dare mention my family, not ever again."

"Calm down, Anderson," another officer said. "This'll all be over soon. No matter what he says about our kids."

The officer—Thompson—was carrying a fully automatic rifle, although Wolfe wasn't sure of the brand, as he only really knew pistols. But Thompson's eyes flickered back and forth between Wolfe and Rhett, and he sat with the easy confidence of someone used to violence—unlike Anderson. Wolfe kept wanting to try to use the key, but he knew if did, he'd be deader than the job of town crier. No way he could finagle unlocking his cuffs and closing the distance to Thompson before Thompson blew him away. He still needed his moment.

253

Rhett sat up as straight as he could while handcuffed to the wall of the van. "Whatever you've done, it can be mitigated if you turn yourself in and stop now. It only gets worse the longer you go."

Anderson rushed over and grabbed Rhett by his blue police shirt, jerking him as close as the handcuffs allowed. "This didn't have to happen! It's *your* fault we had to do this! If you had let it go, not been such a damned Boy Scout, we could all have gone our merry way."

"I didn't force you to do this," Rhett stated. "You could have just done your job."

There was a quiet moment where nothing happened, but then Anderson completely lost his shit. He slammed his gun into the side of Rhett's head, once, twice, three times. The first blow stunned him, the second split his eyebrow open, and the third his ear. Blood poured over Rhett and even splattered the seat and wall slightly.

The two officers who hadn't been involved in the conversation at all leapt up and yanked Anderson back and away from Rhett. Anderson was breathing heavily, his face red.

Wolfe didn't want any part of this—foolish last-minute heroics were for when no other option presented itself, and he still had an option. He had an option so long as he didn't get hit so hard, he dropped the damn key. But no one was paying him any attention as they wrestled Anderson back.

Wolfe's eyes flickered around, but Thompson was still semi-alert to Wolfe, too far away. The situation still wasn't right, and Wolfe almost growled in frustration.

After they'd gotten Anderson under control, the three officers moved toward the cab, near Thompson, leaving Rhett and Wolfe semi-alone in the back of the van, with Thompson's eyes, and the muzzle of his gun, the only thing pointed at them.

The rest of the ride was thick with silence, broken only by the sounds of the van occasionally bouncing and the faint sound of outside traffic. Wolfe could feel each bounce through the metal of the bench he was on, but didn't complain—he knew what that would get him.

Rhett must have finally learned as well, because he too remained silent.

After about twenty, maybe thirty, minutes, the van pulled to a stop. A moment later, the back door was thrown wide, and the unmistakable smell of the river, not that different from last night when Wolfe had dropped Tracy's corpse in it, flowed into the musty van, clearing out the sweat, anger hormone, and blood smell that had been brewing.

If Wolfe hadn't known this particular river held a certain attraction to bad guys thanks to the prolific freshwater crab population, he might have found it refreshing.

The officers came, uncuffing Wolfe and Rhett and moving them out the back of the van. They were in an old parking lot next to a rundown, wooden boathouse with a single speedboat in it.

Wolfe glanced across the river at the city skyline, which was pretty familiar, especially lit up at night as it was. *This isn't the warehouse, but we can't be more than half a mile from it. Ironic if I do end up dying here. Poetic or some shit.*

A tall, thin, stick-like man came walking out of the boathouse. He wore a sleeveless T-shirt and jeans and carried a knife in a sheath at his waist. Wolfe was vaguely impressed at his cold resistance but appalled at his lack of sense. His arms were wiry, but not cut enough to justify the look—and he had been skipping chest day, it appeared.

"Castor," Officer Thompson said, his dislike evident in his voice.

"Charleston got us up to speed," Castor said. "We can take it from here."

Anderson pushed Wolfe forward. "You gotta get whatever information they have. And call us afterward with the details. We need to make sure this information dies with these pricks."

"I said, *Charleston got me up to speed.* You pigs don't need to tell me twice. We're just waiting on the specialist to get here."

Castor motioned to his six buddies to take Wolfe and Rhett. Wolfe didn't struggle—it still wasn't the right time. Plus, they had inadvertently given Wolfe the information that he still had time.

Rhett hadn't gotten the memo, however. He struggled, and most of the thugs left to deal with him, restraining him and putting a gun to his spine.

The thugs walked Wolfe closer to the river, pushing the struggling Rhett along behind him.

"They might as well call this the River Styx, so many dead people have tried to ford it," Wolfe quipped.

One of the thugs laughed. "You're the funny one, then?"

Wolfe chuckled. "Just more relaxed now that I'm not in the presence of cops."

"Yeah, you don't look like one of those fuckers, that's for sure."

The thugs turned them to the side and pushed them up a small ramp and into the boathouse. It was filled with numerous crates, and the walls were covered in all kinds of miscellaneous boat parts, fishing equipment, old radios, and a ton of similar things. The center had a damn speedboat in it, partially disassembled, the blades of its propeller on the boat's floor. Four metal poles kept the center from collapsing in on itself, and the thugs led them to the pole closest to the water at the far end.

Probably just the instinct to keep us from the front door on the off chance we escape, although no one seems to be worried about that.

They made Wolfe and Rhett sit, backs to each other with a pole between them. Then they tied their handcuffs together, trapping them to the pole.

"This place owned by the Grimm family?" Wolfe asked.

"Yeah," one of the thugs replied. "You know them?"

"Once."

"Then you probably know we aren't going to be the ones beating the information out of you. Damian hired a surgeon, and he's on his way. Although if you want to just tell me everything now, maybe he won't be needed."

Wolfe chuckled darkly. "I might, but I'd rather save something for him so he'll eventually leave me alone."

The thug matched Wolfe's chuckle and stood. "You're mighty blasé about this, but suit yourself."

Wolfe was impressed that the thug knew the word *blasé*. He wasn't sure he had heard anyone say that since he had put his father down.

Might have to upgrade my name for this guy to 'Educated Thug.'

Educated Thug and his five thug brethren went over, grabbing some slightly rusted folding chairs and one of the crates, and set up an impromptu poker game they were playing by phone-light. Castor still hadn't come inside.

It was dark outside, and extra dim inside. The thugs were distracted.

It was finally time.

But Wolfe's hands were in an awkward position.

"They've hired a surgeon?" Rhett asked under his breath.

Wolfe laughed quietly. "A torturer, a professional one, to get information from us."

"By cutting into us?"

"Maybe," Wolfe said. "Most guys break after having their fingernails ripped off, but you're fairly stubborn. They might get to the part where they start slicing things up that aren't that important."

Rhett was quiet for a moment. "You're fairly calm."

Wolfe chuckled again, although he was covering for his growing frustration—he couldn't get his hands to bend right to open the cuffs. "Maybe I should be less calm, like you—then we can both get our asses kicked first."

"This isn't a game," Rhett hissed. "Have you given up on life? Is that it?"

"You really know how to win friends and influence people," Wolfe growled out. He still couldn't get the key where it needed to be.

"I can't believe this—you should be more upset. You've put Shel's life in danger."

Wolfe almost dropped the key. "What? Why the fuck would Shel's life be in danger?"

"Because she might know what you know—they can't chance it. You live together, right? If they were willing to dispose of me, they'll dispose of her for sure. And if she were tied up here, she would have indignity added to the pain and death."

Wolfe paused. *Fuck. He's right. I didn't consider that.*

Wolfe took a chance. "I've got the key to my cuffs—but I can't get it in right." *That sounded bad.* "If I drop it, can you grab it and free me?"

"You've got keys? Really?"

"No, this is the dumbest ever 'fooled you' joke. Of course I do."

"I can help, yeah."

Wolfe carefully dropped the key, wincing at the tiny *plink*.

He felt Rhett moving his hands down.

"What was that?" Educated Thug asked, standing from his chair.

"Nothing," said another thug. "Just play the damn game."

"I fold on this one—I'm gonna go check it out."

Wolfe felt pressure on his handcuffs—Rhett being insanely fast and accurate at undoing them, he hoped.

Educated Thug ambled over to Wolfe's position. He was smoking now, although Wolfe hadn't seen him light up.

Just as he arrived, there was a soft *click*.

"What the...?" the thug said, his eyes widening as he watched one cuff fall from Wolfe's wrist.

Then Educated Thug reached for his gun.

CHAPTER 31

RUMBLE IN THE BOAT HOUSE

Wolfe launched himself upward, his free hand touching his chest as he did. He tried to swing his manacled hand around and knock Educated Thug on this ass, but the open end of the cuff caught in something, and instead, Wolfe slung himself sideways, giving Educated Thug the time necessary to get his gun out.

Knowing he was seconds from death, Wolfe didn't even hesitate, simply throwing Cereboo into the space between him and Educated Thug. Wolfe felt like a bit of a douche for letting his doggo take the shot, but, well... Cereboo came back when he died. Wolfe didn't.

The crack of a gunshot, whine, and following enraged barks were painfully loud in the relatively small boathouse, but Wolfe didn't let it stun him. As Cereboo leapt onto Educated Thug—who abandoned his verbosity for screaming—Wolfe extricated his cuff from Rhett's, where it was stuck, and stood.

Then he dropped back down and crawled to the slight protection of the speedboat in the center of the boathouse. A hail of gunfire went through the space he had been half a second earlier.

The other five thugs hadn't been far behind.

He touched his deck again, and red washed over him—the familiar power of his Soul Hunter mantle. Between the increased defense and the resistance to Mortal damage that being Infernal gave him, he would take only about a third the damage from the mooks and their guns as he would otherwise have taken.

Feels like old times—Cereboo and a mantle against a pack of thugs.

Rhett yelled, and a notification popped into Wolfe's view that a deckbearer had pulled their deck.

Okay, not exactly like old times.

Educated Thug went down beneath Cereboo, and Wolfe ran out and ripped the gun from the dying thug's hands, then peeked around the front side of the speedboat.

When he didn't immediately get shot, he wasted a thug and pulled back, rapidly scuttling to the other side.

"Castor, Wolfe's free! We need backup!"

Wolfe ordered Cereboo to attack the thug nearest the water, then lunged around the speedboat himself on the side farthest from water. He shot at two thugs rapidly, dropping them, while Cereboo absorbed bullets and brought another down.

The last one turned and started to run, just as a crazy demon burst into the room. It looked like an insane Koa-Toa had birthed it after mating with some fishing gear, and it smashed the door to the boathouse off its hinges before leaping across the scattered crates. It landed and slashed at Cereboo but did little damage thanks to Cereboo's huge resistance to the Infernal.

Wolfe ran to the side, aiming to go out the boathouse window and around behind Castor, whom he figured was coming in hot on his demon's heels, but when he attempted to push the wooden slats open, they were stuck, briefly halting him.

"Die!" Castor screamed as he entered, firing at Wolfe, who hissed as a bullet went through the meaty part of his left bicep. He hit the ground, ignoring the seven damage—as much as Deputy Charleston's punch, which either said something awesome about the deputy chief or really bad about the pistol Castor was using.

But it also meant Wolfe was half-dead, and he got his first injuries notification—a 1-point penalty to his stats, except health.

"Did that hurt, Wolfe?" Castor called out, faux kindly.

Why do so many of my enemies try to taunt me? Do they think I'm going to suddenly become incompetent?

"Want me to kiss it better? Kiss it better with *my gun*?" Castor continued.

And why are so many so very bad at it?

Wolfe swiped and tried to play Cerberus's Home for Wayward Hellhounds, but nothing happened except a notification appeared. *Insufficient space on field to play that card.*

Huh.

Wolfe instead played a single Angry Hellhound.

Even as he did, another notification appeared. *Malviere has been slain. Her card returns to the deck, and the timer is reset.*

Wolfe was shocked—Malviere was back at his house. With Ms. Timo, Lucy, and Shannon.

Which meant someone was fighting there.

Oh, shit.

Maybe they'll kill the Vengeful Orphan, too, and let Shel know something is going on.

Wolfe tried to put it from his mind as another fish hook

demon joined the fight, snarls and exploding boxes heralding its arrival.

Wolfe looked at his remaining cards. Another Angry Hellhound, a Pack Howl, and his Fireborn Hellhound. He only got one, and that would also bring his cards on field to max.

He opted for another oldy but goody, the Fireborn Hellhound. He wished he had a bit more synergy, but he still had the equivalent of seven power worth of demon dogs on the field.

He stood, his gun and gaze tracking together for Castor, but he didn't see him.

But his mantle made him deadly to other Infernals, so Wolfe spent a moment blasting one of the fish hook demons to pieces. The other managed to get a hook *into* the skin of his Angry Hellhound and ripped it out. His Angry Hellhound yipped and dropped to the ground. But Cereboo and the Fireborn Hellhound hit the demon and began ripping it to pieces.

At the same time, a giant crab appeared and rushed the field.

Castor leapt out from around the side of the speedboat to shoot Wolfe three times in rapid succession. Wolfe was blinded by pain that felt like getting hit in the chest three times with bone-cracking force, but his mantle prevented his death—he was left with huge penalties and three health. Wolfe stepped inside and knocked the gun from Castor's hand, only to have his knocked from his hand in turn. They went chest to chest, wrestling as they pushed each other around, grunts and huffs of exertion as the coppery smell of blood slowly overwhelmed the smell of the river.

Wolfe could normally take a chump like Castor in almost no time, but he was severely wounded. A lance of pain went through him as Castor managed to elbow one of his chest wounds, and his wounded arm gave in slightly. Castor used that to push Wolfe back. In the space, he drew his huge knife and lunged for Wolfe.

Wolfe caught the descending knife by using a cross-wrist block, but Castor pushed him back, and Wolfe tripped over the side of the speedboat. Both went down, and Castor landed on top. Wolfe tried to get the advantage, but Castor had started on top, was younger, and wasn't riddled with bullet holes. The bloody scramble ended in an advantage for Castor, with Wolfe trapped against the metal bottom of the speedboat, Castor above him.

He quickly got his angle, mounted above Wolfe, and tried to stab Wolfe again. Wolfe again caught the knife, but he was in dire trouble. Castor was now pushing down on the knife, with his weight backing his play. Wolfe was nominally stronger, but his weak arm and Castor's superior position meant the knife inched ever closer to his chest, bit by bit. Wolfe's limbs were already shaking with the effort to keep it away. They would give way soon, and then Wolfe's story would end.

"Give in, it'll all be over soon," Castor whispered, his breath smelling of onions.

Wolfe glanced to the side at the disassembled propeller lying in the bottom of the speedboat and gave a last desperate, spasming heave to the side, throwing Castor and rolling. Castor let go of the knife and tried to post, but Wolfe hit him, driving him partially onto the exposed screws with their combined weight. Castor screamed and thrashed, not nearly dead but agonizingly wounded. Now, every thrash they made also wounded Castor more, and Wolfe finally managed to get on top of Castor, their positions reversed from a few seconds ago.

"You give up," Wolfe said back. "I've been *not giving up* for twenty-five years, and I'm not about to change that for a stupid POS like you."

That sounded better in my head.

Wolfe was still tiring, however, and Castor wasn't dead.

Both men also still had cards in front of them, moving in and out of each other's bodies without interacting with them, and Castor managed to swipe, switching his cards.

Wolfe needed to stop him from summoning, and fell chest to chest with Castor, putting all his cards inside Wolfe's body. Castor couldn't get Wolfe off him, half-screaming, half-grunting as each effort pushed the broken propeller parts deeper into him.

It only required a few moments of Wolfe stopping the summon for the air to suddenly reek of brimstone.

Castor looked up into four hellhound mouths. He had time for one scream before he was silenced forever.

Wolfe hit level twenty-five. He dismissed the notification telling him that he had hit the level for a new perk, instead slumping back down onto the metal bottom of the speedboat for a moment, trying to recover.

He had imagined hitting level twenty-five to be more epic, somehow.

He rested for thirty seconds next to Castor's corpse but then managed to half-heave, half-crawl out of the boat. It wasn't over yet. A 'surgeon' would be here soon, and Wolfe was in no condition to fight. He went over to Educated Thug, hoping he would have the keys to the handcuffs.

A quick rifle through his teeth-punctured, burned corpse showed that he did, in fact, have the keys. Wolfe managed to walk his way over to Rhett, barely able to stand. One hand on Castor's gun, one hand holding the keys to Rhett's cuffs.

When he reached the lieutenant, Rhett was staring at Wolfe with wide eyes. "You just killed seven armed men, including a deckbearer, in a couple of minutes."

"Turns out I suck at nearly everything—but I am *stupid* good at one thing, which is being the 'find out' to every evil jackass who 'fucks around.'"

Rhett snorted. "Sucking at nearly everything including one-liners, I take it?"

Wolfe ignored the banter and held his newly acquired gun to Rhett's head in one trembling hand. "We need to have a talk about where this goes next."

Rhett narrowed his eyes, his jolly demeanor gone like a fart in the wind. "Spit it out, then."

"I'm pretty sure you can guess by now that I didn't kill Emmett, and who the real enemies are. So what's going to happen is, I'm going to set you free, and you're going to forget you ever heard the name 'Wolfe.' We make a deal—I get to keep my anonymity, and you get to keep your life. Sound fair?"

Rhett stared at him for a few moments, eyes occasionally crossing to look at the gun pressed to his forehead a mere inch from his eyes.

"Fuck you," Rhett said.

"Really? That's it? Just 'Fuck you'?" Wolfe asked with exasperation. "Maybe your pride is wounded, being beat up by your fellow officers in blue and saved by some random thug, but don't let it stop you from thinking straight."

"You've heard my answer," Rhett growled.

"Why? Why not even just pretend to agree and then arrest me later? Is turning me in worth *dying for*?" Wolfe asked, truly baffled. "Why not even give me the *tiny hope* I might get to lead a normal life, finally, so I won't shoot you?"

Rhett was silent for a moment before speaking. "You think a man like Anderson woke up one day and decided 'I'm going to betray my fellow officers'? Of course not. He did some tiny thing, barely noteworthy, and probably for a seemingly good reason. Maybe his mother was sick, and someone in your line of work offered to take care of all her bills in return for ignoring just one shipment of drugs. And it made sense to him. Victimless crime, save his mother. But it tainted him, and it made him susceptible. The next bribe maybe he justified as his wife deserving it. Then that he deserved it. Then it was just his lifestyle. Even if he wanted to turn back, he can't, because he's a criminal now too. He may not realize it, but he's already ended the life he loved—now it's just a matter of time till it catches up with him. And he's the worst kind of criminal— the one who betrayed the trust of a society he swore to protect. I'm going to do my job, and I'm going to Divine well do it right."

"You can't do your job if you're dead, asshole," Wolfe said.

"Men like you don't understand," Rhett said. "When I die and go before the Divine council, there won't be anything to explain away."

Rhett was the definition of self-righteous. Wolfe's hand trembled as he began to tighten his finger on the trigger, looking in Rhett's eyes.

CHAPTER 32

MORE FIGHTING

C ereboo whined.

Wolfe exhaled noisily and lowered his weapon. *He's a good man, even if he's also a self-righteous prick. He doesn't deserve to die. And I don't want to upset my pooch.*

Wolfe put the key into Rhett's cuffs and turned them.

"You know I'm still going to arrest you, right? This doesn't change anything."

"By all the Infernal, can you please just quietly take the W? You've made that pretty fuckin' clear... I swear to all the archangels, you *want* to get shot. But no such luck, Twinkletoes, 'cuz this fight isn't over yet and I'm pretty fucked up. Turns out I'm not going to be the one to decide your fate —this surgeon character and whomever he brings will be."

"'Twinkletoes'?" Rhett asked.

"I call you 'Self-Righteous Prick' in the privacy of my own head. You want me to use that instead?"

Rhett actually laughed at that, a single bark of what sounded like genuine mirth. "Fine, *Twinkletoes* will do. Privately, at least." He glanced at Wolfe. "Also, you're more than 'pretty' fucked up

—you need a hospital. A morgue, soon, if we don't do something. I know this probably isn't your style, but just fight with your cards from behind cover, please. Let me handle most of this."

"Hey, you're the insufferable hero. I, personally, have *no issue* with letting someone else handle the problems, as long as they actually *do* handle said problems. I mostly do shit because others won't."

Wolfe was saved from whatever rejoinder Rhett might have made by the sound of a car entering the parking lot outside.

"Unfortunate," Rhett said, his voice elaborately casual. "I should have pulled my deck earlier."

He touched his chest and pushed his hand out. Gold, steel, and tan cards sprang into existence in front of him.

Three types, no energies, Wolfe thought, wondering how much utility that would have.

One gold card hung off to the side, and Rhett reached out and touched that one.

Golden light flowed from the card, forming a beautiful, winged angel carrying a lantern chained to her wrist. She had black hair and vaguely Asiatic features but still bore a resemblance to Sorenia, somehow.

No damned way, Wolfe thought, his eyes wide for a moment despite the approaching danger. He stared at the card.

Liurenia
Unique, effective Tier-7 Divine/Light companion
0 Power
Health: 11
Attack: 0
Magical Attack: 10 [**Light**]
Defense: 5

Magical Defense: 5

Special: **Guiding Light [Mortal]:** While in play, all Mortal creature cards gain divine typing and +25% (minimum 1) to all stats.

Special: The benefits to Mortal cards stack with the other three named companion lantern angels. If all 4 are possessed, the card Zarachiel, Commander of the Lanterns, a 4-power mythic Tier-8 equivalent Divine companion card, will be gained as well as a free companion card slot.

"Liurenia was first infused with the Divine and evolved from a base Lantern angel when she slew her tenth demon, and she gained her current rank after the Archangel Raphael saw her save a Mortal's soul at risk to her own existence."

"You've got to be fucking kidding me," Wolfe growled out. "How the hell did you get a god-gifted deck card from the Archangel of Kindness? You might be a good guy, but you're more the Archangel of Ramming a Rod *Alllll* the Way Up There kind of guy."

"I didn't," Rhett said distantly. "This card belonged to my father. Now hush your attempts at humor—they'll be coming for us."

Something about the way Rhett had said it told Wolfe that Rhett's dad probably wasn't in this world anymore.

Wolfe also tossed an Angry Hellhound out to replace the one he had lost.

A sudden thought occurred to him, about the strategy his enemies might use. "Get down!"

Rhett squatted. "Why would I need to—"

Wolfe reached out and grabbed Rhett. Rhett easily batted his hand away, but he did shut up.

Wolfe ordered all his creatures behind boxes, and his three demon dogs slunk there.

Wolfe whispered. "They *might* not know we're free, in which case we might get the jump on them."

"I won't shoot someone without warning."

Wolfe rolled his eyes. "Whatever. If they do know we've escaped, they'll probably—"

Wolfe's talking was interrupted by multiple gunshots through the door and window slats. Most of them hit Liurenia, whose lantern exploded—as did a lot of her body, showering blood everywhere before everything simply turned back into gold energy and flowed back to Rhett.

"And that's why we duck, children," Wolfe said sarcastically. "Any questions?"

Rhett stared briefly at the space Liurenia had been. "Thank you."

A deckbearer has pulled their deck near you.

"It's on," Wolfe said. "Head in the game."

Rhett switched from squatting to a one-knee position, gun held up in front of him. "This is the police! Drop your weapons or I will be forced to use deadly force!"

Wolfe slapped his face and dragged his hand down, but there was a pause in the fighting.

"I didn't sign up to fight the police," came a voice from outside.

A different voice called out, "Jones, get the fuck back to your window or so help me, I'll shoot you myself."

Rhett touched his deck and a large, brass clockwork... device, Wolfe supposed, fell out, blocking a most of the view. It had a ton of clockwork gears, but no visible clock face, was almost ten feet on a side, and square.

Clockwork Penance
Rare Tier-1 Golem Persistent

3 Golem Power

Special: **Embodied Clockwork:** This persistent has 100 Health and 10 Defense as if a creature. This may not be increased by anything that would increase a creature's stats.

Every round this device is out, all Golems, Mortals, and Angels gain +1 to all stats, stacking with each other gain, so long as any Infernal, Elder, Undead, or any card with the word 'criminal' in its title is on the field and controlled by an enemy.

"The law isn't always quick, but it is inevitable."

"Shame Shel isn't here. That would stack with her build wonderfully," Wolfe muttered.

A quick series of gunshots came from outside, but no bullets entered the boathouse.

"I'll be damned. I think your hippie-dippie speech actually did something useful," Wolfe quipped.

"Saying, 'This is the police, get down,' is hippie-dippie?"

"It is in this situation," Wolfe said with a roll of his eyes.

Rhett didn't answer, standing and striding forward. A bullet immediately whizzed barely past his head. Rhett planted his feet, drew his pistol—a Glock-19, pretty standard police model—and fired through the door, three shots in quick succession. *Why didn't he wait for his mantle?*

Something hit the ground with a *thump* outside, and Rhett ducked back behind some boxes.

Wolfe figured it was time and ordered his doggos out. He had bare moments before the Fireborn Hellhound would dissipate for lack of time on the field, but Cereboo and the Angry Hellhound would last until taken down.

Rhett touched another card and threw out a golem—nearly eight feet tall, with a scary, stone mien and glowing eyes.

Enforcer Golem

Uncommon Tier-1 Golem

2 Golem, 1 Any Power

Health: 30
Attack: 9
Defense: 12
Magical Attack: 0
Magical Defense: 7
Special: **Façade [Civic]:** Counts as a 'civic' Mortal card for all purposes.

"A basic but powerful golem guard, its magic and purpose is to assist Mortals."

Guy has a decent amount of power, Wolfe thought as he glanced at the card. *He might be around my level.*

The golem stomped outside, and Rhett followed right behind, using the stone body as mobile cover.

Wolfe sat and waited, near death. He heard some yells, gunshots, guttural growls, and barks from outside. His Fireborn Hellhound actually timed out, and an Angry Hellhound died, but Wolfe replaced those with other Angry Hellhounds and sent them back into the fight. He got two more notifications of dead mooks that didn't give him any experience, and then finally got a bit of experience for the death of what his notification called 'the Surgeon Deckbearer.'

Wolfe watched as Rhett came back in, limping slightly from claw marks to his leg. His deck was still out, with gold, steel, and tan cards interspersed. He wasn't as badly busted up as Wolfe, but he wasn't that far out, either, given the earlier hits to the head from his fellow officer.

Rhett limped over to Wolfe and slid down the crate with a sigh to sit beside the one-time enforcer. "So, should I do a bit now where I put a gun to your head and demand things?"

"I'd like you a bit more if you did," Wolfe responded.

Rhett chuckled tiredly but didn't respond beyond that. "We need to get out of here. One sec."

Rhett touched a tan card from his deck, and a Veteran

EMT appeared. The card healed Wolfe for eight damage—Wolfe felt it as a mending passing through him, his agony lessening and wounds closing. His injury penalties went back to a one-stat penalty.

Wolfe sighed. "That's the good shit."

Rhett dismissed the EMT and swiped his cards.

Wolfe glanced over at him. "Why didn't you use that in the first place?"

"You spent most of the time I *could* have done that threatening me."

"Eh."

Rhett laughed, then hauled himself painfully to his feet. "That's the only one I have—I keep it for emergency healing if I respond to a call with injuries and am first there. But we need to go—I can heal myself on the way."

Wolfe climbed to his feet with barely a grunt.

"Do you think Shel is in danger?" Wolfe asked.

"Not yet—she has no way to know we were in trouble, and the Gala isn't over yet. She's probably pretty concerned neither her primary instructor nor her boyfriend showed up, though."

Wolfe winced.

Rhett glanced at him. "This is where the news gets bad, right?"

"They killed my minion, and probably Shel's, at my house—so now the files are missing, most likely. And Shel knows for sure."

"Was anyone there? Besides your cards, I mean?" Rhett asked.

Wolfe winced again. "Maybe an old lady and two kids."

Rhett grabbed Wolfe's arm. "Let's go. The Surgeon had a car, and we need to get to your house *right now*."

CHAPTER 33

MAN TALK

Rhett walked outside the boathouse, and Wolfe followed him. The lieutenant flipped the cards in front of him to a new set but didn't play any. Instead, he walked over to a man lying dead on the ground on his back, arms almost comically akimbo. He moved one arm across the man's chest and then rolled him over.

Rhett reached inside the man's back pocket.

"I've fondled plenty of things in my day," Wolfe drawled, "but dead bodies isn't one of them."

"Har har," Rhett said drily, and then he pulled a phone from the man's pocket. He dialed 9-1-1. "Hello, there's been a shooting at the Noimoire docks, the"—Rhett glanced up at a sign—"Gavin's Boathouse."

"Like the card-selling company?" Wolfe asked.

Rhett glanced over. "Or another unrelated guy named Gavin."

Rhett flipped the cards still in front of his chest again, then summoned his Veteran EMT, healing himself.

Wolfe snorted. That made more sense.

Rhett pulled a key fob from the man's front right pocket

and pointed it at a dark-green Jeep wrangler. The car's lights flashed, and Rhett opened the driver's-side door. "Let's go."

Wolfe got into the opposite side. He was feeling a lot less damaged after Rhett's card, but now the adrenaline was leaving him. If he hadn't been so worried about the cops at his house, he would likely have tried to sleep, but he was a bit too keyed up for that.

In fact... "You have a cigarette?"

"Shel told me you quit."

Wolfe ground his teeth. Of course they had talked about it. Now he would probably hear something from Shel *and* also not get a cigarette.

"I don't have any."

And part one comes true.

Wolfe sighed and kicked one foot up onto the dashboard.

"Sit normally, please. It's dangerous to position yourself like that."

Wolfe kicked his other leg up out of sheer orneriness and hooked his ankles. "Life's short. I don't give a shit."

Rhett cornered hard, keeping his speed high, and Wolfe had to grab the bar. He glanced over, expecting to see Rhett mocking him, but he saw nothing of the sort. Instead, Rhett was driving intensely and with focus. Cutting seconds competently.

Wolfe would have complimented the man, but at this point, he assumed Rhett hated him so much that all he could think was—*why bother?*

"Why are you relaxing, anyway?" Rhett asked. "Shouldn't you be more—ready, or something?"

"Being too tense can kill you on things like this. You've gotta relax. It's going to be almost half an hour before we're there. I have no idea what happened, anyway, and no way to find out."

Rhett was silent. For a few minutes, the road sped by beneath them as he drove with focused determination.

But after a moment, Wolfe glanced over at him. "Hey, I have a question. Do cops get any say over which prisons inmates are housed at?"

"No," Rhett said. "There's a prison designation board that determines your facility based on your security rating, criminal record, area code of residence, and availability of space in the different facilities. Sometimes a judge can make a recommendation on your behalf, but that's rare."

Wolfe thought about it, but there was nothing really to say.

"Why?" Rhett asked.

"I wanna be placed as far away from Shel as possible."

Rhett turned and stared at Wolfe for a second before going back to focusing on the road. "Why? I thought you were going to be there for her for life, or something."

"I'd planned on it. But we both know I'm gonna go away for a long, long time. I can't take care of her, can't provide her with the family and support she so desperately wants. Shel won't leave her siblings, I think, and I'd rather she not visit. She's got better things to do with her time."

Wolfe was frustrated, but he knew that he had chosen his path when he hadn't killed Rhett. He probably should have, but what Shel had said to him all those months ago, after Big Man Grimm had died, was still true—he had done the right thing the wrong way his whole life, and it hadn't worked out. Wolfe was tired of it.

And even then, he had never killed just to make things easier for himself, and never a true innocent, which Rhett was.

"Look," Wolfe said, "I'm no simp or whatever the term is these days, but maybe you can help her... move on from me when I'm gone."

"You want me to help her 'move on'?" Rhett asked with a bark of a laugh. "What are you implying, Wolfe?"

Wolfe slammed his feet down onto the floor of the car. "You know damn well what I'm implying, you bastard. Don't fucking even *try* to make me explain it further."

Wolfe bit back his rage. This was hard as the Infernal for him, but he wanted to make sure that Shel was taken care of—taken care of and happy. She did everything to make his life better, and now that his past mistakes had caught up with him, he couldn't let his failures drag her down. No matter how much it ripped his soul to think about someone else taking his place.

Wolfe had witnessed Rhett be the most honorable knight ever. Also a self-righteous prick, but a knight nonetheless. And he and Shel had a lot in common.

"I know you want her. You can say whatever you want about your honor and not sleeping with a subordinate, but she won't be one soon. Tell me to my face that you don't want to be with her. I bet you can't."

Rhett didn't answer.

Wolfe continued. "Truth is, at the end of the day, I have to do what's right for Shel. I can't let my past mistakes be what makes her unhappy. So if you're what makes her happy, you self-righteous prick, then that's what needs to happen. No matter how much I fucking hate it."

Rhett didn't answer for a bit, and they drove again in silence for a few moments.

Finally, he spoke. "Humor me. Hypothetically speaking, let's say you are who I think you are. Some gangster lowlife. Now let's pretend that you *didn't* hire someone to kill Emmett. Why would they say you had?"

"Hypothetically speaking?" Wolfe asked.

"Yeah. Pretend. We're pretending this is reality."

"Then I would tell you that no one leaves a gang without

consequences. I would also tell you that some of my hypothetical old associates would be displeased with my current occupation and consider it traitorous. I don't think we need to imagine what happens to traitors, right? I'd say they would go to great lengths, hypothetically, to make sure I was taken out of the picture."

"Some guy would be willing to go to prison to bring you in?"

"You'd be surprised at how far certain influences go. It's always nice to have a middleman in prison. If he was headed there, anyway, why not make it as good a life as possible? Like a sideways promotion."

"Is our prison system really that bad?"

Wolfe shrugged. "It holds individuals fine, but organizations? Not so much."

"Why are you and Shel together?" Rhett asks. "I don't mean, how did you meet, or why did you hook up. I mean why stay together. She's not like you."

"This seems really personal and not something Lieutenant Rhett Walker should be asking me."

"Please, humor me."

"I ask myself the same damn thing all the time. I think Shel thinks she owes me. I saved her once—she's telling the truth about that. She did something dumb, got in over her head, and nearly died. I saved her, at some risk to myself. Then I helped her with some important stuff at a lot more risk to myself. Found out what happened to her dead brother, although we never truly fixed that situation."

"What happened?"

"The Cobra street gang killed him—their head enforcer, Nico, specifically did it. But Shel didn't know that, and so she went and tried to hunt her way up the list of gang lieutenants, at level one and with a brand-new deck, like an idiot."

"Oh? She's an idiot? Let me guess—you're infinitely smarter."

Wolfe sighed. "I'm even dumber. Doesn't change that her thing was retarded too."

Rhett sighed. "You know, this isn't *at all* how I imagined arresting you."

This guy has an odd train of thought. "Sorry to spoil your fantasies."

Rhett frowned and faced Wolfe. "They aren't *fantasies*."

Wolfe laughed. "Let me guess, you wanted me to resist? Kick my ass?"

"You have to admit, your attitude, comments about me, and comments about my co-workers have earned you at least *one* ass kicking."

Rhett said it deadpan, but when Wolfe turned to look at him, a small smile was playing around his face.

Wolfe snorted. "Yeah, probably. My default position is 'torque them off.' Although for the record, I didn't resist because I didn't want to kick your ass where Shel might see. She's soft that way."

"She wasn't there in the garage, and she certainly wasn't there in the boathouse. Why not then?"

Wolfe thought about his life, his patron, and Shel. "Sometimes a man has to follow through with his duty, I guess. You're carrying out yours, and I'm carrying out mine. That's all."

Wolfe wasn't sure if he owed Shel anything. It could be argued that *she* owed *him*. But it didn't matter—Wolfe *wanted* her to be happy, deep in his soul. He had taken the responsibility onto himself.

They were now inside the Joliet city limit, and Rhett sped through the city.

Rhett spoke again, his voice thoughtful. "Why did you join the gang in the first place? Hypothetically, I mean."

"Well, if I am who you think, then my story would go something like this: My dad was a mob lawyer. He beat my mom and raped my older sister. When I was a teenager, I tried to stop him, and he beat me half to death. Two days after I was taken to the hospital, the police who had taken my statement altered records, then testified with a bunch of lies that made me the villain. My dad went free."

"That's why you dislike cops?"

"I dislike most people," Wolfe said.

Rhett laughed. "Continue."

"Eventually, I killed my dad while trying to stop him from harming my family. It was about a year after the first fight. You can look it up, assuming you can get into sealed juvenile files. Maybe some of the bastard cops are still around, and you can get the true story from them. But the only guy who stuck up for me—hypothetically—was a mob boss. He got me out of juvie, right before they tried to try me as an adult for murder. He took care of me, legit. A man who wasn't good but was at least honorable—something those who were sworn to serve and protect me weren't. Tell me—what would you have done?"

Rhett took a corner hard. "You saved my life, back there."

This guy jumps topics like a damned jack rabbit.

"It's fine. You saved mine too," Wolfe said tiredly.

Rhett spoke musingly. "No... not really. I saved *mine*. But you could have left, after the first fight. Instead, you tried to save me."

"I held a gun to your head. Not the same."

"Only to get me to not arrest you *once you had saved me*. Leaving me or shooting me would have done everything you needed."

Wolfe rolled his head over and stared at Rhett. "Rhett... what do you want? Okay, I saved you. You going to not arrest me?"

Rhett didn't answer. Instead, he touched his chest and pulled his cards out again.

Then he took a pile of cards—twenty—from his pocket, split them in half, and passed ten to Wolfe. "These are the Surgeon's cards. Half belong to you."

"All right...?" Wolfe said, taking them and stuffing them in his pants next to the ones he had gotten from Castor.

"You value Shel's happiness more than your own?" Rhett asked.

"I... What?" Wolfe asked, briefly baffled. "Yeah. At least, I think so."

Rhett reached out and touched his companion card. But it didn't summon—instead, one of the ten cards Rhett had kept from the Surgeon's deck disappeared, and the companion card appeared in his lap. He picked it up and passed it too Wolfe. "For saving my life."

Wolfe stared at the card for a moment, then glanced at Rhett. "Are we friends now, or...?"

Rhett pulled into Wolfe's driveway. "We're here is what we are."

CHAPTER 34

UNEXPECTED AID

Wolfe leapt from the car and flew to the front door of his home. He immediately noted that the front door to the house was askew, hanging lopsidedly. It had been smashed in by something. Claw marks in the front lawn, barely visible in the moonlight, suggested a powerful card monster as the most likely culprit.

Rhett followed Wolfe closely as he ran up. "No decks? Is that wise?"

Wolfe gave it brief thought. Usually, he liked to surprise his enemies, but if his enemies were here, they had heard Rhett and Wolfe drive up. "Pull 'em."

Rhett touched his chest and then touched a steel-colored card. His Enforcer Golem sprang into existence.

At the same time, Wolfe pulled his deck. His two companions appeared—including Malviere. Suddenly feeling like an idiot for not bringing her forth earlier and asking what had happened, Wolfe touched her card.

"Who was here?" Wolfe asked as the ten-year-old-looking girl appeared.

"Two men dressed in all black, wearing black masks," she said. "They asked for a box containing information on the cops," Malviere reported. "Are James and Jason all right? The dogs were very scared."

"I don't know yet," Wolfe said, then he pushed into the house, not sure what he would find and terrified he would find someone he cared about dead or hurt.

Just like when I was a child. If I even find either of my idiot cavapoos hurt, I'm gonna go John Wick on someone.

When Wolfe pushed in, he found his front room torn to pieces. Cushions had been thrown everywhere, as if a box of files would have been hiding in a couch. A couple of lamps were smashed. For some inane reason, even the glass door to the back yard had been smashed open.

It took a moment for Wolfe to understand what he was seeing, but a lump, lying between the cushions, resolved into the form of Ms. Timo.

Rhett pushed in and knelt beside her. "Ma'am, are you all right?"

Ms. Timo coughed, a wracking sound. Blood was coming from a huge split over her eye, which was already swelling up. *Someone struck her with a gun butt but didn't finish her off.*

She struggled to rise, and Rhett helped her into a sitting position.

"Where's Lucy?" Wolfe asked, kneeling down next to her.

She struggled to sit upright, almost falling over, and held her hands to her head. "I'm sorry. I don't know. Shannon and Lucy were outside, last I saw. In the back yard, sleeping under the stars. They told me you said it was okay."

Wolfe vaguely remembered that, but mostly, he remembered telling them to check with Shel. It might have only been this morning, but that had been a *long* day ago.

Ms. Timo kept talking, her voice a broken monotone.

"But when the men with guns came, after they killed Sorenia and Malviere, they got really upset. They said that your bedroom was empty, and the box was missing. When I told them I didn't know where it was, they hit me with their gun. That's the last I remember."

Two tiny feet planted themselves on Wolfe's side, and he turned. James, the slightly larger of his two apricot cavapoos, was standing on his back legs, his front pressed against Wolfe. His tail was wagging, as if Wolfe being back meant everything would be okay. Next to James was his brother, Jason.

Wolfe was glad his two dogs were okay, but he still didn't know where Shel's sister was.

"Do you think they're still outside?" Rhett asked.

"Let's check."

Wolfe stepped through the shattered remains of his door, the glass crunching underneath his feet. When his cavapoos tried to follow, Wolfe turned to Malviere. "Keep them back, please. They'll cut their feet on the glass."

They whined but didn't struggle as Malviere picked them up into her arms.

Wolfe and Rhett walked off the porch into the yard proper. A small tent was on the ground under the sole tree in the back yard, nearest the fence. Rhett began searching around the fence and tree, but Wolfe walked over to the tent and glanced inside.

Two sets of blankets, two sets of pillows, a couple of books —*very old fashioned*—and a small pile of snacks, but no girls. As Wolfe's eyes roamed the tent's interior, he saw a piece of paper.

What? Wolfe picked it up.

It was his partially written statement in the *People v. Timo* case.

Ah, shit. Wolfe could already see the situation. Shannon,

desperate to find out what had happened with her parents, must have stolen the box of files and had almost certainly been looking through it in the tent.

But Wolfe didn't see the box anywhere.

"William, take a look at this," Rhett called.

"Just call me 'Wolfe,'" Wolfe said, then, just in case, "It's a nickname."

He backed out of the tent and stood, walking over to where Rhett was examining the fence. Even in the dark, Wolfe could make out what he was talking about. Footprints on the fence.

The girls must have fled when they heard the commotion. Did they actually take the files?

Wolfe wouldn't have put it past Lucy. The girl was far too bright for her own good, but it was at least possible that she might have been bright enough for *Wolfe*'s good in this case.

Or maybe they had left *before* everything had gone wrong, taking the files to look at where no one would find them. Wolfe wasn't sure.

"Where would she have gone?"

"Well, Shannon and Ms. Timo live next door," Wolfe replied, his mind running. "Right here, in fact, over this fence."

He turned and faced the house, glancing at it over the barrier separating the properties.

Rhett huffed out a breath and leapt onto the fence, pulling himself over and jumping down to the back yard next to them without another word.

"Son of a..." Wolfe growled out and leapt over as well, stumbling slightly on the dismount. He still hurt quite a bit, and his body wasn't responding as well as it ought to have.

Rhett ran through the yard and opened the back door. "Shannon? Lucy?" he called into the house.

No answer.

"Lucy?!" Wolfe called out as loud as he could.

Still no answer.

"Let's go," Rhett said, entering the house through a glass door and curtains in the backyard entrance.

"Should you be breaking in?" Wolfe asked as he followed.

"Exigent circumstances doctrine," Rhett muttered. "Kids might be in danger inside."

The living room was empty of people, but the box of files that everyone was looking for was on the coffee table in front of some old, sheet-covered couches in the center. The Timo file was out and open in the center.

On the page describing Shannon's mother's death at her father's hands.

"Fuck," Wolfe muttered.

Rhett picked up some of the police corruption files, glancing through them.

A knock came at the front door before he could process anything further—a small hall connected the living from to the front, and Wolfe could see the thick door from where he stood. He reached out and touched a card—an Angry Hellhound—and tossed it out before walking over to the front door as quietly as he could.

He glanced out the peephole. Shel was standing on the front, her arms wrapped around herself, nervously pacing back and forth on Ms. Timo's porch.

Wolfe opened the door, and Shel flung herself into his arms, hugging hard. After a long three seconds, she pulled back and glanced at Wolfe's blood-soaked form. "Are you okay?"

"Well enough. And you can heal me, so I'll be a lot better soon."

"Where's Lucy?"

Wolfe shook his head. "I don't know. I'm almost positive the thugs didn't get them, but I don't know where she and Shannon are at now."

"Are you two going to look for them?" Rhett asked, glancing up from the pages he was reading. Steel-colored particles also flowed back into Rhett, which Wolfe took to be Rhett dismissing his summons.

"Of course," Shel declared, and Wolfe nodded to her words.

"All right, well, even after a cursory glance, I can see these files are fairly complete. I'm going to take them back to the station, get my own chief on the line. He's a good guy—I know him personally. He'll help me to make sure that every police officer who betrayed his oaths goes to jail for a very, *very* long time."

Rhett picked up the box of files in both arms with a grunt.

Wolfe nodded to Rhett's statement, not entirely convinced after Rhett's insane display of ignorance of the corruption in Noimoire that the lieutenant was the best judge of police misconduct. But Wolfe had to admit, none of Emmett's files had shown any Joliet officer as being involved. Maybe they really were clean.

He wasn't about to gainsay Rhett at this point regardless. Wolfe no longer had the slightest doubt that Rhett was on the side of the angels.

Rhett walked out of Ms. Timo's house, and Wolfe and Shel followed.

Rhett walked down the Timos' driveway and then took the brief jaunt back to Wolfe and Shel's place. He reached the car that had belonged to 'the Surgeon' and hitched the box briefly into one arm, opened the car, and then put the box into the back seat. He straightened with a slight sigh before glancing at Wolfe.

"I'm not sure who you really are, Wolfe, but if you *were*

who I think you are, you might be inclined to seek *personal* vengeance. I would recommend against it. Let the wheels of justice work—they may be a touch slow, but they'll be certain in this case, I promise. Too many people are involved now that we know what's up, and someone will squeal. With the evidence in these files, we could probably get a conviction even without that—but someone always squeals."

Shel raised her eyes at Rhett's declaration, and then stared at Wolfe. He shook his head at her very slightly before addressing Rhett.

"I'm just gonna find Lucy and Shannon, and then sleep for three straight days," Wolfe said.

"Be sure you do." Rhett opened the front door of the vehicle.

Does that mean he isn't going to arrest me?

They watched as Rhett got into 'the Surgeon's' car and drove off, presumably heading to the Joliet Police Station.

Wolfe turned and walked back into his house. Ms. Timo was sitting on the couch now, steadier than she had been. The two dogs ran around, tails wagging now that Wolfe, Shel, and Malviere were all back.

"Lucy and Shannon are gone, but the box of files was at your house. We're pretty sure the girls stopped there, and Shannon read the Timo case files—and then they left. Do you have any idea where they might have gone?"

"Oh, no," Ms. Timo said. "I didn't want her to find out that way. I was going to tell her myself, but—"

"Ms. Timo, *please*," Wolfe said, exasperated. "The point is, she's missing. Do you know where she might have gone?"

Ms. Timo thought for a few moments. "Well... her father used to take her to the local park—it's a municipal card park, and it's always in bloom, and always spring-like. Maybe she went there?"

"Oh, Persephone Park?" Shel asked.

Wolfe had never heard of it, somehow.

Ms. Timo nodded.

"All right, we'll check it out. Hopefully, they're there."

"Please make sure Shannon is safe," Ms. Timo replied, resting her head back. "My son was already so unlucky... It would be a terrible shame for her to be lost as well."

CHAPTER 35

A FEW MORE CARDS

W olfe turned Ms. Timo's old-ass car off and stared
out at the city's card park. It was beautiful, even
in the moonlight, the fields of flowers surrounding
the various playgrounds still in bloom as if it were day.
Two marble fountains girded the formal entrance to the park,
each bearing bas-relief carvings of the various nature deities in
Greek style along the fountain's base.

As Wolfe stared at the park, its card appeared.

Modern Municipal Park
Rare Tier-1 Nature/Mortal Building

This park increases the Health of Nature, Plant, Beast, and
Life cards within it by 100%, and increases the Health of any
Mortals inside by 50%
This park increases the lifespan and disease resistance of all
Mortals within 5 miles by .1%

"A city park brings numerous benefits to a city, even without
magic. With it..."

293

Wolfe dismissed the card, noting that it was one of the rare cards that affected non-deckbearers within the Great Game. *Nice to see that not every card in the Great Game is for murdering other deckbearers.*

He opened the door, stepping out into the cool, night air. A fragrant breeze, incongruous to the dark mission Wolfe was about, blew over him.

Wolfe strode into the park, head down and shoulders squared, the gun he had taken from the dead Grimm goons in his pocket. Shel stepped nimbly after him.

Wolfe walked the park, glancing around at the various playgrounds. No kids that he could see, anywhere, probably because it was almost ten in the evening.

But he did see a few homeless dudes. He wrestled with himself, figuring it was useless, but he knew from his time in the gangs that the homeless were sometimes missed and just heard things. He took a chance on a slight delay.

He walked over to one man lying on a bench, a thick but ratty blanket on him. As Wolfe approached, a rank smell of B.O. with a chemical undertone reached him, powerful enough that it wasn't overwhelmed by the smell of flowers.

He reached out and shoved the man's shoulder. "Excuse me?"

The man snorted and looked up, blinking at Wolfe with bloodshot eyes. "Who're you?"

"Doesn't matter. I need to know something—did you see a pair of girls, about twelve, around here?"

The man nodded his head. "Yeah, I did." He glanced up at the sky. "About an hour ago, I think. Maybe."

"Where'd they go?" Wolfe asked.

"What ya gonna give me to tell ya?"

Shel stepped forward, reaching into her pocket and pulling out her wallet. She fished a twenty out and held it to the man.

"That ain't much," the man said.

"Please," Shel said, her voice raw with emotion. "One of them was my sister. I need to find her."

The man rolled his eyes but took the twenty. "Fine, whatever. They were here, sitting on the swings over there"— he pointed—"and two cops approached. I was under the playground at the time, and didn't want to be seen. Was, uh, you know..."

"Hitting your favorite pick-me-up?" Wolfe guessed.

The man nodded. "Yeah. Anyway, the two men approached and asked the girls about where their families were. One of 'em said she didn't have a family anymore."

Wolfe winced.

"Then the one cop said that the girls needed to come with him. The other girl, who had red hair, said she didn't go with strangers. But then the policeman said that his name was Anderson, and that the girls had to come with him, because they couldn't be in the park at night."

Wolfe winced again. Anderson was the one who had been beating Rhett in the back of the van. Corrupt with a capital C. He wondered how and why the cops had grabbed the girls. Was it pure coincidence? Were they really desperate to grab people to ship off since Wolfe had shut multiple shipments down?

"The girls didn't look like they wanted to go, but they got up. The second cop called someone. Said they had found the two they were ordered to get and were gonna take them to the factory."

"On his police radio?" Shel asked.

"On his cell phone," the man said.

Wolfe glanced over at Shel. Her eyes were wide and her lip trembling.

"That's the place Damian is, where they process the people they ship away, right?" she whispered.

Wolfe gave a single nod, his insides cold. He felt still, in a moment that presaged violence, despite no one being around to attack.

"Thank you," Wolfe ground out as he stepped away from the man.

Once they were out of earshot of the homeless guy, Shel turned to Wolfe. "What now? We have to rescue her."

Or avenge her, Wolfe thought to himself but didn't say.

"First, we fix our decks and I make level twenty-five. While you were partying, Rhett and I were attacked by corrupt cops and then members of the Grimm family. Downside is I'm wounded, upside is we got some more cards—including a fantastic one for you."

"One of them was a Divine deckbearer?" Shel asked, surprised.

"No." Wolfe barked out a single mirthless laugh. "It was weirder than that. Rhett gave it to me for saving his life."

Shel gave a small smile, although she was twisting her fingers in her hair. "So, are you guys friends now, then? I heard him call you by your name. Your real name."

"I have no idea. He started the whole situation by trying to arrest me, and then said he's still going to arrest me, but he's obviously taking his sweet-ass time about it. We'll see."

Shel bit her lip as she mulled that over, then changed the subject. "So what card did he give you?"

Wolfe held out Liurenia.

Shel stared at it for a good ten seconds before she spoke. "He never once mentioned that he had one of the Lantern Angel cards."

"It was given to him very recently, I think, since he got it from his dad."

"Spending those leveling pips now," Shel said with vacant eyes, then refocused on Wolfe. "Done."

She took the companion card in trembling fingers. A

quick touch of her chest, pulling her deck, and suddenly she held a Vengeful Orphan card, and she had *two* golden cards off to the side—both the companions.

"That'll make me *wayyy* stronger for the fight, if we have one," Shel murmured. "I'll put the orphan back in once we've resolved everything."

She glanced at Wolfe. "What did you get? Is your deck stronger?"

"I haven't checked yet, and a lot will depend on my perks when I make level twenty-five."

"Check now—we have to hurry."

Wolfe pulled the cards he had out—twenty-five new ones, ten that were his half of the Surgeon's cards, and fifteen that had been Castor's.

Wolfe pulled the ten cards that was his share of the Surgeon's deck first, wondering what kind of nefarious deck he would have had.

Wolfe was astounded to see that the first card was a Nature card, a faerie specifically.

Unseelie Court Attendant
Uncommon Tier-1 Nature [Faerie] Creature
1 Nature and 1 Psychic Power
Health: 10
Attack: 0
Magical Attack: 8
Defense: 4
Magical Defense: 8

Special: **Unseelie Attendant:** Higher-rarity Faerie cards gain +2 stats when this card is in play

Special: **Power Sink [Any 1]:** When this card comes into play, pick any Power type. Cards of that faction cost 1 more power to play.

"They may play by the rules of the court, but even the servants know how to bend those rules to their will."

"That's a nasty card," Shel muttered. "But it means this deck likely doesn't have anything too crazy good for you in it."

Wolfe snorted, agreeing. He quickly moved through the deck, seeing a Faerie Whisper-stealer that prevented non-creature cards from coming into play, and a Faerie Scion *legendary* that had very high magical attack stats and could add temporary rules to a battlefield that had to be obeyed at risk of Psychic damage. It was likely to sell for a ton but wasn't useful to Wolfe in the moment. *This surgeon had some badass cards.*

But then he reached a different card, a beast one.

Dark Owl

Rare Tier-1 Beast/Nature Creature [Bird]
1 Beast Power
Health: 4
Attack: 2
Magical Attack: 2
Defense: 7
Magical Defense: 7

Special: **Shake it Off:** Any attack must either kill the owl outright or it takes zero damage.
Special: **Rebound All [Faerie]:** So long as the owl is on the field, any faerie that dies becomes immediately available for recast for the remainder of the fight, as if a companion.

A bit more hopeful, Wolfe turned the next card and saw another Beast one.

Litter

Uncommon Tier-1 Beast Persistent
3 Beast or 3 Nature or 3 Life Power

This card will create 3 token copies of any 1 or 2-power creature of the Beast, Nature, or Life type that already had two cards on the field. The power used remains spent until all copies are destroyed.

"The Beast faction is considered weak by many, but quantity can have a quality all of its own."

Wolfe could imagine the monster creature that this would create if two of the Unseelie Attendants were on the field with that crazy-powerful Fae Scion. He shuddered. Either Rhett was way stronger than Wolfe had originally figured, or he'd gotten fairly lucky in his fight—or perhaps having all of Wolfe's doggos as well had been too overwhelming for the Surgeon.

But this was a card he could use—if he could put it somewhere. Wolfe could easily put more than two Angry Hellhounds or Lost Hellhounds on the field, and it would benefit him greatly—although the three-power cost was steep.

And he would need to clear a space in his deck.

"Maybe merge three of your Tier-three Angry Hellhounds?" Shel asked. "I mean, at Tier-four, you get the first merge special—it's slightly different for each deckbearer, depending on their decks and powers. If your Tier-one, three-power card—the Litter card—made three Tier-four, two-power cards, that would be a huge net for you."

Wolfe gave it some thought. Having a ton of hellhounds out and synergizing was his signature, but he could sell most of the cards he had to buy a ton more, as they were extremely cheap. For now, merging three Tier-threes into a Tier-four was almost certainly the right move.

He knelt on the ground and removed the necessary hellhounds, glancing at them.

Angry Hellhound

Common Tier-3 Beast/Infernal(Canine) Creature
Two Beast or Infernal Power
Health: 13
Attack: 8
Defense: 5
Magical Attack: 5[**Fire or Infernal**]
Magical Defense: 5

Special: **Dual Attacker:** When this creature makes a physical attack, it also makes a Magical Attack on the same target.
Special: **Empty Mind:** Immune to all mind-affecting debuffs.
Special: **Canine Tribal [1]:** +1 to all attacks for every other canine on the field.
Special: **Hunter [Escaped Damned 1]:** Gains +1 Attack for every Escaped Damned on the field.

"It could be argued that most things in the Infernal realms are angry, but these hellhounds take it to an entirely new level—and this one has torn many a spirit to the point it needs to reform on many an occasion."

Then he pressed them together and willed them to merge.

Angry Hellhound

Common Tier-4 Beast/Infernal (Canine) Creature
Two Beast or Infernal Power
Health: 14
Attack: 9
Defense: 5
Magical Attack: 5 [**Fire or Infernal**]

Magical Defense: 5

Special: **Dual Attacker:** When this creature makes a physical attack, it also makes a Magical Attack on the same target.
Special: **Empty Mind:** Immune to all mind-affecting debuffs.
Special: **Canine Tribal [1]:** +1 to all attacks for every other canine on the field.
Special: **Hunter [Escaped Damned 1]:** Gains +1 Attack for every Escaped Damned on the field.
Special: **Reformed Doggo:** This card gains type advantage, and loses type disadvantage, against any Infernal, Undead, or Elder card, and any card with the word 'criminal' or 'villain' in its title or type.

"It could be argued that most things in the Infernal realms are angry, but these hellhounds take it to an entirely new level— and this one has torn many a spirit to the point it needs to reform on many an occasion."

"That tracks," Wolfe muttered. He added the 'Litter' card to his deck as well.

Shel briefly kissed Wolfe on the cheek. "Well, it'll almost certainly help us immensely with what's to come. Now see if you got anything in Castor's deck."

Wolfe flipped through Castor's deck next. It was Elemental/Infernal. *Four* of the cards were the stupid fish hook demons. The next three were Third Degree Elemental, which created an Elemental that did Fire damage and could inflict pain—causing a round loss. Two were cards that simply inflicted pain directly on a deckbearer or creature. The real key to the deck came from the next five cards. Three were Flayer Demons. They could also inflict the Pain status, but they got stronger each time any creature on the field suffered pain. Then one was a rare persistent card called 'Post Traumatic

Stress Disorder' that caused the pain status to repeat, and the last was a mantle that gave the user strength from every pain status inflicted as well. All were moderately low in power cost, relying on the pain synergy to achieve the desired effects.

"How was this not the Surgeon's deck?" Wolfe muttered.

"The Surgeon?" Shel asked.

Wolfe waved her off before putting the cards away. Some were nice, but they didn't synergize with his deck. Still, the fourteen cards would probably go for near a million, and he still needed land to place his orphanage on.

Without much hope, Wolfe flipped over the last card.

His eyes nearly popped out of his head.

Hellfire

Unique rare equivalent, Tier-5 equivalent Infernal persistent (equipment)

2 Infernal Power

+3 Attack to the deckbearer or card equipped with this item.

Special: **Paired [Brimstone]:** This card may be equipped with the equipment card 'Hellfire.' They empower each other, adding both totals to their wielder's attack stat.

Special: **Neutral Attack**: This equipment ignores ALL type resistances or immunities.

Special: **Injurious:** Causes damage that is immediately considered injuries for healing purposes.

Special: This card is part of the 'Banisher' card set. If both cards are gained, they will create a single rare pack of Infernal cards and give the deckbearer who possesses both 1 additional pip of Infernal power. Both cards were initially sent to members of the Noimoire underworld who are considered assassins.

"The Infernal use weapons of all sorts during both their internal wars, and their wars against other factions. This weapon started its life as a gift from Aesthma to his favorite assassin in hell and has worked its way into the mortal realm since then."

"That's... That's the other half of your set, Wolfe. You have both, right?"

Wolfe nodded, his own eyes wide. A free Infernal power was huge, as was having an equipment card that added *six* attack.

"Take it," Shel whispered.

Wolfe switched out a single Pack Howl, and as soon as the card entered, a massive feeling of power and sense of completion washed over him. A sulfurous burst of fire popped in front of him, and Wolfe held his hand out.

A rare card pack, titled "Cycle of the Lost and the Lonely I" dropped into his hand. The picture of a small, demonic child in ratty clothes with a tail and horns, running from police through a modern-day alley, was on the cover.

"Open it," Shel whispered.

CHAPTER 36

...AND A FEW MORE LEVELS

Wolfe hesitated. "Do you think it's better to take perks, on the off chance I can improve the cards first? Or should I instead open the pack and see if any card I get might drive my decision on which perk I take?"

"Just check," Shel said. "But don't make a choice unless you have a pull-modifying perk. If you don't have a pull perk, you can open the cards and return to your status after." She grinned. "I can't wait to see what perks the system offers you for how you've played the Great Game so far."

Wolfe pulled his status sheet up but didn't pay much attention to it, instead going to perk selection, next to his name where 'free leveling pips' were listed.

He was presented with a new notification chart, containing six new options for perks.

Alpha Wolf: The deckbearer counts as a Beast [Canine] tribal himself and may have one additional card on the field so long as it is a Beast [Canine] tribal.

Lone Wolf: So long as no creatures are on the field, the deckbearer gains 2 to all stats except Health.

Stray Street: Lose 1 Fire Power, Gain 1 Mortal Power. Bonuses to Mortal [Criminal] cards will benefit Beast [Canine] cards, and vice-versa as well. May have up to one additional Minion card at all times so long as it is an [Orphan]. May have up to one additional Building card at all times so long as it is Mortal [Criminal] type or has 'criminal' in the title. Gain the Stray Street rare building card.

Bane [Infernal]: The deckbearer and all creature cards gain advantage against Infernal and lose any disadvantage. This stacks with anything already possessing advantage or other bonuses against type.

Master of the Lost and the Lonely: Orphans gain +1 Tier when they switch over, and any card packs or non-orphan cards gained from orphan advancement are gained twice. Any one [evolved orphan] card of no more than 2 power may be treated as if it were a free-slot companion card with a 0-power cost.

Fire's Temptation: Gain 3 Legendary Fire card packs immediately, and the first non-creature fire card used each time a deck is pulled does not count against card plays.

Wolfe stared at his screen for a moment. *That is six legitimately good abilities.*

"What did you get?" Shel asked.

Wolfe gave her a quick rundown.

She smiled. "Now *I* can't wait to get to level twenty-five. Damn, those are good—each is a serious power boost."

"Do champions have *four* additional perks?" Wolfe asked.

Shel nodded. "New perks are gained every twenty-five

levels, supposedly based on your style in the Great Game for the previous twenty-five levels."

Shel smiled slightly. "So... you got offered a temptation perk because you've *never* used fire cards?"

Wolfe chuckled darkly. "Probably, yeah. Although the Fireborn Hellhound requires Fire power... It's actually right— it's tempting. That is an *amazing* ability, which would give insane card advantage. But I would have to nearly rebuild my deck to get it—and I have multiple set cards that won't synergize at all, many of which are really good, like the Hellmouth Institute and Malviere, and of course Cereboo."

"Well, the perk is further proof this cycle was power crept, as if companion cards, sets, and orphans weren't proof enough already. I wonder if the gods are working toward anything..."

"Why is it proof this cycle was power crept?" Wolfe asked.

"Because people have not used a type in their deck before and yet have never received a perk option like that." Shel pursed her lips. "As to the perk itself, you'll get three legendary fire packs. That probably means you'll actually get three fire legendary cards. Which would most likely make your deck rather epic, especially with a free cast of a non-creature spell. You tend toward an 'early overwhelm' or 'aggro' style, anyway."

Wolfe nodded consideringly. "You think that's best, then?"

She paused and glanced around the dark park. "Normally, I'd want to weigh every decision and think about it for days, but perhaps you should just open the deck and see what you have first, since you didn't get the option for a card-pulling perk."

"I think you should open it, Shel. *Two* of my six options are for orphan cards—and even though there are common and uncommon orphan cards, they're a lot harder to come by. How often did cards become orphan cards normally?"

Shel held her hand out. "I think I remember any given

card in this set having a two-point-five percent chance of becoming an orphan card. So even a common orphan card is fairly rare."

Wolfe passed the pack over, and Shel tore it open, shook the six cards into her hand, and then passed them without looking to Wolfe.

Two Escaped Damned made up the commons, and Wolfe frowned. Once upon a time, that would have excited him, but at the moment, he had purged them from his deck, despite their synergy with his Angry Hellhounds.

Wolfe had three uncommon cards. First was an Enraged Imp, a one-power imp glass cannon, which he reminded himself to sell to Derek.

The second was, in fact, an *orphan* card, which Wolfe would have bet Infernal packs wouldn't have. But Shel's card trumped, he supposed. Shel and Wolfe stared at it.

Desperate Cult Child

Uncommon, no-tier Mortal minion [orphan, criminal]

0 Power

Health: 7

Attack: N/A

Defense: 5

Magical Attack: N/A

Magical Defense: 3

Special: Will fetch normal objects and such with a decent degree of precision and help carry up to ten pounds.
Special: **Orphan Evolution [Unique]:** If kept 'alive' for five straight years, will turn into a rare, Mortal/Infernal, 1-power-available, Tier-4 creature card called 'Obsessive Infernal Cultist.'
Special: **Ritual Sacrifice [Infernal]:** If in play as a minion, may be sacrificed for 2 Infernal Power that lasts for 30 minutes

"This young girl was abandoned by an abusive family before her fifth birthday and has been raised in a street cult ever since. She has dedicated herself to its every rite since, hoping to find approval from someone—or some*thing*."

Wolfe stared at it, his mind whirling with ideas.

But the first thing that popped out of his mouth was, "Not that all your pulling specialties haven't been amazing, but I can't wait till it makes a rare card into a legendary or turns it into a rare orphan or something."

Shel nodded absently to his words. "These orphan cards are really sad. I mean, I know it's the Great Game and probably not real, but that one hits hard. Especially with my sister lost."

Wolfe rubbed her back. "Yeah, sorry. Don't worry—as soon as I finish increasing my power, we'll rescue her. I just want to be sure we don't die because I forgot to level and deck adjust."

Shel shuddered. "No, I agree. But just check the next card, please."

Wolfe flipped it over. His third uncommon card was named Demonic Portal. It cost one Infernal and five any power. It created of a side deck and added five Infernal creature card 'slots' to any side deck. When the card was played, it allowed any number of creatures, up to five power worth, in any combination, to be quickly summoned.

"That could play well with your deck," Shel murmured beside Wolfe.

Wolfe quirked an eyebrow. "It's a chump move, spending six power for five power of creatures."

Shel kissed his cheek. "In a swarm deck like yours, it could put three to five creatures on the field quickly. Since they'd get all their stacking benefits, it could be worth it. Additionally, you could put some oddball creatures in there for, well, odd situations."

"Hmm... I'll think about it. I don't like total reduction in power. But maybe."

"You *did* just gain a permanent power, so long as Hellfire and Brimstone are in your deck."

Wolfe slowly nodded, but rather than answering, he flipped over the last card—the rare, although it might have gone up to legendary or down to uncommon.

It had remained a rare, which was briefly disappointing to Wolfe.

Deal with the Devil
Rare Tier-1 Infernal Persistent
3 Infernal Power

So long as the deckbearer has any Infernal Creature on the field, he may assign control of any one non-Infernal creature controlled by any deckbearer to any other deckbearer. When the card leaves the control of its original deckbearer, it may take an attack against that deckbearer or their card, obeying normal rules as if it were an enemy card, before it switches. This card's power remains spent so long as the creature is on the field.

"In the abstract, evil should be defeated quickly, as most want to be on the side of good. But there are *always* individuals who will betray the whole for their own benefit, and the Infernal is always there, whispering in their ears."

"This is an Infernal version of your Barter the Soul card," Wolfe said.

"Thanks, I'd missed that," Shel muttered, kissing Wolfe's

cheek a second time, probably to take the sting from her gentle mockery.

Wolfe was briefly embarrassed but was too concerned with the new card for it to last long. "It's notably pricier but is considerably more versatile and doesn't require a sacrifice—and could really switch a fight. But it would take a beefy chunk of my power and it doesn't synergize with the rest of my deck. What do you think overall?"

Shel considered, staring out into the dark park. "Well... As to the cards, I'd recommend putting your spare Angry Hellhounds into a side deck and putting Demonic Portal in, as well as adding the Deal with the Devil card. Since we're rescuing my sister, I'd normally advise taking the ones that gave personal power... but since you have Malviere *and* the Hellmouth Institute as improved, rare cards, I think you might be better off taking one of the two orphan cards."

Shel's face went briefly fierce. "And you have *a lot* of cleanup to make sure things like this quit happening to people like my sister and brother. You should be as strong as possible."

Wolfe slowly nodded. "I agree... absent the tempting switch to actually use Fire, I think the most power I can get is likely with the orphans. But which one? I mean, both sound amazing—one gives me an extra building slot and a free orphan card, which is at least six levels, more if I add other specialty cards, and bonus synergy."

"Not to mention a rare building card," Shel said, pulling out her phone and typing into a search bar, perhaps to check on the stats of the building.

Wolfe nodded. "And the second gives a permanent tier to any orphan cards, which are already very high tier, and also gives me a *third* free companion slot, which is insane in converted levels."

Shel nodded to his words.

"I'm honestly torn, Shel. I don't normally hesitate on shit like this, but... Which one do you think I should take?"

CHAPTER 37

READY AND ONWARD

Shel gave it brief thought, still looking out at the nighttime park, before responding. "As much as Stray Street sounds amazing, I think you should take Master of the Lonely and the Lost. Another free companion card would be nearly impossible to beat, I think, even more than a free building slot. Each Companion card slot is sort of two free power."

Wolfe nodded along with her words, and when she'd finished, he took the perk she recommended.

Before he could do more, Shel chimed in again. "You can always take Stray Street at level fifty."

Wolfe snorted at the idea he would live that long and pulled his status chart up.

"What else should I take? I have five pips left."

"I think you should take an enhancer card slot and take the 'Caretaker of the Lost' card."

"Your card?" Wolfe asked. "It's Mortal."

"It's a zero-cost card. It doesn't matter what type it is. And your orphans will be gaining *three tiers* when they advance, which will make them *way* stronger for their power cost, as if they weren't already. Not to mention the static improvements to any given orphan."

"I suppose I'll want some actual minion card slots for more orphan cards as well, then," Wolfe said. "I'll add another of those, leaving me with two pips."

"Save for a building slot next—we'll try to find an orphan-improving one. If we can attach that to the Hellmouth Institute and get them both settled, your orphan cards will be insanely good."

"I'll also need cards in hand and deck size, and I'll soon need another card in play," Wolfe groused. "These leveling pips spend fast."

Wolfe made the changes and checked his status sheet.

Ethan Madison Wolfe Status:
Level 25 Mortal [2 pips remaining]

Deckbearer Perks:
Deckbearer Perk 1: In the Thick of it: +50% to all numerical benefits gained from mantles
Deckbearer Perk 2: Man's Best Friend's Best Friend: Gain 1 Beast Power. May have one extra card in play so long as it's a Beast (Canine or Hybrid Canine).
Level 25 perk: Master of the Lost and the Lonely: Orphans gain +1 Tier when they evolve, and any card packs or non-orphan cards gained from orphan advancement are gained twice. Any one [evolved orphan] card of no more than 2 power may be treated as if it were a free-slot companion card with a 0-power cost.
Deckbearer Flaw: Fallen: May not gain Divine Power,

nor use Divine cards unless they are also Infernal or Corrupted.

Deckbearer Stats:
Cards in Deck: 15 (1 pip)
Cards in Hand: 4 (1 pip)
Cards in Play: 3 (1 pip)
Length of Play: 5 minutes
Specialty Cards: Companion: 1
Minion: 2 (3 pips)
Total Power: (upgraded 5 times): 8 -1 (Infernal Rift) +1 (Infernal Gun set) = 8. (Total pips 15)
Type 1 and Power: 5 Infernal (5 -1 (Infernal Rift) +1 (Infernal Guns))
Type 2 and Power: 2 Beast
Energy 1 and Power: 1 Fire

Personal Perks:
Inborn Perk 1: Vicious Killer: +25% to all Attack and Defense, check twice for Attack modifier and take the best
Inborn Perk 2: Tough as Nails: +10 Health
Acquired Perk 1: Crafty Street Fighter: +3 Attack and Defense

Personal Stats:
Health: 25/30
Attack: 10
Magical Attack [None]: 0
Defense: 10
Magical Defense [None]: 5

"I think I'll hold off adding the orphan cards for the moment," Wolfe mused. "Everything got reset for both of us.

I'll leave Malviere in, as she can empower my deck as she is, but for everything else, I'll add it once we rescue your sister."

Shel nodded.

Wolfe did some last alterations to his deck, coming up with his final deck for the rescue operation.

He kept Cereboo and Malviere, his companion cards. He kept Infernal Rift and Cerberus's Home for Wayward Hellhounds. He kept both Hellfire and Brimstone, the set guns. He kept his Tier-four and Tier-three Angry Hellhounds as well as one of the two Tier-one Lost Hellhound puppies and his Litter card so that he could generate a fair number of stacking Infernal doggo benefits. He added the Demonic Portal and put his remaining two Tier-three Angry Hellhounds and a Lost Hellhound Puppy in the side deck— he didn't have anything to go in the two spare slots, really. He kept his Fireborn Hellhound as his big hitter. He kept his Soul Hunter mantle. He added the Desperate Cult Child. And finally, he switched his Pack Howl for the Deal with the Devil.

He kept both Pack Howls and the Desperate Cult Child card, to add to Hellmouth Institute and the Caretaker of the Lost card when the time came to focus his deck on making truly strong evolved orphans.

He gave everything else to Shel. "Sell it and add the profit to our cash stash—we're going to need to buy a bigger place for the Hellmouth Institute."

She nodded.

"Ready to save your sister?"

"Of course."

Thirty minutes later, with their car parked a fair distance away, Wolfe and Shel crouched in some bushes and stared across the small patch of grass at the giant, abandoned cannery that was Damian's new lair.

If Miriam and her spies were correct.

"That's a *huge* facility," Shel said.

She was dressed in dark-gray sweatpants and hoodie, almost black but not quite, and the hood was up, hiding her red hair. She had wanted an all-black outfit, but Wolfe had convinced her that it was a touch easier to see in dim light, usually.

At her waist, a belt and holster held her Glock-19.

Wolfe was dressed almost identically, although multiple sizes larger, and he carried a chest holster with, finally, his STI Edge. He would quite possibly try to use Brimstone or Hellfire if the situation called for it, but since his Edge was 0-power cost and didn't take a card play, it would be better in most situations where he would take a pistol in the first place.

His belt carried a large knife in it, something absent from Shel's ensemble.

Both of them had multiple magazines in their deep pants pockets—hardly safe, but it would work for what they were doing.

The giant canning plant Shel was staring at had multiple warehouses near it, and the entire complex sat on what had to have been at least a dozen acres. A huge parking lot led from the street to a central point, with the cannery immediately off the side, and the warehouses forming a huge complex in the back, the closest one flush against the cannery on the side farthest from the street. The complex had a couple of the same style vans Wolfe had seen at both the kidnapping sites, but a lone van was in the smaller parking lot next to the entrance to the cannery as well.

It was nighttime, but there were a decent number of lights about the facility, and Wolfe saw a couple of people walking the place in security guard uniforms.

He would have bet his Cereboo card that at least some of them were Grimm family retainers in disguise. He'd be surprised if it wasn't all of them, in fact.

This is gonna be a whole thing. Fuck.

"Where do you think Lucy and Shannon are?" Shel asked. "The warehouses where the vans are?"

Wolfe glanced at the warehouses, then back at the cannery. "They're in the cannery, I'd bet. The warehouses don't have lights on inside that I can see, but the cannery does. And a single van is waiting there."

"How do we get there?"

"Wait for the idiots walking the place to pass, then sprint for the side nearest the road. Try to find someone with keys, or an unguarded way in. Basic shit."

"Raiding a mob site in the middle of the night outnumbered some ungodly amount to two is basic shit, huh?" Shel muttered.

Wolfe didn't answer, instead focusing on keeping track of the movements of the guards. The security thugs were actually fairly inconsistent and wildly spaced, and an opportunity almost immediately presented itself.

"Let's go," Wolfe said, low and intense.

The two of them leapt from the cover of the bushes. They ran across the couple hundred feet of grass and trees that separated the side of the cannery from the road, moving from tree to tree. Soon, they found themselves in an interior line of ornamental rocks with occasional bushes up against the outside of the cannery.

Wolfe glanced around the side of the cannery at the front door. No one was there. Wolfe rushed around the side and grabbed the front door. It was locked.

Wolfe wasn't surprised.

He went back around the side to Shel.

"No go?" she asked.

"We're going to have to ambush someone and get the key," Wolfe said.

Shel nodded, her face set.

"I'll handle the guard."

"It never crossed my mind we'd do it differently."

Wolfe went until he found a place where the building's exterior wall had an interior corner with a bush in the little rock garden.

Then he waited for a guard to pass by on the walkway around the facility.

About five minutes of crouching in the bush later, a ripped twenty-year-old with a bald head, beard, and face tattoos came ambling around the corner. He was smoking and had headphones in.

Wolfe chuckled to himself. *If this fucker was fat, he'd be the perfect target—but as is, he's not far out from it.*

Wolfe waited a few more seconds for the man to pass his hiding spot, then quickly ran to the corner, peeking back around it to see if anyone was following the smoking thug. No one was.

Wolfe pulled out his knife and rushed up from behind the thug and kicked him in the back of the knee. The thug cried out, "Fuck!" and hit the ground on one knee, but Wolfe kicked him in the back. The man hit the ground, his face bouncing on the concrete walkway, blood spurting from his nose. Wolfe dropped on top of him, landing with his knees to either side of the facedown man, his knife pressed to the side of the man's cheek where he could see the blade.

"Don't move, numbnuts," Wolfe hissed.

The man complied.

Wolfe carefully removed the headphones, surprised when pop music came out as opposed to death metal or phonk or something equally apropos to the appearance of the tattooed man.

"What'd ya want?" the man asked, fear in his voice.

"One sec," Wolfe replied, patting the man down. He extracted a Desert Eagle—*what is it with street thugs and their oversized hand cannons?*—a container of pepper spray, a Taser, and multiple zip ties.

Wolfe almost asked him why he had all the gear for restraining people but then stopped. *Of course. He's guarding to keep the merchandise—people down on their luck—from escaping as much as to keep people from getting in.*

He also had a keyring, which was what Wolfe really wanted.

And he supposed the thug's gear made the next step easy.

"I'm gonna tie you and gag you. If you try to stop me, or shout for help, or anything like that, I'm gonna stab you to death instead. Got it?"

The man nodded, although Wolfe was starting to get a stench from him. It smelled like *scared and angry young man.*

Being extra careful not to give the thug a chance to act on his growing anger, Wolfe slowly started to zip-tie him. Shel joined him, making the process far easier.

Then Wolfe cut part of the man's shirt free, fashioning a gag.

"Oof. I'd hate to have this man's B.O. in my mouth," Wolfe muttered as he tied it tightly.

"'Uck 'ou," the thug said, and Wolfe chuckled, even in the tense situation.

Wolfe grabbed the man and hoisted him into an awkward fireman's carry, then took him and stashed him in the bushes at the end of the road, praying to whatever deity of whatever faction would listen that the scumbag would be held and undiscovered for at least ten to twenty minutes.

He returned to Shel, huffing and puffing, and took stock of himself.

He was still wounded, even after all of Rhett's and Shel's

healing, but basically okay. He was at twenty-five of thirty health but retained a one-point penalty to non-health stats from his injuries.

His deck was as optimized for as many situations as he could make it.

He took a deep breath, held the keyring up, and stared at the front door to the cannery.

Damian was inside, as well as any new lieutenants he had acquired, with his *very* expensive deck. Quite possibly also people from Worldwide Decurion. And who knew how many thugs with guns.

But so was Shel's sister, Lucy, and her friend Shannon.

"Let's do this."

CHAPTER 38

FOUND FAMILY

The door creaked open. Wolfe wasn't sure what he had been expecting, but it wasn't a modern office with a dusty but otherwise pristine tile floor and two reception desks—although there were a ton of footprints leading to a door in the back of the office. The outside had felt a bit more... thuggish, Wolfe supposed.

There was a computer on one of the desks.

Shel walked to the computer and flipped it on, but after a few seconds of banging at the keys, shook her head. "I tried the most common passwords, but none worked, so we're on our own."

"Always are," Wolfe said.

He walked across the floor and opened the door. It led into a hall with a few more doors into respectable offices, although again covered in dust. But the path that had been cleared of the most dust went forward, hit a four-way intersection, and then curved left, away from the center of the factory and back toward the outside wall.

Wolfe followed the footprints slowly until he reached a door that just read, 'Stairwell.'

He opened it into a dimly lit, unadorned concrete stairwell heading down. "This is more of the vibe I was expecting. A sort of modern homage to thugs and horror movies."

Shel giggled nervously.

Wolfe took the steps down until he reached the basement, then exited into an equally dimly lit hallway with concrete floors heading right and left. Wolfe could vaguely make out both connecting hallways and doors.

A lot of them.

"I wouldn't normally advocate splitting the party, as the kids say, but we're on a time limit here. You okay to search for your sister right while I take left?"

Shel nodded, her pupils slightly dilated, but her jaw firmly set.

Wolfe held his knife out. "All right. Take this. Try not to shoot someone or pull your deck if you can help it, although obviously, your safety is what's most important. But either action will put the whole place on alert."

Shel took the knife, nodded once, and headed away from him down the hall.

Wolfe drew his gun—he wasn't sure what he would run into, and as he had told Shel, he'd really rather not fire it. That said, he wasn't dumb enough to walk through Damian's lair unarmed.

He took a couple of hallways, peeked inside the mostly open doors, and passed by more hallways. The place was a maze. Wolfe turned a third corner in the same hallway.

A sudden loud bang—metal on metal, not a gunshot—echoed through the building. Adrenaline dumped into Wolfe's system, and he held his breath and tried to convince his heart to climb back out of his throat.

The bang didn't repeat, but the sound of men laughing replaced it.

"Another, another!" someone yelled.

A doorway ahead of Wolfe erupted with cheering. Wolfe wasn't sure if they were playing a game or what, but he was glad they were occupied.

The door opened, throwing light into the dim hallway. Wolfe quickly stepped back around the corner of the four-way intersection, keeping one eye out.

A man staggered out of the door. "Just play without me. I'm gonna go check the merchandise, see if they're almost ready. Boss wants to move soon. Besides, I'm down too damn much money already."

The thug was wearing a reinforced jacket and jeans, and he staggered in Wolfe's direction. Wolfe leaned back, reversing his grip on the gun to use as an improvised club if needed.

But the thug turned the other way, walking within a few feet of Wolfe without seeing him.

Wolfe sent a half-meant prayer Cerberus's way, then followed after the thug as quietly as possible. The man walked slow, his gait ungainly, staggering as he went, but Wolfe still gave him a fair amount of space.

The man never turned around and never seemed to notice Wolfe. He walked down a side hall, then took a turn and went to another door.

He banged on the door. "Finish up! Boss called down, said they'll be ready to move in thirty minutes, and we need the last two handled quick!"

Wolfe fell back again and hid around the corner of a different hall as the man stumbled back. He continued past Wolfe again, heading back toward whatever-the-Infernal game they had been playing.

Wolfe was half-tempted to end the trafficking asshole now but restrained himself. It would only subject him to risk, not take out anyone who actually needed to die. 'Drunk Thug' would be handled by the police or a different thug.

Instead, he turned and walked back to the room the thug

had banged on. He would bet money that Lucy was there. There were three other doors in the same segment of hallway, and Wolfe could hear activity from some of them.

He would need to be quiet.

Wolfe opened the door, but the room he entered didn't have anyone in it at first glance. It had a medical table heaped with something, some desks, a couple of chairs, and too many bundles of medical equipment to count. Plus a computer haphazardly placed on the very edge of a counter and numerous IV bags on stands. A ton of those.

Also, a door in the back that was closed.

Wolfe realized the bundle on the medical table wasn't bundles—it was a body, hooked up to the computer and an IV bag. Some dude, probably about eighteen, fully naked.

The computer screen was so old, it was a solid square. There was a vitals display on it. The little blips kept going up and down and weren't a flat line, so Wolfe assumed the man was okay. Or at least not dead.

He was glad he didn't have to take a pulse—he might have been old-fashioned, but he didn't want to be touching a naked man.

There were a couple of sheets of paper on a clipboard next to the man. Wolfe grabbed them—they might have been evidence of something that could get Worldwide Decurion in trouble.

The door to the back opened as Wolfe was engaged in his examination. He grabbed the heavy computer screen off the counter and yanked the cord out, and then, as a man walked into the room, slammed the whole-ass monitor against the guy's head.

The dude's face exploded, teeth and blood flying, and he slammed back onto the ground with a mangled grunt. Someone inside let out a very girlish yell. The damage notification from Wolfe's attack didn't say anything about dead or knocked out, and so Wolfe stepped up and kicked the man in his head as hard as he could.

The man stopped moving. Permanently, according to the damage charts.

Fuck. Pretty sure I won't get in trouble for this, but not sure how Shel will feel about it.

Wolfe pushed it aside. It was an issue for later. He stepped into the next room, which was very dimly lit.

"Get back!"

Wolfe stopped, surprised by the command. He lifted his gun but then stopped, surprised by what he saw.

Thank you, Cerberus, or whichever god has my back.

Lucy and Shannon were in the back. Lucy stood farthest forward, a medical syringe held in her hand like a knife in a slasher movie. Lucy wore a white men's T-shirt, which was long enough to act as a dress and barely that, but nothing else at all—even her feet were bare on the concrete floor of the room. No shoes, no socks. She was glaring at Wolfe with a look a honey badger might give a lion that had come for it—the lion might win, but it would be a whole thing.

Shannon, however, was huddled behind her, legs drawn up in front of her and her hair over her face, which in turn rested on her arms, which were crossed on her knees. She too only had a men's T-shirt on.

"I said, *get back!*" Lucy thrust the syringe forward, even though she was a good fifteen feet away, her finger on the plunger.

Does she not recognize me? Wolfe stepped into the light, lowering his weapon.

"Kid, keep quiet."

For once, Lucy didn't object to improper naming. "Wolfe? Is that you? Really?"

"Shh."

Wolfe walked over to Lucy. She fiddled with her long, red hair, hesitating, then suddenly handed over the syringe. Wolfe put it in the front pocket of his hoodie, hoping he wouldn't accidentally stab himself.

Then Lucy threw her arms around Wolfe, hugging him tightly.

She's never really liked me before. I guess everyone likes me when I use my one skill for their benefit. Hell, I don't think she's so much as shaken my hand before.

Wolfe couldn't deny he was happy about the change of heart, though.

Wolfe still hurt a bit, from injury and lesser damage both, but he didn't have the heart to push Lucy away.

Lucy finally let go and stepped back, her face more guarded and her eyes watering.

"Are you hurt?" Wolfe asked. Then he glanced over at Shannon. "Can you both walk?"

Wolfe wasn't sure what to ask, or say. He would hunt whoever had hurt them, but he didn't know how much they had been hurt, or what to do about it... and him killing bad people was a proscriptive measure—it prevented future harm; it didn't fix the ones who had already been hurt.

Lucy grabbed Wolfe's hoodie, her voice high and fast. "There were police officers. They forced us into their car. They took us here, all the way from Joliet. They wouldn't talk to us. I thought we were in trouble."

Lucy spoke quickly, taking short, sharp breaths between sentences. Wolfe was nervous, as they were very much on a timetable, but he didn't want to stop her from getting it out. *Just one minute more.*

"They said we had to wait here," Lucy continued. "And then other people came to see us. They had guns. They told us to take off our clothes. I told them 'no.' Shannon did too. But they didn't listen. They had guns. We didn't want to. We told them 'no.'"

"I understand."

"We didn't want to," Lucy repeated, staring up at Wolfe with glassy eyes.

A whole lot of motherfuckers are going to die. "I believe you," Wolfe said, trying to keep the rage from his voice.

"Shannon cried, and one man... He gave us shirts. A different man asked us questions. He had a needle. He took our blood." Lucy was now speaking in a monotone voice, as if she were reporting facts, and not something that had happened to her.

Wolfe grit his teeth. At least one of the assholes had possessed a tiny shred of humanity. When a little girl had cried, he had handed over shirts.

When Big Man Grimm had been in charge, stuff like this had never happened. Deputy Chief Charleston might think all criminals were the same, but they really weren't. Innocents had never suffered when Big Man Grimm had been in charge, not like this. No children, no one who hadn't voluntarily lived the life.

Wolfe knew the Grimm family had taken a huge dive when he found himself thanking some random, nameless thug for giving kids shirts.

"They didn't hurt you?" Wolfe asked.

Lucy held out her arm, showing Wolfe the inside of her elbow. "Just this. They didn't do anything else."

Thank the Divine.

Lucy continued. "They just left after taking blood. 'Cept the one you hit."

She peeked past him. "Is he okay?"

"Don't worry about that. We need to get out of here."

Wolfe stood. "Let's go. Shel is here, and we need to leave. More bad men will come soon."

Lucy turned and glanced at Shannon. "She's not moving, or saying anything."

Wolfe stared at the girl, who hadn't so much as lifted her head from her crossed arms.

Shit.

CHAPTER 39

THE LITTLE ONES

Wolfe walked over to Shannon. "C'mon, kid, we've got to go. We're seriously in danger here. Don't blow this rescue."

The room smelled like chemicals and fear—and now, a rising undertone of blood. Nothing about the room was an ideal place to stay. Despite that, Shannon remained right where she was on the cold, bare concrete floor and didn't move, although she started to shiver. Whether from fear, reaction to the violence, or the actual temperature, Wolfe didn't know.

Fuck. Now is not *the time for this.*

"No one came for me," Shannon mumbled into her knees. "I was scared, and no one came for me."

Wolfe blinked and glanced back at the corpse in the doorway, surrounded by teeth and shattered screen. "What are you talking about, kid? I'm right here."

Shannon shook her head against her arms. "No. You came for Lucy. No one came for me. Nobody... They don't want me. No one cares."

Wolfe had no idea how to deal with whatever Shannon

was going through. "Look... we have to go. Now isn't the time for this."

Lucy walked over and placed her hand on Shannon's shoulder, but Shannon still didn't move beyond shivering.

Wolfe was tempted to grab Shannon and shake some sense into the blonde-haired girl—tell her now wasn't the time for existential dread, and that everyone had shit they were dealing with.

Before he could act, Lucy spoke. "Talk to her. You knew about her mother."

Gods damn it, I wasn't the one who made the choice to hide things from her.

Wolfe took a breath. He remembered how terrible it had felt when he'd thought he was alone, after being abandoned by the system that was supposed to protect him when his father had been abusive and his mother permissive. It had felt like shit. And he had felt powerless—a feeling he had overcome through training and violence. It had to be worse, being a pre-teen instead of a teen, and knowing that neither your dead mother nor murderer father were going to be in your life—and having a grandma who, however well meaning, wouldn't talk to you.

Not to mention *not* having the option to kick the shit out of people.

Wolfe sighed. "I wasn't going to leave without you. I promise. You need to pull yourself up by your bootstraps and help us, okay? When I was only a little bit older than you, my parents died as well. I can take care of myself, in case you haven't noticed. Sometimes life kicks you in the ass, but you're strong enough to kick back. I know, because I did it. You can too."

"Your father died?" Shannon looked up at Wolfe with wide eyes. "Your mother too?"

Well, I killed him, but... "Yeah. And I'm fine. A little secret —sometimes you make your own family."

Wolfe didn't tell her the rest, of course. He left out the fact that he had made the mob his family, and a mob boss—better than most, but still on the side of the demons—his surrogate father. His life hadn't really been Hallmark movie material. He was pretty sure the details wouldn't help anyone.

"I'm cold," Shannon whispered.

Wolfe took his holster off and put it on the table. Then he pulled his huge hoodie off and held it out. Shannon put her arms straight up, and it took a moment for Wolfe to realize what she wanted. But he carefully straightened the hoodie out and put it over the girl—unlike the T-shirt she wore, it went past her knees and sat on her like a massive tent.

Wolfe was cold in just his T-shirt and sweatpants, but damn if he would say anything when Lucy was in less and hadn't complained.

Shannon stood and then hugged Wolfe hard, much as Lucy had done. She buried her face in his stomach and let out a sob.

"There, there," Wolfe said, awkwardly running his hand over her blonde hair.

As Shannon held Wolfe, there was a crunching sound from behind him.

He whirled, knocking Shannon to the side, where Lucy caught her before she could fall, and was confronted by a gun pointed directly at his face.

Wolfe briefly thought he was dead but still wasn't going to go down without a fight. He reached for his gun on the table at the same time he touched his chest, but the person lowered their gun.

"Wolfe?" Shel asked.

"Shel!" Lucy cried.

Then she flung herself into her sister, hugging her as tight as she had Wolfe. "You came for us!"

"I would never leave you," Shel said. Then she took her own hoodie off and gave it to her sister.

It didn't quite cover her as effectively as Wolfe's giant hoodie covered Shannon, but it helped.

"All right, well, that was a great reunion. Worthy of an old-school Disney movie. But we need to get out of here before this becomes a tragedy," Wolfe said.

Shel looked down at the blood she was now standing in with a sardonic expression. "Yeah, I can think of a few places I'd rather be."

Then her face went deadly serious. "This place is crawling with goons—I swear they seem even less competent then when I was around them nine months ago, but they're everywhere."

Wolfe was surprised—he hadn't run into many gang members at all.

"You found them where you were? Toward the front of the place?"

Shel nodded. "Yeah, there was a sign that said 'garage' on it. I couldn't get any farther without getting caught, though."

Wolfe looked back at the table in the room they were in, and thought about the person attached to the medical machines outside.

"They must be getting a shipment prepared, probably in the garage. Perhaps after I shut two deliveries down at their sites with plausible deniability, they decided to handle the next one in house." Wolfe briefly thought about the pickup of Lucy and Shannon. "And on almost no notice."

"Well, we need to get out of here," Shel said.

The four of them walked out of the back room into the front, Lucy gagging as she stepped over the man Wolfe had killed.

Lucy stopped and pointed at the guy on the table. "Is that... a person?"

"Yeah," Wolfe replied.

"What... What's happening to him?" Lucy asked again.

Shel answered. "They put him in a medically induced coma."

"Why?"

"I..." Shel paused. "Every answer is evil. Bad people doing bad things. I'll tell you more when you're older."

For a wonder, Lucy didn't argue the point, instead asking, "Are we going to save him?"

"I can't carry a dude and fight," Wolfe said. "I might need to fight. So not yet. But when we get out, we'll call the police."

"The police brought us here," Shannon said. "Why will they save this man?"

"We know some good police who take their jobs very seriously," Shel said. "I'm going to be a police officer, and you trust me, right? Well, we'll get people like me."

Lucy and Shannon both nodded. Crisis averted, Wolfe took the handle of the door.

Static sputtered from the man Wolfe had killed, and he whirled. For a moment, Wolfe was worried that a monster had appeared, but the sound was coming from his pocket.

Then a voice he hadn't heard in almost a year came from the pocket, slightly electronic and distorted by the clothing.

"Wolfe has come for us," the voice of Damian said. "He's in the cannery. Everyone not in the cannery get to the exits and guard them, and everyone *in* the cannery, find him and kill him, and bring his cards to me. I want to make damn sure he stays dead this time."

"Fuck," Wolfe muttered. "Fuck, fuck, fuck."

Lucy didn't call him on his language, instead quietly asking, "Are we in trouble again?"

"We need to go. *Now*," Wolfe responded.

He reached out and opened the door.

For a second time in a few minutes, he found himself staring into the barrel of a gun, but this time, it was held in the hand of a man nearly as wide as he was tall—and he wasn't short. The man had thick muscles across his body and a huge, red beard with rings in it but was otherwise bald. His eyes, however, were rimmed in dark circles, and his skin was sallow and pale.

"Wolfe?" the man asked with wide eyes.

Wolfe stared at the man, an apparition of old times whom he hadn't thought of more than twice in the last nine months, now standing in front of him. "Liam?"

CHAPTER 40

REDEMPTION ARC

Liam lowered his gun, but only partially. "What are you doing here? I thought you were dead!"

Wolfe shook his head slightly, keeping his eye on Liam's gun. "That's not important. What are you doing still working for Damian? He's kidnapping *kids*, for the Divine's sake!"

"He gave us the shirts," Lucy said quietly from behind Wolfe.

"He still helped kidnap you," Wolfe growled, staring Liam in his eyes.

There was a brief pause, and Liam's eyes flickered to the corpse in the doorway behind Wolfe.

His gun dropped further, but he muttered, "We're supposed to kill you."

"No way you get both me and Shel," Wolfe said. "And you'll likely fail even one, as we're both deckbearers. But you shouldn't be working with Damian regardless, Liam. Remember when we worked for Big Man Grimm? This shit didn't happen. How come you didn't leave when Damian took over?"

Liam's gun fell until it was almost facing the floor. At this distance, Wolfe was pretty sure he could get to Liam before Liam shot him, but he waited.

"I... I didn't know what to do, after you killed most everyone," Liam said. "I applied to a few jobs, but no one was hiring, and Damian and his people kept calling and telling me to do stuff. Eventually, I just kinda... kept going."

"Well, now's a chance to stop," Wolfe said. "What's it gonna be?"

Wolfe tensed, ready to spring into action if Liam decided to fight.

Liam put his gun away and hung his head slightly before stepping away from the door. "All right, get out of here. I won't stop you."

"Come with us," Shel suddenly said. "Help us escape. Wolfe's going to be a private investigator. Maybe you can work with him."

Wolfe turned and raised an eyebrow at her.

"If you don't work with him, or if it takes a bit until Wolfe has jobs for you, we have enough money to put you up," Shel added.

Liam hesitated again, but his head rose and his face firmed. He glanced at Wolfe with near hero-worship. "Yeah, I will. I hated working for Damian, anyway."

"How do we get out if Damian sent his thugs to all the exits?" Wolfe asked. "Will others switch like you did?"

Liam shook his head. "One or two, maybe, but the vast majority don't know you and were hired after you killed nearly everyone. Or they're ex-Cobra guys who hate you. You're damned lucky it was me who found you."

"Then do you know an alternative way out?" Wolfe asked.

Liam thought, then smiled, an expression that sat a bit uneasily on his face. "Yeah, I do. We can go out the windows of the manager's office on the upper floor of the cannery to the warehouse, and probably use the fire escape down from there. I doubt either will be guarded."

"Let's do it," Wolfe said. "And let's try to avoid any contact with the thugs. One gunshot will tell them almost exactly where we are."

Unknown deckbearer has pulled their deck near you.

"What?" Wolfe and Shel asked at the same time.

Wolfe stepped over and glanced around the corner of the room into the hall. "In a place like this, that could be anywhere."

"Should we pull our decks?" Shel asked.

Wolfe nodded. "Surprise is gone. It'll give them some idea of where we are, but it won't be perfect."

Wolfe and Shel touched their chests and pulled their decks.

Shel touched one of her two golden cards floating beside her and Sorenia appeared. Wolfe touched one of the red cards floating next to him and Cereboo appeared.

Sorenia started to bow to Shel, but Cereboo gave a low woof and ran at her, jumping up and licking her with three heads as he always did.

Shel ignored that, as did Wolfe. He normally found his card-doggo's antics amusing, but the situation was too serious.

Instead, he turned to Liam. "I assume you know who's working for Damian who might have pulled a deck?"

"The only two deckbearers he has left who work for him are newly promoted to the status—Hans Rosario, who heavily favors Fire energy, and Zack Chang, who has a dragon deck. Neither fight like you, but they aren't slouches, either. But Caine Delacruz is also here with him, and that guy has some very strong cards if nothing else."

He wasn't that strong. "Which one just pulled their deck?"

"What?" Liam asked, his eyes wide. "How would I know that?"

"Which one is near us here?"

"Only Hans was down here—everyone else is in the Temple of Corruption."

Wolfe stared, completely floored by the comment. "What?"

"The Temple of Corruption—Damian's building card. He placed it inside the warehouse."

The walkie-talkie sprang to life again, mirrored oddly from Liam's pocket. "Wolfe is still in the cannery, nearer the middle or front. Everyone, converge."

"That's Hans," Liam stated.

Then Damian's voice came. "He's probably listening to us. Use your phones if you know who to call, even if it's longer. And Wolfe, if you're listening to me—I'm going to kill you for mucking my plans up. You have no idea how bad you fucked me, and I'm gonna have a gods-damned gorilla fuck you back."

Wolfe stepped over and took the walkie-talkie, pushing the talk button and bringing it to his mouth. It was time to play psychological games and try to trick Damian, since surprise was lost. "I'm coming for you, Damian. You're a corpse that doesn't know it's dead yet. I'm almost to your little temple, and when I get there, you'll die."

He clicked it off.

"Hopefully, that sends a few guards in the wrong direction," Wolfe muttered.

Figuring the thirty seconds were up from when he'd brought Cereboo forth, Wolfe pulled Malviere.

At the same time, Shel pulled Liurenia.

"You've added one of my sisters to your deck!" Sorenia said, stepping forward and hugging Liurenia before the new lantern angel could say anything.

Then she stepped back. "Did you hurt someone to acquire her?"

Liurenia shook her head. "I was gifted to Wolfe in return for him saving my previous deckbearer's life, and I assume he transferred me over since I see him here peaceably with my new deckbearer. Speaking of, it's an honor to meet you, new deckbearer."

Shel smiled. "Yes, you as well. But we need to go. Please, since both of you have lights, take up the rear. I'll be in the middle with Shannon and Lucy, and Wolfe, I assume you'll be scouting ahead?"

"Yeah. Cereboo, Malviere, with me."

"For the pack," Malviere whispered, taking a spot right behind Wolfe.

Wolfe looked at the old Grimm family enforcer. "Liam, lead us out. If you see anything, try to warn us away before we get caught."

Liam nodded and headed out the door.

Wolfe followed, an entire train behind him—since he and Shel had entered, they had picked up two kids and four cards.

Wolfe reviewed his situation. Cereboo was enhanced by a mere plus one, but Malviere would also give him an additional attack each round. Beyond that, Wolfe could put two whole cards on the field directly, although power wouldn't be a concern at all, since his highest card was a mere three power. Shel was a solid deckbearer with two cards out already, but in the same situation—only two more cards, assuming one was Mortal, would come into play. And they had Liam.

His kept his other four cards cycling.

Hardly an army, but it would have to do.

Liam led them out into the hall and then down a side hall.

Immediately, he came rushing back. "Back up, back up," he stage-whispered.

Wolfe turned and bumped into Cereboo, only to see everyone rush back around the wall in shambolic chaos.

He half-tripped, half-hopped over to them, stepping on Cereboo's paw once, eliciting a whine.

"Sorry, bud," Wolfe said as he hit the wall around the corner.

A moment later, Liam came around the corner. "Okay, I think it's safe to go."

Wolfe started around the side, only to see Liam awkwardly running back to him and a thug coming around the corner of the hall, behind Liam.

I knew we wouldn't sneak out of here with nine people.

Wolfe pointed over Liam's shoulder and shot the thug in the face at the same time a second thug started his way around the corner. Thug One's head was blown through, and Thug Two leapt around the corner, screaming, "Wolfe's here, he's here!"

Probably unnecessary, given the sound of Wolfe's pistol.

"Well, we're well and truly fucked," Wolfe muttered quietly.

"This way!" Liam screamed, running down the side hall, away from the conflict.

"Cover us, buddy," Wolfe said to Cereboo, whose three heads woofed in antiphonal chorus before he loped off after the thug.

"Let's go!" Wolfe yelled.

He ran to catch up to Liam to provide any additional firepower that might be needed, but Liam reached an elevator.

Everyone slammed to a stop in front of it as Liam dinked the *up* button.

Shannon and Lucy clutched Shel, and all three of the adults pointed guns down the hall, but somehow, no one came.

The elevator opened with a chime, and everyone piled in, Wolfe last.

The elevator shut just as he got a *Cereboo has died* notification and red energy flew back into his chest.

The elevator lurched and began to slowly move upward, soft piano music playing.

Wolfe caught Shel's eyes and almost laughed at the sudden, absurd sense of forced normalcy as the crowded elevator slowly reached the top, no one saying anything. After it settled, it dinged and then opened.

A plain, carpeted hallway faced him, with pictures of old-school Noimoire industrial buildings done in black and white. Doors to either side led into meeting rooms with glass windows looking into the hall.

Wolfe led the way out at a jog, not even trying to hide his presence. Rather than waiting for Cereboo, he saw that his mantle was up and put it on—the next five minutes might be crucial. Tiny horns appeared on his head, and red scales crossed his arms.

"You have an Infernal deck?" Shannon asked from behind Wolfe as they ran. "Are you a bad guy?"

"Well, if I am, I'm on your side. Besides, didn't Cereboo clue you in?"

Before she could answer, Liam and Wolfe rounded a corner. Wolfe had the barest vision of a man in a red suit with a gun aimed at Liam.

Wolfe dived sideways as the gun fired.

Chapter 41

Rumble on the Roof

Wolfe grunted in pain as the bullet slammed into his back, taking a step forward from the force.

Hans attacks at 9 (5 +1 trained thug +3 gun +0 random roll) and does 3 damage (81 net damage over 14 defense 14 ((5 + 3 crafty street fighter +3 defense mantle (2 x1.5 for perk)) x1.25 (Inborn killer perk))/2 for Infernal resisting Mortal.)

"You saved my life," Liam said, wide-eyed.

"Regretting it already because you're talking when you should be fighting," Wolfe grunted out while turning and spraying his bullets down the hall at Hans.

Hans yelled and dived to the side himself. Wolfe got a negative modifier to his attack despite his 'take best of two' perk, winging Hans but not hitting him seriously.

Two Light energy beams hit Hans across the chest, nearly vaporizing his shirt and leaving giant, burned gashes on him. He screamed and rolled into a room to the side of the hall.

"Excellently aimed, sister," Liurenia said.

"You as well," Sorenia replied.

"After him!" Wolfe cried, and Sorenia, Liurenia, and

Malviere all ran into the room. Sorenia made it around the corner first and had time for a brief scream as she was consumed in fire.

Wolfe saw the card responsible in the air over the blaze before Sorenia turned into golden particles and flowed back to Shel.

Immolate
Tier-2 Uncommon Fire Immediate
1 Fire, 1 Any power (available)

This power makes a magical attack (fire typed) against 1 target at strength 12. This repeats the next round. This may not target a deckbearer unless he has no creatures on the field.

Wolfe rushed to the corner but hit Liam and bounced back. Liam shot around Liurenia, but Wolfe got no death notification for Hans. More shots and tinkling glass sounded.

"He's getting away, onto the roof!" Liam shouted.

Where we were planning to go. Great.

"Move!" Wolfe growled, pushing past Liam.

He entered into a plush but otherwise normal office room, with a small couch and some chairs and a bunch of corny signs, including a huge piece of wall art that read, "All our jokes are canned" over a picture of the same.

But all Wolfe cared about was the busted window. He saw Hans scrambling across the roof on all fours, trying to keep low enough to avoid bullets. Before Wolfe could end him with his Edge, however, the bastard made it behind some piping.

What the fuck warehouses still have piping on the roof in this day and age? Go home, Noimoire, you're drunk, Wolfe thought exasperatedly before diving out the window at a run.

He hadn't realized there was a tiny gap between the warehouse and the roof, but he sailed over it and hit the top of the building in a roll. His mantle protected him from the normal scuffing that would have occurred from such a move. Wolfe rolled to his feet and charged forward, gun out, and fired a single bullet vaguely in Hans's direction just to keep his head down.

At the same time, he swiped his cards, pulling an Angry Hellhound and tossing it to the ground.

Hans stood, and a card very briefly appeared in Wolfe's vision.

Wall of Flame
Uncommon Tier-1 Fire Persistent

This card creates a wall of fire up to 6 feet wide, 20 feet tall, and 100 feet long that burns hot—anyone within 5 feet takes a true damage per round, and anyone crossing it takes a 10-point Fire magical attack every 6 seconds.

The card did just what it said, and Wolfe screeched to a halt and backed as a towering inferno appeared across his path. He hesitated briefly as some of the plastic on the piping caught fire, and insulation burned away as well.

I've got resistance to fire and an effective nine magical defense...

Wolfe glanced back. Liurenia flew from the window, but a rapid fusillade of bullets slapped into her and she dropped down, behind the cover of the flame wall.

But Wolfe heard Hans's gun click on empty.

At the same time, Malviere hopped across the small gap, calling, "I'm coming, Chosen!"

Neither companion was likely to be much help, Wolfe judged.

Wolfe had the new Demonic Portal card, his Tier-three Angry Hellhound, and a Lost Hellhound Puppy left. Not his best hand, since he couldn't get close enough to summon onto the other side of the fire wall.

I could really have used my Fireborn Hellhound right about now, gods, Wolfe thought sardonically. *I have to do something, or this guy will just use fire cards or creatures to fight me.*

He took a deep breath, anticipating pain, and ran at the wall. Right before he hit, Wolfe leapt through the searing flames, his skin frying. He screamed in agony as he took six damage—something about being burned was far worse than just being hit or shot, and Wolfe thanked Cerberus for his own resistance to fire.

He also slammed into a pipe partway through and careened sideways, away from where Hans had been firing. He hit the ground on the other side of the fire and rolled, then came up to see Hans standing a mere few feet from him, gun in hand as he tried to reload. Wolfe was injured now, taking a die penalty to all non-health stats—he had sixteen health left.

When Wolfe came crashing through the fire, Hans gave a cry of his own and stumbled back across the roof, between two of the pipes that were now burning, dropping the magazine he had taken out on the ground. But he smiled to see Wolfe and touched a card in front of him. "You aren't so tough, Wolfe, no matter what Damian said."

A fiery wolf appeared in front of Hans, growling with a sound half-canine, half-crackling wood in a fire.

Fiery Wolf
Uncommon Tier-1 Beast/Fire [Canine] Creature
1 Fire, 2 Any power
Health 20
Attack: 3
Magical Attack: 9 [**Fire**]
Defense: 3
Magical Defense: 5

Special: **Beneficial Façade [Elemental]**: This creature benefits from all cards, as if it were an Elemental in addition to its other types.

Special: **Thorns [Fire 6]:** If this creature is attacked in melee or by brawl, the attacker takes a magical attack of Fire type at 3 or 6 strength, respective to the type of attack, and if that damage would kill the attacker, they make no attack. This defense scales with all bonuses that would add to Magical Attack.

"Beasts are highly susceptible to magical augmentation, and these wolves were no different."

"Join the pack," Malviere said from behind him, then she *howled*.

Wolfe received a notification. *Fiery Wolf has switched allegiance for the duration of the fight.*

The wolf turned and growled at Hans.

Wolfe pointed his gun at Hans, growling himself, but the thug deckbearer dived behind another of the giant pipes. The wolf howled and chased after him.

Wolfe cussed but didn't waste ammo trying to hit his running enemy, letting the dog handle it.

Instead, he painfully climbed to his feet and took a quick glance around. He saw the fire escape along the side, past the fire he had just run through.

Damn. I really need to kill Hans.

A series of yells and cussing told Wolfe that Hans wasn't dead, but the notifications said he was probably close, absent healing, but he had resistance to fire.

Wolfe turned back to the pipes, crouched low, and tried to rapidly walk through the couple of pipes and venting system on the top. The roof felt warm to him, but he ignored it. Now that he was on the other side, he switched his cards, sardonically noting the Fireborn Hellhound, and summoned it.

Wolfe was pretty sure of impending victory.

Then, as if to spite him, the roof exploded right front of him. His crouched position behind pipes meant he wasn't hit by either the blast or what it had thrown about, but his brief relief was short-lived as the part of the roof he was on cracked.

He got some experience for Hans dying, and his fiery wolf blinked out of existence.

Wolfe stood, flailing his arms, as the roof shifted again, dropping another foot.

He turned back to see Shel staring at him, her hand at her mouth. Although Wolfe was pretty sure every thug in the greater Noimoire area knew where they were, he was still glad Shel didn't shout for him and give herself away.

The roof cracked again and dropped another couple of feet. Wolfe continued to flail his arms and grabbed a pip, but the portion of the roof Wolfe was on gave out, and a twenty-foot section ripped away, one edge falling down while the other remained half-attached to heated metal rods.

But the side only fell another fifteen feet or so before slamming into something, the whole roof segment at a forty-five-degree angle. Wolfe fell down the steep and relatively smooth surface until he caught a pipe, tripped over it, and slammed down on something else.

Another roof? was Wolfe's first quizzical thought. He was staring at a roof with a slight wall around the side, and in that wall were red stained-glass windows depicting horrible tortures and abuses of mortals at the hands of demons. The roof and walls were painted black, and at the far end, there was a portion with stairs slightly down to a door set in the ceiling.

A couple of cards slid down next to him, and Wolfe absently gathered them as he stared in shock at the baffling and poorly designed building in front of him.

As he stared, a card overlay appeared.

Temple of Corruption
Rare Tier-1 Elder Building
0 Power

Special: The owner of this building may pay 1 less of either Infernal, Elder, or Undead power inside their building for all cards.
Special: All of the deckbearer's cards with 'cultist' in their title double their stats, to a max of +6 on each, if within a mile of the Temple of Corruption.
Special: The benefit of all Elder, Undead, and Infernal enhancement cards are doubled, as are the number of enhancement cards the deckbearer may have. However, each one adds a feature and either doubles all negatives, or, if there were no negatives, imposes -1 Health and -1 to any random stat.

"Liam did say that evil hobbit had a temple down here, and I can't wait to see what he looks like now, given what I just read," Wolfe muttered, standing.

The rods twenty feet behind him gave a tortured scream of breaking metal, and Wolfe turned, staring in brief horror as the metal broke and the broken piece of roof fell.

Wolfe leapt off the piece of collapsing warehouse roof and onto the temple roof, grunting as he hit, his wounds painful.

He stood and brushed himself off for the however many-eth time today, noting that his shirt was all but gone, and even his pants were barely holding on to modesty.

He stared at the door in the roof. "I guess Damian and I are gonna settle this today, after all."

CHAPTER 42

THE TEMPLE OF CORRUPTION

Wolfe walked across the roof of the temple, heading for the door in the back wall. The roof itself appeared marble—but a marble run through with worm holes and tracks, organic half-dips like whoever had designed it had finger-painted into plaster in a continuous, intersecting line. They didn't make a pattern that Wolfe could see, and they were made more disturbing by the flickering crimson light filtering through the red stained-glass windows around him, on the inside of a wall that surrounded the top of the building.

"Who builds stained glass windows on the *inside* of the building's walls, where no one could see them?" Wolfe wondered aloud. "Kooky-ass building."

There were stairs leading down a bit to a recessed floor that led to the door—a place where water could get trapped. Wolfe supposed it didn't matter for a magical building, to a degree, but still—*why?*

He reached out and took the handle hesitantly, wondering if there would be some trap.

It opened easily, revealing a hall made of the same worm-track-riddled marble, with old-fashioned candelabra and dark-red hangings on the walls, depicting more demons and elder beings doing all kinds of horrible things to humanity.

"I always hated how open your dad was with his affiliations, Damian," Wolfe muttered. "Way to one-up your old man. Apparently, shooting him wasn't enough."

Wolfe cautiously made his way to the left, turned a corner left, and continued down a similar hall that would logically be on the outside edge of the building. There were numerous doors to the side, but Wolfe kept going.

He didn't encounter anyone, including, fortunately, any thugs sent by Damian.

His deck was already out, and he took advantage of the fact to switch his cards. He intentionally dismissed Malviere and Cereboo, figuring they wouldn't be able to reach him where he was. Seconds later, red energy flowed into him. It would be a few minutes before he could re-summon them.

I have no idea whom he has down here—I should be as prepared as possible.

Wolfe dismissed his Soul Hunter mantle as well—it was about to go away regardless. He pulled Brimstone, waited a moment, cycled, and pulled Hellfire as well. *Two cards down, and plus six to my attack.*

Wolfe was torn between waiting and buffing up, and moving to find Damian before more could go wrong on the roof—he had a buddy, two girls, and his woman up there.

He split the difference between waiting and buffing, settling on creeping forward slowly as he swiped and picked cards.

At the end of the terrible hall was a smaller room. Inside was a spiral staircase, black metal with ornamental human skulls on the knobs at the top of them. Wolfe took it down.

He reached a small alcove—still in worm-track marble—with two doors out. One was open, looking to a front foyer with a matching door and staircase on the far side of it.

Wolfe tried the other one, behind him, and found it locked. A notification popped up, telling Wolfe that he wasn't permitted through the door.

Does Damian know I'm here, or is this just a door no one can go through?

Wolfe swiped his cards. Soul Hunter had popped back up, and he equipped it.

Soul Hunter
Uncommon Tier-1 Persistent (Mantle)
1 Infernal Power
+2 Attack, +2 Defense, +2 Magical Defense

Special: Traitor [Infernal] The deckbearer will do an additional 25% damage against Infernal cards, monsters, and deckbearers.

"Sometimes, the Infernal Realms want their own back. That's when they send a Soul Hunter to do their dirty work."

Wolfe stepped into what he was pretty sure was the front foyer of the Temple of Corruption. The foyer had a similar but even more grandiose set of decorations to that of the previous rooms, including a full-on chandelier hanging from an inverted vault ceiling, the bottom of the chandelier a mere seven feet above the ground. A giant double door, covered in a bas-relief of void-squid monstrosities, headed into the central portion of the lower floor of the temple, and a slightly smaller one headed out what would have been the front.

The door behind him, to the staircase, and the one across

from him to a matching alcove and staircase both swung quietly shut, and a click sound told Wolfe they had likely locked.

The evil hobbit definitely knows I'm headed his way.

There were only the doors to flee, and deeper into the lair. *Way to really rub in the choices, gods*, Wolfe said in the quiet of his own mind.

Just to check if he *did* have a choice, Wolfe turned the handle of the door out and gave it a shove. It creaked open.

A fat man in a huge, leather jacket that looked as if a whole cow had died for it stood outside, long, white hair and a giant ZZ Top beard adorning his florid face. As the door opened, the thug turned and faced the doorway—but when he found himself staring down the barrel of Hellfire, he froze.

"Uh..."

Wolfe stepped outside, glancing around the warehouse interior. There were an absolute ton of the metal coffins around, including quite a few hooked up to a huge generator, near the front of the warehouse. A few people were working around them, mostly thugs moving stuff, but somehow, none had seen Wolfe. He could see an unguarded side entrance out.

"Stay still and quiet," Wolfe said to the man, who frantically nodded.

Wolfe pulled his phone out, took a picture, and awkwardly texted it to the phone number Rhett had given him way back in the day, at the police party with the great beans.

Well, I never did give him anything on Emmett's murder, but I suspect he'll consider this desirable.

Somehow, the thugs working the kidnap victims still hadn't seen him, and he motioned the ZZ Top Thug inside the temple.

The thug complied, and Wolfe shut the door.

Then he put his gun back in the waistband of his pants.

"Thanks, man, I thought you were going to kill me," the

thug replied, wiping his hand across his red and sweaty forehead.

"If I asked, could you guys get me a little girl?" Wolfe asked. "Do you have any children?"

"Yeah, we just got two. I can—"

Wolfe punched him in the side of the head. He caved the thug's head in entirely, blood and brain squirting from him, sending the body careening into the wall with his single punch.

Even without the additional damage of the gun, Wolfe's bonuses stacked to seventeen—and Infernal got fifty percent extra damage against Mortals. That was roughly eighty damage *after* reduction, or four times what it took to kill most humans. And the body reflected it.

"People who traffic deserve death," Wolfe said, shaking his hand hard to sling some of the viscera off it. "Especially those who traffic children."

Wolfe had five of his eight power used, but his own stats were ridiculous. He glanced at the modified stats on his sheet, getting a handle on his capability.

Health: 16/30
Attack: 20 ((8 +6 (Infernal Guns) + 3 (Mantle 2 x1.5 for perk)) x1.25 for perk, -1 wounded)
Magical Attack: 0
Defense: 13 (8 +3 (Mantle 2 x1.5 for perk) x1.25 for perk -1 wounded)
Magical Defense: 8 (5 + 3(Mantle x1.5 for perk))

Wolfe stared at his stats, trying to decide if a frontal charge at Damian was a good idea. Wolfe got a lot of mileage out of being far more aggressive than most people gave him credit for, and his stats were absurd—his attack on par with a mid-rarity, mid-tier power seven or eight card, more against Infernals, and the rest of his stats were roughly that of a power-four creature —especially if Damian was wearing his mantle, which would give Wolfe even more damage.

But he also knew that he would be walking in on multiple deckbearers, most likely, and he already knew Damian's trick —between his mantle, which Wolfe had seen nine months ago, and the building they were in, Damian would be throwing out creatures at two less power cost. He doubted Damian was as high level as him, or had as much power—but he might. And he had a lot of really good cards.

If Rhett gets here first, it's likely that he'll go to jail, and I won't get to take him out. And if Rhett doesn't get here quickly, it's likely that they'll ship out a ton of people for sale and simply switch locations.

Wolfe had three cards in play and could only have one more out on the field. He had a thought about that, though, and rifled through the cards he had picked up from the dead Hans. He noted that there was a Fire/Beast [Canine] *orphan* card, but it wouldn't be useful yet. Wolfe pocketed everything except for the Immolate, which he put into his deck—it was never 'in play' as an immediate. It might be useful.

He had switched enough that Cereboo had returned to his hand, and he tapped his companion's card.

His doggo appeared, not barking, his hackles raised.

Then he summoned his Desperate Cult Child card. "Stay in the corner," Wolfe said, pointing. The creepy little kid moved to the corner closest to the exit and stayed.

"Yeah, it's that time," Wolfe said. "Let's end this."

He reached out and pushed open giant doors with both hands, pushing his way into the central hall of the Temple of Corruption.

For the location of a final showdown with his nemesis, the hall didn't disappoint. It had pews of black basalt stone, with stone spikes on each end leading partway into the main isle, sharp and jagged. There were multiple chandeliers, their flames an unnatural blood color, and smoke disobeyed the laws of physics, drifting down across the room. At the far end was a raised dais with a throne of flesh melded together, eyes and mouths from multiple people adorning the outside. The eyes snapped to Wolfe as he entered, and mouths cried out for release in a guttural tongue that Wolfe didn't know.

Three men were on the platform, and all already had their cards out.

To the left of the throne was Caine Delacruz, wearing a white suit similar to the one that Wolfe had seen him in before, and his mantle was already on—fiery wings extended from his back. With his boy band look and fiery wings, he fit the part of angel quite well.

To the right was a man who looked to be of mixed white and Asian descent, dressed in a faux-Chinese robe of gold silk with dragons carved on it. Wolfe presumed this was Zack Chang.

Sitting on the throne was what Wolfe presumed was Damian. He was nearly five and a half feet tall now, and probably weighed six hundred pounds. He was covered in a robe as well, and it hung awkwardly, revealing arms so pudgy, they were almost two round balls of flesh squished together. His face was also so fat, it was hard to make the eyes out, and nearly round, but for two massive ram's horns curled on top. His skin was covered in pustules that wept pus, and his robe was already stained in it.

The throne itself had two chains attacked to skulls at the end of the armrests, and each led to a beautiful woman wearing a bikini and nothing else but a collar around her neck. Each stood just behind Damian, one with a plate of food, and the other with a towel that was already covered in pus.

He went full Jabba. Never go full Jabba.

He was also wearing his mantle, which Wolfe knew well—it was his 'Gate of the Underworld' set.

Duke of the Legion
Unique Tier-5 equivalent Infernal Persistent (Mantle)
2 Infernal Power
+7 Defense, +15 Health

Special: **Master Deckbearer [Infernal 1]:** All Infernal Cards cost 1 less power

Special: **Versatile [Infernal]:** This card alters to fit its wearer so long as they have at least 2 Infernal Power

Special: **Demonic Empower [1]:** All the deckbearer's Infernal creature cards gain 25% to their stats.

Special: One of the 'Gate to the Underworld' cards. If all 6 are possessed in the same deck, the bearer will gain 7 Legendary Infernal or Beast card pulls. Additionally, the deckbearer may either gain the Mythic 'Gate to the Underworld' Building Card or evolve Cereboo. One card is held by each of the crime families of Noimoire, and the sixth is held within the city by another.

"This person has been chosen to lead the demons of the Infernal, and they have been given the power to do so. Demons come extremely cheaply and are far more powerful."

Damian stood easily and quickly, reminding Wolfe that his hideous appearance was likely the result of the combination of a ton of enhancer cards and his Temple of Corruption, and not a bad lifestyle, per se—and he had the benefits of his mantle, as well.

I still need to be careful with him.

Damian threw his disgusting arms wide, and Wolfe saw some pus fly out, narrowly missing Caine's white suit.

Before Damian could give some grandiose speech, Wolfe said, "Damian no botha'" in his best *Star Wars* impression.

Damian sneered. "I always hated your sense of humor. So be it."

Everyone reached for cards except Wolfe, who whipped Brimstone from his pants and fired.

CHAPTER 43

THREE-ON-ONE

W olfe swiveled and shot Zack Chang in the chest, blowing the man near in half. His enemy collapsed to the ground, red-brown cards spilling around him without so much as a single summon.

But Wolfe wasn't sitting around to enjoy his kill—he dismissed the experience notification and raced to the side, leaping over a set of stone spikes into the basalt pew and crouching. Bullets ricocheted around him, from Caine, but he only took a single point of damage from a slight hit to the shoulder. Caine's toy pistol couldn't do much against Wolfe's net defense, between the actual stat and his resistance to Mortal damage.

Wolfe, on the other hand, had a double strength gun that ignored type disadvantage.

Wolfe knew he could have hit Damian for an *insane* nearly four hundred and fifty damage, but he also knew that with his temple, a mere four enhancement card slots—ten levels— would become eight enhancement cards in his deck that were all double strength. That was a lot of potential power. Plus, Damian had clearly put himself out to be attacked.

Never do what your enemy wants.

As Wolfe was contemplating his moves, he threw his Fireborn Hellhound out, into the center aisle between the pews.

"Fuck, he got Zack!" Caine yelled.

"It won't matter," Damian said. "He's dead, anyway, and now we get Zack's cards and don't have to pay him."

Caine flew on wings of fire to land behind the first row of pews, mimicking Wolfe's defensive moves. The blond bastard threw a card out as he did.

A rune, glowing with white energy, appeared across the floor. It was complex, with numerous interlocking circles.

Preemptive Retribution
Uncommon Tier-3 Persistent
2 Divine, 1 Any Power

This card makes all opposing creatures **Open:** Any round it attacks, its opponent inflicts its damage first, and only if the creature survives will it inflict damage. This does not affect creatures whose attacks are ranged.

"Sometimes, angels don't wait before taking down evildoers."

Damian threw out his own card, and a massive, ten-foot-tall horned demon with all the muscles of an Olympic bodybuilder appeared.

Infernal Champion
Rare Tier-1 Infernal Creature
5 Infernal Power
Health: 35
Attack: 16
Defense: 16

Magical Attack: 0
Magical Defense: 16

Special: **Terrifying Aura**: When this creature comes into play, return any one creature that doesn't have resistance to its type, or is of matching type, to the deckbearer's deck.
Special: **Neutral Defense:** This creature does not take any extra damage from any source due to type disadvantage.

"Infernal Champions are trained to fight the strongest enemies of the Infernal and embody the theory of rule by fear—most flee before their might."

The setup proved too much for Cereboo—he turned into the Infernal Champion, only to be grabbed by his central head. Cereboo stopped with a whine and tried to snap with his other heads. The Infernal Champion slung Cereboo sideways into the stone spikes on the end of one pew. His health and defense were far insufficient to handle the damage, and a triple canine yip of pain, cut off, was his only contribution to the fight.

Caine was behind cover, and Wolfe fired a cluster of shots at Damian, just to get a sense of what he was facing. He didn't have the power to put any more cards out.

Deckbearer Ethan Wolfe and Deckbearer Damian Grimm engage in physical combat.

Ethan makes a Physical Attack at 23 (20 + 3 random roll) against Deckbearer Grimm's Physical Defense of 26. Damage dealt is 28 (23 * 23 (1.375)/26)).

Damian grunted hoarsely as he was blasted three times in the chest, blood spewing from him. The Hutt wannabe coughed more blood as he lumbered backward. He tripped over the chain of one of the 'slave girls' he had—who let out a yelp as she was pulled to the ground—and half-fell, half-leapt off the dais to the back, out of sight.

But he didn't die. Wolfe guessed that Damian's total health bonuses were over eight net, but he was pretty sure they weren't enough to take a second round of damage similar to what Wolfe had just done. *Thank the gods that the building imposed some health penalties on the enhancer cards, or I'd be royally fucked.*

Wolfe was still okay with his choice to start the fight with wasting Zack, though. He didn't think he could have handled a third deckbearer.

At the same time Wolfe was attacking Damian, the Infernal Champion obliterated his Fireborn Hellhound, again without taking damage thanks to the Preemptive Retribution card.

Wolfe shot a few more times, since the ammo of Brimstone was infinite. But he was starting to become concerned about the fight, despite his great opening move.

A second Infernal Champion joined the fight next to the first, and Wolfe winced. Damian must have also gotten a great deal of power or cost reduction from whatever enhancers he had.

Caine also summoned Artenia.

Wolfe swiped his cards, getting a Pack Howl, a Tier-four Angry Hellhound, Cerberus's Home for Wayward Hellhounds, and a Lost Hellhound Puppy. He almost touched the Home but stopped.

Wolfe had suddenly realized how he was about to get himself killed. He needed enough monsters to fight both of them and not let any of the big guys through, as they would kill him. If he threw the Home out, it would need a round, and Wolfe would get owned by the big guy.

Instead, Wolfe threw the Lost Hellhound Puppy out and

took aim at the big guy while quickly leaping from pew to pew. He fired repetitively at one of the Infernal Champions as he did, blasting it away.

Deckbearer Ethan Wolfe and Infernal Champion Card engage in physical combat.

Ethan makes a Physical Attack at 27 (20 + 7 random roll) against Infernal Champion's Physical Defense of 16. Damage dealt is 62 (27 * 27 (1.375)/16)).

The Champion was wasted before it could attack, but the second one slaughtered Wolfe's Lost Hellhound Puppy.

A Light energy magical attack from Artenia hit Wolfe, and he crashed to the ground behind a pew, grimacing as he took another five damage and his wound penalties went to two.

Wolfe quickly glanced over the pew to see that Caine had put a buff on Artenia—Sentence Passed—that allowed her to attack a deckbearer directly.

Shit, shit, shit. I've got one minute before I'm dead, even assuming I draw one creature in the next card hand.

Wolfe leapt up, going for broke, to see that somehow, Damian had pulled *another* Infernal Champion. Damian shouldn't have gotten the power from the first one back yet. It told Wolfe that Damian's Enhancers were somehow reducing the cost of his Infernal Champions even further, or adding power, or both. There was no other way.

Wolfe fired rapidly and wiped one out while it also dropped the Angry Hellhound.

After a moment, Wolfe turned and aimed for the pew that Caine was hiding behind. It exploded, revealing the asshole, who had pulled a Corporate Enforcer.

Wolfe bit his teeth to keep from screaming as another Light beam slashed along his side, burning him deeply despite his mantle.

Caine scrambled back, trying to find cover. His eyes were

wide with fear as Wolfe leapt over pews toward him. He had actually wet himself, his once-immaculate white suit stained yellow around the crotch, and Wolfe sneered at him.

"Wa-Wait!" Caine cried, his hands held out in front of him. "My dad is a billionaire! He can pay you whatever you want, take care of anything! Don't kill me, please!"

Wolfe had no sympathy for Caine, but he needed to get rid of Damian, so he took a chance.

"Then kill Damian, right now," Wolfe said. "Do that, and I'll spare you."

"Don't listen to him, we have him!" Damian screamed from behind the dais.

Wolfe knew they did—but he was pretty sure he could kill Caine at the same time, possibly a round earlier.

He swiped his cards.

At the same time, Brimstone disappeared, and Wolfe got a notification that its time on the field was over.

Caine smiled.

Wolfe had Cereboo back, as well as a Deal with the Devil, the useless Litter, the too costly Demonic Portal, and the Immolate.

Caine was being an idiot. The loss of three attack wasn't significant since Wolfe had another thirty seconds with Hellfire, and that would be more than enough to finish Caine off.

But Wolfe would die as well if he did, since there would be too many creatures on the field for him to handle. He had to kill one of the Infernal Champions to prevent himself from being attacked. Wolfe couldn't see a way around it. But if he didn't kill Caine, Caine would just keep summoning, and Wolfe would be overwhelmed next round.

Fuck it. I'll at least leave Damian with absolutely no followers, a pissed-off boss—whoever this guy's dad is—and a whole situation to explain to the police when Rhett and his boys get here.

Wolfe raised his gun, prepared to drag all of Damian's hopes to hell with him.

CHAPTER 44

I'LL ALWAYS HAVE YOUR BACK

"Wolfe!" the person he most wanted to hear in the world called, and Wolfe risked a brief glance back. Shel, along with Liurenia and Sorenia, was running into the temple after him, a Rookie SWAT card also in play.

"I'm here to help!" Shel cried again.

Wolfe needed a mere fraction of a second to process what the change meant. He shifted his aim, and he exploded the next Infernal Champion with a cluster of shots from Hellfire.

He still needed to shift the fundamental course of the fight, however.

But he saw the move.

He touched his card Deal with the Devil.

Deal with the Devil
Rare Tier-1 Infernal Persistent
3 Infernal Power

So long as the deckbearer has any Infernal Creature on the field, he may assign control of any one non-Infernal creature controlled by any deckbearer to any other deckbearer. When the card leaves the control of its original deckbearer, it may take an attack against that deckbearer or their card, obeying normal rules as if it were an enemy card, before it switches. This card's power remains spent so long as the creature is on the field.

"In the abstract, Evil should be defeated quickly, as most want to be on the side of good. But there are *always* individuals who will betray the whole for their own benefit, and the Infernal is always there, whispering in their ears."

Using its power, he seized control of Artenia—but instead of giving it to *himself*, which wouldn't do much, he transferred it to Shel, hoping that card wouldn't count against her maximum.

He also had her blast the Corporate Enforcer on the way out. It didn't die, but it took some damage.

Caine scrambled away on all fours before leaping into the air and flying over to join Damian behind the dais.

The Corporate Enforcer shot Wolfe, but it was another single point of chip damage, and Wolfe dodged and leapt over the pew again, crouching behind it.

"You're a dead man, Wolfe!" Damian screamed from behind the dais. "You can't compete with the power of my cards, and I'll destroy you and then have your woman!"

"Looks like slavery is the only way you can have any women, slug. You're a disgrace to the Grimm family name."

Wolfe half nodded to the women, who were cowering against the sides of the throne, almost entirely out of view.

"You're dead now!" Damian shouted.

"Way to really vary up your taunts," Wolfe called from behind the pew.

Wolfe knew his mantle was about to fade in a minute or

so, but he had two power left from Brimstone leaving the field, and if he made it another twenty-or-so seconds, he would be at four power when Hellfire dropped back to the deck as well.

As gunfire whizzed over the pew—and occasionally bounced off them—Wolfe quickly reviewed his moves. He had a mere three health left again, and a two-point penalty to all his stats.

I need to keep from getting hit again... but I need to keep the Infernal Champions down! If I stay back, we still lose. Just a minute more of danger.

Wolfe took a deep breath, trying to ignore the burns and gunshot wounds across his entire body. No way was he going to leave Shel without an ally who was giving it his all.

Hellfire faded away, its light rushing into Wolfe, the very thing he had been waiting for.

He touched the Demonic Portal card, which summoned two Tier-three Angry Hellhounds and a Lost Hellhound Puppy in a single move. He sacrificed his hidden Desperate Cult Child for the two extra power as he did.

He ordered the two Angry Hellhounds not to attack the Infernal Champion—if they did, all would die in a single round thanks to the Preemptive Retribution. But he sent the puppy to its doom.

The puppy was crushed by the massive foot of the Infernal Champion, and the Angry Hellhounds *howled*.

"Throw me your gun, and then go for max Mortal power! We need stuff that can fight his damned Infernal Champions!"

Shel managed a near-perfect toss, and Wolfe stood, catching the Glock-17 and turning. He leapt over the front pew with a wince, firing the gun into the Infernal Champion as fast as he could as it raced at a hellhound, punching the poor dog's spine so hard, it broke.

But his other Angry Hellhound ended the Corporate Enforcer with a single move.

Wolfe continued to fire—into the underarm, into its neck, and finally into the creature's head. With his reduced power— from not having both Hellfire and Brimstone—he didn't quite kill it, but two Light beams—from Sorenia and Liurenia —finished it off.

Caine screamed as Artenia leapt into the air and flew to the side of the dais and, presumably, fired her beam into him, able to bypass Caine's dying Corporate Enforcer thanks to his own buff on her.

Caine tried begging one more time, his voice floating up from the dais, which was covered in the two cowering women and a ton of viscera from Damian. "My father will give you whatever you want!"

The field had been cleared of almost all cards, but *another* Infernal Champion appeared.

Wolfe's mantle faded. But he still had one creature on the field, and he was safe from the Champion.

He ran up to the throne, finger on his lips for the benefit of the two chained women. He was careful not to trip or slip, either. He reached the top and leaned over the dais. Caine was hunched over, staring around the corner, firing at Artenia. Most of his body was burned. Damian was standing behind Caine, a pistol in his hand, pointed at Caine's back. His entire over-robe was soaked in blood, and the evil Jabba wannabe trembled where he stood.

Neither noticed Wolfe a mere few feet above them.

"We have to fight Wolfe together!" Damian said, his voice tinged with desperation. "His creatures can't get past mine as long as your field is up, so all we have to do is *shoot him*."

"My own angel is going to kill me! I'm surrendering!" Caine said. "Dad will get me out of whatever trouble I'm in, but he can't do that if I'm dead! You're just some hired goon, not someone I owe anything to. You're on your own!"

Damian shot Caine in his back without another word,

right through Caine's heart. He hit the ground like a sack, and Artenia and the Preemptive Retribution both faded as cards appeared on the corpse's back.

Damian reached down and grabbed the cards.

"Drop them, and your deck," Wolfe said.

Damian started to turn, not even attempting to point his gun at Wolfe but rather putting his hand inside a pocket on his robe, but Wolfe didn't wait to find out what was happening. His emptied his gun into Damian's head and shoulders.

His attack was far weaker as a Mortal shooting an Infernal, and with his modifiers off. But Damian was already wounded, and the shots were like multiple punches to the head and shoulders, plus one that slashed into his collarbone.

Damian hit the ground on his knees, managing to turn and fall awkwardly onto his back. He kept fumbling inside his robe, but he couldn't seem to coordinate his hand.

"Damn," he started to say before coughing. Bloody spittle flew out. "Damn you, Wolfe. May the Infernal claim your soul."

"Probably. Keep someplace warm for me," Wolfe quipped, his voice tight.

"Why... Why did you hate me so much? What did I ever do to you?" Damian asked, blood starting to dribble from the corner of his mouth. His hand fell from his robe.

"Are you seriously this delusional, still?" Wolfe asked, exasperated. "After everything?"

He was about to launch into a diatribe about everything that Damian had, in fact, done... but stopped himself. It didn't matter.

He raised his gun and pointed it at Damian but didn't pull the trigger. Damian's breathing was coming in shorter and shorter gasps, more and more labored as Damian struggled to make his lungs work against his own weight. His eyes were fading, his fingers barely moving.

Shel came walking around the corner, staring at Damian as well. "Is he... dying?"

Wolfe nodded, keeping his gun pointed at Damian.

"What did you do with the card that holds my brother's soul?" Shel asked.

Damian's head rolled to the side slightly, and his eyes focused on her. He gave the slightest smile, a hint of madness to it, his eyes feverish.

Then he exhaled slightly and went limp with finality. A pile of cards appeared on his chest.

Wolfe stared down at the corpse of his nemesis, feeling a deep, and dark, sense of satisfaction.

"One more down," Wolfe said, reaching over and picking up the deck. He also grabbed Caine's, and passed it to Shel. Then he flipped through Damian's deck until he found the set card.

"What about us?" One of the chained women asked, startling Wolfe, who had forgotten about them.

"You'll be freed as soon as the building comes down," Wolfe said. "The chains are part of the magical card. Without it being in my deck I can't free you before then, and I'm sorry. I don't have the space for a building card in my deck."

The woman nodded. "Yeah, Damian said we could never remove the chains unless he let us."

Shel gave the woman a hug. "It'll just be a few minutes."

Wolfe turned from the mini-drama and stared at his new card.

Duke of the Legion
Unique Tier-5 equivalent Infernal Persistent [Mantle]
2 Infernal Power
+7 Defense, +15 Health

Special: **Master Deckbearer [Infernal 1]:** All Infernal Cards cost 1 less power

Special: **Versatile [Infernal]:** This card alters to fit its wearer so long as they have at least 2 Infernal Power

Special: **Demonic Empower [1]:** All the deckbearer's Infernal creature cards gain 25% to their stats.

Special: One of the 'Gate to the Underworld' cards. If all 6 are possessed in the same deck, the bearer will gain 7 Legendary Infernal or Beast card pulls. Additionally, the deckbearer may either gain the Mythic 'Gate to the Underworld' Building Card or evolve Cereboo. One card is held by each of the crime families of Noimoire, and the sixth is held within the city by another.

"This person has been chosen to lead the demons of the Infernal, and they have been given the power to do so. Demons come extremely cheaply and are far more powerful."

Even as Wolfe held the card, it shimmered, shifting, and changed in his hand.

Mantle of the Infernal Chosen
Unique Tier-5 equivalent Infernal Persistent [Mantle]
2 Infernal Power

This card modifies to become one of numerous possible mantles depending on who claims it. This card is stronger if a card that names an Infernal Lord is present in the deck when added.

Special: One of the 'Gate to the Underworld' cards. If all 6 are possessed in the same deck, the bearer will gain 7 Legendary Infernal or Beast card pulls. Additionally, the deckbearer may either gain the Mythic 'Gate to the Underworld' Building Card or evolve Cereboo. One card is held by each of the crime families of Noimoire, and the sixth is held within the city by another.

Wolfe stared at the card. "That's... convenient."

Shel hugged Wolfe hard, and he winced.

She let go of him and stepped back. "Thank the Divine you're okay," Shel whispered.

"Yeah, I'm fine. Your sister and the others? Are they okay?"

"Everyone should be okay. Sorenia and Liurenia flew everyone to the lower fire escape, and then Liam led them away while I came back for you."

"Thanks," Wolfe said. "I wouldn't have made it without you, although I didn't really want you risking yourself for me."

"I'll always have your back. *Always*," Shel said, reaching out and gently squeezing his arm where he was unburnt. "So... it's over, then?" She motioned to Damian's body.

Wolfe shrugged. "It's over with him, anyway. This piece of shit"—Wolfe kicked Caine's corpse lightly—"kept talking about his billionaire daddy, so I'm sure there's more. And the other three houses still exist, so..."

Shel nodded. "So it'll be a whole thing?"

Wolfe chuckled tiredly. "Yeah."

Then he looked down at the card in his hand.

"About this card... should I add it?" Wolfe asked.

"You *must* be hurt if that's even a question. Of course. It's about how the Infernal Rift worked," Shel said. "Whatever the person needed, it became, and Infernal Rift gave you some of your best cards ever."

Wolfe nodded. He touched the card and willed it to replace Soul Hunter in his deck.

Soul Hunter appeared in his hand, and a new card appeared.

Master of the Infernal Hunt

Unique Tier-5 equivalent Infernal Persistent [Mantle]

2 Infernal Power

+10 Health, +3 to all remaining stats.

Special: **Cerberus's Champion:** All other [Canine] Cards gain +5 Health and +1 to all other stats, and all [canine] cards gain advantage against Infernal cards.

Special: **Versatile [Infernal]:** This card alters to fit its wearer so long as they have at least 2 Infernal Power

Special: **Grand Pack [Canine]:** [Canine] cards do not count against cards on the field

Special: **Favorable Façade [Canine]:** Count as a Beast [Canine] card for all purposes except type match penalties.

Special: One of the 'Gate to the Underworld' cards. If all 6 are possessed in the same deck, the bearer will gain 7 Legendary Infernal or Beast card pulls. Additionally, the deckbearer may either gain the Mythic 'Gate to the Underworld' Building Card or evolve Cereboo. One card is held by each of the crime families of Noimoire, and the sixth is held within the city by another.

"Sometimes, the demons call a hunt on other demons, and a hunt master is always chosen to lead the chase."

"That's amazing... but it seems weaker than the other version," Shel said. "Twenty-five percent stats and a power lower on Infernal cards was huge."

Wolfe thought about it. "Well... maybe. It makes me count as a canine, though, so I'll get a bunch of bonuses from my own cards. It opens a lot of interesting possibilities, certainly. And the total stat gain is higher. Either way, it's crazy strong for a two-power card."

Shel nodded. "Also either way, it beats your current mantle."

Wolfe nodded. "Yeah... and I can use the health at the moment."

Wolfe touched his mantle, and it settled over him. He grew a bit larger, stag-like horns sprouting from his head.

"You have red eyes," Shel said.

His health went from three of thirty to eighteen of forty-five, and Wolfe somehow felt himself strengthening, becoming stronger without healing, per se. His penalties went down to just one in each category.

A voice came reverberating through the air, obviously over a powerful loudspeaker, as it made it even into the Temple of Corruption. "This is the Noimoire police! Come out with your hands up!"

CHAPTER 45

OATH ABANDONED

A notification popped into Wolfe's field of view: *The Temple of Corruption will despawn in 5 minutes. Leave now, or make peace with any result thereafter.*

"Well, that was pretty clear," Shel said. "Shall we?"

"Shall we what?" Wolfe asked.

"Turn ourselves in," Shel replied.

Wolfe was flabbergasted. "What? Why would we do that?"

"It's the police. They'll arrest us, but then we'll be released when the fact that we were rescuing my kidnapped sister—and others—comes out. It'll be fine."

"You didn't meet Deputy Chief Charleston," Wolfe replied. "Seriously bad dude. If we survive, he goes down for sure. I mean, at this point, he probably goes down regardless, but he'll do his best to survive and take us down, with no hesitation as to methods. He gives me the same vibes that Damian and Nico did. That 'no loyalty amongst thieves' type vibes. We need to get out of here, away from them, and quickly."

Shel twisted her finger in her red hair. "Okay, I'm with you. Where to?"

"Out the back, or the side, of the warehouse. Somehow."

Shel walked over and picked Caine's cards off his back. She pocketed them and turned to Wolfe. "Lead on."

Wolfe left the huge central area of the temple, stepping past the stone spikes on the pews, clean of the card blood that had briefly been on them. He exited into the antechamber and then went to the front door. As he left, he brought out Malviere and Cereboo, noting with delight that his stats increased by one across the board when she was out. *That'll be extremely handy.*

Shel put her mantle on as well, a glowing third eye appearing on her forehead and starting to weep blood. Liurenia and Sorenia walked beside her, the three looking like a mystic prophet and her angel bodyguards.

"If we're going to run, you should put the lantern angels away," Wolfe commented.

"Yeah, sorry," Shel said. Both of the angels turned into gold light and flowed back into Shel.

My own team looks like a demon, a demon child, and a demon dog—a tiny, screwed-up Infernal family. Appropriate, I suppose. We definitely don't shine, though.

Wolfe's brief musings were broken by the sound of the police. "Everyone, out now! You're all under arrest, and anyone leaving will be considered to be resisting arrest."

"Yeah, yeah," Wolfe said. He reached out and pushed the huge front door of the Temple of Corruption open.

Light, bright and powerful, hit his eyes. Wolfe briefly saw a floodlight pointed at him, with vague outlines of people near it.

Shel's eyes widened in shock as blood spewed from her chest, and the CRACK of a rifle sounded.

Time seemed to slow to Wolfe. Shel started to fall back, her arms wide, but Wolfe was already moving. He reached out and touched the nearest creature card—his Gehenna Kennel

Master—and summoned it, blocking the door just as another CRACK sounded, the Kennel Master grunting and stepping back. At the same time, Wolfe felt magic flowing into him and from his Kennel Master and fired out into the warehouse, aiming for the giant spotlight, which exploded. Wolfe caught Shel with his other arm and let her drop gently to the floor on her back, then dragged her away from the door, her blood leaving a massive smear across ground.

Cereboo, empowered by both Malviere and the Kennel Master, ran howling into the light, charging the enemies of his pack heedlessly.

No thugs had been outside, and the police had already been there—including one with a sniper rifle, Wolfe guessed.

They never, ever had any intention of letting us surrender, and now the thugs have police allies.

"No, no, NO!" Wolfe growled as Shel's body convulsed, blood spewing from her mouth. *If they've killed her, I'll leave a trail of bodies like no one has ever seen through this city.*

But no cards appeared, and Shel's wound stopped pumping blood and started to close, painfully slow.

"Shel? Shel? Talk to me!"

Shel coughed again and blood spewed across Wolfe. She convulsed one more time but then managed to get ahold of herself and rolled over, coughing more blood onto the worm-track floor of the Temple of Corruption.

Wolfe was pretty sure he was 'privileged' to witness a rare event—someone with exactly zero Health, or maybe one, who would have died from bleed damage but for active healing.

"We need to go!" Wolfe said, grabbing Shel and heaving her to her feet as the magic of her mantle repaired her. Malviere pushed her shoulder under Shel's other side.

It was easy, like lifting an empty doll.

Wolfe glanced at his stats.

He was at a massive additional eight to all stats, not just his attack. He was also an Infernal, meaning he took half damage from Mortals. It was interesting that the stats were making him stronger.

Wolfe did quick math in his head. It was most likely he would only take two damage from each officer firing at him every thirty seconds or so, if they were in clear light and without cover. As it was...

Wolfe growled. He could summon one more card, and he knew what it would be. He pulled Shel back into the temple, going to the far back, behind the dais, where he dropped Shel off.

"Heal, and send cards to aid me," Wolfe said.

"I will. What are you going to do?"

"Murder them all," Wolfe growled.

Shel reached up and grabbed his arm. "There has to be another, better way. Please. They'll kill you, and if they don't, you'll go to jail forever for murdering that many police officers, even if you're justified."

"They tried to kill you," Wolfe said darkly.

"They failed. I'll be fine in a few minutes, thanks to Raphael's gift. We can still live the rest of our lives together happily."

Wolfe hesitated. Even as he stopped to think about it, however, another plan formed in his mind. *It's risky, giving the enemy a clear shot if they get the light back up, but only for a few seconds, and we might get away clean...*

"All right—we'll do it your way. Come with me."

Wolfe ordered his wounded Kennel Master to hide as best he could and not engage the enemy. At the moment, the Kennel Master was a walking buff for him, and he needed to keep the bonus.

Wolfe jogged to the side of the Temple of Corruption, between two pews, and knelt, pistol out. He was fast and limber, despite his wounds, empowered by the magic of his cards. He scooted just a bit, positioning himself so he was right next to the outside wall, about a foot away. Shel followed after him, her hand over the slowly healing wound on her chest. She dropped down next to him.

Malviere followed, silently, kneeling on the other side of Shel from Wolfe.

"What're we doing?" Shel whispered.

Wolfe fired a single shot blindly out into the opposite wall, and Shel clapped her blood-covered hands over her ears.

"Warn me when you're going to do that," she muttered.

"Sorry, I'm just delaying them, keeping their heads down. Get in line with me, the same distance from the wall, please."

Shel complied, going behind him the next pew over. "What're we doing?"

Malviere climbed over the pew to the front.

"Avoiding any falling debris," Wolfe responded.

The building around them disappeared. Wolfe fell about a foot but caught himself easily, staying upright even as Shel half-fell and posted her hand against his back to catch herself.

A rain of objects, including modern chairs, computers, paperwork, and some heavy furniture, rained down around them, but none of it hit Wolfe or Shel—Wolfe had positioned himself beneath the empty hall that he had used to get into the temple in the first place.

A string of cussing from what had been the front foyer of the temple a second ago told Wolfe that the police had been coming for him.

"Go!" Wolfe whispered, pointing toward the side of the warehouse.

"Thompson's down. We need a medic!" someone called. "A goddamned file cabinet landed on him!"

"Oh, no, I'm gonna miss him," Wolfe muttered sarcastically as they rushed to the side of the building. But he knew it was a lucky break. Thompson had seemed the most competent of the crooked cops after Charleston himself, and not by a small margin.

The deep, dark voice of the deputy chief called out into the darkness. "We'll get him to a hospital when we're done! Find that thug and his damned woman and *kill* them. Everything else comes after!"

Wolfe turned, letting Shel go in front of him, and then rapidly ran, hunched over, to the side of the building. Malviere trailed behind him.

Thanks to Wolfe's Kennel-Master-fueled shot earlier, the warehouse was still dark, and he reached the outer edge of the building without incident. The two of them rushed along the side until they came to a door in the wall.

"All right, when we open it, run out. If there are still any of Damian's guards, then we need to end them quickly. Ready?"

Shel nodded, her eyes wide, her hand on the handle of the door.

"Go!"

Shel pushed the door open and ran out. Wolfe followed half a second later, and a bullet impacted the wall of the warehouse next to him.

"Wolfe!" Deputy Chief Charleston roared.

Wolfe fled into the moonlit night, and for a wonder, there were no thugs—or anyone else—waiting to stop him. He considered whether they'd fled because they weren't receiving orders, because of the cops, or because Charleston had told them to leave so there'd be no witnesses. Either way, it was a welcome relief, and Wolfe gave a half smile as they ran onto the lawn, between the few carefully manicured trees, heading toward the road and freedom.

"Wolfe!" Deputy Chief Charleston roared again, and he sounded closer. Wolfe glanced back.

The huge man, almost three hundred pounds of muscle, was *running* at Wolfe from the side of the warehouse—at the speed a car might travel down a residential road—with cards circling around him. Brown cards. Wolfe turned and had just enough time to bring his hands up as Charleston clotheslined him, slamming Wolfe back six feet to hit the ground hard.

Wolfe dismissed the two-damage notification, about a third of what he had taken when he had been hit before, thanks to his mantle and canine-stat increases.

Still, Charleston hit as hard as a pistol shot and then some.

Wolfe launched to his feet, firing rapidly at Charleston, hitting him three times. Each knocked the man back a step and caused minor damage, but on the fourth shot, Wolfe clicked on empty.

The two men stood staring at each other across the lawn. Wolfe knew he was wounded, and Charleston looked almost whole, despite the three bullets. His veins were popping out, and he had fur growing across most of his body, despite his bald head. His eyes were red.

One more round, then, Wolfe thought as Charleston growled and charged.

CHAPTER 46

BETRAYAL LEAST FOUL

A golden light flared behind Wolfe, and he assumed that
Shel was summoning creatures to the field.

But that wasn't his problem—the charging
mass of animalistic muscle was. Wolfe threw his gun at
Charleston and dived to the side as the growling, chuffing man
flew through the space Wolfe had been. Wolfe hit the ground
and rolled to his feet, only to find that Charleston had skidded
so hard in the grass, he had ripped tracks in it and was heading
back at him.

Wolfe sidestepped and pushed the first strike away, but the
second caught him below the ribs with a cracking sound and
he involuntarily folded slightly around the blow. He managed
to barely dodge the follow-up and threw himself to the side
again, hitting the ground. He had very little power left,
between the mantle and the still-present Kennel Master.

And he was down to fourteen health.

He reached out to touch a card, but Charleston flew in,
foot raised for a stomp to Wolfe's head.

He felt a sudden rush of energy as Malviere triggered her
power, and with supernatural speed, Wolfe turned and up-

kicked Charleston to his gut as he came in, the brief boost making him hit faster than the corrupt cop.

Charleston took two steps back, his turn to involuntarily bend around a wound, but rushed at Wolfe again.

He touched his Fireborn Hellhound—which would get plus three to all stats from the Kennel Master and another one from Malviere and Wolfe's mantle each. It sent Wolfe to zero power, however.

In a viral-video missed opportunity, the hellhound appeared just as Charleston charged, and he hit it perfectly, flying over the hellhound with a yell and slamming onto the grass past Wolfe, but also rolling the hellhound over Wolfe. The hellhound flailed its legs and yipped.

Wolfe rolled over and tried to scramble to his feet, but Charleston again pivoted rapidly and ran on all fours over the Fireborn Hellhound and lunged at Wolfe before he was fully to his feet.

Wolfe caught the incoming deputy with a vicious elbow over the eyebrow as he came in but was tackled back to the ground, the far larger and heavier cop scrambling on top of him. But Wolfe scrambled himself, at least keeping the officer from getting a stable position. He took two vicious blows, accruing another three damage, dropping him to eleven health.

A Light beam struck Charleston to small effect, and the Fireborn Hellhound slammed into him, taking him off Wolfe to the side.

Wolfe finally managed to scramble to his feet and rushed over to where Charleston was fighting the Fireborn Hellhound on the ground, aiming at Charleston's head with a soccer kick.

The crack of a rifle sounded at the same time wood blasted from one of the nearby trees, and Wolfe was thrown off enough that he hit Charleston's shoulder instead.

Meanwhile, with almost single-minded determination, the corrupt cop snapped the leg of the Fireborn Hellhound and then started pounding it with vicious short elbows on the ground, growling as the Hellhound bit him repetitively in return.

Wolfe ran behind a tree, not wanting to risk being shot with a damned sniper rifle just to try to get a few more hits in on the magically jacked Deputy Chief.

His timing was fortuitous as his mantle faded, precipitously dropping his stats—and removing the health it had granted. For a second, Wolfe thought he might die, but it dropped in percentage terms, bringing him to seven health.

He hurt everywhere and was moving slower since he wasn't receiving the benefits from Malviere anymore.

He swiped his cards, getting a Tier-four Angry Hellhound, the Desperate Cult Child, Cerberus's Home for Wayward Hellhounds, and Hellfire.

A Veteran EMT appeared and healed the Fireborn Hellhound entirely, keeping Charleston occupied.

Wolfe's mind whirled with possible strategies, but he decided to toss his Angry Hellhound, Tier-four onto the field.

He glanced at the warehouse again. Multiple officers had come through the wall and were slowly moving across the lawn toward them. Small-arms fire started up, and Shel grunted from a hit and retreated to the cover of a small tree as well.

Wolfe pulled back again as a near miss from the sniper rifle showered him with wood chips. *Glad Thompson is out—that fucker was a bit too good with the gun, and his replacement is adequate at best.*

Shel looked at him and mouthed, "Plan?"

Wolfe directed his two Hellhounds to keep the pressure up on Charleston, then yelled to Shel. "Keep the cops from getting clear shots on the Hellhounds and keep them healed!"

She nodded, and Sorenia hit a tree next to a cop with a Light beam. The police dived behind trees or into the ornamental bushes, one getting half-stuck.

Charleston managed to climb to his feet, slowly taking damage from the Fireborn Hellhound and beating it half to death, but Shel summoned a Rookie EMT, healing the card again.

That has *to be irritating*, Wolfe thought with a grim chuckle.

When the thirty seconds was up, Wolfe took a chance, dismissing his Kennel Master so he'd have the power, then tossing the second Angry Hellhound—the Tier-three one —out.

Charleston was now taking significant damage, but he touched a card in front of him.

Vitality of the Wild
Uncommon Tier-1 Nature/Beast Card
2 Beast or Nature Power
Any single targeted Beast card fully heals

"Sometimes, the animals of the wild have reserves from hard living that pampered humans can barely comprehend."

Every wound on Charleston disappeared, and he smiled at Wolfe even as he fended off the dogs attacking him.

Yeah, it's utterly irritating, Wolfe thought. *Also, interesting to know he counts as a Beast card. That changes things.*

"Shel, refocus—bring out all your Mortal buffers and Mortal cards!" Wolfe yelled.

"It won't be fast enough," Charleston growled as he slammed the Fireborn Hellhound to the ground, killing it.

That's fine.

Wolfe swiped his cards, almost sure of what he would find

—and he was right. His Litter card came up, as well as Brimstone, a returned Cereboo, the Lost Hellhound Puppy, and the Demonic Portal.

Wolfe could hear sirens in the semi-distance, rapidly coming closer. They were sheltered from sight by the factory from the street, and by the warehouse from the parking lot, but they'd certainly figure out where everything was and join even *more* officers, from a different angle, soon. Wolfe needed to end this.

He threw the Litter card out, and three more Tier-four Angry Hellhounds appeared. Between Malviere and their own buffs, each now had an additional five on all stats—and they were nasty. Praying that Charleston's ridiculous stats didn't extend to a huge magical defense, Wolfe ordered his whole team at the Deputy Chief.

The police gunfire started to rapidly drop the dogs, but they lasted long enough thanks to their type and stat buffs to hit Charleston repetitively. The physical attacks, even buffed, did little, but his magical defense was lower. Charleston screamed as he was burned and bitten, flailing about himself.

Two of the dogs died to his strikes and gunfire, and three were wounded, but the Deputy Chief was covered in wounds.

By now, seven of the corrupt police officers were on the field, firing repetitively.

Wolfe needed to finish Charleston fast.

The sirens were suddenly far louder, and four police cars came around the factory, driving across the lawn between trees, boxing Wolfe and Shel in between the officers who had followed them and the new ones driving up.

Damn. Time's up.

Wolfe flew around the tree, running for Charleston in a last, desperate bid to kill the man despite his incoming reinforcements. If Wolfe was going down, he was taking

Charleston with him. He hit Brimstone, firing at Charleston as he ran up, hitting him twice.

No one else fired at him for some reason, but Charleston charged from the dogs and slammed into Wolfe, who didn't have his mantle on.

He felt things crack and hit the ground hard, dropped to a single health. Brimstone spun from his hand, landing two feet from him.

Fuck. I'd have taken him out if this weren't the fourth fucking fight in thirty minutes that's been dragging me down.

Charleston loomed over Wolfe, his body pouring blood from multiple small wounds, and most of his skin charred. He was huffing but didn't seem to be slowing at all.

"Hands in the air, Charleston!" came Rhett's voice. "It's over! Come quietly and you may still have a life at some point."

Charleston glanced up from Wolfe and screamed. "You fucking idiot, Rhett! This man is scum, just like everyone we remove from the street. Noimoire's crime is down, damnit, because we're taking out the trash!"

Wolfe glanced over. There were another eight officers, but all had the words *Joliet Police Department* on their uniforms. They looked incredibly anxious, licking their lips and glancing around nervously, but all had their guns out to back their lieutenant.

Rhett was still talking to the man whose poster had once adorned his office. "It's illegal and unethical. Additionally, I think that if your actions were counted in the official statistics, crime wouldn't be down at all. Might as well argue that gangbangers shooting each other reduces crime. But that's an argument for a judge. I'm placing you under arrest for attempted murder, conspiracy to commit murder, kidnapping, and about thirty other charges. Stand. Down." He looked up at the other officers. "That goes for all of you, although you may well face lesser charges as mere accomplices."

"We were *winning*," Charleston said, holding his arms out and facing the Joliet officers. "Winning against the lowlifes who won't follow the rules. We can still win, and get rich doing it! Join me! Don't let this vile man get away with everything."

"William will answer for his crimes, just as you must answer for yours," Rhett said. "He won't get away free, I promise you."

"Join me!" Charleston cried again.

No Joliet officer moved.

Charleston's face twisted with hate. "Fuck you!" Charleston screamed, slamming his fist down toward Wolfe's face.

The crack of Rhett's handgun came the tiniest fraction of a second before Charleston slewed to the side, a split in the skin over his cheekbone appearing, and he punched the earth next to Wolfe. Wolfe grabbed Brimstone and placed it against the underside of Charleston's jaw, pulling the trigger rapidly.

Blood and brain spewed across him, and the giant slumped on top of him, almost smothering him.

"Wolfe!" Shel yelled.

"I'm fine," Wolfe replied as he squirmed from under the giant corpse. "That's all him."

He dismissed the notification of the experience, cumulatively pushing him to the next level, and finally pushed Charleston's corpse off himself, slowly standing, his whole body in agony.

"Men of the Noimoire Police Department, we are taking you into custody. Please do not resist," Rhett called.

The men stood in shock for the most part, although Officer Thompson collapsed to the ground, weeping, as he was placed in handcuffs. Wolfe was too tired, and in too much pain, to take much pleasure in watching the corrupt cops get arrested by the Joliet Police Department.

Rhett walked up. "Sorry, William, but I think you're stuck with the damage for a moment. Everyone with healing cards here already used them on you, I think."

He reached down and picked up the cards that had spilled onto the ground when Wolfe had pushed Charleston away. "You'll get your share, once everything is resolved."

"What's left to resolve?" Wolfe asked.

"You're still under arrest. Can I assume you'll come quietly?"

"Are you fucking kidding me?" Wolfe asked.

Rhett gave Wolfe a small smile. "No. Now, care to come with me quietly to the Joliet station?"

Wolfe took stock of his situation, especially his health. "Yeah, I guess I will."

CHAPTER 47

SO MANY REMAIN

Fern

Wachowski walked the giant, ostentatious hallway with slow, short steps, her sandals scuffing the marble floor, her legs and lips trembling at the thought of the news she had to deliver. She was dressed in multiple layers of clothing, all covered in thick, black sweatpants and a giant, black hoodie, but it felt like no protection at all.

She was carrying a folder filled with paper, a manila envelope with postage on it that had been hand-delivered mere minutes ago, and a small thumb drive.

She placed her hand over her chest, feeling the comfortable power of her deck—a deck whose contents she didn't know, as she hadn't pulled it once in the nine months since she'd received it. The deck felt of trickery with a mechanical, cold edge, and she had pulled her status sheet up, so she knew she had Psychic and Golem, but as to the specific cards, she was still ignorant.

It was far too dangerous to risk telling people she had a deck by pulling it, since she had nowhere to go. But the sensation of the cards, a tiny weapon that she could theoretically use to fight against her captor, soothed her.

Her time of escape would come, when she was ready. Prepared.

She walked the rest of the hall as if she were heading to the gallows, but the trembling had stopped. She passed underneath crystal chandeliers, and next to plinths carrying cards inside glass cases—famous cards that Adam couldn't use, a few even legendary, from the many deckbearers whom Adam had defeated over his years. Indigenous chieftains, Nazi generals, and Prohibition mobsters were merely a small sampling of the people Adam had defeated, and the cards he couldn't use were displayed here.

He valued his legacy and vanity more than another paltry hundred million, Fern knew.

The door at the end of the hallway was just as tastefully gaudy as everything else, but its motif was even darker. The entire thing was a bas-relief of the Archangel Gabriel, the Divine Lord of Death, striking down an evildoer with a single blade to the neck.

Fern rapped lightly on the door.

"Enter."

The voice was familiar but never ceased to scare her. It was competent, confident, and filled with power.

She pulled back on the door, hard, and it slowly opened, the crease in the giant double door separating right where the neck of Gabriel's conquest was, so it appeared as if the head were separating from the neck.

Fern shuddered.

When the door was opened enough, she turned sideways and slipped into Adam's office.

It was even more ostentatious than the outside. Adam had

a massive oil painting of himself dominating the back wall, behind the massive mahogany desk he sat at, which was more than six feet deep, and nearly ten wide, inlaid with gold to show Gabriel's sign again and covered in glass.

Around the room were multiple large, leather couches, and Fern was relieved to see that they were occupied. With witnesses, Adam would never lower himself to hurt her. Not even these witnesses, who would likely want to see her suffer.

Because three of the couches were occupied by her once victims, the heads of the remaining Noimoire crime families.

To Adam's left was Benjamin Renfeldt, who was nearly a hundred and looked it. He was an old man, with wrinkled skin; wispy, white hair; spotted skin; and trembling hands. But his brown eyes were quick and sharp, and his grandson and successor, Benjamin Renfeldt III, sat next to him, younger, larger, and more vital, but with eyes no less sharp.

Across from him was Gurjit Singh, a swarthy man in his mid-forties with black hair; a giant, black beard; and eyes so dark, they were also almost black. He wore a traditional red turban with a black gem—an actual onyx, not glass, in his case —representing his allegiance to Asmodeus, Infernal Lord of Lust. His arms were completely free, and corded with muscles despite his advancing age—muscles and scars, proof of victories he had won by the skin of his teeth.

Between them, on the opposite side from Adam, sat Chester Ambroise, the nearly-sixty-year-old head of the 'Weeds,' the vague last gang in Noimoire. He smelled slightly of weed—and weeds too, an odd earthen and medicinal smell. His long hair, kept in a graying ponytail, nearly reached his waist in the back.

Behind Adam and to his right stood his eldest remaining son, Abel Delacruz. He had his father's height and strength and was dressed in a power suit of deep blue with a crimson tie, his black hair cut to military perfection. A bulge under his jacket showed that he was probably the only armed person here—if you didn't count the decks, of course.

Behind him to his left was Nathan Leopold, a tall, black-haired and green-eyed man with the gaze of a killer. Once a Navy Seal, he owed his current wealth and his deck to Adam. But much like Adam, the wealth was a mere perk—Nathan fanatically believed in Adam's goals and supported him wholeheartedly.

But Fern took all the others in quickly, before focusing on the person at the desk: Adam himself. He was nearly six-foot-three, with the frame of a defensive lineman. He was older now, with sun-touched skin and white hair. He wore a stylish if slightly old fashioned suit and carried a cane with a mythic card in a forged diamond on the top next to him—a cane he utterly didn't need.

He appeared to be a vibrant sixty-year-old man, still hale and healthy. But Fern knew he had fought in the Confederate army.

She gave the shallowest bows. "I have the information you requested, Champion, and two more things besides. I'm sorry, there's bad news—personal news."

"You can tell me in front of these men," Adam said. "I have no secrets from them."

Fern knew that was a lie, and a massive one. Adam had nothing but utter contempt for the men of Noimoire's underworld. But Adam liked to keep up appearances, put people at ease. He wouldn't have allowed any information he didn't want shared to be presented in this manner regardless.

"You should have gotten rid of the little thief," Gurjit muttered.

"You got your money back," Adam said, his voice hard. Then, "Give me the files."

Fern handed them over—they were logs of all the dirty

business these men had together, the transactions and whom they had been with.

The money was a mere drop in the bucket for Adam, for whom wealth was a very secondary goal, Fern knew. But it gave him contacts he needed. It was more than half of everything the crime families made these days, however.

Adam didn't open the files. Instead, he glanced with raised eyebrow at the remaining two items.

She passed the manila envelope over with a muttered, "From Gavin's, Champion."

He opened it, turning it sideways until the contents fell out—a single card.

A companion card named Aliel fell onto the deck, a near-match for Artenia, which Adam had bought for his third son, Caine.

"We have the second one. Has the cop become less obstinate about selling?"

"It... won't be an issue, not in that sense. The card is with someone new, a rookie police officer named Rachel Lyons."

"Will she sell? Caine's deck must be perfect."

"I..." Fern trailed off, and the trembling started again.

"Speak, wench," Adam commanded.

"Your son is dead," Fern whispered. "His killers, Rachel Lyons and her boyfriend, William Madison, have the card. Caine was caught with Damian Grimm after kidnapping the rookie officer's little sister."

Adam was still for a long time, staring down at the card on the table and moving it back and forth with his finger. No one dared to speak.

"And the connection to Worldwide Decurion?" Adam asked.

"Their offices are being raided by members of the Noimoire Police Department as we speak. I expect that nearly the entire operation will be wrapped up in days, based on the chatter I intercepted."

"Is this going to be a problem, Mr. Delacruz?" Benjamin Renfeldt asked, his voice soft.

"Don't be ridiculous. There will be very, very little, other than my disappointing and dead son, to link them to me. It may cost me my seat come next November, but it might not. Beyond that, it simply won't matter to what we're doing."

Benjamin Renfeldt inclined his head ever-so-slightly.

"So your pet thief has her uses after all," Gurjit murmured.

"That she does. As I explained to you all, repetitively."

There was another pause.

"I'm sorry for your loss," Chester said. "It's hard, losing a child."

For a moment, Adam didn't speak, but then his face firmed. "He was weak, and undeserving of any portion of my empire."

"Shall we do something about this Rachel and her boyfriend?" Gurjit asked.

"Of course," Adam replied. "But not yet. Immediate retaliation might lead people to suspect me, even with tenuous connections to Worldwide Decurion. But in a few months, perhaps a year at most... we'll remove them."

Adam turned to Fern. "You're dismissed."

Fern nodded and slowly fled the room, trying not to give in to the urge to run. Once she was outside, and the door closed, she sagged with relief.

She hadn't revealed everything she knew... She thought that even if Adam found out, she would have plausible deniability. She had her own plans, however nebulous they might be. And *she* certainly wasn't going to fight Adam.

I hope you survive... Wolfe.

CHAPTER 48

FINALLY BOOKED

Wolfe felt a degree of déjà vu as he stared around the Joliet Police Department for the second time this week.

He still hated police stations.

This time, however, Shel sat on the hard, plastic bench next to him. Shannon and Lucy sat next to Ms. Timo on another bench, both dressed normally and leaning on each other, snoring. Ms. Timo was asleep as well. Having everyone around put him a tiny bit at ease.

But only a tiny bit. Everything else reminded him that he had never yet had a positive experience in a police station, and he was pretty sure after four A.M. when it was still dark outside, being suspected in multiple killings wouldn't be the first time he enjoyed this place.

At least he didn't hurt anymore—or not much. He still had an injury debuff, but his active wounds had been healed by the cops. The good cops, he supposed.

"So what do you think Rhett is doing?" Wolfe asked for the tenth time.

"I don't know. He took you in and booked you, right?" Shel whispered, with a nod at her sleeping sister.

Wolfe lowered his voice. "Yeah, and he got a cheek swab and fingerprints, too—something I've avoided since I was a kid. And that file was sealed a long time ago."

"They cheek swabbed you when you were a juvenile?"

"Just the fingerprints, actually."

Shel was quiet for a moment before softly asking, "But he just let you come out here, obviously... Did he handcuff you?"

Wolfe shook his head.

A man came in, screaming and struggling. He had clear Taser marks on his neck, and his eyes were wild, his pupils dilated.

Shannon and Lucy jerked awake, staring around with wide eyes. Wolfe wished the two could go home, but their statements were needed—and since they were the primary reason he might *not* go to jail, he had resisted asking the police to take them back home.

"When it rains it pours," Wolfe said, looking at the man. "With eighty percent of their force dealing with the Noimoire stuff, they've got this guy going crazy."

"Yeah," Shel said, but she twirled her finger in her red hair and bit her lip. She didn't respond past that.

So much for making some light conversation.

Wolfe took Shel's hand and sat quietly, and the two girls fell back asleep. For his own part, Wolfe tried to pass the time watching the Joliet office around him. Despite the crazy guy with the eyes, nothing else happened, however. It gave Wolfe time to dwell on things that he didn't want to think about.

He was elated, of course, that he had killed Damian, and glad that his minions were all dead as well—not to mention a whole slew of dark deckbearers—assassins, enforcers, and thugs involved in human trafficking. Even a corrupt member of Noimoire's elite Card Police. Over the last three days, Wolfe had bagged ten deckbearers—he was fairly sure that his patron, Cerberus, would be quite excited.

Plus, Wolfe had most of the cards from the dead. Including a ridiculous amount of cards he hadn't looked at yet.

Not to mention half the cards for the 'Gate to Hell' set now.

Shel rested her head on his shoulder and let out a huge yawn.

Wolfe couldn't stop thinking—not normally a problem he had. But everything could go away in the next few minutes, depending on what Rhett did. He had saved Wolfe's life now, even if Wolfe had previously saved Rhett's. Maybe he'd lost his sense of gratitude and would arrest Wolfe.

Wolfe just wished he knew. He let go of Shel's hand and stood, his face darkening.

Shel startled from her half-dozing state and rubbed her eyes. "What are you doing?"

"I'm gonna go see Rhett and figure this out. Whatever he's doing, he can do quickly so I can get on with my life."

"Maybe we should—" Shel began.

But for once, Wolfe didn't listen to her, regretting it slightly but still determined. He strode toward the door in the wall. *I'm not really a wait-and-see kinda guy, anyway.*

Just as he reached the door, it opened, admitting Cara, who looked harassed and tired. She was still quite pretty without her makeup, but the difference was noticeable.

Or maybe it was the lack of sleep everyone was suffering from.

She was glancing down at her clipboard and actually walked into Wolfe, bouncing off him and staring up with startled eyes. But when she saw him, her expression softened.

"Uh... I'm sorry, William," she muttered as Shel came up beside Wolfe. "You *are* William, right?"

Wolfe nodded.

"Okay, well, I was supposed to come get you for the detective. Please come this way."

Wolfe followed her into the back. Most of the desks were empty of police officers, but the ones that had them had multiple calls going at once, and every occupant looked harassed.

"I never thanked you, by the way," Cara said.

"Thanked me?" Wolfe asked.

"For saving Rhetty-poo's life. I don't know what I—we— I mean, the department, would have done if he'd died. It would have been a tragedy."

Shel strangled a laugh, turning it into a weird cough-snort. Wolfe was too surprised to do anything about it, just blinking at her. *Rhetty-poo?*

Cara brought them to Rhett's office and knocked. This time, Wolfe waited for Rhett to call out, "Come in!"

Cara opened the door and motioned Wolfe and Shel inside, and they went. Rhett had two cheap, metal chairs in front of his medium-quality desk, and the poster of Deputy Chief Charleston was missing, but nearly everything else was the same as Wolfe remembered.

Including the picture of the dead officer whom Wolfe knew had had a connection to the card sellers from the Rat Arena, however tenuous.

Shel sat in one metal chair, and Wolfe took the other and spun it around. Before he could sit, Rhett stared up at him, raised an eyebrow, and said, "Please?"

Wolfe sighed, completed the chair's rotation, and sat in it normally.

He glanced at Rhett's desk. There were files for both William and Shel on the table—but none for Wolfe. None for any of the Grimm family, in fact.

"So, have you decided if you're gonna be arresting me?" Wolfe asked.

Rhett didn't respond, instead looking up at Cara. "Cara, hon, would you mind bringing us some coffee, please?"

"Black?"

"Yes," Wolfe and Rhett said at the same time, and, "Sugar and cream," Shel said.

Cara left, shutting the door behind her.

Rhett looked up at Wolfe. He looked as tired as Wolfe felt, with bags under his eyes, but he was smiling slightly.

Wolfe knew he was playing into Rhett's odd game, but he was growing tired of waiting. "So, are you arresting me?"

Rhett turned two files around and pushed them in front of Wolfe and Shel. On each one was a 'promise to appear in court' form, a pen, and a marked place to sign.

"Yes, I am arresting you—" Rhett began.

"You son of a—" Wolfe interrupted, violently grabbing the pen.

"For trespassing," Rhett finished.

Wolfe stopped, holding the pen above the X for signing. "What?"

Rhett smiled sardonically. "I'm arresting you, William Madison, for trespassing, a misdemeanor. The same crime I booked you for—and the same one I got DNA evidence and fingerprints for. With a very complete file on William Madison that I will send to every major police station in Illinois, as well as a federal database. I am also releasing you, with a promise to appear in court when summoned by said court, assuming, of course, that our local district attorney decides to prosecute. I think it's more likely that I get a call from said district attorney telling me not to be an ass and to stop harassing heroes who saved lives and put a stop to a trafficking ring, but that's for her to decide."

Wolfe was at a loss for words. "Why?"

Shel silently clapped her hands beside him.

"Funny thing about the arrest packet. It requires a court order to seal and is never really gone. So, anytime anyone ever looks for a certain DNA pattern, or fingerprints, or anything else, really, they'll find William Madison, and no one else—nor an emptiness that might be suspicious. Prints matching the ones you'll need to provide in your private investigator work."

Wolfe got it—it was an extra layer of protection, making sure that he would always officially be William Madison, no matter what stories any remaining Grimm boys—like Piper— tried to spin.

"What about Shel?" Wolfe asked. "Her career, I mean?"

Shel nodded to his words.

"Well, technically—very technically—it might cause trouble. But I'd bet money I get another call about how much of a, shall we say, 'self-righteous prick' I am," Rhett said.

Wolfe chuckled. "Never going to live that down, am I?"

"Nope. But, the point is, I suspect that case gets dismissed too. No one questions why I only charged you. Regardless, trespass really isn't likely to be a problem for becoming a police officer, absent some really bizarre moral turpitude or associated crimes like stalking.

"Now, hurry up and sign that paperwork. We both have about twenty hours of sleep to catch up on, and I'm sure you have family to take care of. I've gotten enough from everyone to let it go for the evening—we'll take more formal statements in a day or two."

Wolfe nodded and stood, holding his hand out. "Thank you. For the extra safe fresh start."

Shel stood as well. "Yes, thank you. Truly."

Rhett nodded to Shel, then stood and shook Wolfe's hand. "It's a double-edged sword, *William*. You've a fresh life, but you are in the system now. Just sayin'."

Wolfe rolled his eyes. "Right, right. I'll be good."

"In your case only, I think I'm more worried about 'Law-abiding' than good, per se, but I'll take what I can get," Rhett said.

Then his eyes widened. "Oh, before I forget. We were going through Emmett's stuff, looking for evidence, and my boys came upon something."

He held a giant pack of paper slips to Wolfe.

Wolfe took them, rifling through them. They were all dates, times, and case names. "What are these?"

"Three years of time cards from Emmett, showing in meticulous detail all the times, places, and cases you worked for him over the last three years. It's good to see that you didn't spend all seven years since the last lumber mill closed unemployed."

Wolfe looked up to see Rhett grinning at him with a sardonic half-smile. "And welcome, however tangentially, to the side of the cops, since you're a full private investigator now —and I know I can trust you with a ton of jobs for our office and the D.A. both."

"Oof. That made me barf a little in my mouth."

CHAPTER 49

A BREATHER

"I'm sorry I missed your police thing," Wolfe said as he stared at the giant lot, empty but for a large parking lot.

Shel snuggled against his side, her arm around his back. "The ceremony honoring me for being top of a class of two hundred?"

"Yeah, that," Wolfe replied with a grin, stretching slightly, enjoying not hurting for the first time in a week, since Damian, Caine, and Charleston had nearly killed him. The last injury penalty had disappeared only this morning, reflecting the lack of pain when he'd woken up.

Despite the lack of pain, Wolfe wasn't completely sanguine. He might have been stronger than he'd been a week ago, but his deck was far weaker than it had been at that point.

One of the reasons for the new weakness nuzzled against his leg, and Wolfe glanced down.

He had no idea why the Wandering Bulgae Pup, which appeared to be made of fire, didn't burn him. But it didn't, and its fur felt amazing, silky and fine. He reached down and pet the orphan card dog, which was more expressive than he would have figured an orphan card would be.

Wandering Bulgae Pup
Rare Fire [Canine] Minion [Orphan]
0 power
Health: 6
Attack: 0
Magical Attack: 0
Defense: 3
Magical Defense: 3

Special: **Orphan Evolution [unique]:** If kept 'alive' for three straight years, will turn into a rare, fire, 2-power, Tier-5 equivalent creature card called 'Bulgae Moon Chaser.'
Special: **Lost in the Dark:** If in play, the deckbearer does not trigger deck drawn warnings.

The Wandering Bulgae Pup orphan card that Hans had possessed had opened Wolfe's and Shel's eyes to the possibility of canine orphans, and Shel had been scouring Gavin's and far less reputable card sources both for any canine orphan cards. She had even found rumors of *police dog* orphan cards, which intrigued her.

Malviere and the Desperate Cult Child were also in Wolfe's deck now, and out and accumulating growth time.

The various orphan cards had replaced more powerful fighting cards in his deck. Plus, Wolfe had taken the Caretaker of the Lost enhancer card and put the Hellmouth Institute in his deck as well.

Wolfe was almost a hundred percent positive that investing in the orphan cards was the way to bring him to levels of capability in his deck that would be almost untouchable someday, as he could raise orphan cards to extraordinary tiers.

Almost no one had a card of tiers higher than three or four, but the orphan cards could hit absurd levels.

But it really bothered him that it made him weaker in the moment. He was pretty sure that at some point, people were going to come for him, after the things he'd done.

"Stop that," Shel said, lightly shoving herself against Wolfe.

"What?" Wolfe asked.

"Brooding. This is a wonderful moment. Don't ruin it with worry."

"Sure."

They were silent for another moment, and Shel turned to him. "Hey, I wanted to tell you something. I wanted it to be more special, but... I would have hated it if I hadn't told you before, and one of us died. So I'm just going to say it."

She stepped in front of him, staring into his eyes. "I love you, Wolfe. You're my one and only, if you'll have me. I want to be with you forever, to have your back forever."

Wolfe's chest tightened. It was hard, and he didn't know why. Maybe because everyone he had loved once had abandoned or betrayed him.

But he wanted to be a part of a family again, to have someone he could truly trust, who would be there for him forever. An ally against the darkness life could throw at you, always.

Wolfe took a deep breath and unburdened his heart. "I love you too, Shel, and I want the same."

She smiled at him brilliantly, then leaned up on her toes, put her arms around his neck, and kissed him hard.

When she came down, still resting her hands on his shoulders, she had tears in her eyes, but a smile to chase away the night. "Well, shall we look at getting a house together?" she asked playfully.

Wolfe chuckled and nodded, as happy as he'd ever been.

He stared at the huge plot of land in front of them. It was on the very edge of Joliet, bought with money from selling some of the cards he'd gotten from Damian—a pure cash transaction so that it would close almost instantly.

Shel let go of him as he strode across the newly laid parking lot and touched his chest, feeling the usual sense of power and hunger. He pushed his hand forward, fingers splayed out. Shel and the various orphan cards came up behind him as well.

Five cards appeared, and Wolfe touched Cereboo first. The pup had been with Wolfe from the beginning and deserved to be here for this as well.

Cereboo appeared, licking at Wolfe and Shel, then turned and stared, as if he knew what was coming.

Wolfe willed his new building card, the Hellmouth Institute, into existence.

The building that appeared was massive. The card claimed it was twenty-four thousand square feet in size, and Wolfe believed it. The structure was three stories tall, each story nearly three times as large as a good-sized home in America, with a tower climbing up another two stories from the back left. The architecture was clearly gothic, with arches at the top of every window, spikes and gargoyles on the roof, and stained glass, mostly red, across the windows of the tower.

Even the ground around the outside changed, becoming black and cracked, with fire seeping out around the edges. A few planters were below the bottom-floor windows, and each had flowers in crimson or black roses.

"Thematic," Shel said drily as they both stared at the building. The card stats appeared as an overlay in Wolfe's vision.

Hellmouth Institute
Unique, rare equivalent Tier-2 equivalent Infernal Building

No cost

Special: Creates an ostentatious orphanage of 24,000 square feet. It may utilize power and water if hooked to an appropriate grid, and will generate food for up to 100 inhabitants, of excellent quality, every day. Minor magic within the orphanage makes the entire place far easier to live with. Any Infernal deckbearer inside gains 2 Infernal Power.

Special: Any additional Infernal Buildings gained will add bonus benefits to orphan or transformed orphan cards.

Special: **Fast Age [3], Fast Age Infernal [5]** All orphan cards 'age' at 3x the rate, unless they are Infernal or would become Infernal without the aid of this building, in which case they age at 5x the rate.

Special: **Evolve Improvement: Infernal [1]** Every orphan card that transforms that is Infernal or would become Infernal without the aid of this building gains 1 tier of equivalent power as a permanent modifier.

Special: Every Mortal orphan card that transforms becomes Infernal and is modified accordingly but gains no total increase to power.

"A hundred people..." Shel mused. "Do you think that it can house that many?"

"Probably," Wolfe responded. "I mean, a hundred ten feet by ten feet bedrooms would only take up ten thousand square feet, and this *is* an orphanage, after all."

Shel turned to face Wolfe, her fingers tapping together. "So... my mom called. She's decided to move."

Wolfe knew something ridiculous was coming, but he waited.

"She... asked me to keep Lucy."

Wolfe blinked hard. "You want us to raise Lucy?"

Wolfe was floored by the comment, but something about *us* warmed him. It really was *them* now, not just him.

Shel nodded. "I'm sure, with this building, we can have your P.I. business on the bottom floor and Lucy can live in one of the upper floors."

Wolfe shook his head, bemused. "I don't know anything about raising kids."

"Well... you *have* to be better than our parents, and we turned out all right."

Wolfe laughed at the understatement of the year. "Fair enough. We can raise Lucy."

Shel smiled, but she was still tapping her fingers.

"And?" Wolfe asked.

"Well... I was thinking. Ms. Timo and Shannon are poor. And Lucy and Shannon are best friends now. Maybe... Maybe they could come live with us? I mean, you'll need a secretary anyway, and Ms. Timo is good at that..."

"You want us to adopt the old bat and her granddaughter? Seriously?"

"Well, we wouldn't formally *adopt* them. I just want them to live with us. It wouldn't even cost anything. I mean... the electricity and such will already be here, and the building magically makes food, so..."

Shel hesitated. "Plus, you said my half of the job was to save those who deserved it. Obviously, I can't save everyone, but Shannon could really use a champion, and she utterly adores you now, despite your, shall we say, 'rough' exterior."

Wolfe shook his head in bemusement. Still, Shel was right —the 'cost' to him of having them in the Institute was almost nothing. And Ms. Timo and Shannon were good people. "Sure, you can offer them a place to stay. Assuming they'll want to stay in a giant, demonic orphanage."

Shel glanced at the dark building and laughed. "Good point."

Wolfe continued. "I hesitate to ask, but anyone else?"

"Well... Liam will need a job, once he's done serving whatever sentence he gets. It'll probably be pretty light since he turned state witness and helped us both. I mean, he did risk himself to get the girls out when I came back for you, and he did a great job. Maybe he could live here and work at the firm?"

Wolfe shook his head in genuine amazement at the sudden turn his life was taking. But he didn't mind, he admitted. People to protect and take care of, whom he knew were worth the effort, was something he had always wanted. "Sure, whatever, Liam can work here. I'm afraid to ask again, but anyone else?"

"Not yet," Shel said, smiling at him.

Wolfe's smile faltered. "Are you sure about this, Shel? All of it, I mean. I remind you that Cerberus himself, a Lord of the Infernal, showed me that I need to end the remaining heads of the family in Noimoire. I don't think I can stop... and I'm not sure I would want to if I could. If I can take them down the"—Wolfe held his fingers up in air quotes—"'right' way, I will, but it's more likely it becomes another fight. Liam is one thing, and even you're an adult who made her choices clear, and I love you for it. But Lucy and Shannon..."

Shel's smile also faded, and she thought for a moment. "I... I think it'll be okay. Despite your takedown of Damian, almost no one wants to attack deckbearers inside their building cards. Besides... we aren't exactly anonymous, but your mission is. Everyone knows who we are. But your beef with Damian was personal, and the traffickers kidnapped my sister. I think—I hope—no one will come after us, at least till later, and we can move them then if they need to be moved. Besides, someone could get to them more easily in another city than inside your institute, I bet."

Wolfe nodded. "All right. We'll do it your way. Can't say I

don't enjoy the idea." He turned away from the institute. "It'll be a good break, while I prepare again. I need to make two more levels and add another building card slot, and then get a good building for the institute. Then I need to evolve some of these orphans and hopefully other ones you find as well. But afterward, when my deck is stronger... Afterward, I'm going to go back to cleaning up Noimoire."

"*We're* going to clean up Noimoire." Shel hugged him close, staring toward the city of Wolfe's birth. "So nothing like what happened to my brother and sister can happen again. We're going to remove the taint from the city. Together."

End Book 2

THANK YOU SO MUCH FOR READING!

Please consider leaving a review—any and all feedback is much appreciated!

Also, check out these super helpful Facebook groups!
https://www.facebook.com/groups/LitRPG.books
https://www.facebook.com/groups/Dungeonstories
https://www.facebook.com/groups/LitRPGsociety
https://www.facebook.com/groups/litrpgforum
https://www.facebook.com/groups/LitRPGReleases

"To learn more about LitRPG, talk to authors such as myself, and just have an awesome time, please join the LitRPG Group."

About the Author

John Stovall loves Shami, gaming, reading, math, his friends, his family, and his dog, and probably a whole lot of other things he can't think of right now. He obtained his BA in political science, and then later his JD from Humphrey's School of Law, but his real passion lies in writing. When he isn't thinking up number systems for his own homebrew Dungeons & Dragons game, he's thinking up cool plotlines for his books.

MORE STUFF!

If you're interested in more work from me, please check out my author page for other series, or sign up for the newsletter! I have a lot of other books, all LitRPG, but with a great deal of variance therein.

If you'd like to contact me directly, the easiest way is my Discord. You can also find me on Facebook (be prepared for questionable photography skills), or can email me at John.W. Stovall@gmail.com. You can also support me and read advance chapters on my Patreon.